Commitment

USA TODAY BESTSELLING AUTHOR

T.K. LEIGH

COMMITMENT

Published by Carpe Per Diem, Inc. / Tracy Kellam, 25852 McBean Parkway # 806, Santa Clarita, CA 91355

Edited by: Kim Young, Kim's Editing Services

Cover Image Copyright Dmytro Buianskyi 2018

Used under license from Shutterstock.com

To second chances…

Dear Reader,

Thank you for picking up a copy of Commitment! I can't tell you how much your support means to me. Also included in this is an extended prologue / prequel titled Promise. It's more of a mature YA / New Adult novella, whereas Commitment is an adult romance.

I never intended to write Promise. In fact, up until a month prior to the release of Commitment, not a single word had been written of this novella. As I was working on revisions and edits of Commitment, I couldn't stop thinking about the backstory I painted for Drew and Brooklyn, and if there was a better way for me to relay that story to the readers. Thus, Promise was born. In the novella, you'll meet Drew and Brooklyn, the main characters in my Redemption series, during a very poignant time in their lives. Drew is about to head off to college, and Brooklyn is about to enter her junior year of high school.

I understand the mature YA / New Adult genre may not be for everyone, but I truly believe it was necessary to take a step back and tell this story in greater detail than just a few brief flashbacks and/or dialogue between the characters. While Commitment takes place almost seventeen years after the events of this novella, I'm convinced this will help you understand why things are the way they are, why the characters act the way they do.

I've made it so it's not absolutely necessary to read Promise, having included the general details in Commitment, but I urge you to take an hour or two and lose yourself in Drew and Brooklyn's beginnings. Maybe it'll bring back memories of your own first love.

Thank you!

Promise

"We were always meant to say goodbye…"

T.K. Leigh

Chapter One

BROOKLYN

JUNE 2001

THE AVERAGE PERSON SPENDS at least two weeks of their life kissing. When you consider you may live to be ninety, it doesn't seem like that long a time. But if you take into account the average kiss lasts approximately seven seconds, two weeks equals over 170,000 kisses.

I'm almost sixteen and haven't even been kissed once. At this rate, I doubt I'll ever come close to hitting my kiss quota. It's not that I haven't had any offers. I have. But I want my first kiss to be special.

I once read the term "French kiss" came into popularity as a slur against the French culture, who seems to have an obsession with sex and promiscuity, at least according to the indecency experts of the early twentieth century. But the French refer to that deep, all-consuming type of kiss as a "tongue kiss" or, even better, "soul kiss" because, if done right, it should merge two souls together.

That's what I want from my first kiss. To merge my soul with another, not waste it on someone who won't appreciate it.

Even at my young age, I've spent an unhealthy amount of time imagining the day my soul will connect with another in such a beautiful way. I've forced my best friend, Molly, to watch a ridiculous number of romance movies. Whenever I'd witness that first kiss between the leading lady and man, I'd exhale dreamily.

Will my first kiss be like the one between Ingrid Bergman and Humphrey Bogart in *Casablanca*, deep and full of despair? Or will it be closer to the one between Clark Gable and Vivien Leigh in *Gone with the Wind*? All-consuming and needy, as if neither one could go another minute without that connection. I'm beginning to think I'll never know.

"What about this style?" Molly asks, snapping me out of my daydream. I shift my eyes to where she reclines on her lounge chair in practically the same position as me. Back propped up at a slight angle. One leg bent at the knee, the other straight. Chin tilted to the sun in an attempt to prevent the occurrence of strange tan lines. The aroma of coconut-scented sunscreen and briny sea air filters into my senses. It's the smell of summer.

I scan the page of the magazine Molly's pointing to, seeing some famous actress whose layered haircut has become popular over the past few months. "It's cute."

She raises her eyebrows and huffs in annoyance. "Cute? Just cute? That's all? I'm sixteen. I'm far too old for anything cute."

"Okay then." I lower my book. My father insists I work my way through the recommended reading list my honors English teacher provided. I'll soon be starting my junior year of high school. These are important years, especially where college admission offices are concerned. My dad doesn't have a lot of money, so he's depending on me getting some scholarships to help ease the financial burden of sending me to college. "What do you *want* me to say?"

"I don't know," she exhales. "Beautiful. Stunning. Sexy." She waggles her eyebrows. "I want to be sexy. Don't *you*?"

I shrug, looking away. Brightly colored beach towels cover the sand like a Tetris game gone wrong. Off to the right, several guys I recognize from school play volleyball, many of them shirtless, their tanned skin glistening with sweat from the humid temperatures. I try not to stare, but I can't help it, especially at one guy in particular.

"I never really thought about it," I lie.

"Oh, come on, Brook. You can't tell me you haven't swayed those hips of yours a little more whenever you passed a cute boy at school or the mall."

I retrieve my book and flip it back open. My eyes remain glued to the words on the page, but I don't comprehend any of them. It could be written in a foreign language for all I know. There *is* a boy at school I sway my hips for, who I smile shyly at whenever I see him, who makes my entire body warm whenever he steals a glance at me. I can't tell Molly, though. She'd never understand. After all, that boy is her older brother.

"I guess I never really thought of anyone in our class that way." I continue to avoid her eyes.

Up until a year or so ago, I was taller than most boys in our class. There was nothing attractive about having to bend my five-foot, nine-inch frame over just to dance with them during one of the school functions my father begrudgingly allowed me to attend. Over the past year, something happened. *Boobs.* My formerly straight and statuesque frame is no longer shaped like a stick, but now resembles an hour-glass. Along with the boobs came a lot more attention I still don't know how to handle.

"Well, I have." Her voice is very matter-of-fact.

"Who?"

"Brody Carmichael."

I lift my sunglasses off my eyes, narrowing my gaze at her. "He's about to be a senior *and* is replacing your brother as captain of the hockey team."

"So?" she says dismissively.

I shake my head, praying I'm not around when Drew learns of this little development. "Your funeral," I quip. "Or maybe Brody's."

She grins. "Most definitely Brody's."

We both laugh. For the past ten years, Molly and I have been practically inseparable. After we met during our first day of kindergarten, we immediately formed a bond. I still remember that day with alarming clarity. I had watched as all my classmates gave their mother a hug and kiss goodbye in front of the school. I'd kissed mine goodbye forever the previous year after a drunk driver killed her.

Growing up without a mother affects you in ways

you never think it will, especially as a girl. There's no one to teach you how to apply makeup. No one to talk to you after you get your period. No one to tell you about their first boyfriend. Molly and I found a camaraderie in each other, considering her mother left them and never looked back. We figured out things together. And I knew we'd confront the rest of the problems life threw at us the same way.

"Are you hungry?" she asks suddenly, her voice chipper. "I'm hungry. Aren't you hungry?" She grins deviously and jumps up from her lounge chair, her blonde curls springing with the motion. After adjusting her bikini, she assesses her appearance. I can't help but envy her. She's petite and skinny with not many curves. On the other hand, I'm tall with an ample chest and even more ample hips. I'm still not used to this new body I find myself in, but Molly's encouragement helps. Whenever she notices me trying to hide underneath my clothes, she tells me how amazing I look, how she'd kill to have curves like mine. She makes me feel good about myself, a difficult feat for a teenager.

I follow her line of sight across the street toward Kelly's, one of our favorite spots, shaking my head when I see Brody, along with several other guys from our school, approach the food stand. That's what summers are like in the greater Boston area. When you're not working, you're hanging out at the beach. Most days, it's like I'm not even out of school, considering how often I see my classmates congregate here.

"I'll let you work your charms on your own." I return my attention forward. "These books won't read themselves."

It doesn't matter that I can't see her. I feel her roll her eyes at me. "You're always so serious. When are you going to learn to have a little fun?"

"This *is* fun for me."

"Suit yourself. Want anything?"

"I'm good. I'm still full from the muffins you stole from the café." Her father owns and runs a café in the North End of Boston. It's been in her family for generations. They have the best coffee in the city and the best pastries in the world, although I've never left the New England area.

Molly moans, rubbing her flat stomach. "God, what I wouldn't give for another muffin right now."

"You're a fiend."

"But you still love me."

"You bet I do. Now go before your...food walks away."

She shifts her eyes across the street and chews on her lower lip, her cheeks blushing. "Be back in a few, Brook!" she calls out as she runs up the sand. I watch her climb over the short ledge, then hurry across the street, still barefoot.

Once I see that she's made it to Kelly's in one piece, I return my attention to my book, immersing myself in the author's world. To be honest, it's a world I hope I never have to live in. Now that I'm older and am in more advanced English classes, it seems the reading material has become more mature, as well. I can't help but feel bad for Hester Prynne and the secret she keeps at the expense of her happiness. I hope I never put myself in a situation where I have to keep my love a secret.

Sweat beads on my forehead as I continue to bask in the sun, losing track of time, which is often the case when I read. So many people I know hate reading. This is probably why Molly and I get along so well. We can hold entire conversations using book quotes and no one would be the wiser.

It's not until my hair starts to stick to my neck that I put the book down for a moment to tie my long, dark locks into a ponytail. The instant I do, I spy a familiar silhouette heading my way, eyes trained on me, a cockiness about him.

I quickly retrieve my book, burying my nose in it once more in the hopes he doesn't recognize me. I didn't have this problem last year. Next to Molly, with her charismatic personality and infectious enthusiasm, I was practically invisible. Now, thanks to the cleavage that no swimsuit can properly hide, everyone's suddenly noticing me. All the more reason I should keep my cover-up on, just like I tell my dad I do to stop him from worrying. I don't want to consider what would happen if he drove by and saw me in this bikini he doesn't even know I own.

"Brooklyn Tanner," a coy voice croons.

I take a breath, swallowing down my irritation at the interruption, and float my eyes to the source, who's now commandeered Molly's chair. "Damian."

"Looking good." He winks, but it does nothing for me. Damian Murphy is one of the most popular guys in class. He always has an entourage with him, mostly made up of the popular girls, who fawn over him every time he scores a basket during games or makes a tasteless joke, most with some sort of sexual connotation. He can have anyone he wants, but over the past few months, he seems to have made it his mission to get me to go out with him. "Where's your hip attachment?"

"You mean my *friend*?"

"Yeah. It's rare to see one without the other."

I flip the page of my book, brushing off his comment. "Not that rare. She has her own life. I have mine. We just enjoy spending time with each other."

"So much so that you can't seem to find the time to go out with me?" He cocks a brow, then leans closer. "I normally don't ask a girl out more than once." He pauses, considering his words for a moment, furrowing his brow in obvious confusion. "I usually don't have to. I've never had anyone turn down a date with me."

I grit a smile. "Well, there's a first time for everything, Damian."

"Ouch," he teases. "Beautiful and witty. That's one killer combination."

"I'll be sure to add that to my college applications then." I return my eyes to the pages, hoping he'll get the hint and leave. Unfortunately, just like every other time he's asked me out, he doesn't.

He's an attractive guy — sandy blond hair, crystal blue eyes, dazzling smile — but even killer looks can't diminish his pompous attitude. A year ago, he thought my name was Brenda. Now that I have boobs, he seems to have mustered the brainpower to learn my real name.

10

PROMISE
Too little, too late. No thank you, Damian.

"Like I've told you repeatedly, my father doesn't want me to date until I'm sixteen."

"And when will that be?"

"September first, but even then, I'm not sure I want to date." I attempt to give him the cold shoulder, but I can't ignore the heat of his body inching even closer to mine.

"Oh, Brooklyn, Brooklyn, Brooklyn..." His voice is irritatingly sly. "What can I do to convince you to say yes?"

When his hand lands on my thigh, my body immediately grows rigid. I inhale a sharp breath. His fingers sweep up and down my leg as I blink repeatedly, my heart pounding in my chest. Didn't Damian pay attention during our health class when Mr. Ottermeyer went over the importance of verbal consent? Probably not. He was too busy flirting with anything with a pulse.

"Damian," I warn through tight lips, gripping my book, my knuckles becoming white with the force. "Please take your hand off my leg."

"Why?" He smirks. "Is there somewhere else you'd like my hand?" He comes closer still, his fingers traveling up my leg, over my hip, and farther north.

I open my mouth, dread forming in the pit of my stomach, every inch of my body tensing. The hair on my nape stands on end, my palms becoming clammy. I press my elbows into my sides, my teeth grinding. Hearing laughing and blaring music, reminds me I'm in public, that I can get up and leave, but I'm frozen to the spot, unable to move or speak as his hand looms

11

perilously close to my chest.

As I brace myself for what's to come next, he suddenly flies off the lounge chair and onto the sand. I'm disoriented at first, unsure what just happened. Then I see a familiar, yet intimidating figure standing over Damian, his foot pressed against his neck, his dark hair wild.

"Don't you *ever* put your hands on her again!" Drew bellows. His back is toward me, muscles tense, body taut.

Over the past two years, he's gone from a tall, scrawny kid, who perpetually had a pair of ice skates or rollerblades attached to him, into this beast of a man. With his six-foot, two-inch frame and muscles he's built up during hours of training, he's a force to be reckoned with. Couple that with a hot temper, and the entire school has learned not to mess with Andrew Brinks, unless you want to walk away with a broken bone or two.

"Chill out!" Damian says once Drew lets up on the pressure. "We were just talking."

"Really? It didn't look like you were just talking."

Drew glances over his shoulder and our eyes meet. I swallow hard at what I see in his stare. I can't quite explain it. It's unlike the way he typically looks at me. He's no longer looking at me like I'm an annoyance, someone he has to put up with because I'm his sister's best friend. It makes me feel ashamed. I jump to my feet and grab my cover-up lying in the sand, hastily tossing it on my body.

Damian takes advantage of Drew's momentary

distraction and wiggles away, climbing back to his feet. "You got a thing for her, fine," he barks out, brushing sand off his swim trunks. "No skin off my back. You've seen one pair of tits, you've seen 'em all. And I've seen plenty. Nothing special about hers."

In an instant, Drew's hand forms into a tight fist. Damian doesn't even have time to react before Drew reels back, landing a powerful blow to his perfect nose. When blood spews onto the sand, I shriek. Needing to do something to put an end to this before it gets out of control, I dart toward Drew and attempt to pull him off Damian, but he's obsessed, a man on a mission.

"Drew! Stop!" I do everything I can, but I'm no match for his strength. "Please!

Just as he's about to land another punch to Damian's face, I jump in between the two. Drew quickly halts mid-blow. It's the first time I'm actually thankful for my height. If I were as short as Molly, he'd never even notice me standing here.

He stares at me, nostrils flaring. It's just enough time for Damian to get his footing and take off down the beach. The crowd that had assembled to watch the fight disperses and I expect to hear sirens at any minute. It's not the first time Drew's gotten in trouble for fighting, and it certainly won't be the last. His only saving grace has been his father's close connection with many of the boys in blue in this town.

"What the hell, Drew?" I shriek in an uncharacteristic move. I'm normally even-tempered, but I can't be right now, not about this. He may think he's just playing the overprotective friend card, but that's not how I see it. This is an instance of another

13

person in my life thinking they know what's best for me.

"What? I thought——"

"That I need *you* to come in and save the day? I don't! I can take care of myself!"

"Oh really?" He crosses his arms over his chest. I'm so upset, I don't even have time to take in how beautiful he is in just a pair of swim trunks, his chest glistening with perspiration, his chiseled abs disappearing into a V. Just like Damian's arrogance turned me off, I find myself turned off from Drew because of the same thing. "If you call letting some guy put his hands all over you taking care of yourself——"

"Did you ever stop to think that maybe I *wanted* him to put his hands all over me?" I spit out, not caring how far from the truth those words are. "But no! Now, because of you, no guy will ever want to touch me again. They'll all be worried about Drew Brinks finding out and breaking their nose."

"I'm sorry, Brook." His tone softens as he steps toward me, but I back away, collecting my things. "I thought——"

"Well, stop," I bite back harshly. "Just..." I shake my head. "I already have one ridiculously overprotective father. I don't need another." I sling my bag over my shoulder and hurry toward the bus stop, trying to erase the memory of how he looked at me.

But I can't.

Chapter Two

DREW

THE HEAT OF THE day begins to wane as I shuffle down the street I grew up on. Not much has changed in the past eighteen years. A few houses have gotten a fresh coat of paint or new owners, but the feel of the neighborhood is still the same. Everyone watches out for each other here. Everyone knows each other's business, which is why word about Damian Murphy's broken nose seems to have spread faster than a drop of oil in a puddle of water. I spent the afternoon on damage control, thanks to my aunt's insistence I apologize in the hopes he doesn't file charges. I'd like to say I regret my actions, but I don't.

I'm not quite sure what came over me. I'd been hanging out with a few of the guys, playing volleyball, when one of them commented about how hot Brooklyn looked in her bikini. The instant I stole a glance at her, it felt like all the air had been sucked from my lungs. I tried to stop staring, but couldn't. You'd have to be blind to not have noticed the change in her body over the past year, but she always wore relatively conservative clothes, barely showing any skin. That wasn't the case earlier. When I saw Damian Murphy, notorious flirt and player, approach her and proceed to touch her, I lost it. A new sort of protectiveness came over me, one I couldn't quite explain.

One I still can't.

The usual sounds of the neighborhood surround me as I continue down the same route I've walked more times than I can count— children laughing and playing, the five o'clock news blaring out open windows, the sizzle of burgers and hot dogs on a grill. Summer's here and I'm both happy and sad at the same time. I'm done with high school, but unsure how to feel about embarking on the next journey of my life — college.

For as long as I can remember, I've been the star hockey player. First in the town league, then in high school. In a few months, I'll board a plane for the University of Minnesota, where I received a full athletic scholarship and a starting position on their Division I hockey team. I may no longer be the best player, although my father tells me otherwise, considering I've been given a place on the World Junior Championship team and my name's in contention to be selected for the Games next year. Still, I'll be battling for attention among dozens of other players just like me. What if I'm not as good as I've been led to believe? What will I do then? For as long as I can remember, hockey's been my life. It's the only thing that helped when my mother disappeared from my life right after my sixth birthday. I don't know what I would do if I no longer had it.

I slow my steps as I approach my destination. Brooklyn's house looms in front of me. It's a small shotgun-style home, just like many of the houses in this area. A large oak tree sits at the crest of the steep hill in the front yard, and a smile lights up my face when I see Brooklyn sitting on the swing tied to one of the large branches.

Shoving my hands into the pockets of my pants, I head up the hill. She remains oblivious to my presence, her fingers wrapped around the rope, her eyes closed as she basks in the last few hours of sun before it disappears beyond the horizon. A breeze picks up, blowing her long, dark hair around. She looks more at peace than I can recall seeing in recent memory. I almost hate to disturb her.

"Hey," I say.

She startles, her eyes flinging open, a hand flying to her chest. When her gaze lands on me, she blows out a long breath.

"Dammit, Drew. You scared me."

"I didn't mean to, but I had to come talk to you." When I nod toward the setting sun, her mouth curves up in understanding.

"Never go to sleep without making up," she says, reciting what my aunt would say to us whenever we'd argue as kids. It seems like it was just yesterday that Molly brought her new friend from school home to play and she became an honorary Brinks.

Even back then, Brooklyn was withdrawn, quiet, shy. A complete one-eighty from my sister's rambunctious tendencies. Throughout the years, their personalities seemed to complement each other. Molly and I have always been close, and because of that, I grew close with Brooklyn, too. I've always considered her to be like another sister, which is why I feel protective of her. I keep an eye out for Molly, too, but Brooklyn's different. I've lost count of the number of my fellow classmates I threatened when I caught them staring at her ass, chest, or legs. It doesn't matter that she covers herself up by dressing more modestly than most other girls at our school, which is probably due to her father's overprotective tendencies. Every guy notices Brooklyn Tanner. It's impossible not to.

Now that the temperatures are rising, they're all noticing even more. I'm more than aware I overreacted on the beach. I can't stomach the idea of some guy touching Brooklyn. I know I'll have to get used to the likelihood it'll happen. It still brings out my protective nature, though. And that's all this is. My protective nature coming out. Nothing more. At least, that's what I try to tell myself, especially when I feel a burning deep in my stomach as I take in her eyes, her lips, her curves. I've never had this reaction to her before. Why now?

"Exactly." I pull my lips between my teeth, unsure what to say. I hadn't really thought that far ahead when I left my house. All I knew was I *had* to talk to her. Aunt Gigi has a way of making you think horrible things will happen if you disobey any of her rules. I don't want to think what will occur if we violate her admonition that we not go to bed without reconciling our earlier disagreement. "Listen, Brook—"

She immediately holds up her hand. "Just answer one question." Her gaze hardens.

In this moment, I no longer see the girl who's been my sister's shadow for the past decade. I no longer see a girl, period. She looks mature beyond her almost sixteen years. I suppose she always has been. Losing a parent forces you to grow up faster than you want to. I know from experience.

"Are you only here because Aunt Gigi put the fear of God into you?"

"No," I say quickly, then pause. "Well, yes. Gigi *always* seems to put the fear of God into me, especially when I do something wrong and apologize, only for her to point to the sky and say, 'Only *He* can forgive,' or something like that."

Brooklyn tilts her head to the side, studying me. Then she bursts into a hearty laugh, the tension breaking. She knows all too well how Aunt Gigi can be. It doesn't matter that she's technically my aunt. She took Brooklyn under her wing and helped raise her, just like she did with us. She considers all of us her kids, regardless that she didn't give birth to us.

"But *I* wanted to come talk to you," I continue, my voice becoming serious. "To apologize. I just... I care about you, Brooklyn. I know how boys like Damian think. Trust me. It's nothing good."

"I know that. I'm not as naïve as you and my dad think I am." Her voice is firm as she pushes her feet against the ground, swinging slightly. "I have absolutely no intention of going out with him."

I lift a brow. "But you were okay with him touching you?" I lean closer, lowering my voice. "I saw what he was about to do, Brooklyn."

She stops swinging, her mouth tightening as she averts her eyes, staring at the ground.

"Boys like Damian need to learn that no means no."

"And you think you're the person to teach him that lesson?" She slowly brings her green eyes to mine.

"I do." I take a step closer, crossing my arms in front of my chest, my biceps stretching the fabric of my t-shirt. She inhales sharply, then looks away.

"Like I told you earlier, you won't always be around to bail me out of sticky situations." Then she laughs. "But I doubt any other guy will ever come near me again, considering the last one who did ended up with a broken nose."

"Which he deserved."

"Yes. Yes, he did." She draws in a deep breath, then exhales. Brooklyn's almost as stubborn as I am, but in that moment, I see the fear she didn't want to admit she felt earlier. "Thank you, Drew."

"No one touches you unless you want them to. Ever. Got it?"

She nods. "Got it."

"Good."

With the air seemingly cleared between us, I walk around the swing, positioning myself behind her. "Well, go on then."

She glances over her shoulder. "Go on...what?" Her forehead wrinkles.

"Swing. I'll push you."

"We're not kids anymore," she reminds me.

"You're never too old to fly, Brookie," I reply, using the nickname I used to call her.

She considers my response for a minute, then relents. "I suppose you're right, Dewy."

She faces forward and pushes her feet against the ground before straightening her legs as she takes flight. When she swings back, my hands land against her skin and I push, propelling her higher. After a few swings, her laughter fills the air, making me smile.

"Higher," she calls out. Unable to deny her, I use more force to drive her higher. Her hair is wild as it blows in the wind, the sight of her so happy, so carefree, so at ease making my heart full.

Then a pang hits me as I contemplate how this is one of the last times I'll push Brooklyn on this swing. One of the last times I'll inhale her aroma as it wraps around me. One of the last times we'll have *this*.

"Higher! Higher!" Brooklyn's exuberant cries snap me out of my thoughts and I use more force to push her farther into the sky. She swings her legs back and propels herself off the swing, taking flight. I watch as she soars through the air, like she used to when we were kids. Her feet hit the ground, but she loses her balance, tumbling down the hill in her front yard.

I react quickly, hurrying to help. The steep pitch of the hill is too much and I fall, rolling down after her. I reach her, but velocity forces me to keep going, stopping directly on top of her with a grunt.

"Are you okay?" I ask feverishly, scanning her appearance for any cuts or bruises. "I'm so sorry. Did I push too hard? Did I—"

"Relax, Drew," she says with a smile. The anger that had covered her expression earlier in the day has disappeared, leaving the version of Brooklyn I'm accustomed to — tranquil and relaxed. "I wanted to fly."

I lick my lips, glued to my position. I should roll off her, help her back to her feet, then say my goodbyes, but I'm completely mesmerized, unable to look away, to stop wanting to feel her body against mine. She's unlike any other girl at our school. They all seem to be obsessed with the latest fashion trend or hairstyle. Not Brooklyn. She wears whatever she finds comfortable, regardless of whether it shows the most cleavage or leg. She wears barely any makeup, but she doesn't have to. Her skin has a natural glow to it. Her hair is free of any highlights or gels. Her beauty is authentic, not the result of a ridiculous amount of products.

I reach for a strand of hair that had fallen in front of her eyes. The instant my finger brushes against her skin, a charge of electricity pulses through me. I try to blame it on hormones, convince myself I'm just like every other teenage boy who's discovered girls and wants to see them naked, but that's not it. I've been with other girls. I've never felt this surge of need from just a brush of my hand against skin.

"Brooklyn…" I rest on my forearms.

"Yes?" She tilts her head back, licking her lips. I peer deep into her eyes. They're eyes I've seen nearly every day for the past ten years, but right now, I don't know if I've ever seen anything as beautiful. The way they darken when they lock with mine, our stare deep, intense, profound.

"Have you ever kissed a boy?" I have no idea what's come over me, why I'm asking her this, but I only have a few months left with her. It's now or never.

"My dad kisses my cheek every time he leaves." Her voice is low, throaty, completely unlike her usual tone.

I smile at her innocence, doing my best to appear calm and collected when inside, my heart is pounding against my chest at such a feverish pace, I wouldn't be surprised if the next beat forces it outside my ribcage.

"That's not what I'm talking about. Have you ever kissed a boy? Not a peck on the cheek or mouth. I'm talking about a real kiss. A kiss you feel in your soul. A kiss that makes you forget about where you are, who you are. Has anyone ever kissed you like that?"

She shakes her head. I expect her to lower her eyes, as she so often does when forced to discuss something she's not comfortable with, but her gaze remains glued to mine, her eyes shining.

"Why not?"

"You only get one first kiss," she replies in an unsteady voice. "I don't want to waste it on someone undeserving."

I should walk away right now. This is Brooklyn, after all. Brilliant. Smart. Compassionate. With her stellar grades and extra-curricular activities, she'll get a full scholarship to the Ivy League school of her choosing. She has a bright future ahead of her. I struggled to make Bs and Cs. She reads *War and Peace* for fun. I sometimes have difficulty getting through the articles in my *Sports Illustrated*. She cares about what's happening in the Middle East. I don't really understand what's happening in the Middle East. She walks twenty miles during the Walk for Hunger in Boston every year.

I don't like walking twenty feet from the TV to the kitchen to get a snack.

Despite growing up together, we come from two different worlds. Mine is hockey. Hers is doing anything to *save* the world. Not to mention the overbearing father who looks at every boy with suspicion, even me, regardless of the fact that he's known me most of my life. That doesn't matter anymore.

Regardless of all these obstacles, I can't stomach the thought of Brooklyn giving her first kiss to someone who won't cherish it for the gift it is.

"And is there someone you believe *is* deserving?"

Holding my breath, the seconds seem to stretch as I await her response. I know I'm pushing the boundaries and may just ruin our friendship, but I can't stop myself. I have a feeling I know what she's going to say. I've noticed her flushed complexion when I walk around the house without a shirt on. The sly glances when she doesn't think I'm looking. The rapid breathing when I lean over her to grab something as she bakes muffins with Gigi.

Finally, she nods, the motion almost imperceptible.

"Who?"

"You."

One word and my smile widens. One word and my heart soars. One word and I feel like I'm flying.

"Why me?"

"I don't know." She lowers her eyes, but I grab her chin, forcing her gaze back to mine. I don't want her to hide from me. Not now, not after giving me so much hope with that one word. "It just…"

"Yes?" I lower my mouth toward hers, her sweet breath touching my lips. It sends a tingle throughout me.

For a moment, I forget about where we are. That we're lying on her front lawn on a fairly busy street in Somerville, cars driving by, nosy neighbors probably watching us with rapt attention. That her father's truck is in the driveway, meaning he's home. That she's my sister's best friend.

"It feels…"

"Yes?" I say again, inching even closer still.

"It feels—"

"Brooklyn!" a booming voice yells.

I quickly shoot off her as she scrambles to her feet. Both of us look at the other in horror before she darts up the hill toward her front door where her father stands. I wonder if he saw us. By the stern look he gives me as I climb up the grass toward him, I have a feeling he did.

"Evening, Drew," he says, his voice clipped.

It's not that he doesn't like me. He does. He's been like a second father to me, but that's no excuse for why he just caught me in a compromising position with his only daughter, the apple of his eye, his pride and joy. It doesn't matter how much he likes me as a person. He's still the father of a beautiful teenage girl he'll willingly go to jail for.

"Good evening, Mr. Tanner. I apologize for the intrusion," I say, using all the manners Aunt Gigi and

25

my father have ingrained in me over the years.

Despite the close relationship I have with this man, he's always scared me. Being a career firefighter, he gives off the impression of being a no-nonsense kind of guy, not to mention a hard-ass. He's definitely not someone I'd ever want to upset.

I continue. "I just needed to talk to Brooklyn about something."

"It's quite all right." He looks from me to Brooklyn, then back at me again. I shift my eyes to hers, catching them. She chews on her lower lip, her face flushed. When neither one of us makes a move, he says, "Isn't your father expecting you for dinner?" I shoot my eyes back to his and he cocks a brow, crossing his arms over his broad chest, making him appear even more intimidating.

"Yes. Of course." I begin to retreat, this entire situation becoming more awkward. As I walk by Brooklyn, I pass her a sly grin. "'Night." I wink.

"Bye, Drew," she murmurs in a smooth voice.

As I walk away, I can't stop thinking about her, about how amazing she felt in my arms, her breath intermingling with mine.

I'm in trouble.

Chapter Three

BROOKLYN

"**S**MELLS GOOD, DAD," I say, doing my best to steer the conversation away from the topic of Drew and the fact that he interrupted us just seconds before we kissed. I'm still not sure how to feel about it. Did Drew actually want to kiss me? Or was he only doing it to make sure I had the first kiss I always dreamed of? Was I just a charity case to him?

He's *the* guy at school. At least he was before he graduated last week. Handsome. Funny. Star hockey player. And hopelessly out of my league. He's never really paid much attention to me...until earlier today. I have trouble rationalizing the Drew who was seconds away from kissing me with the Drew who can have any girl he wants. Girls who are much more experienced than me. All further proof that I'm probably just a charity project. I absently wonder if that was on the list of approved community service projects for graduation... *Kiss the school geek.*

I grab two plates from the cabinet and go about setting the kitchen table. It's riddled with scratches and marker stains from when I was a little girl, but my father refuses to get rid of this piece of furniture. Most of the items in our house are dated, but he just can't bear to part with any of them. My mother picked out everything, right down to the German figurines they bought in Munich during their honeymoon. I often catch my father standing in front of the display case, staring at the dozens of ceramic pieces. These days, many are worth a small fortune, but he still won't part with them. They're my mother's, and they'll always be my mother's, regardless that she's no longer with us.

The woman who gave birth to me often feels like an enigma, especially with the passing of years. There have been so many occasions I wish I could have a mother-figure to talk to. Lately, I wonder if she had never died, would my dad still be so strict and controlling? I understand why he's the way he is. The heartache of losing the love of your life never goes away. He says he's moved on, that he's no longer affected by her death, but I still occasionally see a pamphlet from a grief counseling session stuffed in his jacket pocket. Because of this loss, he's petrified of the same thing happening to anyone else, namely me. We're all each other have. Whenever I get irritated that I'm not allowed to date or wear clothing that shows even a hint of cleavage, like the rest of the girls in my school are, I remind myself that this is his way of keeping me safe.

Once the table is set, I lift my eyes to my father's, the silence unnerving me. He stares down at me with worry. "Brooklyn, sweetie." He inhales a breath. I can tell this situation is just as uncomfortable for him as it is for me.

"Dad, it's okay. Let's just drop it."

He walks toward the counter to grab the foil-covered plate, the aroma of grilled steaks emanating from it. I blow out a slow breath, thankful to have dodged this conversation. Then he stops himself, leaning back against the counter and folding his arms in front of his chest.

"Do you like him?"

"Who? Drew?" I respond, as if it's completely absurd. "Of course not. He's Molly's older brother."

"I know who he is." Dad's voice is alarmingly calm. "Which is why I'm concerned."

"You have nothing to be concerned about. Promise."

"Are you sure? He's eighteen, pumpkin," he reminds me, using his childhood nickname for me. It makes me feel exactly like a five-year-old. I surmise that's what he intended.

"I know how old he is, Dad." I grab a few napkins out of the holder and go about folding them just to give myself something to do.

"He'll be going off to college in two months."

"Dad…," I groan.

"There's a big difference between a boy in college and one in high school. Trust me. I was in his shoes once. This is why I don't want you dating yet. You're still too young and can easily be taken advantage of."

I groan louder, wishing I could summon a fairy godmother to come and whisk me away from this conversation. These aren't the types of discussions my father typically has with me. Anything of a sensitive nature is usually relegated to Aunt Gigi, but he must realize this isn't something she should handle.

"Boys like Drew are more…experienced."

"Dad," I say once again, rolling my eyes. Regardless of whether he senses my discomfort, it doesn't sway him. He continues.

"They'll expect more, perhaps things you're not ready for just yet, and they may not take no for an answer. You may think you know how to handle yourself, that he's a friend so there's nothing to worry about, but I know boys. They're all the same, friend or not. Their hormones are out of control and they're thinking about one thing and one thing only."

"Dad! Enough!" I whirl around, meeting his eyes. "I get it! You don't like Drew, just like you don't like any boy. It doesn't matter. He's out of my league anyway." Lowering my voice, I add, "He'd never be interested in someone like me."

His expression softens as he approaches, wrapping his arms around me. "What makes you think that? If anything, *you* are out of *his* league." He pulls back, his hands gripping my biceps as he looks upon me with all the love and devotion a father can. Perhaps even more, considering he's made it his mission to make up for the mother's love I'm missing. "I just don't want to see you hurt. That's why I have these rules in place. To protect you."

I swallow hard, giving him a half-hearted smile. "I know. Drew and me… There's nothing there."

I want to believe that's the case, but I still can't stop thinking about the surge of electricity that coursed through me as his breath danced with mine, the

30

anticipation of what was to come unhinging me, making me forget about everything for a brief moment. It was…magic.

Chapter Four

DREW

I HAVE TROUBLE FIGHTING back my smile as I walk into my house later that evening. It's dark, everything silent. After leaving Brooklyn, I was on a high and in no rush to head home. It's irrelevant that we didn't actually kiss. I felt more fulfilled afterward than any other act of intimacy I've ever experienced, even sex. It's crazy to think of Brooklyn this way, but I suppose I've always found her to be beautiful. Now I want more than to simply admire her from afar. I want to be hers, and I want the world to know she's mine. I'd like to see Damian Murphy try to talk to her now.

"Getting in a bit late, aren't you?" a deep voice says, startling me as I make my way down the hall and toward my bedroom. I pause, peering into the den, a small lamp casting a subtle glow. My father's sitting in his recliner, a folded newspaper in his hand as he works on his crossword puzzle. At almost sixty, he's older than most of my friends' dads, but he doesn't look it. His hair is still full and dark, despite a few gray ones beginning to sprout up.

"I guess." I shove my hands into my pockets, rocking on my heels.

"Where have you been?" He arches a brow.

"Out," I say nonchalantly.

"Anywhere in particular?"

I narrow my gaze. My father isn't remotely close to being as strict as Brooklyn's. I don't think I've ever had a curfew, which is why this line of questioning gives me pause. It's completely out of character for him.

"Not really. Just hanging out with some friends."

He assesses me for a moment. I'm waiting for him to call me out on my lies. Then he blows out a sigh and places the newspaper on the side table. "Reece Tanner called earlier this evening."

I try to keep my expression even, not giving anything away. "Is everything okay?"

He opens his mouth, then pauses, formulating his response. "He mentioned you stopped by. That when he went to call Brooklyn in for dinner, it appeared you two were in an…intimate position."

"I was pushing her on the swing and she leapt off," I explain, straightening my spine. "She lost her footing and fell down the steep hill in her front yard. I went after her to make sure she was okay, then fell myself. It was nothing."

"And the fight with Damian?"

I furrow my brows. "What do you mean?"

"How you broke his nose because he was talking to Brooklyn."

"He was doing a lot more than just talking to her, Dad." My jaw tightens.

33

"That's not what Damian claims."

I open my mouth to argue, then stop. It doesn't matter. "Brooklyn's just a friend."

"The fact you even have to say that makes me think she's not. Men don't break someone's nose over a girl who's 'just a friend'."

"Dad...," I begin, but don't know what else to add. I've never liked lying to him. Molly does it all the time, but this man has sacrificed so much to help me get where I am. The least I can do is give him the respect he deserves.

He looks up at the ceiling and I see his lips moving, as if mumbling a prayer. While my father isn't nearly as devout as Aunt Gigi, refusing to attend services except for funerals and weddings, I often catch him praying. In his mind, you can still be close to God without having to go to a building to feel His power. There's something about that theory that speaks to me, too.

When he returns his gaze to mine, he appears more assured. "When you were born, I was grateful you were a boy. Mostly because I didn't have to worry about all the stuff that goes along with having a teenage daughter...even though I found out nonetheless. Still, there are some things about raising a son, especially once they hit eighteen, that are difficult."

I swallow hard, not sure I want to hear what he has to say.

"I've been in your shoes. I guess you can say I've always had a thing for younger women."

"Dad." I look away, feeling a blush building on my face. The last thing anyone wants to talk about with their parents is their sex life.

"Your mother *was* fifteen years younger than me, after all. When I was your age, I thought I was in love with one of *my* neighbors, a girl I practically grew up with. I was eighteen. She was only fifteen."

"It's not like that with us."

He gives me a skeptical look, then kicks the footrest of his recliner back down and stands. "Even I can see that's not true. I may be old, but my eyesight is still as keen as it was when I was in my twenties. I see the way you look at her. It doesn't matter that she's a girl you grew up with. Nothing can happen between you. The age of consent in this state is sixteen. You can argue that it's consensual until you're blue in the face. That won't change a thing. In the state's eyes, she isn't capable of consenting. As Brooklyn's father was gracious enough to point out, this state doesn't have an exception for those close in age."

"Dad, *nothing* happened between us. Whatever Mr. Tanner saw was just a misunderstanding. It wasn't like it looked."

"I hope that's the case. I promised him I'd talk to you, make sure you're aware of the potential ramifications here. You know how he can be. If I were you, I'd consider this a friendly warning. I doubt the next time he calls will be as cordial."

"Yes, sir." I do my best to not appear downtrodden.

"You don't need any distractions right now, Drew," he reminds me. I meet his eyes. "Focus on your training. And that means getting enough sleep." He looks to the clock on the wall and I follow his line of sight to see it's nearly midnight. "We're leaving for the rink at six tomorrow morning."

I hang my head. "Yes, sir." All the excitement has disappeared at the reminder of what's at stake if I pursue something with Brooklyn. It doesn't matter that I've never felt so happy as when she lay secure beneath me, our lips close. For that brief moment, I felt like I was flying. The talk with my dad forces me to come crashing back down to earth.

Chapter Five

BROOKLYN

THE NEW FEW WEEKS are much more uneventful than the start of summer vacation. Just as I suspected, no other boys from school even try to hit on me when Molly and I hang out at the beach. I'm unsure whether to find it endearing or annoying. This is my summer vacation. I'm supposed to be having fun. Instead, part of me thinks I'd have more fun if I were to join a convent, particularly with my father's strict curfew.

As a firefighter, he works twenty-four-hour shifts, then has three days off, so I could easily stay out past my curfew during the times he's on duty. We have a security system, complete with cameras that record all the comings and goings outside my house, but that's not what keeps me from breaking his rules. Every morning before he leaves, he kisses my cheek and reminds me not to do anything that would betray his trust. So I don't.

Instead, I've been relegated to being the token single girl during every group outing. I try not to let it get to me. Still, I *do* get a little jealous whenever I see Molly and Brody kiss, wishing I knew what that felt like.

At the start of the summer, I thought this would finally be the year I'd experience my first kiss. Now, I'm beginning to think it's never going to happen.

I haven't spoken to Drew since our little incident. I'm not sure if he's avoiding me because he's embarrassed we got caught or because he almost kissed me. Even on the rare occasions Molly's lips aren't attached to Brody's and I hang out over at her house, Drew's either not there or locks himself in his room. It's almost like, in his eyes, I don't exist. I wish I could feel the same way about him.

Feeling as if I've been labeled a social outcast, I've begun picking up extra hours at the movie theater where I got a job once I obtained my work permit. Dad's rules. If I want to drive when I turn sixteen, I have to pay for my own gas and car insurance. We aren't so hard off that he can't help with those things, but he wants to teach me responsibility. Plus, having a job looks good on college applications.

"*Pearl Harbor*," Spencer says on a Monday evening in early August as a couple I estimate to be in their early twenties enters and makes their way through the queue toward the ticket counter.

"Nah," I respond, studying them. It's a game we play during our shifts where we try to guess what movie each person or couple is going to see. It makes the slow nights go by much quicker. "That's already been out a few months." I pinch my lips together. "I'm going with *America's Sweethearts*."

"Care to put a wager on it?"

"What did you have in mind?" I waggle my brows, grinning deviously. Spencer's not bad looking. Actually,

38

I think he's kind of cute in a nerdy way. He's thin and brainy, but has this aloofness to him that makes him attractive.

"Loser has to clean winner's children's movies for a month."

I whistle. These are some very high stakes. Everyone who's ever worked in a movie theater knows the theater after a kid's movie lets out is akin to the remnants of a massive tornado. The floor will be covered in popcorn, candy stuck to the back of chairs. If you're lucky, you won't reach under the seat to find some parent decided to leave a dirty diaper under there instead of tossing it into the trash bin. It's the least glamorous part of this job, and Spencer knows it.

"Time's ticking, Brook," he jests, shifting his eyes to the couple who are now fast approaching us. "Lots at stake here, especially your reputation. Unless it's all just been a bunch of crap and you're not as brilliant as we've all been led to believe."

"Fine." I thrust out my hand and he shakes it with a grin. "You've got yourself a deal."

I turn from him, smiling at the couple, then mutter under my breath, "Hope you like scraping gum because you're going to be spending the next month doing just that."

"We'll see." He beams as he faces the couple, my heart pounding in my chest. Spencer *could* be right. It doesn't matter that his guess is a movie that's been out for a while. It's still in theaters for a reason. "Good evening. How can I help you?"

My body tightens as I witness the exchange. Time

seems to stand still as the couple looks at the board containing the showtimes, the man resting his hand on his chin and tapping his forefinger on his bottom lip, deep in thought.

"Two tickets…"

I say a little prayer when I see the man's eyes zero in on *Pearl Harbor*.

"To…"

Then he shifts his gaze to *Shrek*. I know for certain they have no intention of seeing that. This is a college-aged couple here to probably make out away from the overbearing eyes of their parents.

"*America's Sweethearts*."

I breathe a huge sigh of relief, grinning. I wait until the couple leaves with the tickets Spencer begrudgingly handed over, then I break out into a dance, taunting him.

"That's right! Who's the winner now?" I keep dancing, laughing, oblivious to everything else. It doesn't matter. The theater's pretty dead tonight. Monday's aren't exactly a popular night to go to the movies. "You went up against the dragon and got burned!" I reach for the feather duster by the cash registers and hand it to him, although he'll need a lot more cleaning supplies for the task ahead. It's simply a token gesture. "I think *Shrek* just let out. Better get going, Spence!"

"Yeah, yeah," he grumbles as he snatches the feather duster from me, trudging away and toward the theaters.

I'm so lost in my celebratory gloating, I don't even notice when someone approaches the ticket counter until I hear a loud throat clearing. I whirl around, my breath escaping when I see Drew standing there. But that's not what causes a snake to slither up and squeeze my heart. It's the fact he's here with another girl. And not just any girl. Mindy Jacobson. Popular. Beautiful. Head cheerleader. Homecoming queen. It makes sense. Drew *was* Homecoming king.

"Hey," he says, his voice soft. It's the first thing he's said to me since the day he had me pinned beneath him. I wonder how many times he's had Mindy Jacobson pinned beneath him since then.

"Hi." I swallow hard, my face flushing. I do my best to pretend the thought of him here with another girl doesn't hit me square in the gut. I wonder if I'll always feel this pull to him that he doesn't even know exists.

"How are you?"

"Fine." I don't bother to ask him how he's doing. The silent treatment I've received the past few weeks is all the answer I need to know exactly how he feels. He probably just saw me as another notch in his belt, like my dad warned me about.

I hear the things the boys at school say behind my back, especially now that I have a pair of boobs and hips that they, and I quote, "would love to get a hold of and go to town on." After the episode with Damian, I honestly thought Drew cared. He doesn't. He just wanted to have bragging rights himself.

"How can I help you this evening?" I plaster on the fake smile I use with complete strangers, which is precisely what Drew feels like to me…a stranger.

41

As I await his response, I hold my breath, saying a silent prayer like I did with Spencer. This time, it's not because cleaning a dirty theater is at stake. It's because I hate the thought of Drew coming here with a girl for the same reason every other teenage boy does. Certain movies are more advantageous to that kind of thing than others.

"Two tickets to *Original Sin*," he says.

I do my best to not react, not let him see how disappointed I am. I have no claim over him. Gritting a smile, I take his money, gauging his response. I normally don't charge him. But that was before. Before the almost kiss. Before he brought Mindy Jacobson here and asked for two tickets to the steamiest movie we're allowed to show.

Once the tickets spit out, I hand them to him, along with his change. "Enjoy the show."

"Thanks, Brandy," Mindy says with an overabundance of enthusiasm, like every sentence she speaks should be a cheer.

"It's Brooklyn," I mutter as she begins to retreat, pulling Drew along with her.

He glances over his shoulder, his gaze confusing me. It almost looks regretful. I brush it off. It doesn't matter. *He* doesn't matter.

The next half-hour passes slowly. All I can think of is Drew in a darkened theater, making out with Mindy. I don't want to even consider what other things they're doing. I actually wish I had lost to Spencer. Then I would have been cleaning and never would have seen Drew, never would be faced with the reality that I'll never be enough for him.

"Well, that wasn't as bad as I thought," Spencer says as he walks up, removing a pair of rubber gloves and tossing them into the trash. I flash my eyes to his, forcing a smile, but it's lacking. His grin falls and he furrows his brow. "Are you okay? I thought you'd still be doing your little dance."

He starts shaking his hips, moving around the ticket counter, not caring that his dance skills are nonexistent. It doesn't bother him. Nothing ever does. When he does a horrible impersonation of "The Carlton" from *Fresh Prince of Bel-Air*, I laugh at how absolutely ridiculous he looks. There are few things that are certain to bring a smile to my face, but horrible dancing is one of them.

"There's my girl," Spencer says. I quickly shoot my eyes to his, surprised by his words. He sucks in a breath, obviously just as shocked as I am. "I mean… I didn't mean it like *that*. I just meant you weren't yourself. Not that you're my girl or anything. I wouldn't want Drew to get the wrong idea, especially after what I heard happened to Damian Murphy."

My momentary happiness immediately evaporates when I hear Spencer mention Drew. Feeling tears prickle the corners of my eyes, I step past him.

"Can you hold down the fort for a few minutes?" I manage to say through the lump in my throat.

"Are you okay?"

"Yeah."

I keep my head down, doing everything I can to steady my voice. The last thing I want is for Spencer to

43

witness my breakdown. And over a boy. Now I understand why my dad doesn't want me to date. It's too distracting, keeps me from doing what I should be — working and getting ahead with my schoolwork for the upcoming year. I'm already behind on the summer reading list. I can't fall behind during the regular academic year, too.

"I just need to use the little girl's room. I'll be back in a few minutes."

"As long as you're not heading into a theater to mess it up just so I have to clean it."

I glance over my shoulder at him, my lips curving into a sly smile, but it's not as vivacious as it usually is. "I wasn't going to, but now that you've given me the idea…"

His eyes widen. "You better not, Brook!"

I shrug, chewing on my lower lip, then continue walking, grateful for the brief moment of levity Spencer's geeky antics provide. But that levity is short-lived as I pass the theater showing *Original Sin*. I slow my steps, telling myself to stop thinking about him, but my curiosity gets the better of me. I veer toward the theater, slowly opening the door and walking in.

Apart from a few aisle lights, everything's dark. Even the screen doesn't give off much light, considering how dark this movie is. I shouldn't be in here. When they hired me, the management was adamant I not step foot in any of the theaters showing R-rated movies until they were over. I could lose my job if anyone catches me, but that's not a good enough reason for me to leave.

I scan the seats. There aren't many people here, making my perusal easier. As my eyes float over the back few rows, I notice a familiar silhouette, his mouth attached to Mindy's, her hands running through his hair. Jealousy bubbles deep. A voice inside tells me to turn around. After all, I've seen Drew kiss plenty of girls over the years. But this is the first time I've seen him kiss someone after he almost kissed me. A part of me feels like that's *my* kiss Mindy's enjoying.

I step closer, unable to look away. I wonder if Mindy realizes how lucky she is to feel his lips on hers, his body next to hers, his woodsy aroma invading her senses. I notice movement beneath Mindy's shirt and realize Drew's hand is making that motion.

My face heats even more, embarrassed but curious at the same time. Mindy's sitting in the chair against the wall, Drew the next one over, his back toward me. I can make out the expression on Mindy's face as he touches her. I don't think I've ever felt anything that would make me look like *that*, like I'm ready to lose control. I've seen some intimate moments in movies, but they were actors, putting on a show for maximum benefit. Bearing witness to Drew with another girl is yet one more reminder that I could never be what he needs. I would never be so bold as to let him touch me like that, especially in public.

As I begin to slowly retreat, blue eyes meet mine and I freeze in place. I expect Mindy to pull away since I caught them, but she doesn't. She smirks, digging her hands into Drew's scalp. Her stare still trained on me, she leans closer to him, nibbling on his earlobe. Then she palms his crotch, slowly lowering herself toward his waist.

When I faintly make out the sound of a zipper, I abruptly spin around, hurrying out of the theater. I'm smart enough to know what she's about to do. I want nothing more than to erase that, erase *Drew*, from my memory.

Chapter Six

DREW

"THANKS FOR THE MOVIE," Mindy says flirtatiously as I pull up in front of her house. The instant I put the car in park, she reaches across the center console, her hand landing on my crotch. "It was quite enjoyable, although I can't tell you what it was about." She squeezes and I feel a slight twitching in my pants from the gesture.

Mindy's probably every guy's dream. Tall. Long legs. Wavy blonde hair. Mesmerizing blue eyes. She's beautiful and she knows it, but not in an attractive way. She uses the fact that everyone in school thinks she's hot to her advantage. I fell for it, too, although I didn't realize it at the time. Now I can't remember why I asked her out in the first place. She's sexy and always up for a good time, but something's lacking. Something's *been* lacking ever since I felt Brooklyn's body beneath mine. Seeing her again tonight brought up all these feelings I've been trying to suppress for the past month. I'd hoped spending more time with Mindy, even though we're both heading our separate ways at the end of the summer, would help with that. I *need* it to help with that.

Inching toward her, I brush my lips across hers. I want to feel some sort of connection to her, a spark of electricity burning low in my stomach. That doesn't happen. Just as she always does, she grabs the back of my neck, turning the kiss from soft and sweet to erotic and intense. I don't mind deep kisses, but this seems like it's just a means to take things to the next level. Sometimes I just want to kiss for the sake of kissing, not as a way to get laid.

"Oh, Drew," she moans, her mouth moving down my jaw, to my neck. "Let's go to the overlook." Her breathing comes hot and heavy as she nips at my skin. "I leave for Notre Dame at the end of the month. I need you as often as possible between now and then."

I lean my head back against the headrest. Something inside me sparks to life when she rubs her hand between my legs. I was able to forget about Brooklyn briefly when Mindy went down on me tonight. Maybe I need more of that so I stop thinking about her altogether.

"And this time we won't have an audience, so I can really let loose."

"You're the one who wanted to go to the movies," I remind her.

"That's not what I'm talking about."

I bring my eyes to hers. "What do you mean?"

She smirks, leaning toward me. "That little friend of your sister's."

"What about her?"

Mindy grins slyly, her lips landing on my neck, her

tongue tracing circles. "She was watching us," she whispers in a throaty voice.

My chest rises and falls in a faster pattern. Not over what Mindy's doing to me right now, but over the idea of Brooklyn seeing me with someone else. Guilt settles in my stomach, weighing it down. It's never been like this before. Being with Mindy, with anyone else, suddenly feels wrong.

I grip Mindy's biceps, forcing her off me, my eyes fierce. "What do you mean?"

She wipes a finger along her mouth and I release my hold on her. "Exactly what I said. She was standing in the aisle of the theater, watching us. I figured if she wanted a show, I'd give her one. But once I reached for your cock, she disappeared."

My jaw grows slack as I study Mindy. I can only imagine what Brooklyn must think of me right now.

"What? It's not that big a deal. Hell, she's seen us make out before."

I close my eyes, running my hand over my face. I need to smooth this over with Brooklyn. I've tried to avoid her the past month, my obsession with how perfect her tall, lithe body felt below mine unnerving me. Every time I've thought about it, I remind myself how sweet and innocent she is, how I'm not the right person for her, how I'll only hold her back, how she's not yet sixteen. But I need to explain myself to her.

"I have to go," I say curtly.

"Go?" Mindy arches a brow. "What about the overlook?"

"I promised Gigi I'd help cover the morning shift at the café," I lie. "Maybe another time."

She pouts, studying me for a moment, then leans toward me. "Okay. I'll definitely be taking you up on that offer." She places her hand on my crotch once more. "I need more of this."

When she presses her mouth to mine, it does absolutely nothing for me. Finally, she pulls back and steps out of the car. I watch to ensure she makes it into her house safely, as my aunt taught me. Gigi also taught me to never go to bed without reconciling your differences. While Brooklyn and I haven't had a fight, she must be upset. I know I'd be if I were in her shoes, if I walked in on her locking lips with someone else, if I witnessed anyone else putting their hands on her. The last time I saw something like that, I sent the kid to the hospital with a broken nose.

Once Mindy blows me a kiss and closes the front door behind her, I put my car in drive, heading back toward the movie theater in the hopes of catching Brooklyn while she's still there. I don't want to show up at her house, especially if her father's home. After his call to my dad, warning me about getting involved with her, he wouldn't take kindly to me showing up at night.

As I approach the movie theater, I notice a familiar silhouette walking down the street. Reducing my speed, I make a quick U-turn, lowering the passenger side window.

"Brooklyn," I call out.

The instant she hears my voice, she slows her steps, shooting her eyes toward mine. A slight smile builds on her lips before she hardens her expression, facing forward once more.

"Date get cut short?" Her tone is harsh as she continues down the sidewalk.

"Get in the car," I order, driving along beside her. "I'll take you home."

"I'm fine. The bus stop is just a few blocks away."

"Why didn't your dad pick you up?"

"He's working. I take the bus when he can't get me."

"You shouldn't be walking by yourself. It's not safe. You should tell me when you need a ride."

"I do it all the time." She glares at me. "I can take care of myself. I don't need your help." I hear the double meaning in her words.

"I know you don't, and..." I pull my lip between my teeth, pausing.

"And?" When she abruptly stops walking, I step on the brakes. A hand goes to her hip as she taps her foot in irritation. It's absolutely adorable, but I reel in my smile, wanting to give the situation the seriousness it deserves.

"And I'm sorry," I say on a sigh.

She studies me for a minute, then her eyes soften, a smile returning to her mouth. "Jackpot." I haven't seen her smile at me in over a month. I didn't realize how much I missed it until this moment. She looks radiant, vivacious...beautiful.

She steps toward the car and opens the passenger door, sliding in. Once she's brought her seatbelt across her chest and buckled it, I pull back onto the road. Silence settles between us. I'm uncertain what to say. Do I discuss what she saw? It's not like Brooklyn and I are together and I cheated on her with Mindy, even though it kind of feels that way. I wish it didn't. I wish we could go back to the way things were between us before… Before I almost kissed her. Before her dad *saw* me almost kiss her. Before I was punched in the gut with a warning to stay away.

Suddenly, an idea pops into my head. Instead of taking the turn toward the residential section of town, I head in the opposite direction.

"Where are we going?" Brooklyn shifts her eyes to mine.

"It's a surprise." I give her a mischievous grin.

She crosses her arms over her chest, huffing. "We've known each other practically our entire lives. I'm not so sure you're capable of surprising me anymore, Drew. This is the way to the beach."

"Okay, so maybe it's not a great surprise. I just thought…" I trail off, drawing in a deep breath as I steal a glance at her. She's changed out of her work uniform and is in a white t-shirt and a pair of shorts that are unusually short for her. Or maybe they just seem that way because of how long her legs are. It takes every ounce of resolve I have to not gawk at them, the way the passing streetlamps hit them and make them glisten. "I just thought maybe we could go back to the start."

"The start?"

"Yeah. The start."

"Okay." No question about what I mean by that.

No push to talk more. Just a simple acquiescence. There's a comfort in her understanding my thought process without having to say a single word. Will I ever find someone else who can read my mind like Brooklyn can?

After a short, silent drive, I pull my car into a spot in one of the beach lots. I run around to the passenger side, helping Brooklyn out, as my father taught me to do. She blushes and I smile at her. The ocean breeze blows around us, her aroma mixing with the salty sea air. I lean down, my mouth a whisper from her neck. I haven't been this close to her in over a month and it's driving me crazy. I've been warned to keep my distance, but I just need one night, one hour, one minute. I don't care how long. I just need something real again.

"Never date a guy who doesn't open doors for you. You deserve to be treated like the treasure you are. Okay?"

"Yes." She slowly lifts her eyes to mine, our lips close. Just a slight tilt of my head and I'd get a taste of what I've been fantasizing about since I had her body pinned beneath mine. But I brought her here to clear the tension between us. Kissing her would only make it worse.

"Come on." I step back, gesturing across the road to the familiar awning of Kelly's. "Hungry?"

"Not really."

"Then ice cream. You're never too full for sweets."

She laughs, the sound warming my heart as we walk. "Another one of Aunt Gigi's rules for living."

"They're quite poignant," I retort. "Can you really argue with her on this one?"

"No." She shakes her head, shoving her hands into the back pockets of her shorts. "I certainly can't."

After I place my order and am given two chocolate ice cream cones, we cross the street and head back to the beach, strolling along the shore. It's silent between us, the only sound that of the ocean waves and the occasional dog barking as their owners take them for a walk.

"So, you and Mindy?" Brooklyn says after a while.

I shrug, not embellishing.

"How's that going to work with you heading to Minnesota? And isn't she heading somewhere in the Midwest, too?"

"It's not serious between us," I answer, uneasy about talking to Brooklyn about Mindy. "We have an…understanding."

Her mouth forms a tight line as she studies me. "An understanding?"

"Yeah. I guess. We just figured we may as well make the most out of the time we have left before college."

"Getting a blowjob in a movie theater is certainly one way of doing that," she mumbles, then inhales a sharp breath, shooting her wide eyes to mine. "I mean…" She averts her gaze.

"It's okay." I touch her arm, preventing her from going any further. She lifts her eyes. "Mindy told me what you saw."

"I didn't see anything," she responds hurriedly, freeing herself from my hold and continuing down the beach. I follow. "It was dark. I was just trying to get a head start on cleaning up the theaters."

She looks adorable when she's flustered. The full moon gives the beach a subtle glow, shining on her dark hair, and I can see the blush blooming on her cheeks.

"Anyway, it doesn't matter. What you do with your girlfriend, or whatever she is, is none of my business. Let's just stop talking about this because it's really weird for me. Worse than my dad trying to talk to me about sex all those years ago, until he decided it was a lost cause and called Aunt Gigi."

"Dad did the same thing with Molly," I say, chuckling slightly from the memory.

Our house isn't big, so everyone seems to know everyone else's business. When I heard him trying to have "the talk" with Molly, I couldn't help but cringe at how uncomfortable both of them sounded. It was different when my dad spoke to me about the proverbial birds and bees. I'm a guy. Girls are different. I've relearned that fact over the past several years as I've watched Brooklyn become more than just a girl, at least in my eyes. But as my father so nicely reminded me, in the eyes of the law, she's still just a girl.

"I suppose that's the sucky part about not having a mom." She brings her ice cream up to her mouth and I can't stop staring at her lips as they part. Her tongue darts out as she takes a lick of the rich, chocolaty goodness. She probably doesn't even realize what she's doing, but my mind is going to places I wish it wouldn't.

I quickly tear my eyes away and focus on eating my

55

own ice cream, but I'm not concentrating hard enough and some of it falls onto my white t-shirt, staining it. "Shit," I mutter, grabbing the flimsy napkin wrapped around the cone and dabbing at my shirt.

"Can't take you anywhere," Brooklyn jokes. "You seriously need a man bib."

"Man bib?"

"Yeah. Almost every meal you ever sit down to, you spill something."

"It's not that bad. I've done a lot worse."

Brooklyn stops walking and a devilish grin crosses her face. Before I can stop her, she shoves her ice cream cone into my chest, adding to the stain, covering my shirt with chocolate. "Worse than that?"

My eyes fling to hers, fiery but playful at the same time. "You'd better run, Brookie!" I drop my own ice cream cone to the ground.

With a shriek, she darts up the beach, her laughter filling the air. I let her have a little head start, but I eventually catch up to her, wrapping an arm around her waist. Hoisting her up, I toss her over my shoulder as if she were just a sack of flour. Compared to my tall, muscular stature, she weighs next to nothing.

"Drew!" Her screams get even louder, interspersed with infectious laughter. We're making a scene, but I don't care. This moment reminds me of all the times we roughhoused as kids, when she was just like another one of my friends. "Put me down."

She swats at my back, still wiggling against me, but my hold on her is too strong.

"Drew!" she shouts again as I head closer to the water. "Don't you dare! Don't you even think about it, Andrew Vincenzo Brinks! If you do—"

Her words are cut short when I barrel into the ocean, tossing her into it. She yells and sinks below the surface before getting her feet under her and standing.

"You are in big trouble, mister. Big, *big* trouble." Her eyes are on fire as she glares at me.

Then a breathtaking smile lights up her face as she advances, splashing me. She uses every ounce of strength she possesses to try to tackle me. She's no match for me, but I let her believe she can take me and fall into the water, rolling around with her. We continue to splash and dunk each other, heading farther away from the shore, every inch of me alive, alert…happy. This bewitching person makes me so fucking happy.

When we're out of breath, Brooklyn stops, her body bobbing up and down with the small waves. I glance back to the beach, surprised at how far out we are.

"I'm going to miss this," she says thoughtfully.

I return my eyes to hers, her expression serious. "Me, too." Treading water, I swim closer to her, placing my hand on her back to help support her since it appears she's struggling a bit. The reflection of the moon on the water behind her makes her appear almost ethereal.

"Let's not fight anymore." Her brows scrunch together. "I don't like having to walk on eggshells around you. We only have a few weeks left before you go off to college. We should enjoy them…as the *friends* we are."

Although it's lackluster, I smile. She's right. We shouldn't squander these last few weeks. Before I made the mistake of almost kissing her, I genuinely enjoyed spending time with her, seeing her at the house. She's always been a part of my life. And I hope she always will be.

"I'd like that."

Chapter Seven

BROOKLYN

NOW THAT DREW AND I have cleared the air between us, the next few weeks pass quickly. After seeing him and Mindy at the theater, I had thought it best if I steered clear of him the remainder of the summer. It wouldn't have been too hard, considering that Molly seems to be permanently attached to Brody Carmichael these days, despite her assurances it's not serious, that they're just having a little fun. Now I'm grateful for her current preoccupation. It allows me plenty of time to hang out with Drew.

Things are like they were when we were younger. We hang around the café and people-watch. I go to his street hockey games, cheering enthusiastically for every goal he makes. I expect to see Mindy at some of his games, but she never shows. He stops by the movie theater on a regular basis to visit me during my shifts. I've even clued him in on the guessing game Spencer and I play. Turns out, Drew's a lot more perceptive than I originally thought. He can't beat my record, but he gets pretty damn close.

Everything's been great. Better than great. Until

59

today. It's August twenty-fifth. Tomorrow afternoon, Drew will board a plane for Minnesota to start the next phase of his life. This has loomed over us the past several weeks, but we haven't addressed it. It's not like it really matters. Drew's just a friend, like a brother. Maybe that's why I'm feeling like I'm about to say goodbye to a piece of myself.

As I sit on the brick wall separating the parking lot from the shoreline, I steal a glimpse at him. He's staring at the ocean, lost in thought, just like he has been since we got here earlier this afternoon. "Brody's parents are out of town until Monday. He's throwing a big party. The entire school's going. I was even able to convince my dad to let me go since he doesn't have to work until tomorrow morning. Will you be there?"

He looks down, avoiding my eyes. "I can't. I have plans with Mindy."

"Oh." I try not to sound disappointed, failing miserably. He's been seeing her throughout the summer, but he never talks about her much. She's always just been someone in the background who never entered the little world we've created for ourselves. I guess I've simply allowed myself to be blissfully ignorant of the fact that on the nights I don't see Drew, he's with her.

"It's just…" He licks his lips. "It's my last night here and I promised—"

My hand shoots up, interrupting him. "Say no more." I jump off the wall, tossing the remnants of my half-eaten ice cream into the trash. "I should get going. Maybe I'll see you tomorrow morning before you take off for the airport."

Drew clambers after me before I can get too far, his hand wrapping around my forearm. "Brooklyn…"

His tone is heartfelt. It takes every ounce of effort I possess not to break down in tears over the idea that this may be the last time I see Drew.

My Drew.

I'm not ignorant enough to think he won't change. Big things are about to happen for him. He's been selected for the World Junior Championship hockey team. Many of the players chosen eventually go on to make the Olympic team. This puts his name on a lot of important people's radars. He won't have time for anything or anyone else.

"It's okay." My voice catches and I take a minute to reel in my nerves. "You *should* spend your last night here with someone you care about, not at some stupid party. Lord knows, you'll probably have your fill of those at college."

He blows out a small breath and I lift my eyes to his. "I'll miss you, Brooklyn."

I bite my lower lip to stop my chin from quivering. A lump forms in my throat, my heart physically aching at the sincerity I hear. He could just be saying this to appease me, but I honestly believe in the veracity of his words. I try to blink back my tears as my emotions overwhelm me, but one escapes.

Drew reaches for my face, the seconds stretching. The moment becomes more than just two friends hanging out on the beach during a hot summer day. When his finger swipes away my tear, heat rushes through me. He loops his arm around me and presses a

61

hand against the small of my back, bringing my body against his. The sudden move momentarily disorients me. Despite spending a great deal of time together recently, he's avoided touching me. Now that I'm in his arms again, I don't want to leave them.

"Let me ask you something," he says in a soft voice that heats my belly.

I tilt my head back, my eyes glued to his. "Yes." My response comes out breathy, needy, unlike myself.

"That day back in June when I stopped by your house…"

I swallow hard, my heart pounding in my chest. His lips so close to mine make every inch of me come alive with a new sensation I'm not quite sure how to label. I forget who I am, where I am, who he is. None of that matters. All that does is the magnetism to him I've felt for years.

"When we almost kissed…"

"Yes," I say again, my mouth salivating, my chest rising and falling with more intensity. I've completely shut out everything going on around us. I no longer hear the sound of engines roaring by, seagulls squawking, children playing. In this moment, all I hear is my heart pounding a ferocious tempo. All I feel is the electricity filling me at the promise of what's to come. All I see is Drew.

"I wish we weren't interrupted."

I shiver at his words. "Me, too."

"Brooklyn…" His tone is smooth, sensual. He licks his lips, his eyes growing more intense, more heated, more desperate. "My sweet, sweet Brooklyn. You have no idea how much I'm going to miss you." He leans in, his mouth a whisper from mine.

I brace myself to finally feel what I've been imagining all summer. Then, as if a cruel joke, a familiar voice yells.

"Drew!"

We jump away from each other, our eyes flinging toward the source, seeing Molly running toward us. She slows her steps when she notices us together, my cheeks flushed.

"Brook?" With a furrowed brow, she shifts her gaze from me to Drew, then back to me again. "What are—"

"I had something in my eye," I say quickly, praying Molly believes my lie. When she continues to study me, eyes narrowed, I head past her and Drew, avoiding both their stares. "I should get home so I can get ready for tonight. I'll see you later."

I hurry toward the sidewalk, breaking into a run when a bus pulls up to the stop. Not caring if it's the right one, I get on it just so I don't have to face Molly or Drew. I don't remember to breathe until the bus is a few blocks west of the beach.

Twice, Drew has tried to kiss me. And we've been interrupted each time. I'm starting to think it's a sign we shouldn't cross that line.

Chapter Eight

BROOKLYN

B Y THE TIME MOLLY and I arrive at Brody's house that evening, the party is in full swing. I try not to think about the fact that Drew's with Mindy right now. I shouldn't care. Shouldn't think about the excitement of his body against mine, his breath dancing with mine, his lips so close to mine.

"Drew's missing a big party," I say as we walk through the front door, music blaring, bodies dancing. The living room and kitchen swarm with people, the air hazy with smoke. From the looks of it, most of the school has shown up. One last hurrah before the school year begins.

"He wouldn't think so," she responds as she waves enthusiastically to a group of popular seniors. I guess hanging out with Brody has given her a new circle of friends.

"He's never been one for parties, has he?" I comment. Drew's focus has always been on hockey, often forgoing parties in order to get up early to train. He may not be the top of his class when it comes to academics, but his dedication to hockey is admirable.

"Well, it's not that." Molly leads me into the kitchen, grabbing a red cup and filling it with beer from a keg.

It looks like she's done this before. I wouldn't even know how to do what she's doing — tilting the cup and pressing the nozzle against the side to prevent foam. She holds the beer out for me, but I shake my head. I'm lucky my father even allowed me to come tonight. The last thing I need is to walk into the house and have him smell alcohol on my breath.

She shrugs, taking a sip of the beer before finishing her statement. "From what I hear..." She gestures toward the group of seniors she waved to when we first walked in. "Drew's taking Mindy up to the overlook again tonight."

"Again?"

"Yeah," she responds dismissively as I swallow down the bile rising in my throat.

Everyone knows there's only one reason you go to the overlook. The idea that Drew's already been there with Mindy makes me sick with jealousy. It serves as a reminder that I've been fooling myself to think he would ever be interested in me. He'd never be able to take me there. I've never even kissed a boy, so having sex with one? My Catholic upbringing has made me fear the idea of taking things that far.

"I mean, he *is* leaving tomorrow. What else do you think they'd do on their last night together?"

I nod, pretending this news isn't the stab in my heart it is. I feel Molly studying me. Not wanting her to see the truth, I smile. The last thing I need is for her to read too much into this, to tease me for liking her brother.

"You know what? Maybe I will have a beer."

She grins. "It's about time you loosened up!"

And that's exactly what the first beer does. Loosens me up. The second makes me stop caring about the likelihood that Drew's probably having sex with Mindy at this precise moment. By the third, I think I'm the world's greatest dancer. By the fourth, I never want the party to end.

For the first time, I finally relax and stop trying to live up to everyone's expectations of me. I dance with guys from our school who never noticed me before. Now they do, and I like the attention. For someone who's constantly lived in the shadows, who's been known as the awkward, tall girl, the attention from some of the most popular boys in school is all the validation I need. And the alcohol makes me not care about the fact that this validation may come at a heavy price.

Molly stays close by for a while, dancing, but keeping a watchful eye on me, considering I'm usually not the type to act like this. Maybe that's the old Brooklyn. Maybe it's time I finally experience life, as Molly always does. I look at her as she smiles up at Brody. She looks happy. I want that, too.

"You don't have to babysit me," I say after a while, able to sense they both want to take advantage of the fact that Brody's parents are out of town, their dancing having become more sensual. "I'm fine on my own."

Molly narrows her eyes. "Are you sure?

"Of course," I respond, pressing my hand against her bicep. "I'm having a blast." I pull my hair up, perspiration dotting my hairline from the heat of dozens of dancing bodies in such a small area. "You guys should go have some fun, too, if you know what I mean." I waggle my eyebrows.

Molly appears uneasy about the prospect, so I grab both of their hands and pull them toward the staircase. "Go. Get your freak on." Before she can say anything else, I whirl around, disappearing back into the crowd. I'm jostled around a bit, but I move with them, throwing my hands up and singing along to the music.

I'm so lost in the atmosphere, shouting the lyrics to some song about sunshine, I'm taken by surprise when I feel a warmth on my neck, followed by a voice saying, "Care to dance?"

A hand lands on my lower back, yanking me against a firm body. Gasping, I fling my eyes open, staring at Damian. I haven't spoken to him since the incident at the beach. The few times he's gone to the movies, he made sure to approach a different usher to buy his tickets, as if purposefully avoiding me.

"Not worried about another broken nose?" I quip.

He slowly shakes his head. "Drew's leaving for college tomorrow. I'm a free man."

I push away from him, crossing my arms over my chest. "Not quite. It's not tomorrow yet, is it?"

He purses his lips. "Good observation." He looks around the living room. "But I don't see him here, do you?"

"He's not coming." I swallow down my

disappointment.

"Then perhaps we can pick up where we left off back in June before we were so rudely interrupted."

If I hadn't been drinking, I'd probably knee him in the groin and tell him I'm not interested, just as I'd been telling him when Drew took matters into his own hands and punched him. That was before this summer happened. If Drew can get a blowjob in a movie theater and take his "girlfriend" up to the overlook to get laid, I can flirt with Damian.

"What did you have in mind?" I ask, chewing on my lower lip. I've seen Molly do this and guys seem to like it.

"I have an idea."

He grabs my hand, dragging me through the crowd and down a set of stairs leading to a partially finished basement. The lighting is much more subdued than upstairs. I begin to regret being so bold, a chill trickling down my spine. But isn't this what guys like, what they expect? If I don't up my game, I'll never be kissed. And I really want to be kissed. I no longer care about giving my first kiss to someone special. I just want to be kissed so I no longer feel like a leper.

My eyes fall on a small circular table, a half-dozen people sitting around it. Damian places his hand on my lower back, leading me toward one of the empty chairs.

I look at the cards strewn on the surface. "Uno? Really? What are we? Ten?"

"It's not regular Uno," Damian says, holding my chair out for me and helping me sit down. He can't be all that bad if he does that, right? Drew holds my chair out for me all the time. I view it as a chivalrous gesture.

"Then what kind of Uno is it?"

"We add some different rules," one of the girls at the table says. Her name's Elizabeth, a senior and this year's cheer captain. These are not my people, but maybe they can be. "Like, we still do what the cards say and all that, but if certain cards are played and it's your turn, you have to drink."

"I don't know," I respond. "I think I've already had enough to drink. I'm trying to sober up so my dad doesn't ground me for life."

Damian and one of the other basketball players…I think his name is Allen…give each other a look. He's tall, blond, and popular. "Then maybe we can take things to the next level."

"The next level?" I swallow hard.

"Yeah," Elizabeth says, smiling coyly at a redhead named Catherine and a brunette named Gretchen. I take stock of the people sitting around me. It appears they're all coupled up, leaving just Damian and me.

I look at him, my heart thumping in my chest.

"Strip Uno."

"Strip Uno?" The second those words leave my mouth, it grows dry.

"Yeah." His tongue darts out as he leans closer to me, his gaze seeming to undress me without a single card being played. "Similar to regular Uno, with a few changes."

"Like what?"

69

"Well, if you have to draw from the pile, either because of a card played or because you don't have anything in your hand that's playable, you lose an article of clothing," Allen offers. When everyone nods in agreement, I gather this isn't the first time they've done this.

"What else?"

"Same if you get skipped, which includes someone throwing down a skip card *or* a reverse card. So if a reverse card is played and it's supposed to be your turn but reverses direction, you lose an article of clothing. Pretty much anytime you're skipped or have to draw cards, you strip."

"But there are times you get to put clothes back on," Catherine states in a nasally voice. "Like if you play a wild card or a draw four. If you play a draw four, you get to put on an article of clothing, but the person you play it on loses one. Here's the real kicker. If a draw four is played on you, that person gets to choose what article of clothing you lose. If you win a round, you get to put all your clothes back on, while everyone else has to stay as they are. It's a really fun game."

"What happens if you run out of clothes to take off?" I ask.

"We come up with…other ways of making you satisfy your debt," Lucas says, his eyes narrowing in on my chest.

"Come on," Damian encourages, his breath hot on my neck. "You're a smart girl. This game is all strategy. I've been playing all summer and have yet to end up completely naked. What's keeping you from having a little fun?"

70

I meet his eyes, about to tell him *who* is preventing me from doing this. Then I remember he's getting laid right now after almost kissing me. *Fuck him.* If I want to play Strip Uno, I'm going to play Strip Uno. Starting tomorrow, he won't be a part of my life. It's time I do what I want.

I turn my attention back to this group of people I never would have considered friends before, but maybe this will show them I'm not some innocent little girl who needs her best friend's brother to watch out for her. I can take care of myself. And I'm about to prove it.

"Deal the cards."

Whistles and hollers sound around the table as Damian reaches for the deck and shuffles it before distributing seven cards to each of us. When he places the draw pile in the center of the table, he pauses before flipping over the top card. His eyes shift to mine, a devious grin on his face. Time seems to stand still as I keep my gaze glued to that card, knowing it'll be for me. When he finally flips it over, I breathe a sigh of relief. Blue four. Grinning, I place a blue seven on top of it, deciding to play it safe for the time being.

As the game goes on, my confidence builds. Thankfully, I'm dressed appropriately for this game. Two flip-flops. One skirt. One cardigan. One tank top. One bra. One pair of panties. I have to draw or be skipped three times before things get a little risqué. Five times before I have to show some serious skin. *I've got this.*

Ten minutes into the game, I've only lost one flip-flop, while some of the guys are down to their boxers.

Catherine's tied with me, having only lost one article of clothing, but she chose to take off her shirt instead of a shoe.

Damian plays a yellow nine and I look at him, giving him a smile. I get the feeling he's taking it easy on me, and I'm grateful to him for that. Turning my attention to my cards, my shoulders fall when I see I don't have one to play.

With a sigh, I reach for the draw pile.

"Oooooh," everyone at the table taunts as I pull cards until I get one I can play, adding three to my hand.

"Not a big deal," I say with a shrug. "I've still got one flip-flop." I slip it off and hold it up for everyone to see, then toss it onto the pile of clothes.

"What's it going to take to convince you to lose the tank?" Damian asks.

I give him a sly smile. "A draw four card."

The table erupts in laughter, the guys clapping. "I like this one," Lucas states. "She's got some fight to her."

I'm not sure what to make of his statement. If I hadn't been drinking, I may have analyzed it a little more, but the effects of the alcohol have tossed my inhibitions out the window, which also helps me not care when Damian plays his next card, a skip, forcing me to remove my cardigan. Thankfully, this round soon comes to an end with Catherine winning and being able to put her clothes back on. However, she seems a little downtrodden at the idea.

I deal the next round, hoping to get some draw fours or wild cards so I can put some clothes back on, but I don't. I'm at Damian's mercy to take it easy on me. My first few turns are uneventful, then he plays a reverse.

Standing, I look down at my body. Since we're sitting, it makes sense to lose the skirt first. I meet Damian's eyes, which seem to be glued to my every move. No one's ever looked at me the way he is right now. It's primal, animalistic, predatory. That voice inside my head is back, cautioning me.

Instead of listening, I reach for Damian's half-full beer and practically guzzle it down. Then I slowly untie the drawstring of my linen skirt, reveling in the attention from the four guys at the table. Their gazes are intense, glued to my every move. When I leisurely allow the skirt to fall to my feet, I'm met with whistles of appreciation.

"Damn, baby…" Damian grips my hip. It catches me by surprise and I jump. "You have killer legs." He leans closer, his mouth lingering near my belly button as he remains sitting. "Why don't we call this game a wash and find somewhere private where you can wrap those legs around me?"

Anxiety washes over me at his words. I want to grab my clothes, dart up the stairs, and never look back. Isn't this what guys want? Isn't this why Drew has never kissed me? Why he took Mindy to the overlook instead of me? He's barely laid a hand on me all summer…until earlier today. It's obvious he doesn't think I'm the type of girl to do these sorts of things with him. Maybe it's time I prove I am.

"Tsk. Tsk. Tsk." I place my hand on Damian's naked chest. He's not nearly as built as Drew, but his slender frame does have some muscle on it, mirroring that of a typical basketball player. "Then I wouldn't be able to brag about how you lost to me, how *I* got *you* naked." I step out of his hold, not letting him see my relief when his hand no longer scalds my flesh. "Now, where were we? Oh, of course." I lean toward him, my lips hovering close to his neck. "Your turn."

He's speechless for a moment, then snaps out of his stupor, playing a card. Out of the corner of my eye, I notice him adjust himself in his shorts. The knowledge that he's excited just by seeing something as innocent as my legs gives me a boost of confidence, making me continue down this path instead of retreat.

The next few turns are pretty uneventful for me. That's not the case for Elizabeth. She's now down to nothing but a pair of panties, and my discomfort has grown. I try not to let it show. These are some of the most popular people at school. Molly's always been a great friend, but she's been so preoccupied with Brody lately. Maybe this can be my new circle of friends.

Damian plays a card, and I'm grateful it's not a skip or draw. Regardless, I'm still not out of the woods. As I look at my hand, I see my luck has run out. With a smirk, I stand, reaching for the bottom of my tank.

"Holy shit!" Samuel shouts as I pull it over my head. I'm met with louder whistles than when I removed my skirt. I've spent the summer on the beach wearing a bikini. This shouldn't feel any different than that. But it does. I feel ashamed, like I'm selling my body just so people will like me.

As I pretend to bask in the catcalls and cheers, I can't help but wonder what my mother would think if she were still alive. She'd probably tell me I don't need to do something I'm uncomfortable with just to fit in. That real friends would never put me in this kind of compromising position. She's right, but instead of listening to her, I grab the beer that's miraculously appeared in front of me and drink it, hoping it helps with the anxiety. It does, a little.

I'm on edge throughout everyone's next turn, unable to ignore the heated stare coming from Damian as his eyes seem to be glued to my chest. It makes me feel like a piece of meat. At first, I liked the attention. Now, I'm on the brink of throwing up.

When it's Damian's turn, I reluctantly shift my eyes to his, my heart hammering in my chest with the way he's leering at me. By that alone, I know I'm not going to like this.

"I've been waiting to play this card all night," he says, then throws down a draw four, the room erupting in cheers and clapping. I look around the table, then behind me, realizing it's not just us anymore. Many of the people from upstairs have congregated in the basement to watch.

I reach for the beer in front of me and guzzle the rest of it, wincing at the bitter taste. Wiping my mouth, I stand. A warmth fills me when I hear all the cheers, giving me the boost of confidence I need.

"So tell me, Damian," I say coyly. I place my hands on my hips, not trying to hide from him or anyone else. I can feel the heat of dozens of eyes on me. I know I have a nice body. And I'm pretty sure I have the biggest boobs in my class, which is probably why every single guy in this room is salivating right now. "What would you like me to take off?"

He stands from his chair, wearing just a pair of boxer briefs. I steal a glance, noticing a bulge that's grown in size over the past few seconds. He doesn't even try to hide it.

With a devious stare, he lifts a finger to my neck, running it down my collarbone. When he proceeds through the valley of my cleavage, my breathing grows more uneven. I'm hoping he stops there, but he keeps going, his finger circling my belly button before settling at the waistband of my panties.

My pulse spikes, his mouth a whisper away. He sneaks a finger underneath the material for a moment before pulling back. "Your bra."

There's more clapping as everyone begins to chant my name. I draw in a deep breath, summoning the strength to get through this. What does it matter? They're just boobs. Every female has a pair. They're not sexual but maternal, a way for a mother to feed her young. At least that's what I try to convince myself as I close my eyes and reach behind me to unclasp the thin piece of fabric.

One second, my hands tremble, regret filling me for putting myself in this situation, knowing my reputation at school will never be the same. The next, some sort of fabric is thrown over me and I'm hoisted up, disoriented as I watch the basement disappear behind me. I flail and kick, screaming for whomever has me to put me down, worried it's Damian carrying me upstairs for a bit of privacy. I don't know what I expected tonight's end result to be, but it was certainly not that.

Fresh air hits my face, my feet finding the ground. I take a minute to reorient myself when I'm met with a pair of fiery, dark eyes.

"What the *fuck* were you doing?" Drew roars, his neck tense, his jaw clenching. I've seen him angry before, but never like this.

"Just having a little fun." I pull the blanket tighter around my body, feeling sick to my stomach. My skin crawls with what I'd almost done. Still, I don't want Drew to know that. I don't want him to think I need him in my life when he's made it more than apparent he doesn't need me.

"A little fun?" He stares at me, then tugs at his hair, pacing. "A little *fun*? I'm leaving tomorrow, Brooklyn! I won't be around to look out for you anymore!"

"Who said I needed you to do that in the first place?! I'm fine! I know what I'm doing!"

"Oh really?" He stops in his tracks, leaning into me. "And what would your father say if he learned you were about to take off your bra in front of half the male population of our school?"

I swallow down the bile rising in my throat. My dad would never look at me the same way again. He probably *would* send me to a convent. He's constantly warning me about the consequences of bad decisions, particularly on nights he responds to a labor call and the woman is a teenager. Tonight is most certainly the worst decision I've ever made in my life.

"I just wanted one night of fun. *One night!* You can't stand there and talk to me about this when you were at the overlook with Mindy tonight. You have no claim over me."

He screams in frustration. "I never took her to the overlook. That date was over before it ever began!"

My breath hitches at his words. "It was?"

"Yes." His voice softens. "It was."

I'm momentarily speechless, but that still doesn't give him the right to make decisions for me. "Whatever. Doesn't matter. As this summer has taught me, *I* don't matter. I'm just your sister's best friend. Nothing more."

I storm away, never feeling so embarrassed in my life. All I want is to go home, crawl into bed, and wake up in college, where I can leave behind all the social burdens of fitting in.

Before I can get too far, a hand grips my arm through the blanket. I gasp as I'm tugged into Drew's embrace. His chest heaves, his hold on me endearing and powerful at the same time. "Do you really think you're just my sister's best friend?" His voice rumbles like thunder. I swear I feel the ground shake beneath me from the force.

I part my lips, the intensity in the lines of his face catching me off-guard. My muscles weaken, the hairs on my nape rising. A delicious shiver rolls through me, completely unlike the one that trickled down my spine when Damian touched me earlier.

"You could never be just my sister's best friend."

Before I could utter a single word in response, he cups my cheeks in his hands and presses his lips to mine. They're soft, full, in control. I'm completely frozen, my body stiff, not even breathing.

Drew's kissing me.

Andrew Brinks is kissing me.

He's giving me my first kiss, just like I always imagined he would.

Holy crap.

Sensing my surprise at the sudden assault, he pulls away, avoiding my eyes. "I'm sorry. I shouldn't—"

Snapping out of my stupor, I drop the blanket to the ground and lunge toward him, flinging my arms around his neck as I press my lips back to his. He returns my kiss with a passion I've never experienced. It's hot, lustful, wanton. The way he crushes my body against his makes me feel wanted, desired…beautiful. I'm not sure what I'm doing, but this feels natural, feels right, feels perfect.

His hands clutch my hips and he lifts me, forcing my legs around his waist. Lightning strikes deep in my core when he presses my back against the aluminum siding of the house, pulsing between my thighs. The party continues to rage on inside, the sound of Dave Matthews' voice singing "Crash Into Me" filtering outside, but everyone remains oblivious to us as we make out in a dark corner. I've often thought about my first kiss, thinking it would be the culmination of some big romantic gesture. I suppose it is, the past few months just the buildup before the explosion.

His tongue caresses my bottom lip and I open for him, doing everything to bring his body closer to mine, clawing at him, the heat bubbling low in my stomach scorching me. Even a breath of air between us is too much space. Ever since middle school, I've noticed Drew, even when he didn't pay attention to me. For years, I've dreamt of this moment. Not just of my first kiss, but of kissing Andrew Brinks. The real thing is so much more spectacular than I imagined. I'll forever remember what it feels like to have his lips on mine, to feel his unshaven jaw scratch my face, to crave the heat of his hands on my skin. I can only hope this is just the first of a lifetime of kisses I'll receive from him.

He moves from my mouth to my jawline, and I throw my head back, thrusting against him. I may be inexperienced, but I can tell how turned on he is. It makes me burn even hotter for him. He's my first kiss, but in this cloud of lust, I want more than just a kiss.

"Drew," I moan when he hits that spot where my ear meets my neck. I never thought much of it before, but something about the way he uses his tongue and teeth at the same time drives me insane with need. "Please."

My words are desperate, my insides tighter than they've ever been. If he keeps pulsing against me like he is, I'm going to fall apart. I've touched myself before and know what an orgasm feels like, but I've never experienced anything remotely as pleasurable and satisfying as Drew moving against me, his mouth on my skin, his hands gripping me with a craving I didn't think possible.

I reach for his pants, my mind a fog. I'm not thinking, just reacting. Right now, all I care about is feeling more of Drew, feeling all of him. Whenever I've heard girls my age talk about sex and losing their virginity, it never appealed to me, the thought of enduring that initial pain scaring me. But with Drew, I no longer feel that way. I know he'll be compassionate, gentle, giving, just as he's always been in every other facet of his life.

When my fingers find his belt, he immediately pulls back, grabbing my forearm, panting. "Whoa. Wait a minute."

Our eyes meet and he helps lower my feet to the ground. It feels like a bucket of ice water has been poured over me.

"Did I do something wrong?" I ask. "Did I not do it right?"

With a sigh, he cups my face. The way he touches me, admires me, holds me makes me feel secure. "You did *everything* right, which is why I needed to stop you."

I open my lips to protest, but he captures it with a kiss. It's not as deep as his previous ones, but it's just as fulfilling.

"You are amazing, Brooklyn. Everything about you…" The muscles in his face seem to tighten again as he stares at me. "I am hopelessly unable to control myself around you."

With a sly smile, I hoist myself onto my tiptoes and drag my tongue down his jawline. I've seen women do this in the movies and it always looks like the recipient enjoys it. By the way Drew's hold on me tightens, I assume it has the same effect on him. "Then don't."

He groans, then pulls away. "You're making this incredibly hard."

"That's the point," I smirk, surprised at my knack for flirting. I suppose I've watched Molly do it enough that it should be like second nature to me.

"Brooklyn, please." His voice turns serious. "You don't deserve this. As much as I want to, your first time can't be against the wall at some party after you've been drinking. I don't want you to regret it." He lowers his mouth to mine, the heat of his lips gently brushing against me sending a tingle through my body.

"I won't regret it, Drew. I can't regret anything that involves you. I've wanted you as long as I can remember. Please."

He stares deep into my eyes and I see the battle raging within.

"Please," I say once more. "I want my first time to be special. Let me have that with you, someone I know who will respect me."

He exhales a breath, almost resigned, then narrows his gaze on me. "You mentioned your dad's working tomorrow, right?"

"Yeah. A twenty-four. He goes in at seven."

A smile tugs on his lips as he brings his mouth back to mine. "Then I'll be at your house at 7:01. I don't need to leave for the airport until 11:30. That gives me plenty of time to make sure you're taken care of the way you should be."

My eyes roll into the back of my head as his lips land on my neck. I've never had a boy talk to me this way. I suppose there's a good reason. Drew isn't a boy. He's a man. Excitement buzzes deep in my core at the idea that this person I've known since I was a little girl

82

will forever be my first. My first kiss. My first sexual experience. My first everything.

Drew *is* my everything.

Chapter Nine

DREW

"COME ON," I SAY to Brooklyn, retrieving the blanket and draping it over her shoulders, ensuring her body's covered. I don't care that wearing a bra and panties is akin to a bikini, at least according to some. In my eyes, it isn't, and I don't want anyone seeing her like this. I want to be the only one lucky enough to admire the beauty that lies beneath her clothes.

"Where are we going?"

"I'm taking you home," I answer, my voice stern.

She slows her steps. "But my clothes…"

I look from her to the house, releasing a sigh. There's no way in hell I'm going to let her step foot in there. I have half a mind to drag Molly out of there, too, but I trust Brody. Despite giving him shit for his subpar hockey skills, he's a good guy, not someone I need to worry about. If Molly says no, Brody will respect that…unlike Damian Murphy.

"Fine." I usher her toward my car and her mouth opens, about to protest. "I'll go in. You're going to wait for me where I know you'll be safe."

"But—"

"No. This is not up for debate." I stop when I reach the passenger door and open it. "I care about you too much to let you walk back into that wolves' den." I help her into the seat, then step back, resting my hands on the roof of the car as I lean toward her. "I'll go get your things." I place a soft kiss on her cheek. "Lock the doors. Don't let anyone in."

"Drew, I'm fine," she insists. "I can take care of myself."

I cock my head to the side, arching a brow. I don't have to say a word for her to know exactly what I'm thinking.

Hanging her head, she seems to shrink into herself, pulling the blanket tighter around her frame. "I'll keep the doors locked."

"Thank you." I pause as I'm about to close the door. "You don't need to take your clothes off to get people to like you, Brooklyn. And if you do, those aren't the people you need as friends."

She meets my eyes, her chin quivering. In that one look, I can sense the events of the night are finally catching up with her. "I thought it would help me fit in," she confesses, her voice catching as she fights back tears.

I crouch so I'm eye-level with her. "What makes you think that?"

"I don't know." She sniffles. "Molly's always hanging out with Brody. You had Mindy. Everyone around me was part of a couple. I felt like a child, until I ran into Damian. Going to the basement with him

85

was stupid, but... I don't know. I guess I liked that someone finally paid attention to me."

I brush a strand of hair behind her ear, then run a finger down her face, tilting her chin so her eyes are locked with mine. "That's not the kind of attention you need, Brooklyn. Those guys... They're pigs."

I lean toward her, brushing my lips against hers. I don't think I'll ever get enough of her kisses. All summer, I've imagined how her lips would taste, although I did everything not to. Nothing could have prepared me for how perfect, how sweet, how addicting they are. I don't know what came over me, what caused me to finally break down and kiss her. My father's admonition hangs over me like a dark cloud, but I can't ignore my heart anymore. She'll be sixteen in a few days. His concerns are nearly moot.

"You deserve better than that." I'm not sure I'm what she deserves, either, but at least I know I'll respect her, take care of her... *Love* her? I press one more chaste kiss to her mouth, then stand up. "I'll be back in a few minutes. Lock the doors."

"Yes, sir," she retorts, her voice light.

I close the door and dash back up the street, barreling into the house. The crowd seems to part like the red sea as I stride through the packed living room and make my way down the stairs to the basement.

I'd come earlier because I knew Brooklyn would be here. My date with Mindy certainly didn't go as planned, at least according to her. After my almost kiss with Brooklyn this afternoon, the last thing I wanted was to have a hot and heavy make out session with Mindy. I told her as much, and she wasn't happy. The date cut short, I headed here. The instant I stepped into the living room, I'd heard one of the basketball players announce that Brooklyn was about to take her top off, then he excitedly clambered to the basement. I'd never been so angry in my life. That was the moment I saw red.

As I step off the last stair into the basement, back to the scene of the proverbial crime, I see red again. It takes all my restraint not to leave every single guy with a broken bone or two. I was warned. I got off easy last time. I doubt my dad has many more strings he can pull to keep me out of the court system, but that doesn't mean I can just let Damian get away with this.

My eyes narrow on him, my nostrils flare as I stalk toward him. He notices me and jumps up from the couch, letting go of the girl wrapped in his menacing arms. The cocky smirk that had been plastered on his face earlier is replaced with fear. My lip curling, I wrap my hand around his neck, slamming him against the wall. He visibly trembles, clawing at my grip, and I smile at his struggle.

"If you so much as touch her again," I begin, then glower at the crowd of onlookers. My attention is mainly focused on Damian's friends, but I address everyone. "If *any* of you even thinks about it…" I return my eyes to Damian, "I'll get on the next plane home and make you wish all I gave you was a broken nose."

With my free hand, I reel back. Damian flinches, his body stiffening. Laughing, I release my hold on him without hitting him. "Pussy." I turn away, spying Brooklyn's clothes on the floor. The room is silent as I grab them. Then I leave, hoping I never have to see any of these people again in my lifetime.

I retreat out of the house, a smile building on my lips as I think of Brooklyn's kisses, her body, her everything. As I approach my car, her eyes fling to mine, scared and worried. When she realizes it's me, her whole body relaxes. I click on the key fob and duck into the driver's seat. I lean across the console, kissing her, then hand her things over.

"Next time you go to a party, I suggest keeping your clothes *on*." After turning the key, I pull the car into the street.

"Smart advice."

I give her a small smile before hardening my expression. "I'm serious. I didn't like the idea of leaving you to begin with. But now, after tonight, I *really* don't like it. I won't be around to make sure you're okay."

"Well, you have nothing to worry about. I'm never going to another party. It's not my scene. I'd much rather sit at home and read a book."

"If you ask me, reading is a lot sexier than getting drunk." Our eyes meet briefly as I come to a stoplight.

"I'm glad you think so."

"I do. I always have." I reach across the center console and grasp her hand. I've often done this same thing with Mindy, but her fingers intertwining with mine didn't feel like this, like someone's setting off a Fourth of July fireworks display in my stomach.

"I'm sorry things didn't work out with Mindy," she says after a while.

"Don't be. I never should have dated her in the first

place." I run my thumb along her knuckles. Her skin's soft, delicate, angelic.

She contemplates my words for a moment. "Why is that?"

I briefly float my eyes to hers. "Because of you."

"Me?"

"Yes, Brooklyn. You. You're all I want. No one else."

Her body seems to fuse into the seat at my words, her eyes bright, her skin glowing. "I like the sound of that."

"Me, too."

The remainder of the drive is silent. As I pull up in front of her house, I turn my headlights off, not wanting to wake her father. Once I kill the engine, I dash over to the passenger side to help her out, placing a hand on the small of her back. The blanket is still wrapped around her, so I carry her clothes as we walk up the steep incline of her driveway.

"You should probably get dressed before you go in, don't you think?" I whisper as we approach the garage. "What if your dad's awake?"

"It's after midnight. He won't be. He has to be up at 5:30 to go to work."

"You don't know that. He'll lose his shit if you walk into that house wearing nothing but your underwear, a blanket wrapped around you, especially considering this is the first party he's ever allowed you to go to. If you were my daughter and that happened, I know what I'd be thinking, and it wouldn't be good."

"Do you really want me to put my clothes back on?" Her voice becomes low and seductive. There's a subtle slur, but she's not nearly as tipsy as she was when I first found her. She spreads her arms, allowing the blanket to fall to the ground. I've always thought Brooklyn was shy, but I've seen a side of her tonight I never knew existed. She's confident, bold, assertive. I like this side of her.

I bite my bottom lip, my erection springing back to life as I stare at her in just her bra and panties. I pull her to the side of the garage, hiding us from any cars driving by. I press her back against the side of the building, holding her arms above her head.

"That's the last thing I want," I groan, burying my face in her neck, kissing her skin. She's like an aphrodisiac. Now that I've gotten a taste, I'll never be satisfied with anything else. "Tonight is going to be torture, knowing what awaits me tomorrow."

I move to her lips, diving in for another taste. It's heavenly, decadent, sublime. I never want to stop. I'm kicking myself for depriving me...us of this the past few months. We have such little time left and regret fills me, regardless of the reason I stayed away.

Releasing my grip on her arms, I stare at her, running my hand down her face, wanting to imprint everything about her to memory, hoping it'll get me through the lonely nights once I'm thousands of miles away...like tomorrow night.

"Drew?" Her voice is unsteady.

"Yeah?" I furrow my brows.

"What if..." She chews on her lower lip. "What if

I'm not any good?"

"What do you mean?"

"At sex," she whispers. "What if—"

I erase her worries with a kiss, simple but full. Then I look at her once more. "I don't want you to think you have to be someone else just to make me happy. I'm happy with you as you. If you aren't ready, I'll wait. I'd never pressure you into something you're not prepared for."

"I want to. Really bad. I'm just worried I won't be enough for you." She lowers her head. "I'm not nearly as experienced as a lot of girls at school. Hell, Catherine had no problem whipping off her top when she had to strip, even though she still had two good shoes she could get rid of."

"Hey." I grip her chin, forcing her eyes to mine. My mouth inches toward hers, the pull she has on me too strong to ignore. "If I were interested in a girl like Catherine, I'd be with her right now. I'm not. I'm interested in *you*, and no matter what, it'll be enough." I wrap my arms around her, enveloping her as I kiss her forehead. "You'll always be more than enough for me, Brookie."

"I hope so, Dewy."

We remain enclosed in each other's embrace for a while before I reluctantly pull away. "You need to get some sleep," I say, although the thought of leaving her is torture.

She releases a sigh, nodding. "You're probably right." Walking back toward where I left her clothes on the ground, she slips her skirt back on before pulling her tank over her head. Seeing her in just her bra and panties certainly excited me, but she's just as alluring with her clothes on. Anyone who doesn't see that is an idiot.

She saunters up to me and I kiss the top of her head. "I'll see you tomorrow," I murmur.

Her lips curve into a smile. "It's after midnight."

"So?"

"That means you'll see me today."

I beam back at her. "I like the sound of that."

Except that also means I'll be leaving her today.

I fold my arms around her, our lips meeting once more. I just can't stop kissing her. "Sweet dreams, Brooklyn." I leave her with one more kiss, then release her, picking up the blanket. "See you at 7:01."

"Looking forward to it."

Chapter Ten

DREW

SLEEP EVADES ME, MY thoughts consumed with a beautiful brunette slumbering just a few streets away. Every time I close my eyes, I see her breathtaking smile, feel the warmth of her arms wrapped around me, savor in the taste of her lips. There's no way I can possibly be expected to sleep, not after last night, not with the anticipation of what today brings.

I normally dread the breaking of dawn, knowing I have to get up for hockey. This morning, I welcome it, jumping out of bed to finish my last-minute packing before sneaking away to see Brooklyn.

As I'm getting ready, I hear a light knocking on my door. It opens slowly before I have a chance to say anything, my father standing in the hallway. There's something in his expression that's off. I expect him to be a bit downtrodden at the idea of his oldest child leaving for college, but this is something else.

"Drew." His voice trembles. "Can you come into the kitchen for a minute?"

"What is it?" I ask cautiously. "Is something

wrong?"

His shoulders drop and he shakes his head. "I just…" He blows out a breath. "Just come with me."

My heart pounds in my chest as I consider what could possibly be going on. My first thought is that the college found out I landed a guy in the hospital and has rescinded my scholarship. Then my father looks at me again, his expression similar to the one he wore the night he warned me to stay away from Brooklyn. Instantly, my heart rockets into my throat, a heat washing over me. The unease filling me only heightens when I walk into the kitchen and see Brooklyn's father, wearing his uniform, standing there, his arms crossed and stance wide.

"Mr. Tanner," I say, looking from him to my father and back at him. "Is something wrong?"

He tilts his head. "I suppose you could say that." The tone of his voice gives me pause. It's not calm or irate. It's somewhere in the middle.

"I don't understand." I try to play it off. We didn't do anything wrong. We just kissed, nothing more.

"When I went out to get the newspaper early this morning, Mrs. Carhill was walking her dog. You know her. She lives across the street from me."

I swallow hard, remaining silent.

"She told me some interesting things. How she saw a car pull up after midnight and Brooklyn stepped out, only a blanket wrapped around her. Obviously, that didn't sound like *my* Brooklyn, so I decided to check for myself. You see, since I work strange hours, we have a security system that records video from exterior cameras."

Dread boils in my stomach, my mouth becoming dry, my heart echoing in my ears. That could mean so many things, but I'm doubtful he's here to thank me for driving his daughter home.

"I'm sorry." I furrow my brow, confused. "I'm not sure I—"

"She's fifteen!" His voice bellows through the room as he slams his fist on the counter, a stark contrast to the peacefulness that usually accompanies the early morning hours in this house.

"I know that. I didn't—"

"I saw you!" His face reddens as he paces the kitchen.

This man has been a part of my life for years. I've always known him to be rather strict when it comes to Brooklyn. I suppose that's what happens when you lose a wife and are solely responsible for raising your child. Once Brooklyn became a teenager and filled out, he became even more overbearing. But I'm the last person Mr. Tanner should be worried about. I care more about his daughter than I've ever cared about anyone else in my life.

"I don't know what you think you saw, but—"

"You want to know what I saw?" He steps toward me and I shrink into my frame. "I saw you pull up in front of my house and walk Brooklyn up the driveway. You were carrying her clothes!" His lips curl up at the corner, his voice like a snarl as he leans into me. "She had a blanket wrapped around her and was wearing nothing but her underwear!"

My eyes widen as I struggle to find the words to explain this. The way he's describing it certainly makes it look bad. But there's more to the story he doesn't know.

"Then you pushed her against the wall of the garage. You had her arms so she couldn't..." His voice catches as he struggles to regain his composure. "You may not understand what I'm going through. I pray you never have to endure this with a daughter of your own, but that little girl means the world to me. And that's exactly what she is. A *girl*."

"She'll be sixteen in a few days," I reply, hating that Brooklyn's own father doesn't give her the credit she deserves. He's treating her like a child incapable of making her own decisions when she's proven to be more mature than many eighteen-year-olds I know. That's why her decision to play Strip Uno last night took me by surprise.

"That doesn't matter! She's not sixteen yet. I may not be able to protect her forever, but I can protect her *now*. I can do everything in my power to keep bad things, bad *people* as far away from her as possible, and that means you."

A lump forms in my throat. "What are you saying?"

"I'm telling you to stay away from my daughter. I like you, Drew. I really do." He shoves his hands through his dark hair and I can tell how difficult this is for him. "But I won't let you hurt her."

I shake my head, my world spinning. This feels like a bad dream. A few minutes ago, I was on top of the world. Now, it's all been tilted on its axis.

"What if I don't want to stay away?" I ask in a moment of defiance. I care about Brooklyn. Hell, I might even love her. I can't stomach the idea of not seeing her. "I told her I'd come over this morning before I left for the airport."

"Not anymore."

My hands form into fists at my side, anger bubbling in my stomach. I want to scream, yell, cry. But mostly, I just want to see Brooklyn, to bask in the warmth her body gives off when enclosed in my embrace.

"This is ridiculous. You can't shut her away in that house and hope nothing bad ever happens to her. She needs to live, not be so sheltered because you're still not over losing your wife."

"Drew." A hand lands on my arm. I glance at my father, who gives me a knowing look. "Brooklyn's fifteen," he reminds me in a low voice, his tone calm. "Regardless of whether anything *did* happen, what Mr. Tanner saw, what he has video evidence of, certainly gives off the impression something did." He leans closer and whispers. "He's agreed not to go to the police as long as you keep your distance. No contact at all…at least while we figure this out."

"No contact? The police?" I whip my eyes toward Mr. Tanner, bile rising in my throat. His hardened expression cracks momentarily. I'd like to think he wouldn't do that, but I know better. Brooklyn's his entire world. He'll do whatever necessary to protect her. Just like I would.

"I know it sounds unfair and can see how much she means to you, how you'd never do anything to hurt her." Dad shoots Mr. Tanner an annoyed look, but he

97

holds his head high, remaining firm. My dad and Mr. Tanner used to be close. I have a feeling that all may end today. "Regardless, this can still make a lot of trouble for you, even if you didn't do anything wrong. Just the suspicion could cost you your scholarship, your place in the World Junior Championship team. Don't you see the huge opportunity you have? Your name's being tossed around for the Games next year. Professional teams will be knocking down your door. You'll be throwing all that away."

I shake my head, having difficulty processing all this. I tug at my hair, feeling like a hammer has shattered my heart into thousands of pieces. Tears welling in my eyes, I look at Mr. Tanner, pleading with him to reconsider. It was just a few innocent, soul-fulfilling kisses. We could have done a lot more, but I stopped it, not wanting to take advantage of Brooklyn. And this is the thanks I get for doing what I thought was right?

My father taught me to respect the adults in my life, and I always have. But I can't just walk away without getting in the final word. Regardless of whether Brooklyn finds out about this or not, I'll know I did everything in my power.

"You say you're trying to protect her from getting hurt, and I can appreciate that. But this decision is going to hurt her far more than you ever imagined. It's not me you should be worried about. If I didn't show up to that party when I did and hauled her out of there, there's no telling what would have happened to her. *I'm* not the bad guy here."

My anger boiling over, I punch a hole into the wall

of the kitchen as I storm into my room. I flop onto the bed, spying the time.

7:01.

I'm sorry, Brooklyn.

Chapter Eleven

BROOKLYN

THE INSTANT I HEAR my father leave the house and his truck rumble down the street, I jump out of bed and rush into the shower. Butterflies flit in my stomach as I think about what this morning will bring. I take care to shave with more precision than I normally do, even shaving places I usually don't. The magazines Molly brings over say that men like women who are well-groomed…down there. I do my best to do just that.

With a towel wrapped around my body and my hair, I walk out of the bathroom and back into my room, surveying my closet. Not one article of clothing I possess screams sexy. And today, I want sexy. I want Drew to look at me and not see his little sister's best friend. I want him to see a woman he can't go another minute without kissing, touching, loving.

Finally, I decide on a breezy sundress. It has a sweetheart neckline that accentuates my chest. It's fitted through the waist, then flares out. On most girls, it would hit a few inches above the knee, but due to my height, it ends at mid-thigh. I'm not sure it qualifies as "sexy", but it'll have to do.

After drying my hair, I sit in front of my vanity and apply makeup, something I never do. But this isn't a typical morning. This is a special morning, one I'll forever remember as the one when I finally became a woman.

As I finish sliding some gloss over my lips, a chime sounds. I fling my eyes to my alarm clock. 7:00. I hurry to finish, then run down the hall, nervous energy filling me as I sit in front of the window, peering outside.

After five minutes, I figure Drew's just running a little late, as he's prone to do.

After ten minutes, I figure he just wants to make sure the coast is clear before coming.

After twenty minutes, I figure he's packing up a few last-minute things.

After thirty minutes, I figure he's having difficultly sneaking out of his house, although that's never been a problem before.

After an hour, I figure he's gotten waylaid by Aunt Gigi, who probably insisted on dragging him to church one last time before he left for college.

By noon, I realize what I fool I've been. Drew's not coming. Everything he said last night was a lie, but I was so desperate to be noticed by someone, I believed it. Drew knew this and took advantage of the situation…took advantage of *me*.

An ache in my chest, I trudge outside and sit on the swing. I do everything to fight back my tears. Drew doesn't deserve them. He doesn't deserve to know I fell for his charms. I want to believe there's a good reason he's not here, that everything he said last night had meaning, but this all serves as a painful reminder that we live in two different worlds.

After all, he's Andrew Brinks. Funny. Handsome. Soon-to-be star collegiate hockey player.

I'm just his sister's best friend.

I've been fooling myself to think he'd ever see me as anything else.

Commitment

"The ones we love the hardest are the ones we hurt the most."

Chapter One

BROOKLYN

MARCH 2018

"IT ALL STARTS WITH *a decision.*"

Aunt Gigi has said those words to me countless times over the course of my thirty-two years.

"*After all,*" she would continue to say, "*you're always just one decision away from a completely different life.*"

As I sit in my car, I'm unsure why I'm thinking about this right now. Where would I be if I didn't have a father who pushed me to be the best I could be? Where would I be if I hadn't looked up when a handsome man approached me one day, re-igniting something I thought I'd never feel again? Where would I be if my mother had waited five more minutes to run to the store the night she was killed by a drunk driver?

Would my life be any different? Would my father still be as overprotective as he is? Would I have been pushed to excel like I was? Would I ever have formed the friendships I did?

Would I ever have gone to that party before the

start of my junior year of high school?

They say there are certain moments in our life that define who we are. For some, it's when they discover their true passion, like music, writing, or hockey. For others, it's when they see an injustice in the world and decide to make it their life's mission to stop it, to put an end to hunger, poverty, hate.

For me, as silly as it sounds, the moment that defines my life is Brody Carmichael's party the summer of 2001. It's the summer I learned what love is.

It's also the summer I learned what a broken heart feels like. As Aunt Gigi had told me whenever she noticed a tear trickle down my cheek as I followed my best friend, Molly, down the hallway of her house and past the door to her brother's room, *"It's okay to be a glowstick once in a while. Sometimes we have to be broken in half before we shine."*

After that summer, I decided I would shine, even if I was as dark as night inside.

A loud horn blares, bringing me back to the present. I glance up to see the stoplight is now green, cars passing on both sides. "Shit," I mutter to myself, stepping on the gas and rejoining the flow of traffic.

After battling the streets of downtown Boston for fifteen minutes, I pull my economical Honda in front of *La Grenouille* in the Financial District. A valet attendant strides toward me. I can't help but feel him turn up his nose at my choice of automobile. Most of the patrons here drive Mercedes, Jaguars, BMWs. My job at the Massachusetts Department of Children and Families doesn't pay me enough to afford that type of car. I can barely afford the payments on my used one.

COMMITMENT

With a tight smile, I take the ticket from the attendant, then head toward the front doors of the restaurant. Tourists and professionals alike fill the sidewalks in this popular section of the city. Suit-clad commuters hurry from tall buildings and toward the closest subway station, skirting shoppers weighed down by bags, students hauling backpacks, and couples bickering over where to grab dinner. Boston has an energy I love, which is why I've never lived anywhere else. I doubt I ever will.

Approaching the ornate front doors, which appear to be more of a statement than a necessity, I start to pull them open when I stop, staring at myself in the reflective glass. Inadequacy washes over me. I'm about to walk into a restaurant where the price tag on most dishes is more than my mortgage. I don't even want to consider how much the bottle of wine we'll have is going to cost. Everyone will be wearing the latest fashion trends from designers whose names have more vowels than I can pronounce. My simple black dress came from a sales rack at a discount clothing store. Will I ever feel like I measure up?

I fill my lungs with air, doing my best to ward off my nerves. I've been on dozens of dates like this one. Tonight is no different. But I still can't shake the feeling deep in my bones that everything's about to change.

Resolved and calm, I open the door. The instant I cross the threshold, the hustle of downtown Boston disappears, the sound of cars and horns replaced with forks scraping against fine china, low conversation, and ostentation. Such is the life I've been immersed in since agreeing to that first date. I thought things would be different, that we'd be a normal couple who went to the movies or bowling. Then again, we aren't most couples. He isn't like most men. I'm still not sure whether that's a good thing.

"*Bonsoir*," the pretentious maître d' greets in a heavy French accent. "Welcome to *La Grenouille*."

"I'm meeting someone here. He may have already arrived."

"*Mademoiselle* Tanner?" He lifts a brow, surveying my attire.

"That's me."

"*Magnifique*. Your date is waiting. Follow me."

He turns from me, neither smiling nor frowning, and leads me into the intimate dining area. Heavenly aromas assault my nose, making my stomach growl. Steak. Scallops. Garlic. The tables are filled with people enjoying the most delectable food presented so beautifully, you almost hate to eat it.

As I walk farther into the dining room, blue eyes catch mine and my initial worry about tonight disappears. He seems so informal, as if he isn't sitting at a table in a restaurant where a membership fee is required to even dine. Standing, he re-secures the button on his suit jacket, a smile building on his lips. He shaved his face and trimmed his dark hair, but there are still a few curls hanging over his collar.

"My beautiful Brooklyn," his smooth, deep voice murmurs in the refined Georgia accent that soothes and pacifies me. He leans forward and kisses my cheek, then lingers for a moment, inhaling a deep breath. "You look incredible. And you smell even better."

I close my eyes, allowing his words to bathe me with a momentary feeling of contentment. It's not a butterfly-inducing, can't eat, can't sleep sensation I feel deep in my bones. There's only been one person who's ever made me react that way.

"Thank you, Wes." I pull back. "You clean up nice, too." I wink.

The perfect gentleman, he holds my chair out for me, helping me into it. Once I'm settled, the maître d' places my napkin in my lap. Apparently, those who run five-star restaurants don't believe we can take care of that small movement ourselves. It's just another thing I've grown accustomed to since I began dating Weston James Bradford.

"How did court go?" he asks after a few moments of awkward silence. I know not to even bother asking for a menu. Wes has likely already ordered for both of us. When we first started dating, I considered it archaic and overbearing. Now it's just part of what it means to date him. He enjoys taking care of me, making sure all my needs are met. And if he wants to order for me, I won't complain. He's yet to choose something I don't like.

I reach for my glass of sparkling water and take a sip, then return it to the table. "As good as can be expected, I suppose, especially when you're telling the judge the biological parent shouldn't get physical custody of their children yet, and that parent is sitting in the courtroom shooting daggers at you."

His hand clasps around mine, compassion in his gaze. "I understand how hard that must be."

I smile, biting back my remark that he has no idea how difficult it truly is. Sure, he devotes much of his free

109

time to designing and building homes for those in need, but his charitable work isn't the same. He's never had to sit in a courtroom and tell a judge he doesn't think the person who gave birth to a child should have custody of them. As the case manager and therapist to these kids who've been pulled from their homes, the judge listens to my recommendation. I have to remind myself it's my job to look out for the best interests of these children. It's what I swore to do when I began this job. And I've held up that promise for the past ten years.

Just as I'm about to give him one of my standard responses, a waiter shows up, presenting a bottle of wine to Wes. My muscles relax, grateful for the interruption. After my day, I don't want to talk about work, although that seems to be the only thing either one of us talks about lately. After being together for the better part of a year, shouldn't we be comfortable enough in our relationship to share our dreams for a future? What *are* his dreams for a future? I'm not sure.

All I know about Wes is that from an early age, he wanted to design buildings. It's in his blood. His father's an architect and shared his love and fascination for how things are made with his son. Wes has followed in his footsteps, using his Ivy League education to build his father's firm into one of the most sought-after companies in the country, if not the world. Wes grew up in Georgia, but attended Harvard for his undergraduate studies. After moving back home upon graduation, he missed the energy and pace of life up north. So he convinced his father to open a branch of the firm in Boston, one Wes would oversee.

He often travels around the globe, checking in on

one of their many projects, pitching to prospective clients, or overseeing the charity program he started where volunteers from his company help construct homes for those in need. Wes is a good man, one any woman would fall hard for. It doesn't matter how many zeros are in his bank account. He still does good deeds routinely, even donating a huge portion of his annual income to charity. The world needs more people like him.

My eyes gloss over as I consider how fast the last eight months have passed. It seems like just yesterday that a handsome man in a breathtaking suit approached me. I thought he was there to ask out Molly. Instead, his eyes saw me, and only me. It was a welcome change.

When a burgundy hue fills my vision, I snap out of my daze, offering the waiter a smile as he finishes pouring the wine. After he retreats, Wes raises his glass. I follow suit.

"To you, Brooklyn. Thanks for agreeing to date me after months and months of my begging and groveling." With a wink, he sips his wine. I bring mine to my mouth, savoring the robust flavor.

"It wasn't months," I retort coyly as the alcohol coats my stomach.

"Yes, it was. Why else do you think I went to Modern Grounds in the North End when my office is in the Financial District?"

I swirl the wine in my glass, the liquid coating the sides. Before I met Wes, I was never much of a wine drinker. Over the past several months, he's spoiled me in that area, the bottles he orders during dinner sometimes costing several hundred dollars.

111

"Because their coffee is better than any spot in the city," I quip.

"True, but it was to see you...since you're a regular. It took me a while to work up the nerve to talk to you once I learned you're close friends with Andrew Brinks."

My spine stiffens and I inhale a sharp breath. Wes doesn't seem to notice. I've always found his observational skills to be lacking. Or maybe because I've spent my entire life watching and analyzing the world around me, I notice the tiniest things about people. Like the way Wes now seems to take repeated small sips of his wine as opposed to drinking casually. Like the way he doesn't look directly at me. Like the way he chews on his bottom lip.

"I've watched him play." He blows out an anxious laugh. "Worse, I've seen the fights he got into on the ice. I didn't want to be on the receiving end of one of his fists."

"You and dozens of other guys." A small smile cracks on my lips, my gaze unfocused as memories of my childhood rush back. Of sitting in the stands with Molly as we watched her brother play. Watching him grow into a local celebrity, at least in hockey circles. Seeing scout after scout court him when it was time for him to choose a college to attend. The day he signed with the Bruins.

It's amazing to think of the paths our lives have taken. After he left for college, we barely spoke again for years. Every time he came home to visit, he avoided me, as if I carried some infectious disease. If it were anyone else who acted that way toward me, I wouldn't care, but this was Drew. He gave me my first kiss. He was supposed to be my first everything...until I realized they were just lies. It wasn't until he had a daughter that we began speaking to each other again, but neither one of us ever brought up that night or why he never came to my house the following day, as he promised he would.

I wish I could say I learned my lesson after that, but I didn't. I wish I could say I never thought of Drew as anything other than my best friend's brother, but that's a lie. I wish I could say I'm smart enough not to fall for his charms again, but I'm not.

Because I did...only for the same thing to happen.

"He's always been protective of you, hasn't he?"

I know Wes means nothing by it, but discussing my friendship with Drew with the man I'm dating makes me uncomfortable. Then again, I'm not sure friendship is the correct term. Not after everything we've been through. Things with Drew are...complicated. Yes, according to the outside world, he's a friend. Now, I'm constantly skirting the giant elephant in the room Drew doesn't even know exists. I've made it *my* elephant, my burden to bear.

"He has."

"I picked up on that right away. The first day I walked into the café and saw you, I was breathless, Brooklyn. Your eyes were so mesmerizing, the green unlike anything I've ever seen. And don't even get me started on your adorable little freckles. But that's not what caught my attention."

My skin warms as I listen to Wes' words, allowing

113

myself to bask in his obvious affection for me. "No?"

"No." He shakes his head. "It was your laugh. I ducked in to grab a quick coffee before a meeting I had close by." He reaches across the table and grabs my hand in his again. "As I waited to place my order, the sound of your laughter filled the place. I was transfixed. In that moment, I needed to know you. I wracked my brain, formulating what to say to you. It had to be smart, bold, especially since you were sitting with your friend."

"Molly." I nod, briefly closing my eyes as I'm transported back to the day a debonair stranger walked into the café Molly's family has owned for decades. "You'd think she'd be the one you would have noticed first."

"Never," he assures me with a breathtaking smile. "Yes, I've learned Molly can be loud, but something about the way you carry yourself spoke to me from the beginning. But when I saw Andrew Brinks—"

"Drew," I interrupt.

"Right. Drew...," he corrects, still hesitant.

It doesn't matter that we've been dating for eight months. He's still not used to calling him Drew, since only those of us who knew him before he made it big call him that. To everyone else, he's Andrew Brinks, star hockey player forced into early retirement after one too many injuries to his head.

"So when I saw him approach your table and sit down, then kiss your and Molly's cheek, I lost what little nerve I had. But someone was looking down on me because I soon found myself in the same area of the city for another meeting. I didn't want to get my hopes up, thinking there was no way you'd be there, but you were. So I made it a habit of stopping by the café at eight every morning for three weeks on the off-chance you'd be there. That's when I realized you went every Friday morning, and so did I. Finally, after two months, I worked up enough courage to ask to buy you a cup of coffee. To which you replied—"

"'I never pay for my coffee here,'" I answer with a smile, recalling our first interaction. "You must have thought me so self-centered."

"Perhaps." He winks, a twinkle in his beautiful blue eyes. "But when you heard your words, you got so embarrassed. With just that one look, the way your cheeks flushed, you stole my heart." He brings my hand to his lips, placing a gentle kiss on my knuckles. "And I'm so grateful you agreed to go to dinner with me."

"And I'm grateful you didn't walk away after my response."

"Never." He releases his hold on my hand. "You forget, I'd been observing you for the past several weeks."

"Stalking, you mean," I joke, taking another sip of my wine.

"Nuance, my dear Brooklyn. Regardless, I could tell what type of woman you were. I needed you in my life, overbearing hockey player as a best friend be damned," he finishes with a wink, and I lift my wine to my lips, polishing it off.

As if our waiter has an internal alert when one of his patrons needs something, he appears instantly. With a smile, he refills my glass. It's rare for me to drink like this. Normally, I only have a single glass of wine throughout an entire five-course dinner. But everything about tonight has me on edge. The ambience. The way Wes looks at me. The way Drew's name keeps creeping into the conversation when we rarely ever talk about him. I need the wine.

"Will he ever coach in the professionals?" Wes asks, digging the knife a little deeper, unbeknownst to him.

"I doubt it." I take another long sip of my wine. "He's had offers, but has turned them all down. He doesn't want to be away from the girls that much. He already doesn't like being away from them as much as he has to be with coaching college, but he loves the game." A slight smile builds on my lips. "I can't remember a time Drew didn't have a pair of skates on. But he loves those girls more."

"You love him, don't you?"

I choke on my wine, eyes wide. "What?"

"No. Not like that," he corrects in haste. "It's just amazing how close you two still are, even all these years later. Most friends grow apart over time. I can't say I've remained close with any of the people I went to high school with. But you and Drew... At first, I thought he was your brother."

"I suppose that's what Drew's always been," I mutter. "Like a brother."

At that moment, two waiters approach and simultaneously place a dish in front of us in a carefully orchestrated show. The first time Wes took me to an upscale restaurant like this, I marveled at how perfectly timed everything was. Now I've grown accustomed to it and it no longer holds excitement. I stare at the pristine white plates as our waiter rattles off what Wes ordered — a diver scallop with a cauliflower puree. The presentation looks too good to eat, like a piece of art, not food.

Over the course of the next two hours, we eat the exquisite food, keeping our conversation easy. There's no talk of our hopes, our dreams, apart from him asking if I'm excited about starting my PhD program in the fall, to which I answer in the affirmative, with no further embellishment.

After we finish our main course and our plates are removed, Wes clears his throat, rubbing his palms along his pants before tugging at his tie, a slight tremble in his hands. He bites his lip, drawing in a deep breath through his nose. He lifts his eyes to mine, his expression awash with sincerity and yearning.

"Brooklyn…," he begins as he reaches across the table to grab my left hand in his, toying with a very important finger. A sinking feeling forms in the pit of my stomach. I should have known something was amiss with the way he's been acting tonight, the nerves seeming to consume him when he's normally carefree and relaxed. "These past eight months have been some of the happiest I can remember."

"I've enjoyed my time with you, too, Wes."

He's spoiled me in a way most woman yearn to be spoiled. He brings me to the most exclusive restaurants. He buys me jewelry that probably costs more than what I make in a year. He's taken me to places I've only imagined visiting — Paris, Rome, London, Berlin. But they all seem to lack meaning. I'm not like most girls Wes is used to. I don't need to be bathed in jewels and whisked off on a private jet to some exotic location. I just want to feel loved.

"When I first saw you, I remember being so jealous of Drew, of how he could so casually drape his arm across your shoulders or kiss your cheek."

"Wes…," I say, a hint of pleading in my tone. If my instincts are correct, if he's about to propose, the last thing I want to be included in that proposal is a mention of Drew. It would taint the whole thing.

"You were so different from the type of woman I usually dated, but in a good way. They all wore the same type of clothes, styled their hair the same way, every single one of them almost like a cookie-cutter mold. But not you. You were unique."

There's that word, the one I've been called most of my life. Not beautiful. Not stunning. Not breathtaking. Unique. With my pin-straight dark hair, green eyes, fair skin, and freckles dotting my cheeks and nose, I've been called unique more times than I care to count. Other than my father, only one man has ever called me beautiful. Only one man has ever made me *feel* beautiful. And I believed it…until I learned his words were as fleeting as a passing storm, spoken out of desperation and fear of being alone.

"When I first walked into that café, I remember smelling a hint of lavender, not the coffee I expected. As I passed you, the scent only grew stronger. For weeks, I dreamed of that aroma. When work led me back to that part of the city, back to the same café, and you were there again, I had to believe it was a sign we were meant to be together."

I remain mute, willing my heart to skip a beat, my skin to flush, my eyes to sparkle with unabashed adoration for this man and his heartfelt words. Instead, I feel as empty as I have since the first time he kissed me. There's no spark. No jolt. No flutter. I'm just going through the motions, hoping to feel something. I thought it back then, and I still do now. Maybe Drew's already ruined love for me.

Before I know what's happening and can stop this out-of-control train from continuing its journey off the tracks, Wes shifts from his chair, kneeling in front of me. He reaches into his jacket and produces a small box. The room is suddenly silent, dozens of eyes staring at me, at him, at us. When he cracks open the box, a chill washes over me.

My lips part, but no words come. My brain tries to tell my mouth to talk, my voice box to vibrate and make a sound, to tell him to get up. Just like Wes thinks there's a reason our paths crossed, perhaps there's a reason I find myself incapable of forming words at this crucial moment. This feels surreal, like I'm having an out-of-body experience, a casual observer of my life instead of having a starring role.

"Brooklyn Rose Tanner," he begins, his breathing increasing as his pale blue eyes lock with mine, "I've dreamed of this moment since I first heard your voice and you consumed my soul. I'd be honored if you'd be my wife."

My lungs struggle to capture a breath, my face burning, my limbs trembling. Over Wes' shoulder, I spy all the other diners stealing a glimpse at us, everyone seemingly on pins and needles awaiting my response. So many little girls dream of this moment, of the day their own Prince Charming would get down on one knee in front of them and declare their undying love, begging them to consider spending the rest of their lives together.

I've also imagined this moment an unhealthy number of times, mostly when Molly and I would flip through one teen magazine or another, planning our own wedding to whomever was the heartthrob of the month. I didn't think it would be like this, surrounded by complete strangers in a pretentious restaurant. I envisioned it as a private moment, just us, on a beach or somewhere with meaning. This place holds no meaning for us. Then again, I can't think of any place that does. Maybe that's been my problem since the beginning. I never gave him all of me. I've kept my heart guarded, worried he'd destroy it like the last man I let in. But Wes is willing to devote his life to me. Shouldn't that mean something?

Wes is intelligent, has a career he loves, and despite all his money, uses his fortune for good. Best of all, he supports my ambitions. The more I think about it, the more the truth hits me. I've never given Wes a chance. I've never considered us to be serious, even when we went away together, even when he peers at me as if I'm the only woman for him, even when he spoils me and whispers the sweetest things in my ears. I've always viewed him as a stepping stone, someone to bridge the gap between my past and my future. Maybe Wes *is* my future.

"Brook?" His uncertain voice cuts through my thoughts.

I meet his nervous eyes, wishing I could see the answer in them. These are eyes that, over the past eight months, have looked at me with nothing but the sweetest devotion, nothing but the most tender compassion, nothing but the most beautiful love. We may not be an overtly amorous couple who always discuss our feelings, but I know Wes loves me. That's the only thing that should matter.

My lips crack into a smile. "Yes."

"Yes?" Joy fills his expression.

"Yes, Wes." I inwardly cringe at the sound of that. "I'll marry you."

Tension trickles off his body in waves as he jumps to his feet, pulling me up with him. He wraps his arms around me, pressing his lips against mine, the kiss simple, yet full.

With a grin, he removes the stunning marquis-shaped diamond from the box and brings it to my left hand.

"It's beautiful," I breathe as he slides it down my finger, wincing when it doesn't fit.

"Shit, Brook. I'm sorry," he apologizes frantically. "I told the girl at the jewelers it looked small. I…"

"It's okay," I assure him, kissing his cheek, then place the diamond back into the box, closing it and handing it to him. "It's not about the ring."

"But the ring's nice, isn't it? You like it, right?"

Cupping his face in my hands, I hover my lips over his. "It's exactly what I've always dreamed of. We'll get it resized, then I'll wear it for the rest of my life."

He leans closer, resting his forehead on mine. "I like the sound of that."

"So do I."

Chapter Two

DREW

"**D**ADDY," A SMALL VOICE whispers, infiltrating the place between sleep and wakefulness. It's a sweet sound, the perfect one to rouse me from my dreams. It sounds like unwavering devotion and pure, untainted love.

The old me would groan, tell whomever's bothering me to go away, but those days ended eight years ago. Instead, I pretend I'm still asleep. It's become a game, part of our daily routine, one I hope doesn't fade with age and maturity. I treasure these moments with my two daughters. There will soon come a day when I'll wish they'd still wake me up early on a Sunday morning to make them pancakes. When I'll wish they'd still beg me to watch yet another Disney movie with them. When I'll wish they'd still force me to play dress-up. Alyssa and Charlotte have already grown up faster than I like. It seems like just yesterday I held Alyssa for the first time as a bewildered twenty-six-year-old man who thought he had life figured out. Little did I know I had nothing figured out. I still don't.

"Daddy," that same small voice repeats, followed by the sound of snickers.

123

"Do you think he's still sleeping?" a second voice whispers, this one younger. The slight lisp is evidence of a few recently lost teeth.

"No. He's just playing. Like always." I can hear the irritation and a hint of annoyance in her tone. My oldest, Alyssa, is eight going on eighteen, and she has all the attitude to prove it.

"I don't know. He's not moving."

I do my best to stay still, apart from my chest rising and falling with my breaths.

"Daddy?" I sense my two girls hovering over me, inching closer and closer.

Before they can react, I fling my eyes open, bellowing, "Gotcha!" I wrap my arms around them, hoisting them into the bed with me.

Their giggles and laughter fill the room as I tickle them, smiling at how carefree they both seem to be. There was a time I wasn't sure if I'd be a good dad. When my ex, Carla, split, leaving me to raise a two-year-old and six-month-old alone, I had no idea what to do. I worried I'd do something wrong and destroy any chance they had at a bright future. Looking at them now — happy, adjusted, loving — I know I've done a good job, despite the challenges facing me as a single father.

"Okay, you two." I glance at the clock, then back at them. For the longest time, I always saw Carla when I looked at them. But as the years passed and Carla's appearance faded from memory, I no longer do. I see me. In their eyes. In their smile. In their laughter. They're my world, and I know I'm theirs. "Time to get

124

ready for school."

I fling the covers off, then lift each of my girls under an arm, carrying them out of my room and down the hall into theirs, their squeals filling our home. As I drop each off in their pastel-colored rooms laden with stuffed animals, dolls, and books, I marvel at how different my life is than it was ten years ago. Having kids was the last thing on my mind. The only thing I cared about was making a name for myself in hockey. It's amazing how something that weighs less than eight pounds can change everything.

Over the next hour, we busy ourselves with what's become our typical morning routine. Alyssa helps Charlotte get ready while I shower, then both girls appear in the kitchen where we eat our normal breakfast of oatmeal and fruit. I make sure I've signed off on any of their homework, then place the lunches Aunt Gigi has prepared for them into their bags, leaving a note reminding them how much I love them.

Like clockwork, at exactly 7:30, we walk out the door and begin the five-minute journey from our house in Needham, a suburb about a half-hour west of Boston, to the girls' elementary school. During the colder months, I drive them on my way to my job as head hockey coach at Boston College. But now that it's March and the weather is warming up, at least today, we walk, Charlotte enthusiastically clutching my hand. Alyssa refuses, claiming she's too old to hold hands, just like she does every day.

On our way down the sidewalk, the girls entertain themselves. Charlotte sings about a marching duke as she stomps along with the beat, her dark curls springing with each step. Even Alyssa joins in. Trees line the quiet neighborhood, the branches still mostly barren. The bulbs will soon be in full bloom, the browns and emptiness of the winter replaced with greens, everything coming back to life.

As we approach the school, the sound of children grows louder and louder. A line of SUVs and minivans snakes around the block. Several teachers man the drop-off area to keep the flow of traffic moving as smoothly as possible. The instant we turn onto the walkway toward the front entrance, Alyssa attempts to hurry off and join the swarm of kids getting off one of the school buses parked in front of the building.

"Bye, Dad. See you later!"

"Uh-uh. Not so fast," I call out.

She slows her steps and turns around, crossing her arms over her chest. I arch a brow, not saying a word. This isn't the first time we've done this dance. And it won't be the last.

Molly warned me of the things she did to our father when she was a teenager. From making him drop her off several blocks from wherever she was meeting her friends, to the incessant eye rolling, to the constant attitude. I'm unprepared for Alyssa to reach that stage. If I could have my way, I'd keep her eight forever. I'd keep her away from the cruelties of the real world, from people trying to convince her she's anything but the princess she'll always be in my eyes.

With a dramatic sigh and an even more dramatic eye roll, she shuffles back toward me. I crouch down, giving her a hug, which she weakly returns, then kiss her temple.

126

"Auntie Molly will be here to pick you two up after school. You're having a sleepover there tonight." Releasing my hold on her, I stand. "Okay?"

"Okay." She takes off once more.

"Love ya, Lyss!"

"Love you, too, Dad."

Three words can completely melt your heart and turn you into mush. Three words can make even the most secure and macho of men crumble into a thousand tiny pieces. Yes, when the first girl I was serious about said those three words to me, I thought it was the greatest day of my life. But nothing prepares you for the love you have for your own child. Hearing that tiny human you brought into the world say those three words back to you... It makes all the tantrums, fights, and sleepless nights worth it. In a heartbeat, you forget all the stuff that makes you reconsider whether having kids was a good idea, because when your child says those three words, it's the *only* thing that matters.

I turn to Charlotte, lifting her as if she weighs nothing. Compared to my size, she's a peanut. She wraps her tiny arms around my neck, squeezing.

"Tighter, tighter!" I say, a lightness in my tone. "You give the best hugs, Char."

"No. You do!" She giggles.

I hold her for a moment, relishing in the love she has for me. She's only six, still too young to think her daddy's anything short of perfect.

Kissing her cheek, I lower her back to her feet, tousling her hair. "Love you, kiddo. Have a good day at school. And behave for Auntie Molly and Uncle Noah tonight."

"I will. Love you, Daddy." She spins from me, barreling toward one of the teachers ensuring the students make it into the building safely. "Have a good day at your school, too," she shouts back, almost like an afterthought.

"Thanks, kiddo."

I stand there, observing my girls. Being a parent is like riding a rollercoaster. There are moments you believe you have it figured out, then something happens to make you think you're failing miserably. But as I watch my two girls, seeing them smile and interact with other kids their age, it makes me think I must have done *something* right.

Once I see them disappear beyond the front doors, I turn around, about to head home. I come face to face with a group of moms, their eyes raking over me like I'm a pig ready for slaughter.

"Andrew," one of them says. After her months of shameless flirting, I've learned her name is Misty. "You are so good with those two girls." She crosses an arm over her stomach, raising her coffee cup to her bright red lips with her free hand. "I wish I could get my husband to pick up some of the slack."

I grit out a smile, keeping my thoughts to myself. I've been the token single dad of the school long enough to have heard it all before, and from the same people. The group of five women surrounding me makes up what my sister, Molly, likes to call "the cougar den". They spend the hours their kids are at school getting manicures, going out to lunch, and gossiping about everything and anything while their husbands work, some of them two jobs. They wear skin-tight workout clothes, their hair perfectly coifed, makeup expertly applied. They make it clear that the school drop-off is akin to a meat market...and I'm the prize filet.

When I moved here two years ago and enrolled Alyssa and Charlotte, I became the hot topic. And I suppose I still am. These women constantly flirt with me, even at school events with their husbands at their sides. The men don't seem to notice. They're too excited about having their photo taken with me, Andrew Brinks, retired star center for the Bruins who led the team to win the Stanley Cup twice during my short career.

"Big game tonight, huh?" one of the women asks, biting on her lower lip as she inches toward me, placing a hand on her hip.

I nod, unpersuaded by whatever charms she thinks she possesses. "First game of the Frozen Four."

"Well, I'm sure your team will win. After all, they have you for a coach." Misty winks.

"We'll see. We're playing Cornell. No matter what, it'll be a good game." I give them a congenial smile, then open my mouth to excuse myself when she cuts me off.

"Will your good luck charm be by your side? That little dancer for the Celtics?" She steps toward me. "I saw the photos of you together at some charity function last weekend. She's a very lucky girl." When she places her hand on my bicep, I back away.

129

"She's just a friend."

"Mmm-hmm." The way she looks me up and down makes it more than clear she doesn't believe me.

"If you'll excuse me, I need to get going." I skirt around them before having to explain myself any further. News travels quickly in a small town, especially news about any pseudo-celebrities, as it appears I still am, even though it's been six years since I've played professionally. My relationship with Skylar is none of their business. It's not even a relationship. Just a mutual understanding between two consenting adults.

"Okay, Andrew," Misty huffs. "But if you ever need a new 'friend', call me."

I glance back at her, trying to hide my disgust when she gives me an exaggerated wink. The other women chortle and giggle. The sad thing is, every single one of them would gladly invite me into their bed. They may think their brazen flirting and advances are cute, even attractive. But not to me. Not when I know how it feels to have the shoe on the other foot, when you learn the person you'd built a family with is cheating.

I push away the memories and continue down the street toward my house. I don't even turn around when one of them shouts, "Go Eagles!"

Chapter Three

BROOKLYN

I ALWAYS THOUGHT I'D feel like a different woman once I agreed to marry someone, to spend my life with him, to cherish and honor him until the end of our days. But I don't. I still feel like Brooklyn. My Friday morning routine is the same it's always been, even before Wes entered the picture. I get up early, shower, then am on my way to the North End to meet Molly for a cup of coffee at the café.

The entire drive, I don't even think twice about today being any different from every other Friday that's come before it. But as I near the café and am moments away from telling my best friend I'm getting married, my stomach tenses, uncertainty washing over me. What will she say? Will she think it's too soon, like I did at first?

As I lay awake last night, staring at my left hand where a ring would soon sit, I reflected on the handful of men I'd dated in the past. They were all like Wes — serious, professional, and anything but spontaneous. They were all charming, respectful, and devoted, the type of man I would have been proud to marry and have a family with. But something always happened.

Drew always happened, cutting the relationship short before it had a chance to take off, unbeknownst to him. I can't let him ruin this one, too.

I pull into the alley behind the café and park, then step onto the damp pavement, the smell of coffee and sugar invading my senses. Cars roar by, the familiar sounds of the city surrounding me as I make my way to the sidewalk. Despite it not yet being nine in the morning, the North End is already bustling with locals and tourists alike. Mom-and-pop restaurants line the streets of the renowned Italian section of town, the delectable aromas infiltrating the air enough to make anyone's stomach growl. The people who live and work here are like one giant family...including Molly's family, who have owned this café for over a century.

But as I stare at the familiar glass doors of the place that's always been like a second home to me, I feel like I'm sneaking in after doing something I shouldn't have. I'm probably over-analyzing the situation, as I'm prone to do, but I'm unusually anxious and on edge this morning.

"This is just like every other Friday," I remind myself, filling my lungs with air, which has the pacifying effect I'm hoping for.

With my nerves temporarily at ease, I open the door and enter the trendy café that's abuzz with activity. The walls are all dark brick, industrial-looking lights hanging from the high ceiling. Wooden tables of various sizes fill the space — some small bistro tables, others long, communal style. The focal point is the large glass display cases showcasing every delectable treat known to man, all family recipes handed down through the generations.

"Good morning, Brooklyn dear," a petite woman with dark graying hair calls out from behind the coffee bar. She barely even looks up, cashing out a man dressed in a suit. It reminds me of Wes and how we met in his very café. Last night, he told me how I'd caught his attention almost immediately. Well, he certainly caught mine.

I've always prided myself on being such a permanent fixture here. I tend to know most of the people who come through that door. The ones I don't are usually tourists. But Wes… He was neither a regular nor a tourist. Dressed in a breathtaking navy blue pinstriped suit that clung to his muscular, tall physique, he certainly got my pulse going. Then again, I had been reading a rough draft of one of Molly's books, and being the romance author she is, it was exceptionally steamy. When I kept seeing him here, I thought perhaps he'd recently moved. I never would have imagined he stopped by just to work up the courage to ask me out. It's sweet, the type of story you tell your kids years down the road when they ask how their parents met. And what makes it better is that it's pure, free of pain, of heartache, of regret.

"Morning, Aunt Gigi." Heading past the long line of customers, I duck behind the display cases and pour myself a cup of coffee.

While she's technically Molly and Drew's aunt, not mine, I'm closer to her than some of my own aunts and uncles, whom I barely see. Gigi, short for Giorgina, has been a part of my life for as long as I can remember. When Molly and I became fast friends our first week of school and her aunt learned I'd recently lost my mother, she took me under her wing, offering me all the love and affection a mother would…just like she did for Molly and Drew.

"Busy today, huh?" I ask, making small talk, smiling at a few of the other employees as they diligently fill the influx of orders. The coffee and espresso machines whir and steam while patrons wait off to the side for their lattes, cappuccinos, or whatever else they ordered.

"It's Friday. It usually is." She glances over her shoulder, giving me a smile as she seems to analyze me. It's ridiculous, but I wonder if she knows Wes proposed. She's always had an uncanny ability to see things most people can't, see things I try to hide from everyone. Sometimes I feel like she's the only one who knows the real Brooklyn. "How was your date with Weston last night?" She turns back to the customer, writing his order on a paper cup before handing it off to one of the baristas.

"Good." Coffee in hand, I dip back under the counter and snag an empty table before anyone else can. I lower myself into the chair, dropping my heavy bag laden with files to the floor. The aroma of coffee gets even stronger as I raise my mug to my lips, my entire body relaxing as that first taste of the best coffee in the city hits my tongue.

"Just good?" Gigi asks. I look at her. When our eyes lock, she squints the way she always does when trying to peer into my soul, to read my mind.

"It was like every other date." I shrug, playing it off. I don't want to tell her yet. I want Molly to be the first person to know. I'm the first one she shared her news with when Noah, her fiancé, proposed to her. Molly's always been the first person I've told everything to. Well, almost everything. Some things I can't share, the words too painful to say.

"You don't sound very excited about the prospect," Gigi comments.

"I am. I just…" I take another sip of my coffee, trying to collect my thoughts so I don't say anything she'll read too much into. But it *had* been just like every other date. Pretentious restaurant. Expensive bottle of wine. Sex that can be described as blissfully adequate. A nip here. A suck there. A bit of effort to bring me to orgasm, but falling just short of reaching that finish line, at least for me. "I don't need fancy caviar and champagne to be happy. Sometimes it's the things that don't cost a penny that have the most meaning." The words leave my mouth before I can stop them. I brace myself for her next intrusive question. Thankfully, the whirlwind known as Molly Brinks bursts through the door, saving me from further interrogation.

"I need chocolate. Stat." A woman on a mission, she hurries toward the display cases, her blonde waves streaking through my vision.

"Good morning, Molly Mae," Gigi greets in playful irritation. "It's wonderful to see you, too."

With one of the café's famous chocolate chip muffins in her hand, Molly takes a large bite, her entire body seeming to relax as the chocolate and sugar hit her taste buds. "God, that's almost as good as sex," she breathes, then smiles. "Morning, Aunt Gigi." She heads toward her, placing a kiss on her cheek.

"How's my favorite niece and great-nephew doing

T.K. Leigh

this morning?" Gigi places a hand on Molly's protruding stomach. She's only four months pregnant, but her short and slender stature make her appear much further along. It doesn't help that, according to Noah, he was over nine pounds when he was born. Of course, when Molly found out, she joked she would have preferred to know that little piece of information before she allowed him to knock her up.

"We're doing great. Hungry." There's a glow about her as she points to her stomach. "This little guy likes his chocolate."

"You're sure it's him?" Gigi pinches her lips together before returning her attention to the line of customers. "I seem to remember a certain niece of mine having an obsession with those chocolate chip muffins *before* she was ever pregnant."

Molly takes another bite and heads toward me. "They're good, Gigi! You need to stop putting crack in them. Then maybe I wouldn't be so addicted." She turns her attention to me. "Morning, Brooklyn." She places her muffin on the table as I stand, squeezing her, all the tension slowly rolling off my body.

"Morning, Mols." I release my hold on her and meet her eyes. She narrows her gaze on me.

"What is it? You seem…different."

I blink, wondering if there's a giant flashing sign attached to me I don't know about. "Actually, there's something I need to tell you." I steel myself, swallowing hard.

"What is it?" She slides into her chair and I return to mine.

Tapping the side of my mug, I take a sip of coffee as I glance around the café. Laughter and excited voices, along with the occasional sound of fresh coffee beans being ground, echo against the walls. It's the look and sound of home. I hope it always will be.

When I return the mug to the bistro table, I meet her gaze. Concern overtakes her features, as if she's preparing to hear I have cancer or am moving far away.

"Last night, Wes asked me to marry him."

She inhales a sharp breath as her eyes widen, immediately shooting to my left ring finger. When she sees it's vacant, her shoulders fall. I withdraw my hand, hiding it under the table.

"Oh, Brook. I'm sorry." From the gravity in my tone and lack of a ring, I know she assumes I said no and we're no longer together.

"I said yes," I add quickly.

She frowns. "You what?"

"Yes." Growing more and more uncomfortable by the minute, I fidget with the napkin in front of me. I'm not sure how I expected Molly to react to the news. If I'm being truthful with myself, she responded how I assumed she would — in complete and utter shock. It almost mirrors my reaction when Wes got down on one knee last night…until I analyzed the situation and realized this is the next step for us. It's what I need to move on, to bury the past and stop holding out hope for the impossible to happen.

"Wow."

I lift a brow. "That's it? Just a wow? When you told me Noah popped the question, I was thrilled."

"I know, and I'm happy for you." She covers my hand with hers. "As long as it's really what you want."

"What makes you think it's not?" I pull my hand away from hers, toying with my mug.

"I guess I didn't realize it was that serious between you two. The way you've always talked about it made it sound like you were just having some fun. No expectations."

"Well, it is serious." I straighten my spine, staring at the dark shade of my coffee, the queasiness in my stomach becoming stronger. "So I'd appreciate your support and hope you'll stand next to me as my maid of honor during the most important moment of my life."

Her stunned expression falls away, a brilliant smile forming on her mouth. Her blue eyes brighten, everything about her oozing happiness. Still, it doesn't seem genuine. She stands, taking the few steps toward me. "You know I wouldn't miss it for the world." She holds her arms out and I rise, walking into them. "I'm so happy for you. You deserve this." She pulls back. "Truthfully."

"What are you happy for?" a deep, booming voice cuts through. We whip our heads toward the source, both of us seeming to jump back like two errant children who just got caught doing something they shouldn't.

My face heats, a feeling of breathlessness overtaking me, as it does every time I stare into Drew's chestnut eyes. His dark hair is a bit shaggy, curling over the collar of his suit, but it's not as unkempt and out of control as it was during his hockey days. A bit of scruff dots his jawline, and as much as I prefer how he looks clean-shaven, there's something about the facial hair that still makes my pulse race, even though I wish it didn't, wish I could forget the way his arms felt around me, the way his lips warmed mine, the way his body molded to mine. And that's precisely why I need to marry Wes. To forget. To cleanse myself of his toxins.

Pretending Drew's mere presence doesn't send those butterflies fluttering in my stomach like they did during my teenage years, I look at him with a serious expression. "She's happy for me," I state with determination, summoning every ounce of confidence I can muster. "Wes proposed last night."

Drew remains completely still, his eyes seeming to penetrate every fiber of my being, infiltrating my soul, invading my heart. "And you said no, right?"

"I said yes." I stand taller, but my height is no match for Drew's imposing six-foot, two-inch muscular stature.

"You agreed to marry him?" His pitch rises, disbelief filling every syllable. "After less than a year?"

"You're one to talk, Drew. If memory serves, you got drunk with your ex and decided to fly to Vegas to tie the knot after only knowing each other a total of what?" I place my hands on my hips. "A month? How'd that work out for you?"

"And that's exactly why I'm trying to stop you from making the same mistake!" He tugs at his hair, leaning closer to me. I catch a whiff of his woodsy, earthy scent, the aroma causing so many memories to flash before me. We've known each other most of our lives. We have some really good memories, but also some really bad ones. I can't let him be the cause of any more bad memories.

"Our situations are vastly different. I'm not making the same mistake you did."

"But you admit it might be a mistake," he shoots back, not missing an opportunity.

"I didn't say that." My jaw clenches as I try to remain as calm and collected as possible. Part of me wants to agree with him, but I've done that before, allowed him to poison my rationale. I won't let him ruin yet another one of my relationships. I don't have to defend my choice to someone who's supposed to be a friend.

Then again, both of us have been fooling ourselves for years, claiming we're only friends, that there's never been anything between us, no desire for anything more. Maybe he doesn't feel it, but I do. And I don't want to anymore.

"You were twenty-four when you got married. Pretty much every decision you make at that age can be considered a mistake."

"Not all of them. Plus, I was twenty-five." He crosses his arms in front of his chest, widening his stance. It makes the arms of his suit bulge. It doesn't matter that he no longer plays professional hockey. He's still in amazing shape. But I refuse to be distracted by the broad chest, muscular shoulders, or sculpted torso that I know hides underneath his clothes. Not when I've finally found a man who loves me, who will do anything for me, who won't make me promises and then forget them the next day.

"Fine. Twenty-five. I'm thirty-two. Wes isn't someone I met at a hotel bar and asked to come back to my room with me. We're both mature adults who are more than capable of making mature decisions. And I've decided to marry him."

He seems to assess my response, then narrows his eyes. "Is it because of his money?"

My face heats from his accusation, my blood boiling.

"Drew," Molly whispers frantically, her tone evidence of her disbelief at his suggestion.

He darts his gaze to hers and back to mine. "No. Seriously. I want to know."

My lips curling at the fact he thinks the only reason I'd marry Wes is because of his money and success, I lean into Drew, my face less than an inch from his.

"You know damn well that doesn't matter to me," I hiss. "It never has and it never will. I'm still the same girl who's just as happy stuffing my face with whole belly clams off a paper plate at Kelly's as I am eating duck served by white-gloved waitstaff at a five-star restaurant."

Grabbing my bag, I storm past him, pausing as I'm about to leave the café. All eyes seem to be on us...including Aunt Gigi's. Hers aren't stunned, like everyone else's are. Hers are more intrigued, curious.

"In fact, I still prefer the former." I meet his gaze as those words spill from me, a hidden confession laced with meaning only few people will understand.

Then I hurry out the door, cursing Drew for ruining this moment, like he's ruined everything else.

Chapter Four

DREW

"**W**HAT THE HELL WAS that?" Molly bites out. I snap my stare away from the door where Brooklyn had just disappeared. When I meet her blue eyes, they're narrowed, her irritation loud and clear.

"What do you mean?" I rake my hands through my hair, feeling like I'm living in an alternate universe. Sure, Brooklyn's been dating Wes for almost a year now, but I thought it was casual, like things between Skylar and me. Or maybe I simply hoped it wasn't serious. She rarely speaks of him, but I don't make it a habit to ask, either. Still, if she's in love with him, shouldn't she be shouting it from the rooftops instead of speaking of her engagement as if it's a business negotiation?

"I'm talking about how you just called Brooklyn a gold digger." She places her hands on her hips, bringing attention to the baby bump that seems to get bigger every day. "You know as well as I do that she's the *last* person on this planet who would marry someone for money."

"I know. I just…"

"What?" she presses, leaning into me.

You'd think a man of my size and height wouldn't be intimidated by a woman as short and petite as Molly. But what my sister lacks in stature she makes up for in attitude and perseverance. Once she sinks her claws into something, whether it be a person or an idea, she never lets go. She's not going to let me leave this café until she gets what she wants out of me.

"It's like I told Brooklyn. I don't want her to make the same mistake I did." My voice lacks the determination I need to demonstrate that my words are true. "That's all."

"That's a load of crap and you know it. Brooklyn's your friend. One of your best friends, really. She just made one of the biggest decisions of her life. She needs our support."

"But what if I don't support her decision?"

"Then you need to grow a set and tell her why instead of skirting around the bush."

"What are you talking about?" My brows pinch together, my tone uncertain.

"Oh, come on." She rolls her eyes. "I wasn't born yesterday, Andrew Vincenzo Brinks. I see the way you look at her. In fact, I've *seen* the way you've looked at her since high school." She points her finger in my face, her tone sharp. "If you don't do something, you'll lose her. And this time, you won't be able to get her back." She hardens her stare. "Let that sink in."

"She loves you, Andrew," Aunt Gigi says as a hand

rests on my arm. I spin around to see her behind me. She gives me a knowing look, wordlessly reminding me of everything I've struggled to forget over the years.

"Who? Molly?" I joke, trying to lighten the atmosphere and avoid having to endure this conversation. They're seeing something that's not there, something I've done everything in my power to bury. Now, as I look back at that summer, I no longer feel the vice squeezing my heart. "I know she does." I nudge my sister.

Aunt Gigi lifts her hand and lands a light smack against the back of my head.

I duck away. "Ouch! Why did you do that?"

"You've suffered too many hockey injuries. I'm talking about Brooklyn, you fool." She clasps my hands in hers. "*Brooklyn* loves you."

"Of course she loves me. She's told me on more than one occasion that she loves me like a brother."

She shakes her head. "Sometimes, my sweet, sweet boy, women say things they don't mean. They say things they want to think, want to believe."

I look from Gigi to Molly, who simply nods. "We do. All the time. I can't even tell you how many orgasms I faked before I met Noah."

I grimace. "Jesus, Molly!"

Gigi lands another slap against one side of my head, then the other.

"Hey! I wasn't the one who said it!"

She shoves her finger into my face. "You know

better than to take the Lord's name in vain, Andrew, and I can't hit Molly since she's pregnant." She takes a deep breath, pinching the bridge of her nose. "I should have insisted your father take the two of you to church more than a few times a decade."

"Funerals and weddings," Molly and I say in unison, recalling our father's response to Gigi anytime she harped on him for his lackluster attendance record at church. Apart from those two events, our father refused to go, although Gigi attended once a week, sometimes more.

"But seriously, Drew," my sister continues. "Gigi's right. We lie all the time, myself included. After I began spending time with Noah, I couldn't remember ever feeling that way about another person. It scared me, so I did everything I possibly could to fight it. And I fought it *hard*. No matter what I did, he was still on my mind…and in my heart. I love Brooklyn like I would a sister. I will support her decision to marry Wes, if that's what she truly wants. But I get the feeling she's been trying to convince herself her love for you is simply like that of a sister loving a brother. I don't think that's the case at all. I never have. And I don't think that's the case for you, either."

"Those pregnancy hormones are affecting your brain." I head toward the counter to grab my morning coffee, my steps slow as the reality of the situation hits me.

Brooklyn's been a part of my life for as long as I can remember. She's always been there when I've needed her, even after everything that happened before I left for college. I wonder how much longer she *will* be there,

146

if I'll gradually see less and less of her until Wes consumes every part of her life and I'm nothing more than a distant memory.

"They are not. You're deflecting," she argues, following me.

"Have you forgotten that I'm seeing someone?"

She bursts out laughing. "I'm not so sure getting together for an occasional booty call qualifies as 'seeing someone'." She holds up her hand, counting on her fingers. "One, you don't talk about her. Two, you claim it's not serious, that she's more than welcome to see other people. And three, you've never brought her home to meet the girls."

"They've already been through enough with Carla leaving." I add some milk to my coffee, stir it, then turn to Molly, Gigi peering over her shoulder, a smug look on her face. "They don't need to go through that again."

"They're not the ones who went through it," Molly argues. "Sure, Alyssa asked for her mama a lot at first, but she was only two. After a while, she stopped. Charlotte can't remember ever having a mother, so there's nothing for her to miss." Her expression turns compassionate, her brilliant eyes piercing through me. "It's not the girls, is it?"

I open my mouth, but she cuts me off.

"*You're* the one who doesn't want to go through that again. The girls are just a convenient excuse."

"They are not," I protest, although my words lack certainty.

147

After Carla left, I put all my energy into my family, my girls included. My father was diagnosed with Alzheimer's at an early age and it progressed rapidly. I bought the café from him, saving it from being turned into yet another Starbucks. Once I no longer had hockey in my life, I devoted everything I had into making this place as successful as possible. When I wasn't running the café, I kept myself busy with my girls, doing everything to make sure they had as normal a childhood as possible and didn't want for anything. I didn't start coaching hockey again until two years ago, which was when I handed over the reins of the café to Gigi.

"If I were worried about going through all that again, would I be dating?"

"I don't consider you and that bimbo to be 'dating'," Molly retorts without missing a beat. "You won't be able to use those girls as an excuse forever. At some point, they'll grow up and start building relationships of their own. Then where will you be? Alone."

"Not this again," I groan, walking away from her, but she's quick on my heels. I expect Gigi to have something to say at this point. Instead, she remains suspiciously silent, observing me through small eyes, analyzing, assessing, judging.

"Yes, this again. I just… I don't get you these days, Drew. I've been trying to understand. I really have. But for years now, you've successfully caused Brooklyn to shun nearly every guy who was remotely interested in her."

"What?" I squint at her, my tone evidencing my

disagreement with her statement. "No, I haven't."

"Yes, you have. You may not notice it, but I have. We *all* have. So unless you're willing to finally admit you have feelings for her, feelings strong enough for you to fly off the handle at the news of her engagement, you'd better grow up and support her."

"I don't have time for this right now. I have more important things to worry about today, like getting my team into the championship game." My voice grows louder with each word I speak. "So, Molly, if you're done pretending you know what's best for me when just a few years ago, you probably couldn't even remember the name of the guy sleeping in your bed, I'll be on my way."

My temper getting the better of me, I storm out of the café before Molly or Gigi can say anything else. They don't know what they're talking about. Yes, perhaps I overreacted to Brooklyn's news. I just don't want her to make the same mistake I did. That's all. Nothing more. That ship sailed when I got on that plane and left for college.

Chapter Five

BROOKLYN

MY MOTHER USED TO wear a gold locket around her neck. It was small, in the shape of a heart with a diamond in the center, and opened to reveal two photos — my dad on one side, a baby photo of me on the other. I can't remember much about her. Even if I close my eyes and try to recall the sound of her voice, the feel of her arms, the smell of her perfume, I can't. But I remember that locket. I imagine her wearing it as she sang me to sleep, as she kissed my head, as she whispered how much she loved me.

In my childhood, I'd often have déjà vu where I'd see that locket. It wasn't until the day of high school graduation I knew it was real, not a product of my overactive imagination. Just before I was about to leave for the ceremony, my father handed me a long, white box. When I opened it and saw the locket, I was overjoyed, grateful to be able to carry a piece of my mother with me always. The instant he secured it around my neck that day, I felt her — her fire, her strength, her love.

As I toy with that very necklace, about to walk into the house Molly shares with Noah, I try to summon all those things once more. I've avoided this all day — her calls, her texts, her voice messages. And there were a lot. I just wasn't ready to face what she had to say after witnessing my argument with Drew. I'm still not.

Taking a deep breath, I use my key to let myself in. "Hello, hello," I call in a sing-song manner. The sound of laughter hits me instantly, interspersed with that of an announcer's voice blaring from the television.

"Auntie Brook!" two voices shout. I turn the corner to see Alyssa and Charlotte jumping up from the floor of the den, rushing toward me.

"Are you here to watch Daddy's team win?" Charlotte asks.

"Of course." I force a smile. They're too young to read too much into my lackluster response.

"Well, come on." Alyssa tugs me toward the oversized sofa. "It's about to start!"

She plops on the floor in front of the screen, not wanting to miss a second of the action. She's sporting the school's colors, wearing a kid-sized hockey jersey with Brinks above the number 19, Drew's old number, on the back. Their father's influence is clear in the way both girls love everything about hockey. Yes, they play with Barbies and their princess castles, like most other girls, but they also know how to hold a hockey stick, throw a baseball, and shoot a basket. Despite all the challenges facing Drew as a single father, he's given them everything they need.

Molly's eyes find mine as I continue toward the couch where she sits with Noah, his arm draped comfortably around her shoulders. As our gazes lock, I see a thousand questions etched within. I subtly shake my head, wordlessly telling her I don't want to talk about it. Thankfully, she knows enough not to push the matter, at least not while we're in the presence of curious ears.

"Good to see you, Brooklyn." Noah raises himself to his feet, only having to bend slightly to kiss my cheek. "I hear congratulations are in order." His tone lifts at the end, almost questioning.

"I suppose they are." I still don't understand why our engagement is such a shock to everyone. We've been together for eight months. I know women who married their spouses after only dating them for a substantially shorter amount of time and they're happy. I can find happiness, too. Can't I?

I hate that I'm unable to enjoy this moment. The day should have been spent laughing and smiling with my best friend as we flipped through bridal magazines, circling the dresses I liked. In fact, we did that when we were teenagers. Molly claimed she was planning her wedding to one of the actors from *ER*, Noah Wyle. It's ironic she ended up engaged to a doctor named Noah.

When she asked me who I imagined marrying, I lied, claiming some singer in a boy band or hot actor. In reality, whenever I fantasized about my wedding, I pictured walking down the aisle to Drew. It took me years to realize my adolescent dream of marrying my best friend's brother was just that — a dream. Now, as I stand on the precipice of planning my *actual* wedding, I'm uncertain whether I've bid farewell to that dream. I'm not sure I want to, although all rationale says I should.

"Why are you congratulating Auntie Brook?" Alyssa asks.

I snap my eyes to hers, unsure what to say. Telling Drew I'm marrying Wes was difficult. I never imagined having to tell his kids. Hell, I've been engaged for twenty-four hours and still haven't shared the news with my own father.

"Because I'm getting married." My voice is even. Shouldn't I be squealing the news at the top of my lungs, ready to burst from the excitement?

"To Daddy?" Charlotte pipes up, no longer interested in the puzzle beginning to take shape on the wood floor.

"No. To Wes. You met him a few months ago when he came over for Christmas. Remember?"

"Why are you marrying him?" Alyssa presses.

I open my mouth, struggling to come up with a response. What do I say? That I'm still not quite sure myself, but figure it's the next logical step? That seeing Wes on one knee made me realize I never allowed him in, never allowed any man in, except the one who never wanted me, who still doesn't want me? That marrying Wes is the only way I can free myself from the hold that man still has on me?

"Because she loves him." Molly brings herself to her feet, standing next to me. I glance at her, seeing her arch a brow. "Isn't that right?"

"Yes." I address Alyssa once more. "Your auntie Molly's right. Because I love him." I swallow hard, acid churning in my stomach.

153

"Does this mean you won't spend time with us anymore?" Charlotte asks in a small voice, her face long.

"What makes you think that?" I crouch to her level. My tone is serene, reminiscent of the one I use with the kids I see on a daily basis, assuring them they're safe from the abuse they've suffered for too long.

"Because you won't need us anymore. You'll want to have a family of your own and will forget about us."

"Oh, Charlotte." I envelope her in my arms, doing everything I can to ease her fears. "I could never forget about you two. It doesn't matter I'm not related by blood." I pull back, meeting her brown eyes. They have small speckles of gold in them, a bit of light in the darkness. Neither Drew nor Alyssa have those. It's something unique to little Charlotte. "You will *always* be my family. Nothing will ever come between that. Just because I'm marrying Wes doesn't mean I'll spend any less time with you girls. I love playing with you two. That's not going to stop."

"Or you can marry Daddy so you can play with us all the time."

My breath catches at her words. It's a strange observation for a six-year-old, but in my experience, we don't give kids the credit they deserve. Their inquisitive and eager little minds pick up on more than we think. I wonder what else she's picked up on from me...and from Drew.

"These things don't work that way. Like Auntie Molly said, you get married when you love someone."

"You don't love Daddy?"

154

I pinch my lips together, this conversation taking a turn I'm not prepared for. "Of course I do," I answer honestly. "But in a different way than I love Wes."

I pause, my words ringing truer than I anticipated, leaving me stunned. I blink repeatedly, doing my best to stay focused and not think about how different my love for Drew is than my love for Wes. Can my feelings for Wes be labeled as love? Respect. Devotion. Admiration. But love? Love isn't a word to be tossed around idly. It's a word that should be given the weight it deserves. It's the most beautiful and most tragic feeling in the world. I'm not quite sure the way I feel about Wes measures up to that level, at least not yet.

"There are so many kinds of love. I love your aunt Gigi, your auntie Molly, your uncle Noah. But I don't love your uncle Noah the same way auntie Molly does."

"Damn straight," Molly mutters under her breath so only I can hear, and I'm thankful for the levity.

"So even though I love your daddy, it's not the same."

"Oh." Charlotte's shoulders fall at the news.

"But I promise you, both of you…" My eyes float to Alyssa, who stands behind her sister. "Nothing will change. There may just be an extra person at my side on occasion. It'll be fun." My voice brightens and I smile. "And you two will get to wear a pretty dress during the wedding as my flower girls."

"Really?" Alyssa asks.

"Of course! There's no one else I'd rather have."

I raise myself to my feet, looking down at them.

Their concerned expressions lifting at the thought of getting to play dress-up for a day, they return to their puzzle, both of them talking excitedly about what kind of dress they want to wear for the wedding.

Blowing out a breath, I look back at Molly and Noah.

"Wine?" He arches a brow.

"I could use some."

"Red or white?"

"I'll get it myself. You guys sit." I turn away from them and head into the kitchen, pausing at the island.

My hands grip the counter, my arms supporting my weight as I exhale a long breath. I try to compose myself, to swallow the lump in my throat at how concerned Alyssa and Charlotte were that I'd no longer be a part of their lives. I don't think that will be the case, but what if it is? What if Wes wants kids right away? How will I juggle that and starting a PhD program? What if Wes doesn't want children at all? We've never discussed it. There's so much I don't know about him, about what he wants out of life. My world spins, the walls closing in on me as these questions fill me with unease. What have I gotten myself into?

"Want to talk about it?" Molly's voice cuts through and I whip my head toward her.

"About what?" I ask in an even tone, pretending she hadn't caught me on the edge of a nervous breakdown.

"I don't know. Everything." She leans against the counter, crossing her arms in front of her chest. "You didn't return any of my phone calls or texts today."

I avoid her eyes. "My schedule was filled with home visits. Within the span of eight hours, I had over ten kids to check in on. I barely had time to eat, let alone answer a text or phone call. Not to mention submitting a few of my guardian ad litem reports to the court."

"That's never stopped you before." Molly steps toward me, her eyes seeming to analyze everything about me, from the way my gaze darts, to the way I chew on my bottom lip, to the way I try to shrink into my frame so I can disappear. I'm normally an open book with her...except when it comes to her brother. Some wounds are too painful and are better left scabbed over. "We used to talk all the time between home visits. That's when I used to bounce story ideas off you."

I spin from her, opening the refrigerator door and grabbing an uncorked bottle of chardonnay. "Well, you haven't seemed to need me lately, have you?" My words come out harsher than I intended, but the events of the day have finally taken their toll on me — Drew's reaction to my engagement, trying to convince a few of my kids that their foster parents won't hurt them like their biological parents had, Alyssa's and Charlotte's line of questioning. I've reached my boiling point.

"Is that what this is about?"

I find a wine glass in the cabinet and pour a healthy portion. "What do you mean?" I face her.

"Your engagement." She lowers her voice. "You have to admit it sort of came out of the blue. Are you only marrying Wes because *I'm* engaged, too?"

"Molly..." I roll my eyes. "No offense, but you two have been engaged for almost a year now and haven't set a date."

She rubs her stomach, grinning. "Well, my baby daddy knocked me up before we could get around to that. He must have some super swimmers because the month I stopped birth control...*bam*. Preggers." All it takes is a wink to lighten the atmosphere between us. She's always had an uncanny ability to do that. No matter how serious I try to be, no matter what I'm going through, she's always able to put a smile on my face.

Squeezing her bicep, I meet her eyes. "I'm happy for you, Mols...even if you did put the carriage before the horse."

"And it's a carriage I *really* enjoy riding, especially with all these pregnancy hormones." She leans closer. "I've always had a healthy sex drive. Hell, I write romance novels for a living and used Noah as a muse for one of my books. But lately..." Her voice grows softer, more secretive. "I'm like a fiend. I swear, I'm wearing poor Noah out." She pauses, a thoughtful expression crossing her face. "It could be the book I just started playing around with."

I arch a brow. "And what would that be?"

"A reverse harem."

"Reverse harem?" While I read every single one of Molly's books and offer my opinion, I'm not up-to-date on all the trends in the publishing industry. Most of my reading lately has been scholarly articles and other professional development books about working with high-risk children. "What does that entail?"

"Exactly what it sounds like. Instead of one guy

sleeping with a bunch of girls…"

"It's one girl sleeping with a bunch of guys?"

Molly shrugs. "More or less. Of course, it's not just sex. There's usually a reason for it."

"Please don't tell me you're fantasizing about sleeping with six guys at once."

"God no!" she shoots back. "I'm not sure my vagina can take that kind of pounding. It's already overly sensitive because of the pregnancy."

I shake my head, my face burning in embarrassment. "T.M.I., Molly."

She laughs, the sound chipping away at the stress that's been drowning me all day. I raise my eyes to hers, my lips turning up slightly. This is what I need right now, to laugh with my friend and cringe at her lack of brain-to-mouth filter, like we always have.

"Thanks, Mols," I say once her laughter wanes.

"You bet." She squeezes my arm, sympathy in her eyes. "Whenever you're ready to talk about why you're marrying Wes, I'm here. I'll listen."

Instead of insisting my engagement is everything I've hoped for, I say the only thing that makes sense. "I don't think I'll ever be ready for that."

From there, the night only gets worse as we all sit on the couch and watch the Eagles get their ass handed to them. Every time the cameras cut away to Drew in the box where his team sits, he seems to be tugging at his hair and shouting at his players, something he's always claimed isn't effective in getting them to play the best game they can. I've seen him lose important games before, but tonight's different. He's not the Drew I know. I can't help but think the bombshell I dropped on him earlier contributed to his lack of focus.

When the final buzzer sounds and the opposing team swarms the ice in celebration, I slump against the couch, silence ringing in the room once Noah turns off the TV.

"Well, you can't win them all," he states, catching my eyes.

He must be thinking the same thing I am. Did I cost Drew's team their shot at the championship? Sure, he isn't on the ice, but as the coach, he leads by example. If he has a bad attitude, the rest of the team will, as well. The number of fights that broke out between the players had to have set a record, and not a good one.

"It's my fault," I breathe, a lump forming in my throat.

Molly reaches for my hand, squeezing it. "No, it's not, Brook. It just wasn't their night."

"They've played this team countless times. They usually win."

"All the more reason they'd lose tonight. You had nothing to do with this."

I bury my head in my hands, despair eating away at me. "I never should have said anything. Not today. I should have waited until the playoffs were over."

"You had no idea he'd respond the way he did," Noah encourages, indicating Molly told him everything. Not just about my engagement, but also how Drew reacted to the news.

160

"No, but I should have known." I lift my eyes to his. "I didn't even know if I was going to tell him. I was just grateful I wasn't wearing a ring in case—"

"Speaking of which," Molly interrupts, her brows furrowed. "Where *is* the ring? I figured the rock's so massive you wouldn't feel comfortable wearing it to your job."

"They do recommend we not wear jewelry of any kind, but it didn't fit."

She stares at me, her lips curving into a smile.

"Don't even," I warn in a harsh tone. "I know what you're thinking. That it's a sign or something that I shouldn't be marrying him."

"That wasn't what I was thinking."

I form my mouth into a tight line, giving her a knowing look.

"Okay. Maybe it was, but none of that matters, as long as you're happy and this is what you want. *Is* this what you want?" she asks yet again.

"We've been together for eight months," I begin with a sigh. "A proposal is a natural progression."

"You're avoiding the question. Look at me, Brook."

The seriousness in Molly's tone makes me turn my eyes toward hers.

"Is this what you really want?"

Straightening my spine, I stand. "Of course it is." I look from her to Noah, then to the two sleeping beauties slumbering peacefully in each other's arms on the love seat, dead to the world. "Thanks for having

161

me. I really should get going. Wes is expecting me. I'll see you all Sunday for dinner."

I begin to retreat, praying they can't read through my lies. Wes isn't expecting me. I have no idea if he's even home or if he's working late tonight, as he so often does. It's never bothered me before. His busy work schedule gives me space and time to devote to my career and friends. Now, I'd love to be able to go to his house, have him wrap me in his arms and assure me this is the right thing for us.

"Brook, wait!" Molly calls out, jumping from the couch and hurrying toward me as fast as her pregnant little body can carry her. "I didn't mean anything by that. And I'm sorry I keep asking if you're sure about Wes. I trust you know what you're doing. I trust you're smart enough not to just marry someone because you don't think you're deserving of better."

Her words are kind and full of compassion, but within them lies all the hidden meaning necessary to make me doubt everything. And that doubt stays with me as I make my way home, as I draw myself a bath, as I struggle to fall asleep. I need to do something to make that doubt disappear, and there's only one person who can help do that.

Damn Aunt Gigi and her admonition to never go to sleep without reconciling your differences.

Chapter Six

DREW

MY SHOULDERS HANG LOW as I walk from the athletic center toward my car. The campus is quiet, no late-night revelry to celebrate the team making it to the championship game. I've spent the last hour in my office, staring at my desk, beating myself up. I allowed my anger to consume me, and my team paid the price. We were favored to win not just tonight, but the entire Frozen Four. But by the time they dropped the puck, the events of the day had reached a boiling point. I couldn't stop thinking about what Aunt Gigi and Molly had told me, how they said I've been using my daughters as an excuse not to get close to anyone, how I may have just lost the one woman I could love. And I do love Brooklyn, just not like that. I can't. Not after the last time.

I hop into my car, but instead of driving home to an empty house, I text Skylar, telling her I'll be at her place in fifteen minutes. No question to see what she's doing. No checking to see if it's okay that I come by. That's not how we work. There's no small talk. It's better that way.

After the short drive, I climb the steps of Skylar's

brownstone in the Back Bay and knock on the door. Within seconds, a slender body appears in the doorway.

"Tough break, Andrew." Her voice is low and husky as she crosses her arms in front of her ample chest.

I rake my eyes over her. Her long blonde hair is curled, falling to her mid-back. She wears a black kimono robe, loosely secured with a sash. The short cut of the flimsy garment makes her legs look like they go on for miles. Her makeup is fresh, obviously applied right after she received my text. Sultry red lips. Dark shadowing around her eyes, almost swallowing them. Shading on her cheeks to accentuate her high cheekbones.

"Can't win them all," she adds.

"I suppose you're right. I feel like I let the team down tonight," I say in an uncharacteristic move, at least where Skylar's concerned. We don't get personal with each other. There's no talk of feelings, hopes, dreams. Our conversations are kept light, a means to an end — her bedroom. It's worked for both of us for the past several months. We have an understanding. No promises for a future. No hope for something more. Just a physical connection when we need it.

Instead of offering a compassionate word like most people would, she reaches for my crotch and grabs. "I'll help you get back up."

Snapping out of my momentary lapse of judgment, my eyes narrow on her, becoming heated. "That's why I'm here." I lean into her, brushing my lips against hers.

There's no fluttering in my stomach. No

uncontrollable need to spend my time with her. No undeniable craving forming deep in my core when her skin touches mine. I feel nothing, other than a primal desire to lose myself in her and forget everything else. Am I using her? Maybe. From the beginning, I was blunt and straightforward, saying this wasn't about romance, about sweeping her off her feet and offering her the world. She didn't care about any of that stuff when we began our arrangement. She still doesn't.

Gripping her hips, I push her into the living room, our kiss harsh but without depth, jarring but forgettable, needy but lacking. That's how it's always been with her, with every other woman. It's not that I don't care for her. I do, but not in a way that will have me picking out window treatments or place settings. Not in a way that will have me offering my heart, only to watch her smash it to pieces.

I pull away, peering at Skylar. Her hazel eyes sparkle and gleam, returning my gaze with a coquettish look I imagine she uses on every other guy she brings back here. The idea should bother me, but it doesn't. Instead, I harden my stare.

"Get on your knees," I growl, then flinch.

While we're not the type to whisper sweet endearments to each other, the second I hear those words come out of my mouth in such a derogatory tone, I feel like an asshole. But isn't that what I am? A player? The type of person I'd threaten if Molly brought him home claiming it was research for one of her books. The type of person whose life I'd make a living hell if he ever laid a hand on Brooklyn with no intention of offering everything she deserves. The type

T.K. Leigh

of person I'd never let near my little girls, at the risk of going to prison. How did I get to this place?

Without saying a word, Skylar lowers herself to her knees, reaching for my belt, her fingers quick. Her tongue skims along the flesh of her lips as she unzips my pants, freeing me. I'm not rock hard, but she works her magic, her hand moving up and down my length, bringing me to life.

"There's my boy," she coos when I harden.

I peer down at her, her gaze trained on mine as she parts her lips, bringing them to my tip, her tongue teasing me. A hiss escapes and I fist her hair, pushing into her mouth. All the tension that's built up throughout the day melts away. I need this. Need to live in the moment, to think about nothing but her mouth on me, bringing me close to orgasm, as she does so well.

Her robe falls open, nothing but smooth skin on every inch of her body. When her legs part, she reveals the slickness forming between her thighs. I'm desperate to bury myself deep within them, but right now, I need this feeling of control more.

Closing my eyes, I lean my head against the wall behind me. The instant I do, green eyes, hardened and angry, flash before mine. Brooklyn's voice filters into my subconscious, telling me she's getting married.

I fling open my eyes, my motions becoming quick and intense. I don't want to think about today. I should only be concentrating on Skylar's mouth on my dick. Nothing else. But I can't stop thinking about Brooklyn. Why now? I thought I'd moved on, made peace with what happened all those years ago. After all, we were just teenagers. It was just one night. One night that

166

sealed our fate.

Desperate to focus on the present, I thrust harder and deeper, over and over until I'm ready to explode. I yank Skylar's head back, forcing her mouth away from me.

"That's enough," I pant, my chest heaving. "I need to fuck you."

"How romantic," she jests, but I'm not in the mood. Not tonight.

I grab her hand, bringing her to her feet, then pull her toward the couch, retrieving a condom from my wallet at the same time. Sitting, I roll it on, not even removing my pants. This is cheap and dirty, but I don't care. When I tug her down, she straddles me. I tease her with my erection, trying to draw things out before I unravel. And right now, that's what I need. To feel something other than the numbing ache that's consumed me for too long.

Skylar loops her arms around my neck, bringing herself toward me. Her chest in my face, I clamp my mouth over a nipple. She throws her head back and moans. I wonder if she enjoys it or is pretending, as I so often do with her. As I trail my mouth along her skin, I grip her thighs, finding her center and pushing her down on me. I go slow, stretching her to take my size. Then I meet her eyes.

"Ride me."

With those two words, she moves against me, circling. Any other time, that would be fine, but all I can think of tonight is if Wes makes Brooklyn fuck him like this. If she's sitting on his dick right now, moaning, screaming his name. In all the months they've been together, I've tried not to think about that. Now I can't stop. It makes me want to screw Skylar even harder.

Fire in my veins, I tighten my grip on her hips, forcing her up and down on me faster, more punishing, more brutal. Her moans fill the room, interspersed with my occasional grunts. My lips are tight, my jaw clenched, every muscle in my body ready to snap with the building tension. I do everything in my power to think of Skylar, not Brooklyn, but it's impossible. Even when I come hard and fast as Skylar shatters around me, I have to bite back my desire to scream out Brooklyn's name, waves of ecstasy washing over me.

Twenty-four hours ago, I was content with the way my life was going. I have two little girls who mean the world to me. I have a great job where I can finally pursue my passion again. I have the perfect arrangement with a beautiful young woman who's happy with what I'm willing to offer. Now it all seems lacking, superficial.

In less than a day, my entire world's been tilted on its axis. All I hear is Brooklyn's voice.

"*Wes asked me to marry him. I said yes.*"

It brings me back to the day I left for college, Brooklyn's father warning me to stay away from her. His words crushed my soul that morning, just like Brooklyn's did today.

The warmth of Skylar's lips on my neck brings me back to the present. I look at her. "Stay?" she asks in a languid voice.

I shake my head, lifting her off me. "Rule number

one," I remind her as I stand, removing the condom and throwing it into a nearby trash can. "No spending the night." I zip my pants.

"Of course. Rule number one," she hisses, stalking across the room. She grabs her kimono from where it fell to the floor and shoves her arms into it, violently tying the sash. "God forbid you stay the night for once."

"Let's not fool ourselves, Skylar." I sound like an asshole, but that doesn't stop me from continuing. "We entered this arrangement knowing what we both wanted. I don't do romance."

"You can at least stay the night once in a while." She glares at me, her arms crossed in front of her chest. "You come here, make me suck you off, fuck me harder than you ever have, then leave? Makes me feel like a whore."

I still, cursing under my breath. Even if I'm not interested in a committed relationship, I hate for her to think of herself that way, hate that I *make* her think of herself that way.

Softening my expression, I approach her and rub my hands down her biceps, soothing her as I kiss her forehead. "I'm sorry. You're anything but. You're a strong, independent woman who knows what she likes. I appreciate your offer to stay the night. Maybe another time. It's been a difficult day."

"Then let me help you forget." She wraps her arms around my shoulders, rubbing her body against mine.

"I'd love to, Sky, but—"

"Let me guess," she interrupts, stepping away. "You can't. You need to get home to your girls. Or, better yet, you need to get up early to hit the ice."

I shrug. "Yes."

She shakes her head, blowing out a breath. "You know, I haven't slept with anyone else. Since we started...whatever this is..." She gestures between our two bodies, "it's only been you."

"It's only been you, too," I say, masking my surprise at her admission.

A thoughtful expression crosses her face. "No, it hasn't. It's never been only me."

I remain unmoving, my eyes fixed, not reacting to her words. I should have known we'd be getting to this point in our arrangement. In my experience, women are only happy with no commitment for so long before they want something more. All their other friends start getting engaged, and they want that rock on their left hand, too. That's why I usually go for younger women. Twenty-five seems to be my target age. Old enough to be done with the college scene. Young enough to just want to have some fun.

Commitment isn't in the cards for me. Dating is difficult enough, let alone finding a woman I connect with who'll welcome my kids with open arms. Even if she does initially, at some point, it will become too much, too real. I can't let my girls get attached to someone who will eventually leave them. Then they'll wonder if it was their fault. I won't put that on them, not when they're still so young.

"Those girls are my life. Nothing will ever change that. Not even a ridiculously hot rack and dripping wet pussy." My statement comes out harsher than I want, but it's the truth.

"I'm not asking you to make a choice, Andrew. Just leave yourself open. That's all." She lifts herself onto her toes and leaves a soft kiss on my cheek. Then she turns and heads toward the staircase. "You can show yourself out. You usually do anyway."

I watch her disappear, then walk out the door. A part of me feels like shit for never staying, but it's not enough to keep me here, the memory of explaining to a two-year-old Alyssa where her mommy went overshadowing everything.

Chapter Seven

DREW

I CAN NAME THREE places that have always felt like home. The first, of course, is the house I grew up in. My father wasn't well-off, but he did everything to give us a happy childhood free from worry. The next is the café. I remember Molly and I sitting at one of the many tables when we were younger, watching as our father interacted seamlessly with the many patrons, telling one of his stupid jokes or bragging about Molly's or my accomplishments to anyone who would listen. The amount of pride he had for everything we both achieved throughout our lives was obvious, even when those achievements came in the form of getting an A on a short story Molly wrote or me being picked for the traveling hockey team.

The last is the ice rink where I find myself skating this morning, the one that now bears my last name. The same center where I first laced up a pair of skates. The same center that was nearly bulldozed several years ago before I stepped in and bought the place. The livelihood of every junior hockey league in the greater Boston area depends on this rink. I refuse to let that die. Hockey was the only thing that helped me through my mother's sudden disappearance from my life when I was barely six years old. I need to keep this place open for all the other kids who need hockey in their lives as much as I did back then, if not more.

My focus remains glued on the stick in my hands, moving the puck around the ice, passing it from side to side as I speed down the rink. After leaving Skylar's, I struggled to fall asleep, unable to stop thinking about Brooklyn. After hours of restlessness, I drove out here, laced up my skates, and lost myself in the game of hockey, hoping to shrug off the past twenty-four hours. And it's working. Out here, I find a sense of clarity, of peace, all my worries forgotten as I fixate on maintaining control of the puck. The net comes within scoring distance and I draw back my stick, quickly swinging it toward the ice. The puck rockets straight through the imaginary goalie's legs, as so often happened during my too-short career, and into the net.

I can almost hear the long-forgotten crowd cheering me on as I score the game-winning goal. I skate a victory lap around the ice, pretending as if I had, then come to an abrupt stop when the sound of clapping hits my ears. I take off my helmet, shaking out my disheveled, damp hair, and search the stands.

Lifting my eyes beyond the penalty box, my heart drops to the pit of my stomach when I see Brooklyn walking down the steps toward the ice. I'm confused at first, thinking she'd never want to speak to me again, especially after the way I treated her yesterday. Then my aunt's words from when we were kids ring in my ear, making me laugh to myself. No wonder I couldn't sleep.

I skate toward the edge of the rink, unlatch the door hidden in the wall, and step onto the cement. I remove my gloves, placing them next to my helmet on the bench in the front row before leaning my stick against it.

"Hey," I say as she descends to the bottom.

"Hey." She smiles, looking everywhere but at me. Her dark hair is pulled into a knot on the top of her head, her complexion refreshingly free of makeup.

"Gigi?" I lift a single brow.

She nods. "Yeah. Gigi. I couldn't sleep. All I could think about was…" She trails off, then takes a moment to collect her thoughts. She returns her blazing green eyes to mine, the same green eyes I imagined when I was with Skylar. I bury the idea of that having any hidden meaning. "I guess I just wanted to talk to you, to apologize."

"Apologize? If anyone should apologize, it's me." I run a hand through my hair, blowing out a long breath. "I was a prick yesterday morning. You didn't deserve to be treated the way I treated you. I should have congratulated you, told you how happy I am for you, not fly off the handle and accuse you of being something I know you could never be."

"You didn't mean anything by it." She pulls her oversized cable-knit cardigan sweater closer to her body, the sheer size of it seeming to dwarf her slender frame. "I should have told you differently. If I had, then maybe your team—"

"No, Brook," I insist, my voice forceful. Just the thought of her trying to place the blame for my team's loss on her shoulders makes me sick to my stomach, the guilt for how I treated her yesterday festering even more. "You don't get to put this back on you." I hold her gaze, then lighten my expression. "You always do that."

"Do what?"

"Shoulder the blame…hell, the world. You deserve better than that." I pause, collecting my thoughts. "I've done a lot of thinking, especially after last night's game. But not about what I could have done differently regarding how I coached my players, although there's certainly a lot, starting with keeping my temper in check."

"Ah, that famous Brinks temper," she comments, her lips lifting in the corners. "It is hard to control, especially once it's unleashed."

"True." I return her smile. She's seen it first-hand, especially during our high school years. "But all I could think about was us."

Her brows crease, uncertainty dripping from her. "Us?"

"Yeah. Us. Our friendship. Our history."

"Oh." She chews on her lower lip, her shoulders falling.

If I didn't know Brooklyn this well, I wouldn't have noticed it. But I do. I notice everything about her. Like the way her hair always smells like lavender. The way her eyes light up whenever she's excited about something. The way she always lets out a sigh of appreciation after that first sip of coffee in the morning.

"I've taken you for granted, Brooklyn," I say thoughtfully. "Taken our friendship for granted. I assumed things would always stay the same between us."

"Nothing stays the same forever, Drew. Things change. People change. We're not in high school anymore. You can't be like the overprotective brother whenever some guy tries to hit on me. You can't keep breaking noses when..." She stops short.

One look and I know exactly what she's thinking.

That summer.

That night.

That kiss.

What I wouldn't give to tell her the truth, to tell her *why* I didn't show up at her house like I promised I would. There's been so many times I've come close, but I could never bring myself to say those words that would destroy the way she views her father. He's the only family she has. I can't take that from her. I'd rather her think I'm an asshole before I do that.

"You've always been a big part of my life." I grab her hand in mine, running a finger along her knuckles. There's a peacefulness in her eyes when our hands connect. It's familiar, and right now, I need that. "I hope you always will be. You deserve my support, and I acted like an adolescent jerk instead of the almost thirty-five-year-old man I am. You're not shallow enough to marry someone because he has money." I drop her hand, looking away. "This is supposed to be the happiest time in your life. I should have been thrilled for you. And I am..."

176

"You are?" She tilts her head.

"Why wouldn't I be? The man of your dreams asked you to marry him. You deserve that happiness."

She smiles, but it doesn't reach her eyes. "I do, don't I?"

"Yes, you do." I wrap my arms around her, pulling her into my chest.

"Marrying Wes won't change anything." She pulls away and I reluctantly release her from my embrace. "I'll still be at your place every weekend playing with your girls. I'll still be at all their school functions. I'll still be their auntie Brook. It'll be like things have always been."

"I hope so. They need you in their lives. They don't know any other way."

"It'll take a lot more than a ring on my finger to keep me away from those girls." Her expression brightens. "Trust me."

I want to believe her, but it's like she said. Things change. People change. She may be around now, but for how long?

Not wanting to think about there soon being an empty seat at our Sunday family dinner, I start toward the rental booth, pulling her along with me. "Well, come on then. Let's get you laced up."

She comes to a dead stop, pulling her hand from mine. "Laced up?" She looks at me like I have three heads.

"You're at a skating rink. Why else would you be here?"

"Because I needed to talk to you. Not skate. Skating never entered the equation. Like, ever."

"Oh, come on." I sling my arm around her shoulders, dragging her with me. "We used to skate together all the time."

"No. *You* skated. I clung to the walls of the rink for dear life as I tried everything in my power not to fall."

"What's the worst that can happen? You hit your head?"

"I'd rather not get concussed," she jokes, her voice light and breezy, reminding me of the Brooklyn she used to be when we were younger.

"Concussed?" I give her a sly grin.

"Yes. Precisely." This conversation is the perfect example of our dynamic. Brooklyn is serious, straightforward, even-keeled, never showing much emotion. I'm the one trying to do anything to get her to smile.

"And that means?" I lift a brow.

"You've just proven my point." She stops walking and crosses her arms over her chest. "You've taken a few too many hits to the head. Your brain must be impaired."

I shake my head, my motions slow. "According to my latest checkup, my brain's fine." I tap at my head.

"Obviously not if you fail to remember what a complete disaster the last time you forced me to put on a pair of ice skates was," Brooklyn jabs. "I seem to recall your father having to drive me to the hospital and I ended up on crutches for six weeks."

I furrow my brow. "That was in high school. I felt so guilty, I persuaded all my teachers to let me out of class early so I could carry your books for you."

"Exactly."

"You haven't skated since high school?"

She remains silent.

"Well, that changes today." Before she can react, I throw her over my shoulder in a fireman's hold, carrying her slender body as if she weighs nothing. I remember doing this exact thing so many times when we were younger as I carried her toward the shore, throwing her into the ocean. She'd feign anger and irritation, splashing at me, but I knew she loved it. I miss those days.

"What are you doing, Drew?" she shrieks, hitting my back, just like she used to do all those years ago, as I continue toward the rental counter. I find a pair of figure skates in her size and grab them before heading back toward the ice.

"This place opens for the first practice soon. We don't have much time." I deposit her onto a nearby bench.

She stares at me, a hint of indignation crossing her face. "I'm not putting those on."

"Yes, you are. Live a little, Brook. I'll do everything in my power to make sure you don't get hurt." I wink. "Scout's honor."

She eyes me for a moment longer, her lips pinched. Then she blows out a long breath, unzipping her boots. She knows all too well I don't back down until I get

179

what I want. "That line may work with all the other girls you force onto the ice, but not me. I'm well aware that you were never a scout, Andrew Brinks."

"Your memory is impeccable as always, Brooklyn Tanner." I kneel in front of her, helping her into the skates, tightening them and securing them around her ankles. As I'm about to finish, I look up and meet her eyes that seem to watch my every move. "And you're the only girl I've skated with." I pause, allowing that to sink in, then stand.

"Not even that little pixie you've been carrying on with lately?"

"Pixie? You mean Skylar?" When I hold my hand out to her, she takes it, allowing me to help her to her unsteady feet. My arm loops around her waist and I guide her toward the opening in the rink.

"Yeah. I mean, if you're happy with her, I'm the last person to judge, but you can do better. You don't give yourself enough credit, Drew. You're a smart guy. You need someone who's as intelligent as you are. I might be wrong, but she doesn't seem the intellectual type."

I chuckle, her words alarmingly accurate, although she's never met Skylar. "Things aren't serious. We have an…understanding."

"Like Molly used to have?" She arches a brow.

I shrug. "I suppose you can say that."

"And you gave her a hard time about it, saying it was time she settled down. When are *you* going to settle down?"

"I *am* settled down," I argue. "And to answer your question, I've never skated with Skylar or any other woman, except for Alyssa and Charlotte, of course. You should take a lesson from them. They're just kids, but they're not scared of falling."

"It's not falling that scares me." Her voice is soft, contemplative, sincere. The carefree atmosphere becomes more charged, more solemn. "It's hitting the bottom so hard I'll never be able to put the pieces back together again." It's a response I never expected, laced with hidden meaning. She looks up at me, searching my eyes. "I mean—"

"I know what you mean, Brook." The tension between us builds as I keep her in my arms, everything about this moment surprising me. "I've been there, too."

When I'm with Brooklyn, things are different. I can be me. I don't have to keep my guard up, like I've been doing since Carla left...since leaving for college. She knows my scars, has even helped wipe up some of the blood herself. Yet she's still here. At first, I thought it was because of Molly. Now I wonder if there's a different reason, especially after what my sister said yesterday.

"I won't let you fall." My tone is soft, full of promise. "And if you do, I'll help you put the pieces together again. Like I always have."

Her expression drops as she pushes away from me, grabbing on to the wall of the rink. "Of course, Drew. Like you always have," she repeats despondently. It's like a giant bucket of ice water has been poured on top of me. I open my mouth, about to argue that things

181

aren't as they seem, when she interrupts, holding her head high. "Well, you've gotten me on a pair of skates. Now what?" Her voice is bright once more, like she's turned the switch and dismissed part of herself.

"Now we skate." I grin, holding out both hands. Her entire body tenses up, her grip on the side of the rink tightening as she stares at the ice in horror. I glide toward her, my tone calm and eyes soothing. "You have nothing to worry about. I won't let anything happen to you. You can trust me."

"It's hard to let go." She closes her eyes.

"It always is, but once you do, I promise you'll never look back." I hesitantly reach for her hands. Sensing me close the distance, she opens her eyes and lifts them to mine. "It's normal to be scared when faced with the unknown. But if you live your entire life afraid of falling, of getting hurt, you'll miss out on what could be the best thing you've ever experienced."

Her gaze locked on mine, she gradually loosens her grip on the edge of the rink, quickly placing her hands in mine.

"Sometimes the best thing that could ever happen to us has been staring at us all along, but we've been too stupid or scared to realize it." My words fall from me uncontrollably. It's like someone else has taken up residence in my brain, telling me what to say.

"I don't want to be afraid anymore," she murmurs in a small voice as I skate backwards, leading her toward the center of the ice, her soft hands so small compared to mine. It brings out this inherent urge to protect her from everything and anything that could hurt her.

"You have nothing to be afraid of, Brooklyn. I won't let you fall. I promise." I give her an encouraging smile, then pick up my speed, pulling her along with me. She's unsteady, as I expected, but I keep a firm hold on her. "You're doing fine," I assure her. "Straighten your back a little. That will help your balance."

She shakes her head, but eventually follows my instructions. "Humans weren't meant to have blades on their feet. If they were, we would have been born that way."

"You're a natural. Stop thinking about what could happen and enjoy the moment. Feel the rush of the ice below you, the wind against your face. Just glide, one leg, then the other."

"You make it sound so easy." She laughs, breaking the intensity, still clinging to my hands as if afraid she'll perish if I let go.

"Skate enough and it becomes as innate as walking."

"At least when you walk, you're on safe ground."

"True, but when you first learn to walk, you fall a lot. Don't you?"

"I suppose," she replies. Lost in conversation, she doesn't realize when I loosen my grip on her hands.

"Yet that didn't stop you from walking, then running, did it?"

"Of course not."

"Then that shouldn't stop you from flying on the ice, either, Brookie," I say, using the name I called her when we were kids. Before she can tighten her hold again, I let go.

Her eyes widen, every inch of her becoming rigid as panic seems to take over. I'm quick to react, skating behind her and placing my hands on her hips, keeping her upright.

"You're fine," I murmur, leaning toward her. Her entire body relaxes as I steer her around the net and back toward the center of the ice, the motion causing her lavender aroma to overwhelm me. "I've got you."

My words are all she needs. With more confidence than I've seen from her in a while, she continues placing one foot in front of the other, picking up speed as she circles the rink. When I'm certain she'll be okay, I let go of her once more, moving beside her as she glides across the ice in a way that would make anyone think she's been doing it for years.

Sensing me next to her, she shoots me a wide grin. It's the first real smile I can remember seeing on her face in months, perhaps even years. It's like she can forget about everything hanging over her head. Her work. Beginning her PhD program in the fall. Her engagement. We've traveled back in time to when we were kids. To when we would stay up all night watching scary movies. To when we would take the T out to Revere Beach for a Kelly's roast beef sandwich or a plate full of whole belly clams. To when I would push her on the swing hanging from the tree in her front yard and she'd tell me to make her go higher.

"There you are, Brookie," I murmur.

She meets my smile with one of her own and it melts my heart in a way usually only Alyssa's and

Charlotte's smiles can. "There you are, Dewy," she replies, calling me the name she had so many times in our childhood. I used to pretend I hated it, but I never did. I liked to think it was her way of showing her affection toward me. And I like to think the same holds true even all these years later.

Lost in the moment, her eyes still glued to mine, she's not paying attention to where she's going until it's too late. When she notices she's about to ram into the net, she tries to change direction, but she's not as quick or nimble on her skates yet. I do my best to bring her to a stop, but she loses her footing, falling fast and hard to the ice, taking me down with her. I land on top of her with a grunt.

"Are you okay?" I'm frantic as I scan her face, looking for any obvious signs of discomfort, but at the same time trying to think of anything other than the somewhat compromising position we currently find ourselves in.

Heat fills me as a memory comes rushing back, knocking the breath out of me. The summer before I left for college. Pushing Brooklyn on the swing in her front yard. Brooklyn leaping off it and losing her footing, rolling down the hill. Chasing after her, slipping, tumbling down on top of her. Staring at her lips. Pink. Full. Luscious. Unable to control myself as I leaned closer and closer, dying for a taste. It's like we're back there, like I'm getting a second chance.

She meets my eyes, her breath coming quicker. The way she's looking at me makes me think she's remembering that day, too. She makes no move to get up, seemingly content to stay pinned beneath me. I fear

185

if she moves, she'll know exactly how much the heat of her body against mine turns me on. I wasn't this stimulated with Skylar, at least not without some extra effort, even when she was on her knees in front of me. But with Brooklyn… I can't remember the last time I've been this aroused. A tiny voice in my head tells me to retreat, to pull back, to keep my distance, but I'm inexplicably drawn to this woman. I can't let her go.

"Never better," she breathes.

"Good."

"Good," she repeats, licking her lips as she peers at me. A tendril of hair had escaped her knot and fallen in front of her eyes. Instinctively, I brush it behind her ear, her skin soft. A craving to feel even more of her overwhelming me, I graze my fingers along her cheeks, admiring the freckles dotting her complexion. Brooklyn's always hated them, but I've always loved them. They make her stand out, her beauty unmatched by anyone else.

As I savor the smoothness of her delicate skin, a spark shoots through me, low and deep in my core. Her familiar aroma invades my senses, bringing back even more memories of our times together. Sitting on the beach. Exploring the Common. The feel of her legs wrapped around me when we finally did kiss. God, I love the way she smells, the way she feels, the way she always seems to easily break through every wall I've erected without even trying.

My heart pounding in my chest, my gaze focuses on those lips. Lips I've watched kiss too many other men when they should have been kissing me all along. Lips I was lucky enough to be the first person to ever kiss. Lips

I've almost kissed a few times since, but something's always stopped me. I don't want anything to stop me now.

"Brooklyn." I dart my tongue out, forgetting where we are, who we are. All I can think about is getting a taste of what I've deprived myself of for too long now. I don't care that she's a friend. I don't care that she's engaged, although I should. All I care about is feeling her lips on mine.

"Yes," she exhales, her breath dancing on my mouth, making it tingle with the promise of what's to come. Her tone isn't questioning. More like confirmation she wants this, too.

I cup her cheeks, rubbing the pads of my thumbs along the pink flesh of her lips. She plumps them out, her body trembling beneath mine. Every inch of me burning with need, I slowly erase the little space left between us. My heart pounds against my chest, wild and savage. My nerve endings ignite, a fluttering low in my stomach.

"Brooklyn," I say once more as my lips almost skim hers, giving her one last opportunity to say no.

"Yes." She closes her eyes, jutting her chin toward me, preparing herself, moistening those perfect lips I'm dying to taste. But I know I won't be able to stop at just a taste. I'll need more. Brooklyn isn't the type of girl you kiss, then forget. Even though I was forced to do just that over sixteen years ago, I never did. How could I? Brooklyn's the type of girl you love, you cherish. The type of girl who captures your mind, heart, and soul.

I close my eyes, time seeming to stand still. Just as I'm about to finally experience Brooklyn's kiss, a loud bang reverberates through the rink, snapping both of us out of our trance. Our bodies become rigid, the moment breaking as quickly as it began...just like all those years ago.

She blinks repeatedly, then a look of horror crawls across her expression. "I need to go," she says hurriedly, pushing against me. I roll off her, raising myself to my skates.

Unsure what to say, I wordlessly help her back to a standing position. The instant she has her balance, she takes off, skating toward the edge of the rink. I chase after her, catching up with ease. Guilt seeming to ooze from every pore in her body, she keeps her head lowered. I hate that she won't look at me. Acid burns deep in my stomach at what we almost did, how I almost kissed my sister's best friend. My sister's *engaged* best friend. I've been cheated on and it's a horrible feeling. How could I put Brooklyn in that position?

I follow her back to where she left her shoes, smiling a greeting at the swarms of kids filling the rink for this morning's practice session. There's so much I want to say, but don't even know where to start.

"Listen, Drew," she begins when I remain awkwardly silent. Her trembling fingers make it difficult for her to undo her laces, so I kneel to help her. She withdraws her hands, allowing me to unlace her skates. "What we almost did..." She lowers her head. "I'm sorry."

"Don't," I respond, my voice firm. Neither one of us speaks as I effortlessly remove both skates. Then I meet her eyes. "You have nothing to be sorry about," I add softly. "It takes two to tango."

She grabs her boots and yanks them back over her skinny jeans. "But I should have known better. I *do* know better. What just almost happened…" Standing, she gestures to the rink. "It can't happen. It *won't* happen. I don't know what came over me. I guess I was lost in the rush of skating. Wes has been nothing but good to me." She avoids my eyes. "He deserves better than me almost kissing someone else." When she returns her gaze to mine, I see the remorse clear as day. It looks like she's on the brink of tears. "Especially you."

She spins around and hurries toward the exit, skirting kids gearing up for their lesson, their parents helping with their skates.

"Brooklyn, wait!" I call, darting after her, the thin blades on my feet no impediment. Reaching for her arm, I force her to stop. "Don't run away from this."

"From what? There's nothing here. At one time, I did think there was, but I've learned from that lapse of judgment. Yes, you were my first real kiss, but that was years ago, when we were young and made some really bad mistakes. So if you don't mind, I need to get ready for lunch with Wes' mother, who's flown into town so we can start planning our wedding."

Those words hit me square in the gut. I'm on the brink of finally telling her the truth of what really happened, why I broke the promise I made her, but don't. It's not worth it. It won't change anything.

When I drove to the rink, the last thing I expected was to almost kiss her. Now it's all I can think about — the feel of her body against mine, the heat of her breath intermingling with mine, the way every inch of me craves her in a way I didn't think it ever would again.

189

"Is that what you want?" I press, my voice unsteady.

She opens her mouth, her eyes glistening with unshed tears. There's a subtle tremble in her lower lip as she responds. "It's too late for what I want."

The sincerity in her answer surprises me, although it shouldn't. She's always been one of the most honest people I know. I drop my hold on her. "And what's that?"

She shakes her head, shrugging. "It doesn't matter anymore." Then she turns and disappears out the doors, still ignorant of the truth.

Chapter Eight

BROOKLYN

"SORRY I'M LATE," I say breathlessly as I hurry toward a small private table in the dining room at the exclusive country club where Wes is a member. Wes and his father, James, immediately stand when they see me approach.

"No worries," Mr. Bradford states jovially, leaving a kiss on my cheek. "We just placed our orders. Wes took it upon himself to order for you."

I smile at Wes, allowing him to kiss my cheek, as well, his being much more sensual and endearing. "Thank you." He pulls my chair out for me and I take my seat.

"Pleasure to see you, Mrs. Bradford." I reach for the sparkling water in front of me.

"You, too, Brooklyn dear," she replies with a touch of superiority.

During my relationship with Wes, I've come to expect this from her. By the lack of any offer of congratulations, I'm confident his mother isn't thrilled with the idea of him marrying me, a girl from

Somerville, a middle-class town she probably considers to be the slums. While my father has a noble profession as a Boston firefighter, one he still enjoys, it isn't exactly a high-income job. Yes, he does well for himself, but it isn't even close to the same level the Bradfords are accustomed to.

As much as Mrs. Bradford has tried to mask her distaste, it hasn't worked. I'm certain she'd rather Wes date any of the women she's paraded in front of us when we've attended one of the myriad of charity dinners together. Such as the subtle hints that Scarlett rowed during college, like Wes. Or that Deborah enjoys the Museum of Modern Art where Wes is a high-level donor. Or that Caroline is an avid runner, like Wes. He may not have noticed what his mother was trying to do, but I did. It must be eating her up that he proposed to a woman who doesn't come from among the country's wealthiest families.

"I understand the ring didn't fit. Such a pity."

I grit a smile, smoothing my skirt. Wes grabs my hand and my eyes float to his. Without saying a word, he lets me know that she doesn't matter, that nothing she says can make him feel anything less than the unequivocal adoration he's bestowed on me since our first date. And that look, that compassion, that *love* makes me feel even worse about what almost happened between Drew and me a few hours earlier.

Knowing he'd be there, I went to that rink to clear the air between us…to stop thinking about him. But since leaving him, he's all I think about. Not Wes. Not the thought I'll soon be marrying the man of my dreams. It's all Drew and how a part of me wishes we hadn't been interrupted by a group of rowdy kids.

"I dropped it off at the jewelers on the way here," Wes declares with authority. "It will be ready in plenty of time for the engagement photos."

"Engagement photos?" I furrow my brow, my mouth feeling drier than the Sahara. I reach for my glass and take a large gulp of water, nearly finishing it.

"Of course, dear," Mrs. Bradford says. "I've called in a few favors and was able to book *the* premier photographer in New England, if not the country, to take your photos one week from today."

"One week?" My eyes widen and I swallow hard, my lungs struggling to get a full breath of air. It's one thing to have agreed to Wes' proposal. I thought we'd have a long engagement, time to get used to the idea of spending the rest of our lives together. "Isn't that premature? We haven't even discussed a date, let alone where we want to get married. Shouldn't we have that taken care of before we announce our engagement?"

Mrs. Bradford reaches into her oversized purse and withdraws a large planner with Post-it notes sticking out from the pages, placing it on the table in front of her. "Wes has provided me with a copy of your schedule when you begin your PhD program this fall."

"And?" I straighten my back, a heat building on my face, my defenses kicking in.

"The curriculum looks to be extensive. Do you intend to work, as well?" She arches a superior brow.

"Of course I do."

"Then it's settled. I've spoken to the woman in

charge of events here and she can fit us in August twenty-fifth, since Wes has insisted the wedding be up north instead of back home in Georgia. Lord knows why. A southern wedding is much more charming. Everything southern is much more charming, if you ask me."

"Mother…" Wes' voice is a warning. His hand finds my thigh and squeezes, trying to comfort me, but all I hear is August twenty-fifth…

Five months.

But that's not the worst. It's that date. It's stupid, considering it's been nearly seventeen years, but I'll remember that date for the rest of my life — the date I gave Drew my first kiss. The date he gave me so much hope, only to rip it away the following day.

"That's around Molly's due date." I look at Wes, burying the memory, coming up with any reason why we can't get married on that date. "She's agreed to be my maid of honor. I can't get married without her by my side."

"I wouldn't ask you to." He faces his mother, an air of confidence about him. "There must be another date to choose from, something more convenient for all involved. Even if we have to get married somewhere more private, less sought-after."

"Brooklyn begins her PhD program in September," she shoots back. "I don't see her finding time for all the fittings and pre-wedding requirements when she's defending a thesis." She shifts her cold eyes to mine. "Do you?"

I can't help but feel her presence here is just a way

to persuade me not to marry her son. I wish I had considered his family when I said yes. I should have expected Mrs. Bradford to fly in and take control of everything. From the few times I've visited with them, I quickly deduced she's all about appearances. And her baby boy getting married? She'll want to turn it into the social event of the year, even if it doesn't occur in the south. Would I have answered Wes any differently if I had stopped to consider his mother? Yesterday, I would have said no, that I'm marrying him, not her. But now, I'm a mess. I can't answer anything with absolute certainty.

"I'm sure I can find the time." My voice lacks any conviction. I've already started stressing about how to balance my job and the requirements for my classes. Due to budget cuts and being short-staffed, I work over sixty hours a week. I have no idea how I'll be able to find enough time in the day to give my cases the attention they need, prepare for my classes, and plan a wedding.

"You know you won't have to work once you marry into this family, don't you? Perhaps you should reconsider your plans for the fall semester. Or your current employment." Mrs. Bradford pinches her lips. "Or both. That would solve the problem of rushing to get this wedding taken care of before you return to class."

"I love what I do." My response is pointed and sharp, particularly after Drew's snide comment yesterday that I'm only marrying Wes because of his money. If I quit my job and pull out of next semester, he'll think that's the case. "I don't care that it pays less in a year than what your family probably makes in a day. I didn't agree to marry your son because he's well-off. Hell, when he asked me to marry him, I was wearing a dress I got off a clearance rack at a discount clothing store."

"And you looked stunning," Wes chimes in, leaning toward me, his breath on my neck warming my skin.

I steal a glance at him, my heart expanding at how much this man has supported me since the beginning of our relationship. "I'd rather have a fulfilling career that allows me to support myself. Wes understands this."

"Yes, but what about children?"

"Dear," Mr. Bradford interrupts. He gives me a comforting smile before looking at his wife. "It's admirable Miss Tanner plans to continue her education to better herself. They're both young. It's common for couples to have children later these days." He returns his gaze to mine, his eyes practically identical to his son's. For being in his early seventies, he's a rather handsome man — a full head of gray hair, brilliant smile, and kind eyes. If Wes ages half as well as his father, I should count myself as lucky. But looks aren't everything. "When the time is right, they'll have kids."

Seemingly nervous about the direction the conversation has taken, Wes attempts to steer us back on topic. "I'm sure we can come to an agreement. Perhaps something before the start of the fall semester but not so close to Molly's due date?"

I fling my eyes to his. "Like, *earlier* this summer?"

He shrugs, trying to play peacemaker between his mother and me. I have a feeling he'll spend the rest of his life doing that very thing.

"That's not an adequate solution," Mrs. Bradford says, much to my surprise, which is short-lived when she speaks again, revealing her reasons. "What about the pictures, and Molly's…condition?"

"Condition?" I repeat, unsure I heard correctly. "You mean the fact that she's pregnant and will be bringing a beautiful life into this world?"

"I don't have a problem with it," she interjects. "I've been pregnant, too. Twice."

I have to stop myself from returning a sarcastic remark along the lines that she should get a medal.

"But think of your wedding photos."

"What about the wedding photos?" My voice rises in pitch, an uncharacteristic move for me. I can feel dozens of pairs of eyes fling toward our table, the low murmur of the dining room evaporating. I typically never allow my anger or frustration to show. After this morning, I'm not myself. Everything feels like it's ready to implode, like I'm on an out-of-control freight train barreling toward a cliff.

Drawing in a deep breath, I return my eyes to Mrs. Bradford. She's as calm and collected as always. Her dark hair is cut to above her shoulders, not a single strand out of place. She wears a respectful amount of makeup, just enough to give her a feminine flair. Her light pink sheath dress is perfectly tailored to her slender body. As the wife of a man who is worth millions, she looks and acts the part, more so than her husband.

"Molly's my best friend. Regardless of her 'condition'," I state, using air quotes, "I'll cherish those photos and will be able to show my nephew the day he went to his first wedding."

"Mother…" Wes finally speaks up, noticing my composure waning. "It seems the only one who cares about the photos is you. Let's move on."

With a sigh, she returns her eyes to her planner. "This doesn't leave us with much of an option. I wish you'd consider getting married at the family home down south. Our estate is large enough to cater to several hundred people, and then we wouldn't have to worry about it being too close to Molly's due date."

"We could wait." I turn to peer at Wes. "Live together a while first. Get married after I finish my program."

"That's in three years." His brows wrinkle as he stares at me. "I'll be thirty-seven."

"Noah, Molly's fiancé, is forty, yet they put their wedding on hold when she got pregnant. In the long run, does it matter whether you get married? The important thing is that you're with the person you love and cherish. The wedding is more for everyone else. Don't you agree?"

Wes lowers his voice, his face long. "You're not having second thoughts, are you?"

"Of course not." I avert my eyes, not wanting him to see I've been having second thoughts all morning. I promised myself I'd give Wes the chance I never have over the past eight months. I need to show him I'm serious about us. Straightening my spine, I address Mrs. Bradford. "What other dates are available here?"

"Not many, as I'm sure you can imagine at this late stage. But they did just have a cancelation. June ninth."

My heart catches in my throat as I try to hide my shock, not wanting anyone at the table to read too much into my reaction. "That's only a little over two months away."

"It's not optimal, but it's doable."

Just then, our server approaches and places a bowl of tomato soup in front of each of us, my mind spinning at the notion of marrying Wes so soon. All my preconceived ideas of a long engagement evaporate as I listen to Mrs. Bradford plan a wedding for June of this year. Wes and I don't even live together yet. I don't know if he has any weird habits. If he's easy to live with. If he puts the toilet seat down.

Minutes ago, our marriage was more of an abstract notion, something that would eventually happen. Now, it's real...a little too real.

With shaky limbs, I stand from the table. Mr. Bradford and Wes do the same, a sign of the manners they've learned over the years of wining and dining wealthy clients.

"Is everything okay?" Wes peers at me, concerned.

"I need to get some air." My voice is even. "Excuse me."

Dazed, I make my way toward the back patio overlooking the pristine manicured greens. The instant I emerge into the chilly March air, I inhale a deep breath, my lungs expanding. Leaning against the stone ledge, I close my eyes, not caring that my attire of a simple green dress and light white cardigan does nothing to fight against the frigid temperatures still plaguing us, even though it's technically spring.

I toy with my mother's locket secured around my neck, hoping for some sort of clarity. It's moments like these I wish she were still alive. Sure, Aunt Gigi helps in that department, and my father's long-time girlfriend, Ana, is easy to talk to, but it's not what I need right now. I need guidance from a woman who loves me unconditionally, who wants nothing more than happiness for me. Wes *does* make me happy. But is it the kind of happiness I've dreamt of since I was a little girl? Am I willing to settle for whatever I feel when I'm with him? Or am I having second thoughts because I almost kissed Drew earlier? Is this just the Catholic guilt I grew up with rearing its ugly head?

As I stand there, trying to make sense of the strange combination of remorse and uncertainty, I sense a presence approach from behind. A jacket is draped around my shoulders and I tilt my head to my left to see Wes beside me.

"Hey," he breathes, hesitant.

Straightening, I pull his jacket closer. It smells like him, like spice and wood. It offers me a slice of comfort in a world that seems to be spiraling out of control.

"Hey." The corners of my lips lift, treating him to a small smile.

"I'm sorry about all of that. I had no idea she was planning to go all Mom-zilla on you. I thought we were getting together for lunch to celebrate our engagement. I had no idea she was already looking at dates for the ceremony."

"It's okay." I stare at the unnatural green lawn that goes on for miles, the occasional golf cart driving along the paths carrying golfers getting a jump-start on their game for the season. I've never understood the attraction to the game, but Wes claims it's relaxing. I much prefer the excitement of a team sport...like hockey. "It's a bit overwhelming." I glance back at him. "Don't you think it's fast, planning a wedding for June?"

He seems to assess my question, then states, "No, I don't."

His response isn't what I expected. Wes is a very methodical person. He isn't impulsive or spontaneous. The craziest thing he's probably ever done is go out of his way to stop by the café to see if I was there. He has a routine, and he sticks to it.

"You don't?"

He grabs a hand in each of his and I face him. "Brooklyn, I love you. Ever since you finally agreed to go out to dinner with me, I've been the happiest I can remember. There's something about you... I don't know what it is. It's the same thing that's drawn me to you since the first day I saw you, heard your laugh, felt your soul. When I asked you to marry me, it wasn't about having a wedding. It was because I want to spend the rest of my life with you. The wedding is just an excuse to play dress-up." He brings a hand to my lower back, dragging my body into his. When he leans down, his breath warms my neck. "Then take you back to a ridiculously expensive hotel suite where I can strip you down to nothing but your wedding ring."

The way his body feels against mine, coupled with his deep, sensual tone, causes a tingle to spread through me. It's not the hurricane of butterflies that flapped their wings in my stomach when Drew had me pinned on the ice, but I can't think about that. I *shouldn't* think about that.

Wes pulls back, his entire expression brightening. "If you want to wait until you're done with your PhD program, I'll do that for you. It will be torture to wait that long for you to have my last name, but your happiness is what's most important to me."

I stare into his calm eyes, physically able to feel his adoration for me. Should it matter when we get married? I agreed to be his wife. The wedding is just a way to make it official. Maybe it's for the best we marry sooner rather than later. I fear the longer we wait, the more complicated things will become.

"I don't want you to have to wait, Wes," I finally say, cupping his cheeks in my hands, bringing his lips toward mine. "Like you said… It's just a wedding. I already agreed to marry you. So let's plan for June."

All the tension seems to roll off his body as he presses his mouth to mine, his arms swallowing me. His tongue skims my lower lip, asking for permission, and I open for him. Our kiss is simple, but full, his embrace offering me warmth and love.

But there's no charge of electricity like there was when Drew's body was against mine. No unquenchable need pulsing in my core when his dark eyes gazed upon me, piercing my soul. No racing of my heart when his mouth drew closer and closer, agonizing, torturing, teasing.

Am I resigning myself to a lifetime of mediocrity?

Chapter Nine

DREW

"HELLO, HELLO!" A FAMILIAR voice calls out as I maneuver around the kitchen, sampling the sauce that's been simmering the past few hours. It tastes perfect, the right blend of spices. Of course, the real test is if it lives up to Aunt Gigi's standards. She's the one who taught me the family recipe, after all.

"Auntie Molly!" Alyssa and Charlotte jump up from the floor of the family room, abandoning their Play-Doh project and running toward the foyer.

"Hey, lovebugs," she says, beaming as she turns the corner. Noah is right behind her, carrying a few bottles of wine, their weekly contribution to Sunday dinner, placing them on the large island.

"Your belly's getting even bigger!" Charlotte observes enthusiastically.

"Char," I warn, looking up from the stovetop built into the island. Placing the cover back on the pot, I head toward the open living area. The place we moved into a few years ago isn't as big as the house I bought after I hit it big in hockey, but I was young and stupid back then, thinking the money would last forever. After several mistakes, my father talked some sense into me, helping me with a few smart financial decisions, which have kept me very comfortable since I was forced into early retirement. "That's not very nice."

"What?" She spins around, furrowing her brows at me. Her six-year-old brain can't grasp what's wrong with her statement. "You told me the baby's in there. That my cousin's getting big and will come out when it's time."

"Yeah!" Alyssa chimes in. "You said Uncle Noah put the baby there." She shifts her gaze toward Noah. "Didn't you put the baby there?"

Uneasiness filling his blue eyes, he runs his hand through his dark hair. "Yes, but—"

"How?" she presses.

Alyssa, like Charlotte, has always been an inquisitive child. That inquisitive nature has only grown with age. After everything I went through with Carla, I promised to always be upfront and truthful with them, that I would do my best to answer their questions honestly. That was before I had to explain why their auntie Molly's belly was growing. Ever since they learned they'll be getting a new cousin at the end of the summer, they've been curious about how the baby got inside her.

"Yeah, how?" Charlotte chimes in. Then her eyes widen, as if having an epiphany. "Did you eat your baby?"

I stifle a laugh at her grave expression.

"Yeah, Charlotte. Something like that," Molly

responds, having difficulty holding in her own laughter at the ridiculousness of Charlotte's questions. I'm surprised she doesn't go into detail. As a romance author, she has quite the vocabulary, particularly when it comes to sex. All I can do is hope she doesn't pass any of her knowledge on to my girls...even when they turn eighteen. Auntie Molly's books will always be very off-limits.

"Why did you eat your baby?"

"So he has a warm place to grow until he's big enough to survive outside."

Charlotte seems to consider Molly's answer, then looks at me. "Daddy, did you eat Alyssa and me and give us a warm place to grow?"

"No, peanut," I respond, wanting to end this conversation. "Only mommies carry babies."

"So did Auntie Brook eat us?"

"No, Char. Brooklyn is your auntie, not your mother." I swallow hard, the mere mention of her making my heart rate pick up, my body heat, my fingers ache to brush her delicate skin again.

After we almost kissed yesterday morning, I haven't been able to think about anything else, not even losing the playoff game we should have won. Hell, I haven't even returned any of Skylar's messages inviting me over. After my close brush with Brooklyn, Skylar seems inadequate in so many areas. Her immaturity and lack of conversational skills has never bothered me. In my opinion, the ability to hold an intellectual discussion on current affairs doesn't directly correlate to being stellar in the bedroom. Before, that was all I cared about, was all I *wanted* to care about.

"Then where's our mother?" Charlotte's voice forces my attention back to her.

"Probably skanking it up," Molly mutters under her breath. I shoot her an irritated look. As much as Carla hurt me, I don't want to instill any of that animosity onto the kids. They need to form their own opinion.

"She left right after you were born, kiddo."

"Why?"

I run my hand through my hair, wishing my dad were still alive to give me advice on how to handle this conversation. No one prepares you for these types of things when you're getting ready to have kids. No manual covers how to talk to your children about why their mother abandoned them six years ago and made no effort to be a part of their lives. My dad went through it with Molly and me, and we turned out fine. Still, I would love his expertise on how to tell my kids their mother didn't want them, didn't want any of us.

"I wish I knew, sweetie." She deserves a better answer. I doubt I'll ever be able to give her one.

"Here." Noah's voice cuts through as he hands me a glass of a red wine. "Figured you could use this."

"They don't teach you any of this stuff in parenting classes," I mumble, taking the wine from him. "Hope you're ready."

"Is there such a thing?"

I raise the glass to my lips. "Definitely not."

"I want a baby in my belly," Alyssa declares.

I glance at Molly as she takes a sip of water. "A little help here?"

"Oh, no. I'm wearing my auntie hat tonight. This is all you, Drew."

With a deep breath, I turn back to my two girls, both of whom look excited over the prospect. "You need to be a little older before you can have a baby in your belly." I pray this explanation works. I don't want to go into the technicalities of *why* they have to be a little older.

"Okay," Charlotte says. "Can I have some juice?"

Relieved that their questions about the proverbial birds and bees are done, I walk to the refrigerator and pour some apple juice into two cups, then add a straw.

"When I'm older, I'm going to have lots of babies in my belly," Alyssa states, grabbing one of the cups.

"Not if I can help it," I mutter under my breath so only Molly and Noah can hear, to which they both laugh. "Just wait. Your time's coming."

"Eh. We've got it easier," Molly replies as Noah drapes an arm over her shoulders. "We're having a boy. We only have one penis to worry about instead of one million. Times two."

I groan. "Great. Way to make me feel good about this, especially considering Alyssa will be in middle school in three years." Yes, eleven sounds young, but I remember how I was at that age. Remember when I realized girls weren't filled with cooties, as I originally thought.

"Glad I could help." She grins.

Giving serious consideration to buying a firearm to use as a ploy to scare any boy who so much as looks at Alyssa in a way I don't like, I resume preparing our traditional Sunday dinner, checking the sauce every so often. The second Aunt Gigi and Uncle Leo arrive, she kicks me out of my kitchen. I try to argue, to tell her to relax, but she won't hear it.

Every week, it's the same thing. So many other people I know rarely see their families, especially once they began having children of their own. I see mine constantly. If Molly isn't stopping over to see the girls, I'm dropping by the café to visit with Aunt Gigi. We're as nontraditional as a family can be, but I'm eternally grateful for the amount of positive influences my girls have, for the strong support system I've had throughout all the trials in my life.

"Is Brooklyn coming?" Gigi asks as I make myself useful and slice the loaf of bread she brought from the café.

"She's supposed to." I keep my eyes lowered, trying not to reveal anything by the way I can feel my entire body heat from her name alone.

"And Wes?"

I stare at the bread. "She texted this morning to tell me he may be coming."

"I'll be sure not to hold my breath, though," Gigi remarks.

One of the many things I love about my aunt is the way she holds nothing back. She lets you know exactly what she's thinking. As I've learned throughout my life, it's both a blessing and a curse.

"I can count on one hand the number of times that boy's shown up here for our family dinner."

"Brooklyn's not technically family." I meet her eyes, bringing the blade back up to the bread, about to slice.

Gigi's gaze becoming fiery, she points an indignant finger at me. "Just because she doesn't have the same bloodline as us doesn't make her any less important. She's family." With a dramatic huff, she returns her attention to the sauce. "I'd hoped she'd have our last name one day."

"Gigi...," I warn. "You're worse than Molly."

"What? I'm just stating what you're thinking, Andrew. Perhaps if you weren't as stubborn as your father, you wouldn't find yourself in this position."

I place the knife on the cutting board and cross my arms in front of my chest. "And what position is that?"

"About to watch your soul mate marry another man."

"You've been reading too many of Molly's books," I retort, brushing off her comments.

She's in front of me in an instant, forcing my eyes to hers. "You can't avoid me forever, Andrew Vincenzo Brinks. I kept my mouth shut Friday morning when you and Molly were getting into it. I didn't want to bring up what happened all those years ago since not many people know."

"That doesn't matter anymore. Like you said, it was years ago. Brooklyn's moved on. So have I. Need I remind you, I got married and have two kids."

"And now you're using those kids as an excuse for

209

why you refuse to date anyone. But those girls should be the *reason* you pursue a serious relationship, not run from it. Don't you think they deserve to have a mother's influence?"

"They do. They have you." I give her a sly smile, winking. "It was good enough for Molly and me. There's no one better with kids than you, Gigi."

"Stop buttering me up. I'm too old to be persuaded by your charms. Yes, your father made the best of a bad situation, and I'm so grateful I had the chance to be a mother to you when your own mother refused. But don't you think your girls deserve something more meaningful than visiting with their crazy aunt? They should learn what love is. *Real* love. They'll never know that if you refuse to know it for yourself." She lowers her voice. "Don't you think Brooklyn might reconsider if she knew what *really* happened?"

I briefly close my eyes, repeating the same words I've told myself countless times. "It doesn't matter. It won't change anything."

"Andrew, darling. It could change *everything*."

"Gigi, please. I can't just go up to Brooklyn, tell her she's making a mistake, declare my undying love, and beg her to give me a chance. It's more complicated than that."

Suddenly, a loud throat clearing rips through the space and I whirl around, shocked green eyes staring at me. It's evident by the uncertain expression on Brooklyn's face she overheard us. I wonder how long she's been standing there...and if Gigi knew. I look to my right, meeting my aunt's eyes. She shrugs, neither admitting nor denying my suspicions, which only heightens them.

"Sorry I'm late." Brooklyn breaks the awkward silence. "Wes hoped to make it, but—"

"Something came up, didn't it, dear?" Gigi interrupts.

"He sends his regrets. He wanted to be here tonight, but he ran into a few problems with one of his buildings in Florida and had to fly down to see it for himself."

"It's quite all right." Gigi comes around from behind the large kitchen island, placing a kiss on Brooklyn's cheek. "Drew, why don't you pour Brooklyn a glass of wine."

"I can get it," she insists, starting toward the cabinet where I keep the glasses.

"Allow me." I jump in front of her, my nerves at being around her after yesterday clear in the slight shakiness in my voice. "Cabernet okay?" I retrieve a glass, then reach for one of the bottles on the counter.

"You know it's my favorite."

"That I do." I open a bottle of the full-bodied wine and pour it into a glass. I wonder what kind of wine Wes orders when they're out to dinner. Does he know what she likes? Or does he just order whatever he feels like having?

"Thank you." Meeting my eyes, she reaches for the glass. As she grabs it, our fingers brush, the subtle feel of her skin on mine sending a jolt straight to my heart, jump-starting its erratic beat. The same jolt that shot through me as I had her pinned beneath me yesterday. The same jolt that heightened when I was a whisper away from her lips.

I tear my hand away, trying to do everything in my power to forget about the way this woman makes me feel. And that's the thing that scares me the most. After years of going through the motions with woman after woman, I'm feeling again.

I lift my glass off the counter and raise it. Brooklyn follows suit and we clink glasses. She brings the wine to her lips, her motions slow, languid, deliberate. I should look away, but I can't, mesmerized by everything about her, from the way her eyes remain locked with mine, to the way her breathing seems to become more uneven, to the way her lips plump out as she prepares to taste the wine. I've never been so jealous of an inanimate object before in my life, but right now, I'd give anything to be that damn wine glass. I almost wonder if she's putting on this show for me, teasing me, torturing me. Every muscle in my body hardens as she takes a long sip, then lowers the glass, licking the few drops of residue off her lips. Primal instinct kicks in, my muscles clenching…including those in the hand holding my wine glass.

Instantly, the sound of shattering fills the space, followed by a sharp pain in my hand. I look down at the same time Brooklyn shrieks, rushing toward one of the drawers and grabbing a towel.

"What happened?" Molly hurries into the kitchen area. A scene of pandemonium erupts around me, everyone focusing on my hand. Blood drips onto the white tile flooring, red wine mixing with it.

"I guess I don't know my own strength." I laugh, my face flaming.

"Noah!" Molly calls to him. I hear him jump up from where he's playing with the girls in the living room. "Get in here."

"It's okay. It's not that serious," I protest, but no one will hear it.

Brooklyn presses a towel against my hand to stop the flow of blood. When I meet her eyes, she gives me a flirtatious grin. I can't help but smile in response, feeling like this is an inside joke between the two of us. The tension that originally filled me after she walked in and eavesdropped in on my conversation is gone. In its place is a sense of familiarity. No matter the arguments we've gotten into, no matter the years I tried to avoid her for fear of her father, we always seem to find our way back to each other and pick up as if nothing happened.

"Let me see." Noah reaches for my hand, taking it in his. I've always liked him, but right now, I want nothing more than to push him away so I can continue to feel Brooklyn's skin on mine. Nothing has ever felt so damn perfect. What the hell is wrong with me? Why am I even thinking about her this way? She's engaged. *Engaged*. Not just dating someone. I shouldn't even be entertaining the thought of flirting with her, not after what I went through with Carla.

Noah pulls me toward the sink, running my hand under the water to wash away the blood. Once it's clean, he brings it back up to his eyes, surveying the slashes and cuts with the analytical eyes of the doctor he is. Then he grabs a clean towel, wrapping it around my hand.

"Looks to be a few superficial wounds. No glass got

in the cuts. Nothing requiring stitches. Just cover it with some bandages and change them regularly. Do you have a first aid kit here? Or I can grab my bag from the car."

"I've got one," I reply, pulling my hand from his. "It's just a few scratches. I'm fine." I turn, keeping my head lowered, the heat of everyone's stare on me as I round the corner and duck into the bathroom.

Once alone, I inhale deeply, closing my eyes. The instant I do, Brooklyn's coquettish smile flashes before me and I curse under my breath.

I'm in over my head. But I'd rather drown with Brooklyn than live without her. This time, there's no overbearing father to threaten me if I were to pursue his teenaged daughter…just a wedding.

Chapter Ten

BROOKLYN

SILENCE FILLS THE SPACE as we all watch Drew disappear down the hallway. I assume everyone's looking at him, but when I turn around, they're all staring at me. My lips part, my gaze searching theirs, eyes blinking repeatedly.

"What?" I ask sheepishly, the way they're gawking making me feel like I'm naked in public.

Molly's lips form a tight line as she gives me a knowing look, placing a hand on her hip. "You know what. I was watching you two." She steps closer, her voice a low whisper. "You were flirting with him."

My face heats as I lower my head. "I was not," I insist, but there's no conviction in my voice. I *was* flirting with Drew. I don't know what came over me. It wasn't my intention at all. After our near-kiss at the rink yesterday, then Wes' heartfelt words making the guilt fester inside me, I resolved to do everything in my power to stop thinking of Drew this way. To stop looking at his lips and the way they move every time he speaks. The way his eyes light up every time I walk into a room. The way a charge fills me the instant I inhale his woodsy scent.

But when I walked into his house and overheard the tail end of their conversation, something happened. The way he spoke, the fever, the passion... Part of me is desperate for more of that. The other part reminds me what awaits me on the other side of that passion. Heartache. Confusion. Inadequacy.

"Oh, really?" Molly arches a brow. I scan the rest of the assembled crowd. Gigi wears a similar expression to Molly's, whereas Leo and Noah seem interested only because their better halves are. Thankfully, Alyssa and Charlotte still play off in the family room, not listening in on our conversation. After their questions Friday night, it would only confuse them.

"Yes. Really." I straighten my spine, then offer a slight smile. "If you'll excuse me, I'll go check to see if he needs any help." I spin, heading down the hallway where Drew just disappeared.

"Is that what they're calling it these days?" She laughs. I simply shake my head, not responding. I know how it looks, but I *do* want to check on Drew, make sure he's okay, make sure *we're* okay. I can't help but wonder if the hand injury is punishment for failing to reconcile our differences yesterday, as Gigi would probably have us believe.

Just as I approach the open door to the guest bathroom, Drew's deep voice sounds. "Molly, I'm not in the mood for your snarky comments or crazy theories about why I broke a wine glass. It was just an accident."

My lips curve and I lean on the doorframe, crossing my arms over my chest. "Really?"

Once he hears my voice, he flings his eyes toward me. They're wide, shocked, flustered. I chew on my bottom lip, the mere sight of him sending my heart into overdrive. The tension between us mounts as we simply stare at each other. He's nervous. Much more nervous than I ever remember him being around me. It's adorable and chips away at the ice his past actions have built around my heart.

When the strain becomes almost unbearable, I burst into a hearty laugh. God, it feels good. I can't remember the last time I've laughed this hard, this full-belly, gut-wrenching laugh that gives my abs a workout. Wes has certainly never made me laugh like this, never made me smile like this. And I want to laugh again, smile again. That should be the only clue I need to tell me maybe I'm jumping into things with Wes too quickly. But as I meet Drew's eyes, ones that have only disappointed me in the past, I'm reminded exactly *why* I chose Wes. How can I ever learn to fully trust Drew when I'm still coughing up water from the last time he allowed me to sink below the surface?

Reaching for his hand, I grab a cotton ball from one of the canisters on the counter and dab at the blood. "I shouldn't laugh, but it was kind of funny." I lift my eyes to his. "I like to think it was karma paying you back for making me put on a pair of skates."

I rub a little antibacterial ointment over the wounds, making Drew wince in pain. It's endearing to know he's not this macho man, unaffected by anything. But I've always known this. Drew's suffered innumerable injuries during his hockey career. I was often there to tend to his wounds then, even when we were kids. But it never felt like this, not that I can remember. Something about taking care of him now, of the heat in his eyes as he watches my every move, makes me want to forget the past.

My cheeks flush as I attend to his cuts, placing gauze over his palm and wrapping it. The feel of his hand in mine stirs something I've been trying to forget for years now. Something I hoped Wes' proposal would help me bury, never to be resurrected again.

When I lift my head, I notice he's staring at my lips. I can only imagine what he's thinking. Probably the same thing I am. I clear my throat and he brings his eyes back to mine. I give him a knowing look, making it clear with my expression I caught him ogling my mouth.

"You'll be fine," I say, my fingers lighting over the bandage. I should release my hold on him, but I can't. He makes no move to pull his hand back, either. "Don't get into any fights and try not to crush any more wine glasses with your pure brute strength." I wink, enjoying this playfulness between us. This is what I need right now. For things to be the way they were when we were kids, although I doubt we'll ever be able to return to that again.

"What can I say?" He peers down at me, bringing his body closer to mine. I swallow hard, the buzz building between us. Enclosed in this small space, I can't avoid it. His voice turns deep, throaty, husky. "You bring out a side of me I never knew existed."

"Drew…," I caution, but don't tear my gaze from his like I normally would.

"Shouldn't that be worth something? Shouldn't that mean something?" He leans closer.

I stare at him, shaking my head. I want to tell him it's not, that it doesn't, but my brain can't form the words. As I inhale his scent, allow myself to be consumed by his proximity, I'm transported years into my past. For a moment, I forget about the pain and hurt he's caused me. Of all the times he's made me promises, then broke them. Of all the times he made me feel invisible. The way he's looking at me right now makes me feel like I'm the only woman he's ever seen.

"Drew," I say again, licking my lips. My tone is no longer cautioning but pleading. For what? I'm not sure. I know this is wrong, but I can't stop myself from erasing the distance between us. It's like our mouths are two magnets, drawn to each other, a force outside our control urging us together.

"You want this, Brooklyn. I know you do," he murmurs. The timbre of his voice forces an electric current to run through my body. I'm no longer thinking about the possible repercussions of kissing Drew. In this time and space, none of that matters. It's just us. Nothing else. All I want is to feel his lips on mine again, to experience the passion I've been missing in my life for years, to have him consume me completely, even if for just a moment.

"Tell me to stop. Tell me to walk away."

His hand lands on my hip, tugging me against him. I whimper, the heat of his body against mine causing fireworks to erupt in my core. I can feel how much he wants me, how much he needs me. It's unmistakable. And I want him, too, even though I know he should stop. *I* should stop. I'm the one with so much at stake here. He's at risk of losing nothing. I'm at risk of losing everything.

"Tell me," he begs once more.

"I… I can't."

"Oh, Brooklyn." His voice comes out like a growl as his hand goes to my hair, fisting it, forcing my head back. The way he holds me is possessive, controlling, endearing. Wes has never held me as if he has an animalistic need to claim me, mark me as his.

His eyes fiery, he erases the final distance between our lips at the same time as there's a knock on the doorframe. We both jump away from each other, snapping our heads to see Aunt Gigi standing there.

"Dinner's ready."

"We'll be right there," Drew clips back through a tight jaw.

She lifts her brows, her eyes darting between us. My face reddens in embarrassment that she caught us in this compromising position, especially considering how devoutly Catholic she is. She gives me one last look, then retreats.

Drew turns back to me, but I keep my eyes lowered, ashamed that we'd almost kissed yet again. How could I let him cast a spell over me so easily that I would dishonor the commitment I made to Wes? And it's not just a commitment to be his girlfriend anymore. I've agreed to be his wife. I can't hurt him like this anymore.

I *won't* hurt him like this.

"We should go eat." I push past Drew, not looking back. "Don't want to keep your aunt waiting."

Chapter Eleven

DREW

"HOW ABOUT FLYNN?" ALYSSA asks as we sit around the table after finishing the feast of pasta that is our traditional Sunday evening dinner.

"Flynn?" Molly arches a brow in her direction.

The entire meal was filled with conversation about what Alyssa and Charlotte thought Molly should name her baby, since she found out she's having a boy last week. Some were outrageous, and I marveled at their imaginations. Thankfully, as if everyone knows better, there's not one mention of Brooklyn's engagement or the wedding. We've resumed our regular routine, acting like nothing has changed.

Alyssa nods enthusiastically. "It's a great name. That's what you should name our cousin."

"That wouldn't have anything to do with a certain character from a certain Disney movie who you find dreamy, would it?" Molly teases.

"I don't think he's dreamy," Alyssa shoots back.

"Yes, you do," Charlotte pesters in a way only a

little sister can. I should know. Molly did it to me when we were their age. Come to think of it, she still does. "You told me you can't wait to find a Flynn Rider of your very own."

Laughter breaks out around the table as everyone looks at me to gauge my reaction to this news.

I narrow my gaze on Alyssa, all brown curls and toothy grin. "You're never dating, so don't get any ideas."

"But what about Kenny?"

"Who?"

"Kenny. He's been going to school with me for, like, ever."

"You're eight. You've only been going to school for three years. Not to mention, you just started at your current school last year."

"Right." She looks at me with all the seriousness she can muster. "That's a wicked long time."

"Wicked? Where did you learn that?"

"We do live in Boston," Brooklyn reminds me under her breath. I shift my eyes to hers from across the table. They're the first words she's spoken to me since running away after we almost kissed. The tension between us during dinner has been thick, but no one seems to have noticed. Or maybe they did but kept it to themselves. "Everything's wicked here."

"Exactly," Alyssa agrees.

"And what is going on with you and Kenny?" I return my attention to her.

"He likes me."

"You're too young for a boy to like you."

"I like him back."

I bury my head in my hands. First, the discussion about how the baby got in Molly's belly, and now this. I love watching my little girls grow up, but it's happening too fast.

"What makes you say that?"

"Because he picked me first for volleyball."

"That's it?"

She shrugs. "Isn't that what you do when you like someone? You put them first? Like how Uncle Noah takes time off from work to go to Auntie Molly's doctor appointments."

"Yes, but that's different."

"How?"

"For one, they're both adults. You're only eight. That's far too young to like a boy."

"Did you like Auntie Brook when you were eight?"

I do my best to keep my expression even and not react to her question. "That's not the same thing."

"But you did, didn't you?" Alyssa pushes. For the first time, I regret raising such a headstrong, independent little girl. I've always been awed by how smart and perceptive she is, but today, it will be my undoing, particularly with this line of questioning.

"Well…yes. I've always liked your auntie Brooklyn." My brown eyes meet soft green ones from across the table. I hold her gaze. "And I always will."

"Then I can like Kenny," Alyssa retorts matter-of-factly, ignoring the obvious shift at the table as Brooklyn and I stare at each other. The electricity is back, the spark and sensation of breathlessness. I wonder if she feels it, too. How can she not?

When I sense several pairs of curious eyes on me, I tear my gaze from Brooklyn's, taking a long sip of my wine. "I am so not ready for this."

"No one ever is," Uncle Leo assures me, tipping his glass toward me.

"On that note," Molly interrupts. "I'm exhausted and want to crawl into bed." She rises from the chair, Noah jumping to his feet to help her. "This kid is taking a lot out of me lately."

"You're a trooper." Noah leans down and kisses her nose. "And the most stunning pregnant woman I've ever seen."

"And you're the best baby daddy I could ask for," she jokes, beaming. I can always count on my sister to make light of a serious or tender moment.

"Before you go," Brooklyn pipes up, standing from her chair. "Do you have time to go dress shopping this week?" Her voice lacks the enthusiasm it should have when discussing the prospect of choosing a wedding dress. I shouldn't read too much into it, but everything about this engagement seems off. "Mrs. Bradford was able to get me an appointment on Friday."

"Friday?" Molly furrows a brow. "Don't you have to work?"

"I'll have to move some things around, but—"

"What's the rush? I'm happy to go, but I know how important your cases are to you. I can't remember the last time you took a day off."

"Yes, well…" She fidgets with her shirt, chewing on her lower lip. "We've set a date," she announces after a brief hesitation. She remains motionless, gauging our reactions.

"That's wonderful news, dear," Aunt Gigi says, flashing her eyes to me, almost in warning. "When's the big day?"

"I hope you've picked one that gives me enough time to lose some of this baby weight." Molly gestures to her stomach, laughing. I expect Brooklyn to at least smile, but her apprehension only heightens.

"That's not going to be possible." She lowers her head, her voice becoming softer. "We're getting married June ninth."

Everyone seems to zero in on Brooklyn at that moment, me included. Silence settles in the room, a stark contrast to the usual boisterous ruckus that fills this space every Sunday during our family dinner.

"Of *this* year?" Molly says after the shock of the news wears off.

Brooklyn smiles, but it wavers. "I was just as wary of it as you are. Probably more. But after thinking about it, it's for the best."

"The best?" I ask, having trouble wrapping my head around the idea that Brooklyn will be getting married in a matter of months. Why is she rushing into

225

this?

"Yes." She holds her head higher. "My PhD program starts this fall. I'll still be working full-time, as well. I can't plan a wedding on top of that. And my studies will only become more intense during the course of my program. I don't want to wait three or four years to marry Wes. His mother wants us to get married at the country club. They had a few cancelations. One was around Molly's due date in August." She nods at my sister. "I refused. There's no way I'm getting married without you by my side." She turns back to address the rest of us. "The other option was June ninth. I know it's rushed, but like I said, it really is for the best."

She straightens her back, her expression fixed. It sounded like she was delivering a recommendation to the court on the disposition of one of her cases, not like she just set a date to marry the man she should be excited to start a life with. Why does she think it's for the best? I can't wrap my head around this.

After another prolonged moment of strained silence, Molly steps toward Brooklyn, hugging her. "I'm happy for you." She meets my eyes, giving me a look that says everything she wants to but won't, at least not in present company. Then she pulls back, releasing her hold on Brooklyn. "What time Friday?"

"My appointment is at ten. On Newbury Street."

"Oh, fancy." Molly waggles her eyebrows. "Do you want me to meet you at the café and we'll go from there?"

"I can pick you up at your house. No sense both of us driving into the city. Nine o'clock okay?"

"You bet." She hugs Brooklyn once more, then retreats, passing me another look before shifting her attention to Noah. "Let's get going. It's way past my bedtime."

"Says the woman who only a few months ago stayed up half the night writing."

She rubs her stomach. "That was before you knocked me up. Now all I want to do is sleep."

"Speaking of bedtimes," I say before my girls can ask what their auntie Molly means by "knocked up". "Come on, munchkins. Say goodnight to everyone."

"Can we stay up for ten more minutes?" Alyssa asks. "We'll help clean."

"I've seen your version of cleaning. It usually entails making an even bigger mess. You've already stayed up an hour later than normal. So let's go. I want butts in bed."

"We'll leave you to fight this battle on your own," Noah comments, holding out his hand.

"Don't worry," I warn as we shake. "Your time's coming. Better sleep all you can now. In a few months, you'll wonder what sleep is." I walk Molly and Noah toward the foyer, watching as they say goodbye to Alyssa and Charlotte. Then I scoop my two girls under either arm and carry them back into the kitchen. "Okay. Say goodnight to Auntie Brook, Aunt Gigi, and Uncle Leo."

"Goodnight," they sing in unison. Everyone comes up to give them both a hug and kiss, then I carry them up the stairs, depositing them in Charlotte's bedroom.

I go through the normal routine of getting them ready for bed and reading a few books. After tucking Charlotte in, I leave her with a kiss on her forehead, then bring Alyssa into her own room.

"Are you sad Auntie Brook's marrying someone else?" she asks as she settles into her bed.

I inhale a sharp breath, caught off guard by her question. "What makes you think that?"

"I just do. I'm sad she's marrying Wes."

"Don't you like him?"

"He's okay. But I wish she was marrying you."

I lean down and kiss her forehead. "Go to sleep, Lyss." I stand and turn off the lamp on the bedside table.

"Do you love her?"

"Very much." I don't know why I answer so honestly.

"Then why don't you marry her?"

"It doesn't work that way, sweetheart." I kiss her forehead one more time, inhaling. She still has that baby smell to her, even all these years later. "Now, go to sleep."

"Okay." She snuggles beneath the covers. "Love you, Dad."

"Love you, Lyss." I head toward the doorway, pausing for a moment as I admire my daughter's face. There's nothing more satisfying than watching your child sleep peacefully, not a care in the world. It doesn't matter how stressful the day was, the arguments you got into. At the end of the day, it's not important.

With a sigh, I close the door and head back down the stairs. The kitchen that was a disaster, covered with pasta, sauce, and breadcrumbs, now sparkles and gleams.

"You didn't have to clean up," I say to Uncle Leo as he places the last plate in the dishwasher and starts it.

He turns around and passes me a knowing look. "You understand how your aunt can be. Do you think it's wise to tell her no?"

I shake my head, feigning fear. "Absolutely not."

"Then you know why I had to clean."

"Ah, there you are," Gigi calls out, turning the corner from the living room. I look over the area, all the toys normally scattered throughout neatly placed in the kids' chests.

"Are you ready to go?" Leo asks.

"Yes. Go start the car. I'll be right out." She narrows her gaze at me. "I need a word with my nephew."

"Yes, ma'am." He kisses my cheek, as he always does, then continues out of the kitchen.

"Did Brook take off, too?" I shift my eyes around the space.

She shakes her head, gesturing toward the French doors. I follow her line of sight, seeing Brooklyn sitting in front of the fire pit in my back yard, a glow coming from it.

"My darling Andrew," Gigi begins. I turn back to

her. "You remind me so much of your father." She cups my cheeks in her hands, forcing me to bend over to meet her short height. "Every day, I see more of him in you." She stares at me, penetrating, before releasing her hold. "Before Alzheimer's took his memories, he often spoke of his biggest regret."

"What was that?" I press, knowing too well where this conversation is going.

"That he never put himself out there."

"He dated." I cross my arms in front of my chest.

"But he was never all in. He kept his heart guarded because of how much your mother hurt him." She gestures outside once more.

"Are you telling me to pursue a woman who's engaged?" I ask in disbelief. It's shocking my aunt, the devout Catholic she is, would advocate this course of action.

"All I'm telling you is that regret is a bitch."

My eyes widen. My aunt never swears. To hear her use a word she normally won't makes me realize how serious she is. This isn't another ploy to play matchmaker as she's been prone to do.

"Don't regret this. You have the power to stop it."

"But at a huge cost to her." I shake my head. "I can't hurt her more than I already have."

"Always so noble, my dear Andrew." She stands on her toes and places one last kiss on my cheek. "I love you." She turns around. "I'll see you tomorrow."

Dazed, I watch her leave, pondering her words for a

moment. I fear this is a battle that will never be won, that it's not a battle I *want* to win. Sure, my life isn't remotely close to what I imagined it would be, but I've found my happiness. My girls are my happiness. That should be enough. Weren't Molly and I enough for my father? Isn't that why he never remarried? I wish he were still alive so I could ask him.

When I hear the front door close, I draw in a deep breath and head toward the back patio off the kitchen. The instant I emerge outside, Brooklyn looks up, her eyes brightening when they fall on me.

"Hey," she says, running her hands down her jeans, looking away. "I hope you don't mind I'm still here or that I started a fire."

"Of course not. You're always more than welcome here." I sit beside her, a little uneasy. "I'm sure your father would flip if you ever put a fire pit in at your place, so you may as well enjoy it here."

She laughs, the glow of the fire bringing attention to the blush building on her cheeks. I like to believe it's my presence that does it, not the heat coming off the flames. "You can say that again." She rolls her eyes. "He's been a firefighter for over thirty years. In his opinion, everything's a potential fire hazard, especially a fire pit."

I smile, looking at the flames dancing in front of us. The air is chilly, but the fire keeps us warm. I have to resist the urge to put my arm around her and pull her against my chest. I used to do that very thing whenever we sat out here. But that was before she was engaged. Before we almost kissed. Before I realized I'm not over her like I thought.

231

"About yesterday..." Brooklyn's voice cuts through the silence. I gaze at her, but she keeps her eyes glued to the fire. "And earlier..." She slowly lifts her eyes to mine. "It's best if we pretend that never happened." She swallows hard, her eyebrows squeezing together.

"Is that what you want?"

"What I want is irrelevant." Her tone is clipped. "What I *need* is for things to be the way they've always been. I don't want there to be this awkwardness whenever I'm around because we almost kissed. Twice. In two days."

"Do you regret it?"

"I'm engaged."

"That doesn't answer my question." I lean closer to her, my eyes intense. "Do. You. Regret. It?"

She flounders, looking anywhere but at me. She doesn't have to utter a single syllable. I have my answer. It's almost like her brain wants her to say one thing, but her heart wants another. I should know. I feel like I've been going through that same thing for years.

She jumps to her feet, heading toward the doors. "I should get going. It's late and I have a busy week ahead of me."

I dart after her, blocking her escape with my wide stance. "Answer my question, Brooklyn. Do you regret almost kissing me?"

Her breath hitches, her eyes glued to my chest. She could easily tell me yes, because that's the ethical answer for a woman in her position. But that's not who Brooklyn is. Unlike most women I've dated or slept

232

with, Brooklyn's honest, even if that honesty isn't what people want to hear. After being in a marriage that was filled with nothing but lies, deceit, and betrayal, Brooklyn's unwavering truthfulness has always been a welcome breath of fresh air.

"I should," she finally answers, lifting her eyes to mine.

"But you don't." There's a twinge of hope in my voice.

She stares at me, neither confirming nor denying my statement.

When she remains silent, I relax my stance. "If you don't, maybe you need to re-evaluate why you're marrying Wes, why you're settling." The impulsive side of me wants to tell her to call off her wedding, to convince her I can be everything she needs, that everything that's been keeping us apart has just been a bunch of misunderstandings. But that impulsive side is what landed me in Vegas with a wedding band on my left hand, what brought me to the brink of kissing her twice this weekend, what took Brooklyn from me in the first place.

"Not this again..." She sighs, trying to push past me, but I don't let her.

"Yes, this again." I run my hands down her arms. "My reaction on Friday was immature. I recognize that. And I'm so sorry for what I said to you. But my thoughts on your engagement stand. We grew up together. We've stayed friends through everything. What happened to the Brooklyn who wanted to find her true love? Who wanted to find the man who would give her the stars and moon? Who would make her heart beat a little faster, her breath come a little quicker, her stomach flutter from the wings of a million tiny butterflies? Because I've seen you and Wes together. He doesn't make your skin flush, doesn't make you smile, doesn't breathe life into those eyes."

"And you think *you* do?"

"It doesn't matter what I think. Isn't that what you still want?"

"Those things aren't real. It's time I stop trying to live out my adolescent dreams and live in the real world."

I shake my head, unable to believe the words I'm hearing. They don't sound like the Brooklyn I know...or who I *thought* I knew. "What happened to you, Brooklyn?" I ask in a soft voice, fearing the answer.

"Nothing." She exhales a defeated sigh, then pinches her lips together. Her gaze floats to mine. "Some of us have to settle for good enough. And that's okay. Because with real love comes real risk."

"Risk of what?" I press, my Adam's apple bobbing up and down.

She looks forward, her mouth forming a tight line in steely determination. "Of having your heart broken in such a way you'll never find all the pieces to put them back together." She meets my gaze, a few unshed tears forming in the corners of her eyes. "Settling is better for all involved. Good night, Drew."

I hesitate for a moment, then reluctantly release my hold on her, letting her go once more.

234

Chapter Twelve

BROOKLYN

I STARE OUT THE front window of my house Wednesday morning, a cup of coffee in one hand, my free arm over my stomach. I don't know how long I've been standing here. Long enough to watch one of my neighbors leave to drop her kids off at school, stop at Starbucks, then return home. From experience, the wait for a coffee on a weekday at the neighborhood caffeine dealer is easily ten minutes. Add the time sitting in the school drop-off line and we're looking at around twenty minutes, if not more. But I can't stop peering out the front window. I like this neighborhood. The houses are quaint, set on tiny lots, but there's a charm to it. My two-bedroom townhouse isn't much, but I paid for it on my own. Am I ready to leave this place I've turned into a home?

"Morning." Wes' voice startles me and I jump. Recovering quickly, I force my lips into a small smile as he makes his way toward me from the foot of the staircase.

His dark hair is damp from a shower and he's dressed in his normal attire — black suit, conservative tie, crisp white shirt. He leans down, kissing my cheek, his face smooth from a recent shave. He couldn't be any more different from Drew if he tried. Perhaps that's why I dated him in the first place.

Where Drew forgoes the routine haircut, Wes goes every Friday during lunch. He shaves every day, sometimes more than once. If the Bruins make the playoffs, Drew won't shave until they're eliminated. I chuckle to myself, wondering how Mrs. Bradford will react if the team keeps playing like it has been. I can imagine the horror on her face if Drew shows up at the wedding with a big, bushy beard.

"What's so funny?" Wes asks as he turns from me, heading toward my small kitchen to prepare his morning cup of coffee. It's strange to have him in my house, using my things. He spends the night on occasion, but he's typically gone by the time I get back from my morning workout. I prefer it that way. We don't feel obligated to sit together over a cup of coffee and pretend we have something to talk about. At least when we're out to dinner, I can people-watch to distract me. But here, the lack of connection to the man I agreed to marry suffocates me.

"Nothing." I head to the kitchen table and sit. "I was just thinking of something Molly said yesterday," I lie. It's uncomfortable discussing Drew with Wes. What if he's able to see through the front I've been putting up for months...years?

"Oh geez." He takes the seat next to me, pulling out his smart phone and tapping at the screen. "I'm not sure I want to know."

"You probably don't."

Silence settles between us, as awkward as a cow on

roller skates. It shouldn't be like this. We should be comfortable with each other, not trying to fill the stiff silence with meaningless conversation.

"Looking forward to dress shopping later this week?"

"Can we not discuss the wedding?" I float my eyes to his, disappointment shrouding his expression. "It's not that I'm not excited," I assure him quickly. "I am." I shift my gaze, staring at my half-drunk coffee. "But that's the only thing we've talked about all weekend. At least the one day I saw you this weekend anyway."

"I know. I'm sorry." His voice oozes with sincerity and he grabs my hand. Bringing it toward his mouth, he places a soft kiss on my knuckles before releasing it. "Things at the firm are crazy right now. We were just awarded a contract to design and construct a multi-million dollar hotel in Dubai. It's going to require a lot of extra hours from me, considering all the time I'll have to take off for the wedding."

His phone dings and I spy an incoming text pop up. Not wanting to pry, I sip my coffee, but can't help noticing the wide grin cross his lips as he reads it, his eyes darkening. He clicks his screen off, then rises from his chair.

"Speaking of which, I should get going."

"Want to come over tonight?" I ask as he collects his commuter bag from where he left it by the staircase. "Or want me to go to your place? We can grab something to eat—"

"I wish I could," he interrupts. "I already ducked out of work early yesterday to meet you for dinner."

I bite back my response, thinking he makes it sound like I'm someone he *has* to spend time with, like I'm just another item on his lengthy to-do list. His words at the country club were so sweet and heartfelt. Now, ever since getting back from his impromptu trip to Florida, he seems like a different person. I try to shake the sinking feeling in the pit of my stomach I made the wrong decision. Shouldn't we be growing closer together instead of feeling like the divide is widening? This is why I'd hoped for a long engagement, so we would have the time to strengthen our bond before walking down that aisle. Or maybe I'm looking for any reason this isn't the right path for me.

Wes is a good man. He's always been devoted and caring. He loves his family and his job. I can't fault him for wanting to ensure the success of his projects. My career is my priority, too. At least I'm trying to see him more than once a week for dinner and sex, though.

"I need to make up for that lost time." His voice brings me back to the present. "Plus, I have to give up my weekend for the photo shoot Mom's arranged. I promise, it'll get better after the wedding."

Once he shrugs on his jacket, he heads back toward me, giving me a chaste kiss on my cheek. "I'll text you." No I love you. No attempts to squeeze me into his busy schedule, even if for just a coffee. Only a promise to text me, as one would promise an acquaintance. It leaves a sour taste in my mouth.

I watch him head toward the foyer. As he's about to walk out the door, he pauses, facing me. I perk up, thinking maybe he's had a change of heart, that he's going to suggest something incredibly romantic that will reaffirm why I said yes to his proposal.

"I left my suit from yesterday upstairs. Can you drop it at the cleaners by my house sometime today? I'll be working late and won't have time to get there."

His words are like ice on my momentary feeling of hope. "And you assume I have nothing better to do than run your errands for you?" I shoot back, my tone harsh.

"Your work takes you all over the city."

"Most of the families I visit can't exactly afford a Victorian in Cambridge."

"No, but it's not that far from Chelsea and Somerville. You have lots of visits in places like that."

I narrow my eyes on him. "In case you forgot, I grew up in Somerville. My dad still lives there."

"I didn't mean anything by it. Just stating a fact."

He adjusts his tie, ignoring the heated glare coming off me. "Tell them to put a rush on it. It's my lucky suit and I want to wear it to meet a new client this Friday. See ya, babe."

Without a thank you or any other sign of gratitude, he disappears out the door, leaving me to stew alone. This kind of thing never pissed me off before. Then again, he's never asked me to do such menial tasks as dropping off his dry-cleaning. Does he assume I'll do these things just because we're engaged? Does he think my role as his wife is to support him, not vice versa? Does he expect me to put my plans on hold so I can stay at home, run his errands, and raise children I'm not even sure I want with him?

I have half a mind to ask the girl at the cleaners to add too much starch or do something else to ruin his precious suit. In the end, I don't, dropping it off like he requested, going out of my way from my townhouse in Medford. Because of this added errand, my typical fifteen-minute commute takes forty-five, putting me behind all day.

Just as I gather my files for the home visits and assessments I have scheduled, having no time to review my notes, there's a knock on my office door. I glance up to see Michelle, one of the social workers, bursting through, carrying a huge bouquet of roses.

"These came for you," she sings, placing the large vase on the little free space on my desk.

"From who?"

"I'm assuming Wes."

Spying a card with my name scrawled on it, I reach for it, sliding it out of the small envelope. A part of me hopes they're from Drew. I haven't heard from him since Sunday night. It's not unusual for us to go this long without speaking to one another, but considering the way I left things, this silence is eating away at me.

My dearest Brooklyn,

A thousand apologies for my behavior this morning. I must have sounded like an inconsiderate jerk. That's not the way I want to start our engagement. I'll make it up to you. Dinner. Friday night. Anywhere you want to go.

Yours,

Weston

"Engagement?" Michelle asks. I shoot my eyes to her, seeing her staring over my shoulder. "When did you get engaged?"

"Last Friday," I say nonchalantly. I return the card to the envelope, stashing it away in my desk, as if it's a piece of incriminating evidence.

Her eyes practically bulge out of their sockets. "Last Friday? It's Wednesday! Did you not think to share this little piece of information with me?"

"I know," I say with a sigh, eyeing the time. I reorganize all the files spread over my desk, making some sort of order out of them before placing them into my bag. "I haven't told many people yet, other than Molly, Drew, and Aunt Gigi. I haven't even told my father."

"Why not?" She tilts her head to the side, crossing her arms in front of her chest.

"He's been working all weekend. I'm sure he already knows, but this isn't the kind of thing I should tell him over the phone."

She stares at me, remaining silent as she seems to assess this news. No congratulations. No shrieks of excitement. No demands as to where the ring is. She behaves like everyone else I've told.

"Do you think it's a bad idea?"

"What? No!" she answers quickly. "I mean, I don't know him that well. I've only met him once. It does seem a little sudden, but I guess when you know, you know, right?"

I stop organizing my files, leaning back in my chair.

"How long did you date Jonathan before he proposed?"

She rolls her eyes, tossing her dark locks over her shoulder. "Too long. I pretty much had to tell him to put a ring on it or I was leaving."

I laugh, standing, thankful for the brief moment of levity.

"What did he do this morning that required him to send you flowers? No offense, but I don't even think he sent you flowers on Valentine's Day. That would have put Jonathan in the doghouse for at least a month."

"Why? It's only a stupid holiday made up by greeting card companies to pad their pockets after Christmas."

"So? I still deserve flowers. I gave birth to his three kids, one of them without an epidural because it was too late. The least he can do is go to the store and buy me flowers. And, if he wants to get lucky, some ice cream, too."

Smiling, I wonder if I'll ever be able to have conversations like this about my own marriage. Michelle can act annoyed all she wants, but I know the truth. I've spent time with her and her husband. Every woman deserves to have a man look at her the way Jonathan does Michelle.

"So…," she prods.

I focus my eyes on hers. "Wes stayed at my place last night. Before heading out this morning, he asked me to drop off his dry-cleaning. In Cambridge."

Michelle pinches her lips together, the look of annoyance on her face mirroring my own earlier. "You didn't do it, did you?"

"Yeah. I stopped on my way in."

"So you drove from Medford to Cambridge before driving back out here? That had to add on... What? Thirty minutes?"

I nod.

"Oh boy." She shakes her head in disbelief. "That is not the way to start an engagement. That man has a lot to learn. If Jonathan ever tried to have me run his errands for him because he's the main breadwinner in the family, his balls would be shoved so far up his ass, he'd have a permanent falsetto."

"This is new territory for both of us," I explain, not wanting Michelle to think the entire situation has me second-guessing myself even more than I already have been. "But the important thing is he realized it was a mistake without me saying a word. That's got to count for something, right?"

"Of course." She places her hands on my arms, trying to reassure me, but it doesn't. I hate feeling this way. Are these just pre-wedding jitters? Or is it something else?

God, I hope it's not something else.

Chapter Thirteen

BROOKLYN

ERSPECTIVE IS A FUNNY thing. It often finds me when I need it most, when I've lost sight of what's important. My job gives me that perspective on a daily basis. When I find myself complaining that my cable bill went up or the battery on my iPhone drained faster than usual, I reflect on some of the kids I see during the day.

Yes, some of my cases are routine visits to conduct a home study in advance of an adoption. But there are many others where the children suffered various levels of physical or emotional abuse, necessitating the state taking them from their biological parents. It's when I see these kids I'm reminded that my own troubles pale in comparison. They wish their biggest problem could be whether the man they agreed to marry is a good fit for them. They'd gladly drop off someone's dry-cleaning every morning if it means not cowering in fear whenever they hear footsteps outside their door.

The end of the day brings me by Massachusetts General Hospital, having to do an emergency intake of a six-year-old landed there by her mother's boyfriend. By the time I finish and the foster parents she's being placed with arrive, it's almost eight o'clock. All I want is to go home, order sushi, and relax on the couch. But the fire station where my father's currently working a twenty-four-hour shift is only a few blocks away. So instead of making my way back to my house, I pay him a visit.

The instant I walk into the truck bay, I'm surrounded by a familiar smell. Rubber. Fuel. And something else I can't quite explain. It reminds me of home, of family, of happiness. Of the days I'd come visit my dad and marvel as he slid down the pole. Of the days he propped me behind the wheel of the ladder truck and placed a helmet on my head. Of the days he'd have me help him wrap the hoses, although I knew he and his crew would have to redo it once I left.

"Brooklyn!"

I lift my head to the wide window peering into the bay to see a familiar face pestering whoever's manning the dispatch office tonight.

With a smile, I head toward the office and am met in the hallway, vibrant green eyes waiting for me. "Hey, Mike."

"Good to see ya, sweetheart," he says in that Boston accent most find annoying, but I love. His arms envelope me in a short hug before he releases his hold. Mike's one of the newer guys in the department, about the same age as me. He did the college thing, but decided he no longer wanted to work a nine-to-five job. He enrolled in the fire academy and is now happier than he ever was working in investments. "Come to see your pops?"

"Is he around?" I don't know why I bother to ask. I

just walked past the ladder truck he's the lieutenant on. If the truck's here, he has no choice but to be here, too.

"Sure thing." He turns from me and heads into the dispatch office. I smile at the man sitting behind the desk that contains various radios and other communication equipment. Mike leans over him and presses a button. His voice booms throughout the entire station. "Lieutenant Tanner to the front, please. You have a package."

I lift a brow. "A package?"

Mike shrugs, walking toward me and leaning against the doorjamb of the office. "I could have said a singing telegram."

"Is that even still a thing?"

He scrunches his nose. "I have no idea." Folding his arms in front of his chest, he eyes me up and down. "Still dating that guy?"

I tug on the hem of my jacket, a hint of nerves settling in my stomach from the reminder of why I'm here, what I need to tell my father. "I am."

"Damn. Too bad. I was going to ask if you wanted to get a few beers with me this weekend." He winks, always the flirt.

"Even if I weren't still dating him, you know it would never work between us." I smile, my tone light. "If you thought my father gave you hell for being the rookie, imagine if you were to date his only daughter. The apple of his eye. His pride and joy."

He seems to consider my response for a minute. "Yeah. You're probably right."

"No," a thunderous voice interrupts. "She's *definitely* right."

In an instant, the tension in my shoulders melts away. On a slow exhale, I spin around to see my father descending the staircase, wearing the typical navy blue shirt and pants I've seen him wear to work my entire life, Lt. Tanner printed on the left side of his chest.

"Dad." I wrap my arms around him when he reaches the bottom, squeezing him tightly.

"Hey, beautiful," he responds, resting his hand on the middle of my back, returning my hug. His touch makes my entire body relax. It's different from how I feel when anyone else hugs me, even Wes or Drew. It's a feeling of completeness only possible when enveloped in a father's love. I hold on for a little longer than normal, breathing in the man who will always be my first love.

When I don't let go, Dad pulls back, his brows narrowing in concern. "Is everything okay, sweetie?"

"Of course," I assure him, my eyes prickling with tears. "I miss you, that's all."

A smile lights up his handsome face, the wrinkles around his eyes becoming more pronounced. He doesn't look like a man in his sixties. While the years have turned his hair gray, he still has a healthy amount of it. Thanks to his disciplined workout regimen, he's in great shape. He's even trained for and run a few marathons. While most guys in the department seem to put in their twenty years and retire, my dad can't remember a time in his life when he didn't want to be a firefighter. As long as he's still physically able to do the job, that's what he'll do, even though he's been up for retirement for nearly fifteen years now.

"I miss you, too. What brings you here after eight on a Wednesday night?"

"I got called in to do an assessment at MGH."

My father's face momentarily falls. As a first responder, he knows what that means. "Sorry to hear that."

"It's the job." I hesitate, sensing Mike hovering off to the side. "Can we go somewhere to talk?"

He squints, scanning my face, then gestures toward the truck bay. "Sure. Come on."

I wave to Mike as we head away from the dispatch office. When he winks at me, I stifle a laugh, inwardly rolling my eyes. Most women may find his flirtatious ways annoying, but they suit him. It's all harmless fun. I've seen him in action. Mike talks a big game, but inside, he's a complete softy.

We continue past the engine truck, heading toward the ladder truck. Several pairs of boots sit by the passenger compartment, their bunker pants arranged over them so they can suit up in a flash. My dad likes to brag that his crew can be geared up and out of the bay faster than every other crew in the city. After witnessing them jump into action when a call comes in, I believe it.

I follow my dad to the back of the truck and he sits on the ledge, patting beside him for me to do the same. It seems like it was just yesterday that I'd visit him as a little girl and sit on the back of this same truck, my feet unable to reach the ground. I'd marvel at all the buttons and nozzles, asking what each one did. I'm not sure whether he made stuff up, but I loved listening to him tell me about all the tools and gadgets I thought were magical.

Not much around here has changed since those early days. A few more helmets hang on the wall in memorial to their fallen brothers. I've grown up around this life, so it never dawned on me that my father had a dangerous job until a classmate asked how I handled saying goodbye to him before he left for work, not knowing whether he'd come home. It's a part of my life. I don't know any other way. Either does my dad.

"What's going on, Brook?" he asks, cutting through the silence. I cast my eyes toward his. He's never been one to beat around the bush. With him, there's not much idle talk, no assessing the situation to determine how best to approach it. He confronts everything head-on. Sometimes I wish I could be more like that. Instead, I tend to weigh how everyone else will respond before I choose a course of action. I'm always more concerned with other people than my own needs.

Drawing in a deep breath, I run my hands down the legs of my dress pants. "I'm sure you already know, considering Wes must have spoken to you, but I said yes."

His brows furrow as he frowns. "What are you talking about?"

"Wes." I swallow hard, my palms becoming clammy. "He asked me to marry him."

My father's expression becomes even more confused. "He did?"

"He didn't talk to you first?" I chew on my bottom lip.

"No, he didn't."

"Oh." I turn away, my voice laden with unmistakable disappointment. Granted, the idea of asking permission to marry one's daughter is outdated, but there's something about it I like. It's a sign of respect. I'm not sure how to process the knowledge that Wes didn't think it important to ask my father. Hell, when Noah planned to propose to Molly, he came to all of us — me, Drew, Aunt Gigi, Uncle Leo — and asked for our blessing, since her father had already passed away.

"So, you're getting married?"

I sheepishly glance back at him. "I am."

He stares ahead, absorbing this news. I'm waiting for him to tell me it's a bad idea, that we're rushing things. When he finally speaks again, all he says is, "Okay."

"Okay?" My voice rises slightly in pitch. I cock my head to the side, my gaze unfocused as I stare at the calmness in his features. "That's all?"

"You're an adult now, Brook. I trust your judgment. You must have strong feelings for him if you agreed to marry him."

I open my mouth, unsure what to say. After learning Wes hadn't asked for his blessing, I thought he'd try to talk me out of marrying him, like everyone else has. If anyone should question this, it's my father, the man who just so happened to have a display of gun enthusiast magazines on the coffee table when Spencer picked me up for my first date my junior year of high school. The man who repeatedly warned me about the disastrous consequences of teenage pregnancy. The man who never allowed me to leave the house with a skirt that was too short or a top that was cut too low.

"You don't think it's too soon? That we're moving too fast?"

He chuckles, shaking his head as he looks at his feet. "I'm the last person to give anyone a hard time about that." When he returns his eyes to me, there's a hint of nostalgia in them. "Your mother and I were married less than eight months from the day we met. There's no hard and fast rule about how long you should date someone before you get married. When you know, you know."

I nod, absorbing his words. I almost don't ask my next question, but my curiosity gets the better of me. "When did you know with Mama?"

With a shallow sigh, he wraps an arm around me, pulling me close. This is what I need. To feel my father's love and assurance that everything will be okay, that whatever I'm going through will work itself out.

"The minute she opened her mouth and declined my invitation to take her out for ice cream." There's a lightness about him as he recalls the woman I can barely remember now that nearly thirty years have gone by since she died.

"She turned you down?"

"I like to think she was playing hard to get."

"Well, it must have worked." I try to mask the longing in my words, but it's impossible. My dad's a damn good man and the best father a girl could ask for. But it doesn't make up for the empty place setting at the dining room table. Life isn't fair, but I've had a much better life than some people. Regardless, I still get angry that someone could be so careless as to get behind the wheel after drinking, and because of that carelessness, I never had an opportunity to know my mother.

"It did." My father's tone matches the despondency I feel in my heart.

We sit in silence for a while longer, the peacefulness intermingling with the crackling of the radio and a few cheers coming from the second floor where the guys are watching either hockey or basketball. Probably hockey. It makes me think of Drew, of the heat in his eyes the other night when he almost kissed me. Again. And how a part of me wishes he did. Again.

"You still miss her, don't you?" I look to him, my voice contemplative. "Is that why you've never asked Ana to marry you?"

His body seems to deflate. "I love Ana, but not like your mother. When your mother passed, she took a piece of my heart with her, one I'll never get back. One I don't want back. Ana understands this. She lost her husband, too. When you lose someone like that, it changes you. Changes your perspective." He drops his arm from around my shoulders and grabs both of my hands in his. "*You* became my focus. You were all I needed, and through you, her memory will always live on in my heart. I guess that's why I was always a bit overprotective of you. I couldn't stomach the idea of losing you, too."

I consider his words, unable to stop my next question from spilling from my mouth. Everything he just said reminds me too much of another single father I know. "Do you think you'll be able to learn to love with your entire heart again? Even after having it broken?"

Suspicion swirls in his eyes, which I should have expected. This man raised me. He had to hear the real question hidden within — whether Drew would ever lower those walls he's erected around his heart after Carla left. I shouldn't care, but a part of me needs to know the answer. Maybe if I know there will never be a chance for him to be the man I once thought him to be, it will make my decision to marry Wes feel like less of a mistake.

"I've learned a lot in my sixty-two years, most notably that anything's possible." He stares into the distance, deep in thought. "Sometimes we let our own prejudices or fear cloud our vision and it blinds us to the truth, to what's right." With a smile, he returns his eyes to mine and kisses my forehead. "Sometimes we make mistakes. We think we're doing what's best, but we end up hurting the people we were trying to protect."

I open my mouth to ask him what he means by that when an obnoxious alarm echoes loudly through the truck bay. In the blink of an eye, he's no longer my father but Lieutenant Reece Tanner. He jumps into action, ushering me away from the truck and out of the way as the place swarms with firefighters. They all suit up in what seems like seconds.

As my dad's about to hop into the passenger seat next to the engineer, he nods in my direction. "Love you, Brooklyn," he shouts over the alarm before disappearing into the truck.

Within a matter of seconds, it pulls out of the

garage, lights flashing, siren blaring, taking my father away to the call that could be his last. In my heart, I know it's not. I just wish my heart could be as certain about Wes.

"Love you, too, Dad," I whisper as the truck gets smaller and smaller in the distance.

Chapter Fourteen

BROOKLYN

"**M**OLLY?" I CALL OUT as I step into her house on Friday. I expect to see her sitting at the small table in the breakfast nook, as she usually is when I drop by in the morning.

"In here," she responds. I follow the sound of her scratchy voice.

"Are you okay? You sound like hell." I come to a stop when I see her curled up on the couch in the den, Noah hovering over her, his hand on her forehead.

"I feel like hell," she admits.

"She's running a fever," Noah explains, his concerned eyes floating to mine. "And she's been having trouble keeping any food or fluid down."

"It started last night. There's nothing I can take because of this." She points to her stomach, scowling playfully as she meets Noah's gaze. "You just had to get me pregnant, didn't you?"

He leans down and places a kiss on her temple. "I didn't hear you complaining at the time."

Longing fills me as I witness their exchange. It

seems so natural and easy. I've never felt that way with Wes, like I can say whatever pops into my mind. Yes, he's sweet and tenderhearted, but also very serious and somewhat intimidating, like his entire life is one board meeting or client dinner. I'm not sure I've ever felt like I can be myself around him. At least not the person I can be with Molly…and Drew.

"I'm sorry, Brook," Molly says, bringing me back from my thoughts. Her complexion is pale, her normally pink lips lackluster. When a visible shiver rolls through her, Noah drapes a blanket over her, rubbing her arms. "I hate to disappoint you, but I can't go today."

"I need to keep an eye on her temperature," he adds. "If it gets too high, it puts the baby at risk."

Molly smirks, but it's not as lively as usual. "I always knew dating a doctor would come in handy. If I weren't feeling like death warmed over, I'd be all over some doctor-patient role-play."

"Doesn't that usually require you taking on *different* roles than real life?" a familiar deep voice calls out.

My spine stiffens and I suck in a breath. When I snap my head toward the large eat-in kitchen, Drew rounds the corner from the stairs. The instant he sees me standing there, he comes to a dead stop, his reaction identical to my own. We haven't spoken since I left him Sunday night, when I couldn't even tell him I regretted that we'd almost kissed…twice. As I stare at him in a white t-shirt that leaves a few of the tattoos on his arms visible, jeans that fall from his hips perfectly, his hair a bit messy, his jaw unshaven, I still can't say with certainty I regret it.

When he crosses his arms in front of his chest, it seems every muscle in his body tightens from the motion. His biceps stretch the sleeves of his shirt and I can make out the definition in his chest. It's superficial, but I've always loved his body...even when he was a teenager and had just started building muscle. The years have been great to him. More than great. Fantastic. Magnificent. Stupendous. I shouldn't be thinking this way, but I can't stop imagining how perfect it would be to fall asleep enveloped in those arms. Then I remind myself I did...once. I thought it was our second chance. But I was wrong. Again.

A smirk forms on Drew's lips, having caught me ogling his muscles. I tear my gaze from him, focusing on the hardwood floor, as if there would be a test on the pattern of the grains later on. I curse myself for not paying attention to the cars in the driveway or along the street. If I had, I would have noticed his SUV. Would that have changed anything? Not likely, but at least I would have been prepared to see him.

"If I remember correctly, Noah's a doctor," Drew finally finishes.

"But *I* was never his patient," Molly argues.

"You're crazy enough to need to see a neurologist," he jokes.

"That's not what a neurologist does," she states. "I'm crazy enough to need to see a *psychologist*. So, Brook..."

When she says my name, I whip my head toward her, pretending as if this situation were normal. Last week, it would have been. But so many things I thought I buried years ago have resurfaced. I wonder if Molly

257

senses this, too. How could she not feel the tension?

"Be sure to keep some space open in your calendar in a few years once you get your PhD."

"Will do," I say with a smile, then sigh.

All week, I've been looking forward to some girl time with Molly, some time when we could talk, just the two of us without anyone else listening in. Ever since she moved in with Noah and got pregnant, we've seen each other less and less. I'm thrilled she finally found someone who makes her happy, but right now, I need a normal day with my best friend. Instead, I've never felt so alone, like a fish swimming against a current with no relief in sight.

"I guess I'll just go by myself today."

"No. Don't do that. I'm sure this will clear up over the weekend. We'll go next week."

I shake my head. "I cleared my schedule for today. With everything else going on, I'm not sure when I'll have another chance to go shopping. I'll already be cutting it close to the wedding as it is in regard to the dress being ready in time. I don't even want to think what Mrs. Bradford will have to say if I skip today." I roll my eyes.

"I'm so sorry, Brook. I hate that I'm letting you down." She reaches for me, and I take her hand in mine.

"You're not, Molly. I promise. You're turning food into a human. You need to take care of yourself and my nephew. That's more important than you watching me try on dress after dress. I'll just go by myself and text you the photos."

"Okay." Her lips turn into a frown, her remorse-filled expression making it obvious she hates having to miss today as much as I hate she can't be there. I give her a reassuring smile and begin to retreat when she calls out, "Brooklyn, wait! You don't have to go by yourself."

I turn back toward her, giving her a skeptical look. "Who d'you have in mind? Gigi?"

"Drew can go with you."

On a quick inhale, my eyes widen. I'm already questioning my decision to marry Wes. The last thing I need is to have Drew with me as I try on dresses for my wedding to another man. The idea doesn't just make me uncomfortable. It makes my stomach churn. Yes, to the outside world, Drew's just a friend. I've been fooling myself to think we can ever truly just be friends. Our history is too tainted.

"You're not doing anything today, are you?" Molly looks at her brother.

"I have to pick up the girls at two," he answers, his quick response evidence he's just as uneasy about the idea.

"She'll be done before then." Molly glances at me. "Won't you?"

"Well, yes, but——"

"Then it's settled." Her face brightens, at complete odds with the misery prevalent just moments ago. "Drew, you'll take Brooklyn."

I lift my eyes to his, fidgeting with my hands. "I'm sure you have plenty of other things to do today.

There's no reason for you to waste it shopping with me. You don't have to come."

"Yes, he does." Molly grits out a smile, giving Drew what I can only refer to as "the look". I've seen it before, usually on Aunt Gigi's face. She's a master at "the look", and Molly learned it from her. "If you thought I was a pain in the ass in an argument before, you haven't seen anything now that my hormones are out of whack. If you don't take Brooklyn, it could be the start of the zombie apocalypse."

She shifts her hardened stare between the two of us, a long moment passing while we both struggle to come up with a valid reason this is a bad idea, one Molly won't read too much into. I want to tell her my friendship with her brother is a ticking time bomb, but I don't. I stay silent, like I always do. A part of me *does* like the idea of spending the day with Drew.

"Well, since I don't have my ax or machete handy," Drew begins, facing me, "we should probably do as she says." His lips lift in the corners, his slight smile chipping away at my annoyance with the situation.

"And since I don't possess any skills that would help me survive a zombie invasion, I suppose I have no choice, either." I glance at my watch. "But if we're going to do this, we should get going. My first appointment is in a half-hour."

Drew gestures toward the front door. "After you."

"Thank you."

"Have fun, you two," Molly calls out as we walk toward the entryway and into the crisp air.

As I make my way down the front steps, a hand

260

lands on my lower back. Drew probably doesn't even realize he did it, this gesture common between us, but the warmth of his hand on me makes my breathing increase, my cheeks heat, my body hum. Every inch of me sparks to life, a rush I haven't felt since he had me pinned on the ice, since we were enclosed in his bathroom as I tended to his wounds. I haven't felt this needy and alive even when Wes made love to me the few times I've seen him this week. It solidifies my original reaction. Today is going to be a complete disaster.

"I'll drive," Drew offers in the thick silence.

"You don't have to. You're generous enough to do this when I'm sure you have better things to do today—"

"But you need me. That's what friends do. They drop everything else to help someone they care about." He leads me across the street toward his large, silver SUV, opening the passenger door for me.

I pause, meeting his eyes. "Thanks for being so cool about this. Not just today, but with everything. With letting Alyssa and Charlotte be my flower girls, even though it might be during the Stanley Cup."

"There are more important things in life than hockey. *You've* always been more important than hockey, Brooklyn."

Staring at him, I consider his response, then blow out a breath as I duck into the car. I want to believe him, but too many painful memories resurface, reminding me that his words aren't true, that I've never been and never will be a priority to him.

Chapter Fifteen

DREW

"YOU MUST BE MS. Tanner," a voice says as we step into a small boutique on Newbury Street. The hustle of the city has disappeared, and we're now surrounded by nothing but quiet interspersed with low-level classical music.

A petite woman stands from an ornate wooden desk, the wall behind it showcasing black-and-white prints of brides in extravagant wedding gowns. She's slender, and the combination of her chic business attire and blonde hair pinned into a low bun makes her look every part the professional stylist the clientele here on Newbury Street want.

"We were worried whether you'd show. My name's Judy." She holds her hand out to Brooklyn and they briefly shake. "I'll be assisting you today."

"I'm sorry I'm late." Brooklyn's voice is soft and apologetic. There's something so musical about the lilt in it. I've always thought her voice to be pacifying, but lately, I've found it even more soothing. "We hit traffic and had trouble finding a close spot, so we had to park at the Common." Brooklyn looks back at me, and Judy notices me for the first time.

"Ah, I see you've brought your groom with you." She lifts a brow, assessing my appearance, her nose wrinkling in displeasure.

I scan my wardrobe — jeans with frayed hems, a white t-shirt that's seen better days, and sneakers with worn treads. With the college hockey season at an end, I no longer work on Fridays and had planned on catching up on everything I've avoided the past few months...until Molly called insisting I bring over the bouncer and swing from when the girls were babies. Now I can't shake the feeling it was a ploy to force Brooklyn and me to spend the day together.

"It's a bit unusual, but I guess more brides are breaking from tradition these days."

"Oh, no," Brooklyn corrects quickly. "He's not the groom. Drew's a friend. More like a brother," she adds, her cheeks turning pink.

Judy looks at her with skepticism. I wonder if she can sense our history is much more convoluted than that. "Typically, the bride brings her mother or maid of honor to help choose, but I suppose it doesn't matter since Mrs. Bradford stopped by last night and pre-selected dresses for you to try on. I have your room all prepared." She spins, heading from the reception area.

"She what?" Brooklyn's frozen in place, obviously taken aback by this news.

"Yes." Judy stops in her tracks, looking back at us. "Oh, don't worry." She smiles, surveying Brooklyn's oversized sweater and jeans tucked into worn boots. Her expression is similar to the distaste the saleswoman showed Julia Roberts' character in *Pretty Woman* when she tried to go shopping. This boutique is on the higher end, but I hate the idea of anyone looking at Brooklyn like she's not important. "She requested to be charged for the cost of the dress, as long as it's one she selected," she assures her, mistaking her surprise for concern about the price. "The dressing room is this way."

Brooklyn remains in place for several more moments, then shakes her head. Her eyes losing what little excitement they had, her shoulders slump. "Of course," she mumbles, shuffling behind Judy and through a large showroom, me close on her heels.

Racks fill the cluttered space, all of them stuffed with wedding dresses spanning every style, from simple and elegant to exceptional and over-the-top. As we head farther inside, I feel out of place, like a priest in a brothel. Yes, I've been married before, but there was no big wedding. Hell, there was no engagement. After a month of incredible sex, I couldn't think of a reason not to marry Carla, so we hopped on a flight to Vegas and tied the knot. In retrospect, there were a lot of reasons we shouldn't have married, but the young, stupid version of myself wouldn't have listened, particularly to the voice inside saying I was only doing it in the hopes of finally forgetting about Brooklyn.

Judy heads toward the back of the showroom, pulling back one of the half-dozen dark curtains that hang in sections along the rear wall, revealing an intimate fitting room. An ornate divan and a few chairs make up a sitting area in the center, a pedestal placed in front of the large three-way mirrors a few feet away. In the corner is another curtain, which I assume leads to a private dressing room for the bride-to-be. Every wall is lined with racks full of white dresses. And not simple dresses, either, as I have a feeling Brooklyn prefers. These are the quintessential Cinderella-style gowns, complete with more tulle, sequins, and feathers than any dress should have. The extravagance makes me itchy, and I rub the back of my neck. If I feel this way, I can't imagine what's going through Brooklyn's mind right now.

"Mrs. Bradford arranged these in order of preference," Judy explains as she scurries toward the rack closest to the mirrors and grabs the first few dresses, hanging them in the fitting room. She looks back at us, waiting for one of us to react. When we both remain locked in place, uncomfortable expressions on our faces as we stare at all the white, she grits a fake smile. "I'll let you get settled and will be back to check on you in a few minutes." Then she heads away, bringing the cloud of perfume surrounding her.

The instant we're alone, Brooklyn's entire body relaxes and she blows out a long breath, assessing the scene in front of us. She lifts her eyes to mine, giving me a small smile. "Well, if I'm going to have time to try on these dresses before you need to pick up the girls from school, I better get moving." I can't help but notice the slight quiver in her voice.

When she starts toward the dressing room, I grab her arm, forcing her to face me. Her eyes widen in surprise. I'm not sure if it's from my hand on her skin or from her abrupt stop. I wonder if she feels what I do whenever our bodies touch, this unrelenting electricity burning so hot, nothing can put it out.

"You don't have to do this," I say, placing my hands

on her biceps. Her skin is soft, smooth, perfect. "You don't have to try on a bunch of dresses the Brooklyn I know wouldn't be caught dead wearing. This is *your* wedding. You deserve to have whatever dress you want. Not some ridiculous garment your future mother-in-law dictates."

"I can't afford anything here," she whispers. "I can't afford a dress at all. Not on my salary. If I had a few years to save up like I thought I'd have, it wouldn't be a problem. But since I got railroaded into agreeing to a June wedding, I don't have a choice but to pick a dress Lydia likes." She steps away and I drop my hands with a sigh.

I hate everything about this, but I don't know what else to do. I'd love to offer to pay for whatever dress she wants, but she'd see it for more than it is. Brooklyn and I seem to be treading dangerous waters these days. I don't want to add to the tension.

"It doesn't matter what the dress looks like on the hanger," I assure her when she's about to disappear into the dressing room. It's a bold move, but I can't help myself. The way every inch of her seems to be devoid of life makes me not care. She needs to know how amazing she is. "You'll make it beautiful. You make everything you wear beautiful."

She glances over her shoulder, her lips curving up slightly. "As much as I should tell you not to say things like that, it's nice to know someone thinks I'm beautiful." The large velvet curtain closes behind her, her words ringing in the air.

I'm on the verge of asking what she means by that, why Wes doesn't tell her she's beautiful every day, every minute, every second, but decide against it. This is already difficult enough on her, on both of us. The last thing I need is to make it worse. Now, more than ever, Brooklyn needs my support, to smile and laugh. If my dad were still alive, he'd tell me as much.

"Hey, Brooklyn?" I call out.

"Yeah?"

"Why don't cannibals eat clowns?"

Her laugh fills the room, the sweet melody as refreshing as hearing birds chirping on that first warm day after a long winter. "I don't know, Drew. Why don't cannibals eat clowns?"

I pause, remembering my father's assertion that the art to telling jokes is in the delivery.

"You don't want to blow your wad too early, Drew," he would say in his thick Boston accent. *"Get to the punchline too soon and you'll waste the opportunity to make someone smile. There's no greater feeling in the world than seeing someone's entire disposition brighten and know you're the reason for it. Never forget that. Anyone can buy flowers or jewelry, but making someone happy by words alone… There's no greater gift."*

A warmth fills me as my father's voice sounds as clear as day in my head. It's like he's here with me, standing over my shoulder, encouraging me. I wonder what he would think about this situation, if he would approve of Brooklyn's marriage to Wes. If he would want me to tell her the truth of that summer. When he was still alive, he was like a second father to her. Would he side with Gigi, as he was prone to do? I'll never know.

Refocusing my attention on the curtain, I imagine

Brooklyn standing in front of the mirror, holding whatever monstrosity of a dress she's trying on first, uncertainty in her expression. "Because they taste funny."

It doesn't matter that my view of her is blocked, I can feel Brooklyn's smile fill the room. "Good one. Your father would be proud. You used to hate his jokes."

"Perhaps." I shrug. "Maybe I never appreciated their purpose." I lower my voice, my tone becoming sincere. "I do now."

Silence settles between us once more, but this time, it's even more pronounced. The space isn't just devoid of conversation. There's no more rustling of fabric as she tries on the dress she's supposed to wear on the happiest day of her life. The only sound is dull background chatter coming from the reception area.

"Hey, Drew?" she whispers.

"Yeah?"

"Can you tell me another joke?"

"Anything for you." With a smile, I wrack my brain for yet another one of my father's notorious jokes the regulars of the café flocked to hear, regardless of the fact they heard them all before. "How do you make a tissue dance?"

"I don't know. How do you make a tissue dance?"

"You put a little boogie in it."

She laughs again, this time with less life, more sadness, as if she's barely keeping it together. After a moment, she blows out a heavy sigh. "Okay. Here goes

268

nothing. You ready to see?"

"I'm on pins and needles."

"Promise not to laugh?"

"I'd never laugh at you."

"Okay."

The curtain pulls back and Brooklyn steps out, wearing an extravagant white gown. It has a sweetheart neckline, the sleeves set off her shoulders. The satin fabric hugs her curves, then flares out at her hips into a flowing skirt, complete with a long train. Jewels dot the dress, picking up the light every time she takes a step, making her look like a princess out of a fairy tale. It's stunning, a dress many women would fawn over, but from how stiff she's walking, it's obvious she's uncomfortable. She doesn't give off the appearance of a woman overjoyed to be trying on a wedding dress. Her expression is more of a woman being led to the gallows in a pair of handcuffs.

"It's bad, isn't it?" She scrunches her nose, looking down at it.

"You look beautiful, Brook," I assure her. "And I'm sure you'll look beautiful in every single one of these dresses."

"But…" She lifts a brow, sensing there's more.

"But you're not glowing."

"Am I supposed to glow? It's only a dress I'll wear for a few hours of my life."

"True, but shouldn't they be the most important few hours?"

She looks away, shrugging.

"Close your eyes, Brook."

She shifts her gaze back to me, skeptical.

"Come on. Humor me for a minute."

"You're not going to do anything stupid are you?" She places her hands on her hips, tilting her head to one side. "I seem to remember when we were kids, you used to tell me to close my eyes, making me think you had a surprise for me. Instead, you'd put mud down my shirt."

A lightness fills my chest at the memory. "It was my lame attempt at flirting with you."

"When you were ten?"

"Close your eyes, please," I beg. Now isn't the time to rehash the past. "Today is about you finding your perfect dress. I'm trying to help."

"And you think you can do that by asking me to close my eyes?"

"I do." I smirk.

She bites her lower lip, trying to fight a smile, then sighs, obviously curious as to what I have in mind. This can go either way. I half expect her to run from me again, as she has the past few times we've seen each other. But if she's serious about marrying Wes, she deserves to have the wedding of her dreams, including the wedding dress of her dreams.

She closes her eyes and inhales a deep breath. "Okay. Now what?"

I raise myself from the chair I've been sitting in and

make my way toward her. As I near, the scent of lavender becomes stronger, bringing forward so many happy memories. I can't remember a time when she didn't smell like this. Lavender, honey, and baby powder. That's Brooklyn. All sweet and fresh.

"Do you remember when we were kids and Molly forced us to have a fake wedding?" I murmur, convinced the beat of my heart is deafening in the small space.

She swallows hard, lifting her chin. Her chest rises and falls in a quicker pattern, a blush blooming on her fair skin. Brooklyn's never been one to wear much makeup, and she doesn't need it. Her complexion has a natural glow to it, and the pink on her cheeks makes her even more stunning than I thought possible.

"Yes."

"Do you remember walking down the makeshift aisle in our back yard that led to the gazebo?"

"I do," she responds, breathy.

"And do you remember holding a bouquet of flowers and weeds Molly picked for you, which we later realized contained poison ivy and you broke out in a horrible rash?"

Her laughter fills the space, the sound comforting to my soul. To see her this at ease reminds me of when we were kids and had our lives before us. When we didn't have a care in the world. When we thought things would always stay the same.

"I doubt I'll ever forget that."

I allow the light atmosphere to linger for a moment

271

before asking my next question. My eyes trained on her, I continue toward her. The electricity in the room builds with each step I take. She feels it, too, her lips parting, her skin becoming more flushed.

"Do you remember what you were wearing?"

She nods, her voice low and even. "We found an old apron and tied it around my waist. Then we added long streams of toilet paper to it, after wrapping my chest and stomach in it. Your dad was furious we wasted all that toilet paper."

"He certainly was." I come to a stop in front of her. "And you're correct. That was what you were wearing. But in your mind, when you walked down the aisle with the most exquisite smile on your face I've ever seen, what did you imagine you were wearing?"

Her shoulders relax and a peacefulness washes over her. For a minute, she's no longer standing in the dressing room of an upscale wedding boutique on Newbury Street. She's in our back yard, carrying a bouquet of poison ivy, walking toward me. I can feel it.

"A champagne-colored gown," she begins. "Not pure white, but not gold, either. Somewhere in the middle. It had a floral lace overlay." The more she speaks, the more animated her voice becomes. "The shoulders and back were bare, apart from the lace."

I grin, knowing she must have imagined this dress more recently. These aren't the dreams and wishes of an eight-year-old girl. They belong to the woman standing in front of me. And she deserves to have those dreams come true.

"It was fitted through the bodice and past the hips,"

she continues, her hands following the line of her imaginary dress, stopping at mid-thigh. "Then it flowed out in a subtle flare."

Happiness seems to ooze from every inch of her, making me realize I've hit the jackpot. When I grab her hand in mine, she's awakened from her momentary trance, her eyes flinging open.

"That's the dress you deserve, Brooklyn."

"But——"

"Look at yourself." I turn her toward the mirror, keeping my hands on her shoulders. "You're glowing, but not because of the dress you're wearing right now. Because of the dress you were describing. *That's* the dress you should be wearing. Not this ridiculous getup."

"I can't," she insists, despondent. In an instant, she's retreated into her shell, the vivacious, excited woman she was moments ago now a distant memory. Her shoulders droop as she heads back toward the dressing room to try on the next gown her future mother-in-law picked out.

"Why?"

She faces me, exhaling loudly. "It's not worth the eventual argument with Mrs. Bradford or Wes if I don't choose one of her pre-approved gowns. I'm not marrying a normal guy. This family has money and social standing. The wedding of their only son needs to fit into what's expected of them...of me. I just need to get through these next two months and make as few waves as possible. Then things can get back to normal and I can put this behind me."

She disappears into the fitting room and closes the

curtain. The rustling of tulle and whatever other material they use to make these gowns fills the room once more. At first, I didn't want to intervene, didn't want Brooklyn to read any more into this than necessary, but hell if I'll stand by and let someone else dictate what's supposed to be the happiest day of her life.

With conviction, I retreat into the showroom, scanning the space for Judy. When she sees me, she excuses herself from her discussion with a few of the other girls I assume work in the boutique.

"How's everything going in there, Mr…?" She lifts a brow.

"Brinks," I answer in a firm voice. "And things aren't going well. Every single one of those dresses is completely wrong for Brooklyn. They're not her style. She's not a girly-girl who likes jewels and frills. Hell, I'm pretty sure she wore Converse to her senior prom."

Judy's dark eyes widen, her expression a mixture of surprise and disgust over the idea of someone wearing anything other than heels with a dress. "And what exactly *is* her style?" She rests her hands on her hips, her lip curling. "A pair of jeans and a worn t-shirt?" She scrunches her nose at my attire, making no move to hide her contempt for my choice in clothing.

"No," I respond evenly. "She's not a tomboy, if that's what you think. I've known her most of my life, and she's always had her own style. She's beautiful and confident enough that she doesn't need to make a bold statement. She's elegant, but simple. That's what Brooklyn needs here. A simple, elegant gown, not something that makes it look like a unicorn threw up tulle and feathers all over it. And it needs to be champagne colored."

"Oh, no." Judy shakes her head, everything about her giving off an air of indignation. "Mrs. Bradford specified it was to be white. Not off-white. Not ivory. Not alabaster. And certainly not champagne. White. No exceptions."

I lean into her, having difficulty keeping my temper in check with each second I have to listen to what Mrs. Bradford wants for Brooklyn. She doesn't deserve a say over what Brooklyn wears, regardless of how much they're spending on this wedding, which I can only imagine is some ungodly amount.

"I don't give a damn what Mrs. Bradford said," I grit through clenched teeth, my eyes on fire. "I want you to find a dress in a champagne hue. But not just any dress. It needs to be her style. It should be fitted through the body and flare out slightly at mid-thigh. Preferably something with a lace overlay that exposes her shoulders and back. *That's* what she wants. Find something like that, not something that distracts from how beautiful that woman is."

Judy crosses her arms in front of her chest. "And who will be paying? I'm not putting any dress on Mrs. Bradford's card unless it's one of the gowns in that room right now."

"I'll pay for it," I say nonchalantly.

She scoffs, rolling her eyes. "The dresses here are *very* expensive. These aren't just $300 gowns from a discount bridal store. These are all designer dresses, made to order. Most of them run at least ten times that amount, if not more. I doubt—"

"I can afford it." Reaching into my pocket, I grab my wallet, then slam my AmEx Black card on the jewelry display case beside us. "Whatever dress she wants, you can put it on that card. I don't care the price."

The sight of that particular card catches her attention and she reaches for it, holding it in front of her with a furrowed brow. "Andrew Brinks." When she returns her stare to mine, she almost does a double take, as if her eyes are playing a trick. I don't expect her to know who I am. Hockey players don't seem to have the same notoriety as, say, professional football players do. Then again, this is Boston, a city with a reputation of worshipping its teams and the athletes who play for them. "You're not the same Andrew Brinks who used to play hockey, are you?"

I smile, the tension shattering in an instant. "You follow hockey?"

Her entire face reddens as she chews on her bottom lip, avoiding my eyes. "My boyfriend's a big fan. He was beside himself when you retired. He says the team hasn't been the same since, and he'd know. He has season tickets. He'll never believe you were in my store today." She pauses, still seemingly bewildered. It's been a while since anyone has recognized me outside of a hockey game. It's nice to know I haven't been completely forgotten. I suppose coaching, as well as the occasional commentating and endorsement gigs, has helped.

"So…" I cut through the silence. "The dress?"

"Right." She snaps back to the present, a conniving expression crossing her face. "I think I may have something that matches your description." She gives me a conspiratorial wink. As she's about to retreat, she meets my eyes. "And I apologize. I never should have assumed you couldn't afford the dress."

"Find something for her and all will be forgiven."

"You got it." She scurries away, and I head back to the dressing room, praying she's able to pull through.

When I enter the sitting area, Brooklyn's still behind the curtain, swearing under her breath about something. "How's it going in there? Need anything? Water? Coffee? A bottle of vodka?" I joke.

She sighs, her aggravation with the situation evident. "Unless you have the power to fast forward the clocks to the day after the wedding, I'm not sure you can help. This is just a giant waste of time. I should just close my eyes and pick one. They're all the same."

"Don't give up. We'll find the perfect dress. I promise."

My reassuring words are met with silence, apart from the rustling of fabric. I get antsy the longer I sit there, worried Judy can't find a dress close to what I described. Finally, after a few more minutes, she rushes in, carrying a garment bag. She hangs it on one of the racks and unzips it, revealing a gown that fits Brooklyn's description almost to the letter. I don't know how she did it, but Judy knew the exact dress, even with my lackluster descriptive abilities.

Thank you, I mouth as I head toward her, admiring the dress.

She leans close, whispering, "It's seven thousand dollars."

"I don't care."

Judy nods with a smile. "You're a good person, Andrew Brinks." She allows that to linger for a moment, then slips away, giving me some privacy to fight what I expect will be a battle.

"What's that?" Brooklyn's voice rings out and I whirl around. She's in yet another frilly gown with layers of tulle and silk that swallow her slender frame.

"A dress," I respond coolly.

"I see that." She steps toward me, her gaze narrowing. The downside of having grown up together is her ability to read me. And right now, she knows, just by the combination of my darting eyes and rocking back on my heels, I'm not being honest with her. "But what's it doing here? I didn't see it here earlier."

"It was," I argue, although my voice lacks any conviction.

She closes the distance even more, now only a few inches away. "Are you sure?" She scans the racks of dresses, all of them bright white and larger than life. The dress behind me couldn't be more different. Not to mention it looks suspiciously similar to the one she just described. "I find that difficult to believe." She crosses her arms over her chest.

"What?" I shove my hands into my pockets. "It's here, isn't it? I thought it odd, too, but you may as well try it on, don't you think? You can't be blamed for an employee mistake."

"Drew...," she starts.

"Doesn't hurt to at least see what it looks like off the

hanger." I lift the dress and hold it out so she can get an unobstructed view.

She opens her mouth to protest when her eyes catch a glimpse of the detailing on the lace overlay. There are a few beads and sparkles, but nowhere near the over-the-top style of the dresses she's been trying on. Longing fills her expression, her eyes glistening as they rake over the elegance before her.

"Come on," I encourage, my voice softer. "Try it on."

Unable to resist the temptation, she murmurs, "Okay."

"Okay." I hand her the dress, our eyes meeting before she turns around and disappears behind the curtain. She doesn't even stop to peer in the mirrors to see how she looks in the current dress. It doesn't matter. Once she tries on the one Judy brought in, she won't want to give any other dress a chance.

As I'm about to head to the divan and sit, my phone buzzes in the pocket of my pants. I pull it out to see a text from Molly.

> *How's it going? Did Brooklyn find a dress yet? She hasn't sent me any photos.*

> *That's because she hasn't found any she likes. Mrs. Bradford came by the shop last night and pulled a selection of dresses for Brooklyn to try on. She left instructions she'll pay for the dress, but only if it's one she picked out. And they're all hideous.*

I sit down and bounce my legs as I wait for Molly's

reply. I almost expect her to call.

What? That's utter horseshit. Doesn't that old shrew realize this is Brooklyn's wedding, not hers?

I'm handling it.

A longer than anticipated period of time passes as I wait for her response.

How are you handling it?

Don't worry. I promised I'd help her find the dress of her dreams. I'm not letting her walk out of here without it.

You'd better not. Keep me updated.

I will. Oh, by the way, I'm on to your scheming ass. I know you're not sick, that this was your way of forcing us together. Remember that payback is a bitch...especially my version of payback.

I hit send. A few seconds later, my phone buzzes at the same time Brooklyn pulls the curtain back. Without looking at it, I shove my cell back into my pocket and lift my eyes to her. All the oxygen is instantly sucked from the room, my jaw growing slack as I soak in how unequivocally stunning she looks. When I saw the gown on the hanger, I thought it was beautiful. But the way it clings to her curves and seems to bring out the small flecks of gold in her green eyes... I'm stunned, mesmerized, hypnotized.

Blood rushes through my body as she saunters toward the podium, stepping onto it. The way she sways her hips, the confidence she exudes… I've never seen anything so attractive. I open my mouth to say something, to tell her how amazing she looks, but mere words won't do it justice. There isn't a single word in the English language to adequately relay how bewitching Brooklyn is in that dress.

As I watch her, her eyes bright, I can picture her on the big day. She wouldn't want some extravagant hairstyle. Just a few curls in her dark locks, maybe pinned at the side of her head, cascading in front of her shoulder. Her makeup would accentuate the color of the dress — golds and browns.

From the instant I learned of her engagement, I've been against it. But now, jealousy fills me, raw and ugly. I hate the idea of her walking down the aisle to Wes. He's a decent guy, but Brooklyn's special. She's special to me. And she deserves someone who treats her like the treasure she is. I'm not sure Wes truly appreciates her. I'm not sure I've ever appreciated her, either. I certainly could have fought harder for her, regardless of how naïve I was as a teenager. That doesn't mean I'm willing to give up on the idea of us now.

"Wow." Judy's voice breaks through the tension as she hurries inside, a shoe box in her hands. "That looks *fantastic* on you. How do you feel?"

Brooklyn studies her reflection in the mirror, unable to tear her eyes away. I don't blame her. I can't, either. The cut is perfect for her body type — ample chest, slender waist, curvy hips. I'm no fashion expert, but I don't know many women who can pull off a dress like this, the silk clinging to every curve. But Brooklyn can.

"Like a princess," she murmurs, meeting my eyes in

the full-length mirror.

"Then I think we've found the dress." Judy beams as she approaches her. Gathering the loose fabric, she clips it to give her a sense of how the dress will look once it's ordered in her size and fitted to her body type.

"Are you certain this was one of the dresses Mrs. Bradford approved?" Brooklyn chews on her lower lip.

Judy opens her mouth, catching my gaze out of the corner of her eye. I subtly shake my head, hoping she's smart enough to pick up on what I'm trying to tell her. I don't want Brooklyn to know I'm paying. She'll never accept. It's inevitable she'll eventually learn the truth, especially once she tells Mrs. Bradford about the dress. I need her to believe otherwise for a little while, hopefully until it's too late to get a refund.

"Of course," Judy responds with a bright voice. "Why don't we get your measurements and I'll place the order for it right away. If we put a rush on it, we can get it in time." She peers into the mirror as she continues adjusting the fabric around Brooklyn's frame, meeting my eyes once more. "Of course, there's a fee for the rush."

"There is?" Brooklyn asks as I subtly nod at Judy, indicating it's okay. I don't care what it costs. Brooklyn deserves this. She's worked hard her entire life, making sacrifices most other people her age wouldn't. It's time she's rewarded for it.

"Yes, but don't worry. Mrs. Bradford agreed to pay the rush fee, as well."

A moment of hesitation passes. I sense the wheels turning in Brooklyn's head. She looks away from Judy and catches my gaze. "How very generous of Mrs. Bradford."

"She's a peach," I add.

She squints at me, her lips formed in a tight line. "She certainly is."

I hold my breath, waiting for her to refuse the dress. When she refocuses her attention on the mirror, her expression brightens. Now that Judy has clipped the dress in a way that's closer to how it will fit once it's been altered, Brooklyn's even more stunning. Wes is one lucky bastard. If nothing else, I'll make it my mission for the rest of my life to ensure he knows this.

"Okay." She nods, her smile growing wider. "This is the one. Let's do it."

"Perfect!" Judy steps back, clasping her hands together. "I'll send one of our seamstresses in to get your measurements. We'll both give you some privacy while she does that." She gestures at me as she heads out of the dressing room, pausing, waiting for me.

"I'll be out front whenever you're ready." I approach Brooklyn, leaning toward her. After the past week, I expect her to withdraw from me, but she doesn't. I take a moment, inhaling her lavender scent as I gently kiss her cheek. "You look gorgeous," I murmur against her ear, then step back, following Judy toward the reception area.

I'm not sure how much time passes as I watch her fill out form after form, punching a bunch of numbers on the calculator to come up with a grand total. It all seems a bit archaic. I'd prefer she just scan a barcode and run my credit card without me seeing her push all those buttons.

"To place the order, we normally only require a fifty percent down payment, in addition to the rush fee, but I don't think that's possible here, especially if you don't want her to know you're paying for it."

"Which I don't."

"You do realize she'll eventually find out, correct? Mrs. Bradford will wonder why there's no charge. I promised I'd forward an email copy of the receipt this afternoon."

"I understand. I just need her to believe Mrs. Bradford bought it for a day. Not even. I'm assuming you don't have a return policy, do you?"

She chuckles. "Not on rush orders. They'll have to go into production right away."

I nod at my credit card sitting on the desk, then at the four-figure total scrawled on the paper beside it. "Put the charge through."

She picks up my card, pausing as she studies me. With a smile, she refocuses her attention on the credit card machine and swipes the card, a sales receipt spitting out almost immediately.

"It's a shame." She shakes her head as she hands me the slip and a pen.

"What is?" I ask as I sign.

"You love her."

"It's not like that," I argue, my face heating. If she could pick up on that after only a few minutes, what does everyone else think?

She narrows her eyes, giving me a knowing look. "You can't fool me. I make a living off love. I know it when I see it. And you love her. I see brides and grooms on a daily basis. I've yet to see a groom look at a bride the way you looked at Ms. Tanner when you saw her in that dress."

"Like I told you..." I avert my gaze. "She's just a friend."

Judy places her hand on my forearm and I peer at her. "And I've never seen a bride look at a groom the way *she* looked at *you*." She withdraws, giving me a comforting smile. "For what it's worth."

"Thanks." It's all I can manage.

"I hope it works out." She takes the signed receipt from me, then hands me my copy and my credit card.

"Me, too," I mumble.

"What's going on?" We both snap our eyes to see Brooklyn walking toward us, her brows furrowed.

"Nothing." I shove my card into my pocket. Brooklyn looks at Judy, then back at me as I struggle to come up with a reason as to why she caught me signing something.

"I just realized who your friend is," Judy flounders, coming to my rescue. "My boyfriend is a huge hockey fan. Andrew was gracious enough to give me an autograph for him. Of course, I'd like one for myself, as well."

She reaches into the desk and produces a blank notecard, pushing it toward me.

I grab the pen and scratch out my name once more,

285

scribbling the signature I use when signing autographs.

"Tell him I said thanks. I'm glad someone still knows who I am."

"Are you kidding me?" she scoffs, playfully jabbing me. "Everyone knows the name Andrew Brinks. You're hockey royalty. Not many players can go from barely seeing any ice time to being star center and leading his team to the Stanley Cup in just a few months. That's like saying no one knows who Gordie Howe is."

She walks across the reception area, leading us toward the door. I get the feeling this isn't the first time she's done something like this. Then again, she *is* in sales. Learning how to read people and say what they need to hear is essential in that profession.

"That's sweet, but I'm no Gordie Howe."

"You're just modest." She winks, then turns to a stunned Brooklyn. "Ms. Tanner, it was a pleasure. I'll call you when your dress comes in and we'll arrange your fitting. I expect it will only take about six weeks or so with the rush order on it." She reaches into her pocket and withdraws a business card, handing it to her. "If you have any questions in the meantime, don't hesitate to contact me."

"Thanks."

Judy meets my eyes. "Mr. Brinks. Have a nice day. I'll be rooting for you."

I simply smile as I hold the door open for Brooklyn and exit the shop.

"Typical salesperson," she scoffs as we head toward the Common where I parked.

"What do you mean?"

"Oh, come on. She said she was rooting for you after fawning all over you. She didn't even realize you were no longer playing professional hockey."

"Yeah." I play along. "Typical salesperson. Hungry?"

"Starving."

"Want to grab lunch somewhere?" I pass her a devious smile.

"What did you have in mind?"

I look at the sky, the sun trying to peek through the clouds. "I think it's the perfect day for a trip to the beach."

Her laughter fills the air. "How did I know you'd say that?"

"Because you know I'm a nostalgic bastard." I sling my arm around her, grateful when she makes no move to push away. Just like old times.

"That I do."

Chapter Sixteen

BROOKLYN

BLISSFULLY CONTENT WITH A belly full of greasy food, I steal a glance at Drew as he turns down Molly's street. After leaving the dress boutique, we drove out to Revere Beach, where we gorged on whole belly clams, lobster rolls, and roast beef sandwiches, much like we used to nearly every weekend growing up. For the few hours we spent staring at the small waves in the chilly air, things were the way they used to be. Before life got complicated.

When Drew pulls into the driveway, we both scrunch our brows as we stare at the house, not a single light on, Molly's and Noah's cars gone.

"That sneaky little shit," Drew mutters.

"You think she planned this, too?" I ask as he puts the SUV into park.

"I don't think. I *know*." Bright eyes meet mine, surrounded by chiseled features — high cheekbones, strong nose, jutted chin. It's a face I've seen thousands of times in my life. A face I've always loved...but in a way I doubt I'll ever admit to anyone again, perhaps even myself.

288

"I'm glad she did."

"Really?" Drew lifts a brow, my statement obviously taking him by surprise.

"You're not?"

"Spending the day with you? Of course I'm glad. I just figured you'd—"

"Be upset?" I interrupt. "I guess a part of me was at first, but... I don't know." With a sigh, I lean against the seat, then glance back at him. "I think we needed a day to remind us what great friends we are. How we should never let anything come between that."

Drew pulls his lips between his teeth, his shoulders falling. "Of course. Friends." His voice sounds resigned.

"Yes." I swallow hard. "Friends." With a smile that doesn't even come close to reaching my eyes, I open the door, stepping onto the driveway.

He's quick to follow, walking me to my car. "Well, as your *friend*, if you need help tasting wedding cakes, I can make myself available for that. I'm sure Alyssa and Charlotte would also take one for the team."

I lean against my car, laughing. "How very charitable of all of you."

"Always happy to lend a hand, especially when cake is involved." Winking, he crosses his arms over his chest. It doesn't matter that he's wearing a jacket. I can still make out the definition beneath. Wes is in decent shape. He works out and takes care of himself, but his arms don't envelope me the same way Drew's do.

I stare at him, hesitating. I don't want to leave. What if, the second I pull out of this driveway, we lose everything we gained today? I don't want to go back to the way things were before — having to walk on eggshells around Drew or avoid him altogether for fear I won't be able to control my impulses.

Both of us unsure what to say, the moment builds, his stare deepening. Transfixed, he has that look again, the need I see pulling me toward him when I should be backing away. I can't keep putting myself in this position, can't allow the power he has over me to cloud what's important, what's right, what's safe.

"Well..." I clear my throat, breaking the tension. "I guess I'll see you Sunday night." I reach for the door of my car and open it, about to duck behind the wheel when his voice stops me.

"What are you doing tomorrow?" he blurts out.

I pause, turning to face him. "Why?"

"No reason." He shoves his hands into his pockets and shuffles his feet. There's a hint of vulnerability about him, at complete odds with the macho hockey player most people know. But I know the real Andrew Brinks. He can knock a guy out on the ice, but when his daughters ask him to don a tiara and have a tea party, he doesn't hesitate. I consider myself lucky to know that side of him. I guess that's the side of him that's helped me bury the hurt he's caused.

"The girls want to go to the science museum. I was planning on taking them tomorrow. I thought you could come with us if you weren't busy. They'd like that. You know... *Friend*."

My shoulders fall. I'd love nothing more than to spend time with the girls. I barely see them much these days. But every free minute I have over the next few months is filled with wedding preparations. The schedule of events Mrs. Bradford sent earlier in the week probably rivals the royal itinerary.

"I'm sorry. I can't. Our engagement photo shoot is tomorrow. After that, we're meeting with the caterers to go over the menu, then with a florist to decide on centerpieces and bouquets."

He smiles a small smile. "Say no more. I understand. Another time."

"Yeah," I respond in a low voice. "Another time." I would love to blow off Mrs. Bradford's plans, but I vowed to make an effort with Wes. I can't ignore my wedding responsibilities to spend time with Drew. What kind of message would that send? I already don't want to consider how Wes will react to the idea of him being with me today.

Drew checks his watch, then sighs. "Well, I should go get the girls."

When he leans toward me, I still, the warmth of him so close making me forget how to breathe, how to move, how to think. I wish I didn't react this way every time he was near, but I can't control the way my body is hyperaware of every expansion of his lungs, every beat of his heart, every dart of his eyes.

"I had fun today, Brooklyn," he murmurs as he plants a soft kiss on my cheek. A shiver rolls down my spine, his scruff on my skin making me feel more alive than I ever have with Wes. God, I hate this. One minute, I'm convinced Wes is the man for me. The next, I'm trapped in Drew's spell once more. A spell that's only caused me heartache time and again.

"Me, too."

He lingers for a moment longer, then steps back, heading toward his SUV.

As he's about to get behind the wheel, I call out to him. "Hey, Drew?"

He meets my eyes, not saying a word.

"Thanks for buying me that dress."

His brows scrunch together. "What are you talking about? Mrs. Bradford—"

"Didn't pick out that dress for me to try on. There's no way." I smile. "I appreciate you wanting to make sure I'm able to wear the dress of my dreams on my wedding day. You really are a great friend." I say the last part more for myself than anything else. A reminder. "Thank you."

A thoughtful expression passes over his face, the corners of his lips turning up slightly. "You deserve nothing less." With that, he ducks into his car, a little sadder than he was moments ago.

A tightness settles in my chest as I watch him drive away, then stare into the distance after his car disappears from sight. I bring my hand up to my cheek, the feeling of his kiss still lingering on the skin. Will I ever stop doing this? Am I torturing myself by spending all this time with him?

My dinner date with Wes tonight can't come at a more perfect time. A romantic night out is exactly what I need to remind me that marrying him is good, is right. I need to sit across the table from him at an exclusive restaurant as we dine on beautifully prepared dishes and drink exquisite wine. I need to feel his lips on mine as he makes love to me. I need to fall asleep in his arms, cocooned in his unwavering devotion, forgetting about whatever's going on with Drew. What I don't need is to fantasize about something that will never be a reality...at least not *my* reality.

I get behind the wheel of my car and turn the key. As I go to shift into drive, my phone rings. I reach into my purse, almost relieved when I see Wes' name appear on the screen. It's like he knows how much I need him right now.

"Hey," I answer. "I was just thinking about you."

"Oh really?" His tone becomes flirtatious, a huskiness in his timbre that makes my insides clench. "What exactly were you thinking about?"

Pulling my bottom lip between my teeth, I smile coyly, even though he can't see me. "About tonight. Maybe we skip dinner and order takeout instead. You can have me for dessert."

"Actually..." He hesitates. "I hate to do this, but I have to cancel."

"Oh." My posture slumps. Wes has canceled on me before and it never upset me. But I'm finally willing to work on us, on rekindling the spark I'm sure we had at the beginning. If we didn't, why did I date him for so long?

"I know, baby. I'm sorry. It's just..." He trails off as a female voice I don't recognize sounds in the background. It piques my curiosity. I know his secretary's voice. She's an older woman with a voice that evidences her lifelong cigarette habit. That voice does not belong to Susan. It belongs to someone younger, someone much more chipper.

"I'll be right there," I hear Wes say, his words muffled, as if he placed his hand over the speaker so I couldn't hear. "Let me take care of this real quick."

His tone sounds different, almost borderline sensual. Or maybe I'm imagining it. Wes has never shown me anything short of complete devotion, even when I constantly fail to offer him the same. Am I so stressed that my brain is playing tricks on me, trying to convince me my devoted fiancé is cheating on me? Nothing could be more absurd.

"I'm sorry, sweetie," he says, his voice clear once more. "One of our clients didn't like the designs, so we're scrambling to get something approved before they break ground on construction next week."

I sigh, my shoulders sinking. I'm not sure if I'm more upset over the fact I won't see Wes or because I hoped tonight would be the turning point in our relationship, the night I solidified my resolve that this is the path for me. I *need* that. I haven't seen him since Wednesday morning when he asked me to drop off his dry-cleaning. Yes, it's only been two days, but with each day I don't see him and spend time with Drew, the fluctuation of my emotions becomes even more unstable.

"I can't tell you how sorry I am. If it makes you feel any better, I'd much rather be with you than pull an all-nighter at the office. I promise, I'll make it up to you."

"When?" I press as that same female voice sounds in the background again.

"Soon," he replies in haste. "Listen, I have to go."

"Okay." I pause. "What if I brought dinner and dessert to you? Or maybe just a quick dessert?" My tone is seductive.

"Baby, I wish I could. You have no idea how tempting that offer is. Any other time, I'd take you up on it, but this is a huge contract for our company. We could lose millions if we don't get this done."

"Of course." I try to mask my disappointment. "I'll let you get back to it."

"Thanks, baby."

I linger on the line for a moment, waiting to see if he'll say he loves me. Nothing but dead air. When I glance at my screen, I see the call has disconnected. Doing my best to shake off the doubt filling me, I put my car in drive and pull away from Molly's house.

As I sit at a stoplight on my way back to my place, I think of Wes and our relationship, how different it is from Molly and Noah's. I can physically feel the love they have for each other. I have since the beginning. While Wes is courteous and affectionate around me, I'm not quite sure I feel his love. That's probably why everyone was surprised to learn of our engagement, why I was surprised when he got down on one knee. We're not the kind of people to show our affection through grand romantic gestures. But maybe we can be.

Pulling a U-turn, I head in the opposite direction of my house and back toward downtown Boston. Knowing Wes like I do, he hasn't stopped to take a break to eat lunch or dinner, so I pick up sushi from one of his favorite places near his office in the Financial District, then walk the few blocks to his building. If I really wanted to surprise him, I should have gone home and grabbed one of my long trench coats, stripping off everything else except the coat. Heat rushes through me at the thought. Maybe another time.

I enter the large skyscraper, feeling dreadfully underdressed compared to everyone else coming and going, most of them wearing designer suits and expensive shoes. After signing in with the security guard in the lobby, I proceed to the elevators, wondering how Wes is going to react to seeing me. I've never done anything like this, never surprised him at work or at home. Noah surprises Molly all the time when she's out at one of her favorite writing spots in the city. He brings her a chocolate chip muffin from the café or lunch he packed just for her. It's such a simple gesture, but I know how much Molly loves and appreciates how he takes time out of his busy schedule to see her. Wes surprised me with flowers a few days ago. It's time I return the favor.

When I reach the floor where his architecture firm is located, I step off the elevator and into the frenzied reception area. The phone seems to ring incessantly as employees hurry by. I've been here before, but never unannounced. Wes was always expecting me. I'd even been marked in the receptionist's calendar. I'm not sure how to feel about the idea that I'm just another item in Wes' schedule. Will I always just be someone he has to make time for, not someone he genuinely wants to see?

"Can I help you, miss?" the bubbly, red-headed receptionist asks as I approach the front desk. I don't recognize her from the few times I've been here.

"My name's Brooklyn Tanner. I'm Wes Bradford's girlfriend."

She waggles her eyebrows. "Don't you mean fiancée?"

I shake my head. "Yes. Sorry. I guess I'm still getting used to it. I know he's busy on a project, but I wanted to stop by and bring him something to eat." I hold up the bag.

"That's sweet of you." She frowns. "But Mr. Bradford isn't here."

I swallow hard, my heart dropping to the pit of my stomach. "What do you mean?"

She looks at the computer monitor in front of her. "Yes. It says right here that he signed out as unavailable for the rest of the day."

"When?"

Hesitant, her eyes float back to mine. "I can't be sure, but I haven't seen him since I got back from lunch at one."

"Did he go to a client meeting?" I start to grasp at straws.

"No. He wouldn't mark himself out for something like that. It would say where he was and who he was meeting so we'd have it for our records."

"Huh." I stare off into space, wondering why Wes would lie…and who belonged to that voice on the other end of the phone. The thought of him cheating on me had crossed my mind earlier. Now it's back. Why would he cancel our dinner and tell me he had to work late unless he's doing something he shouldn't be?

"I'm sorry," the receptionist says, looking uneasy.

Smiling, I return my eyes to her. "Don't be. I may have misunderstood when we spoke earlier. I've been so frazzled with planning the wedding, I'd forget my brain if it weren't attached to my head."

Her shoulders relax, relief seeming to wash over her. "If he pops back in, I'll tell him you stopped by."

"That won't be necessary." I turn, my mind reeling as I make my way out of the building.

The instant I'm outside, my eyes zero in on a nearby trash can and I head toward it, tossing Wes' food into it. I look up at the cloudy sky, feeling like I'm at a crossroads. I never thought Wes to be the type of person to cheat on me, but maybe I was wrong. Maybe I've been wrong about him all along. No one can be *that* perfect all the time, can they? Truthfully, if I didn't hear a female's voice on the other end of the line, I wouldn't be thinking this way. But the sensuality in her tone and huskiness in his response make me rethink everything.

I pull my phone out of my purse and dial his cell, hoping to give him a chance to explain. His voicemail kicks in on the second ring, indicating he purposely sent my call there instead of answering. I stare straight ahead at the busy city plaza, not really seeing anything.

Perhaps this all happened for a reason. Perhaps this is exactly the wake-up call I need. Perhaps this is the universe's way of steering me in the direction I've been fighting against for years.

It feels like a weight's been lifted off my shoulders. A smile crosses my lips at the thought, remembering something Aunt Gigi often said to me.

COMMITMENT

"You'll know you made the right decision when you feel stress leaving your body."

Her words pushing me forward, I glance back at my screen, dial another number, and bring my phone up to my ear.

After a few rings, the call is answered. "Brooklyn? Are you okay?"

"I'm great." I pause, drawing in a deep breath. Shouldn't I be upset over the idea that Wes could be cheating on me? Even if he isn't, shouldn't I be angry he lied, angry he canceled our date? But I'm not. I feel...free. "Is that invitation to go with you and the girls tomorrow still open?"

"I thought you had engagement photos and other wedding stuff." I can hear the surprise in Drew's tone.

"I do."

"Then..."

"I'd rather spend the day with you."

He exhales a short breath. I imagine a smile building on his lips, forcing his dimples to pop. Few people can make those dimples appear. His girls definitely can, but so can I. That has to be worth something, right?

"Want to meet at the café at nine? Gigi will throttle me if she finds out I took the girls to the city and didn't stop by to see her."

"Sounds perfect. See you then."

As I'm about to end the call, Drew speaks once more. "Hey, Brooklyn?"

"Yes?"

"Is everything okay? I mean, is there a reason you're skipping your engagement photos? Are you prepared for the potential backlash?"

"I don't care about that anymore. The wedding is in less than three months. By the time the photos are ready, we'll be married. It's pointless."

"And the caterer? Choosing the flowers?"

"Mrs. Bradford will choose what she wants regardless of what I say. So, please, let me spend the day with you. I need this." *More than you know.*

"There's no one I'd rather spend the day with."

I clutch the phone tighter, allowing his words to bathe me in comfort.

"See you tomorrow?" he asks when I don't respond.

"Of course. Have a good evening. And give those girls a big squeeze from their auntie Brook."

"I will. Sweet dreams, Brooklyn."

"Goodbye, Drew."

Chapter Seventeen

DREW

"GOOD MORNING, AUNT GIGI," I call out as I enter the café, Alyssa and Charlotte in tow.

She looks up from behind the counter where she's taking a customer's order. It doesn't matter I officially handed her the reins of the café when I began coaching hockey again, even though I'm still technically the owner on paper. Like my father, she loves interacting with the people who come through that door, says the personal contact with the owners gives the place a feeling of familiarity and keeps them coming back, instead of going to Starbucks. With a quick look around the busy café to see nearly every table full and a line almost out the door, I have to admit she may be onto something.

"There are my little angels!" She beams, gesturing for one of our employees to take over for her. She makes her way out to the dining area and holds her arms out for Alyssa and Charlotte.

"I'm not that little anymore," I joke, both of my girls giggling as they snuggle against Gigi's petite frame.

"I wasn't talking about you, *Andrew*." She glares playfully at me. "I raised you. I know from experience you are no angel." She shifts her eyes back to Alyssa and Charlotte. "But you two... Well, you certainly are angels, and don't let anyone ever tell you otherwise. *Capisci?*"

"*Capisci!*" they both respond.

Even though Gigi is second-generation American, certain phrases have stuck over the years. It doesn't matter that my great-grandfather has been gone for quite some time now. We still hold dear many of the traditions he began when he came to this country with barely a penny to his name — from our weekly Sunday dinner, to treating everyone who walks in those doors like a long-lost relative, to calling a colander a "spaghetti-a-stoppa-da-water-go-through", as I learned he did during his life. And we still say it in a thick Italian accent, imitating him as best we can.

I beam with pride at Alyssa and Charlotte, hoping they'll someday pass our stories and traditions on to the next generation. As I see the bond they share with their great-aunt Gigi, I know I've already passed on how important family is.

"Do you girls want a chocolate chip muffin before you go?" Gigi asks, peering at them with all the love in her heart. Like the rest of us, my darling aunt can be hardheaded and stubborn, but she's fiercely loyal to her family. It doesn't matter we aren't technically her kids, that Alyssa and Charlotte aren't technically her grandchildren. She still spoils them as any good grandmother would, with sweets, presents, and unrelenting adoration.

"Like they'll say no to that," I mumble as we follow her toward the display cases, showcasing every sugary concoction possible — muffins, pastries, cookies, cannolis. She ducks behind the counter and retrieves two muffins, handing one each to Alyssa and Charlotte.

"They need to enjoy their childhood. And that includes the occasional sweet."

Crossing my arms in front of my chest, I roll my eyes. "It's more than *occasional* around here."

She shrugs, dismissing my comment as I glance around. There are several familiar faces, regulars who come to the café every day, even Saturdays. Some have been coming since my father ran the place before the Alzheimer's took him. As grateful as I am for their loyalty, they're not who I'm looking for. The only person I care about seeing is one stunningly beautiful brunette whose mere presence lately seems to make my heart beat a thunderous rhythm.

I look at my watch. 9:15. It's not like Brooklyn to be late. She's alarmingly punctual. Is she having second thoughts about ditching her wedding responsibilities today? I'd be lying if I said I wasn't surprised that she not only called me yesterday afternoon, but is willing to put her relationship with her future mother-in-law and Wes at risk just to spend the day with me. This doesn't sound like the Brooklyn I know. The one who always puts other people's needs ahead of her own. Who always does what's expected of her. I wonder what prompted the change.

"Everything okay, Andrew?"

Gigi's voice pulls me from my thoughts and I snap my eyes back to hers. "Everything's great."

303

"Are you sure?" She looks at me through narrow eyes. I feel like she's using her mystical aunt powers to penetrate my thoughts. When I was younger, I was convinced she was a witch. I'm not quite sure that juvenile thought ever died.

"Of course." I retrieve my cell from my pocket and check my messages. Nothing. When I shove my phone back into my jeans, I meet Gigi's eyes. "Has Brooklyn stopped by?" I ask, although I know I'll regret it.

"No...," she drags out, placing her hands on her hips. "Is there a reason she'd be stopping by on a day she normally doesn't?"

I lean closer, lowering my voice. "She said she wanted to go to the museum with us."

"Why are you whispering?" she asks quietly, her tone mimicking mine.

"Because I don't want to tell the girls in case she doesn't show." I gesture toward where they each sit on a stool in front of the bar. The area isn't lit since it's still too early to serve alcohol, but that doesn't bother them. They eat their muffins, staring at the framed photos of famous sports stars lining the wall above the liquor shelves, able to name every single one of them.

"And why wouldn't she show?" Gigi presses.

"Because she was supposed to get her engagement photos done today, then meet with the caterer and florist."

"Supposed to?" She lifts a brow, her posture perking up. A slow smile crawls across her lips as she tilts her head, inching even closer.

"Yeah." I could embellish further, but I'm not sure what to say. All I know is one minute, Brooklyn was happy to continue with the wedding planning; the next, she started shunning her responsibilities.

"Interesting." She pinches her chin, tapping her forefinger against her lips. I can sense the wheels turning in her head.

"What is it? Do you know something?"

She seems to contemplate for a moment before she returns her eyes to mine, clasping her hands together. "You've still got a shot, my boy." Then she retreats, heading toward the dining area to clear some tables.

"A shot?" I repeat, following close on her heels. "What do you mean?"

She grabs a few plates off a recently vacated table, bringing them toward the bus bins. I help her, hoping the less distracted she is, the more likely she'll explain what she's talking about.

"Exactly what I said. It's not over yet. You didn't screw things up." She heads back toward the coffee station and grabs a dish towel, wiping the counters free from coffee and sugar residue.

"Screw things up? It wasn't my fault in the first place."

Gigi stops what she's doing and clutches my cheeks in her hands, pulling me toward her so I no longer tower over her like I usually do. "That's exactly what I'm saying." Her bright smile falls, her expression turning severe. "So don't ruin it."

"You're not making any sense," I say in

305

exasperation when she releases her hold on me, walking away. "How can I ruin something that's not there?"

She bends over to wipe a table, then shoots me a sly look. "Oh, it's there. You just have to work a little harder for it this time around."

I throw my hands up, this conversation seeming to go nowhere. "I give up."

"No, no, no!" She hurries toward me, grabbing my hands. "Don't give up. Just keep doing whatever you have been because it's working!" There's an excitement in her eyes as she bounces on her feet. "You're getting to her. You're getting through to her!"

"To who?" I ask, confused.

"To Brooklyn." She releases an exasperated breath. "She's blowing off her engagement photos today. It may be due to something Wes or his mother did, but if that's the case, she could just as easily stay home. She's not. She wants to spend the day with *you*. That must count for something."

"I told you, Gigi," I say in a serious voice. "Brooklyn's a friend. Nothing more."

"So you've been saying, but you can't hide the truth from me, even if you try to hide it from yourself. You love her. You always have. You always will. She's the reason you married Carla, how you hoped she'd help you forget how you feel about Brooklyn. You never have. And you never will. Your love for her is too deep, too strong, too powerful. It's time you finally—"

"Drew?"

I whirl around to see Brooklyn standing just a few

feet away, her expression unreadable. When I glance back at my aunt, she smirks, obviously satisfied with herself. How many more times is she going to goad me into a conversation about Brooklyn knowing she's probably listening?

"Brooklyn." My eyes dart around as I run my hands through my hair. "You made it. I was beginning to wonder—"

"There was traffic. An accident on the bridge had everything backed up."

I nod, my heart pounding in my chest, worried Brooklyn will turn around and leave at the knowledge that my crazy aunt's trying to play matchmaker. Things have returned to some semblance of normalcy. I don't want to lose that again.

"Coffee, dear?" Gigi asks, giving her a sly look. "Perhaps you and Drew would like a moment to yourselves, head to the roof like—"

"No, thank you," she interrupts with a smile. "I'm sure the girls want to get to the museum."

As if on cue, Alyssa and Charlotte come barreling through the café, flinging their arms around Brooklyn. "Auntie Brook! Are you coming with us today?" Alyssa asks.

She crouches to their level. "Is that okay?"

"Yes!" they both squeal simultaneously.

"Can we do the mirror maze first?" Charlotte presses.

Brooklyn raises herself back to a standing position, her eyes floating to mine. "You'll have to ask your father."

"Of course, kiddo." I tousle Charlotte's curls. "Ready?"

"Yes!"

The girls bolt toward the door, thanks to the sugar rush my aunt provided them.

"Shall we?" I hold my elbow out for Brooklyn.

With a smile that seems to penetrate deep inside me, she hooks her arm through mine, allowing me to lead her out of the café.

"Have fun, you two!" Gigi calls out as we're about to leave.

"Thanks, Yenta," Brooklyn shoots back. "Try to refrain from playing matchmaker with anyone else who stops by the café, will ya?" When she passes me a sly grin, we both break out laughing at the ridiculousness of the situation. The mere sound makes all my tension and stress melt away. I'm pretty sure Brooklyn's laugh could bring world peace.

It brings me peace.

Chapter Eighteen

BROOKLYN

"GOSH, IT'S BEEN A while since I've been here," I announce, taking in everything as we make our way past the central hub of the museum, a hint of nostalgia filling me. The crowd is thick, voices reverberating against the tile flooring. "I think the last time may have been in college to see the Pink Floyd laser light show."

"The girls love it here." Drew offers a smile, then looks at Alyssa and Charlotte as they gaze up in awe at the giant T-Rex skeleton. "She could surprise us, but I get the feeling Alyssa's going to be involved in some sort of science when she gets older. You've seen her at the aquarium. She can't get enough of everything to do with science, especially marine science."

"And Charlotte?" I ask, my voice light. I thought it would be awkward to be here with Drew, to spend my day with him, but it's not. It feels just as natural as yesterday did, although I didn't want to admit it at first.

"A rocket scientist." He meets my eyes, everything about him relaxed and familiar. It's a stark contrast to how I feel with Wes.

"Naturally," I retort, as if that makes all the sense in the world.

"Of course, if you were to ask her, she'd tell you she's going to be the first professional female hockey player, but only if she can play for the Bruins."

I laugh, meeting his whiskey eyes that seem to gleam as they peer down at me. "Smart girl."

"She's certainly one of a kind." He holds my gaze for a moment longer before looking back at his girls. There's a change in his expression as he watches them listen to one of the museum employees talk about how a Tyrannosaurus Rex could sprint at speeds of up to twenty miles per hour and grow to be forty feet long.

All it takes is one look and I see how much this man adores those two little girls. Every parent loves their kids. Well, *almost* every parent. Unfortunately, in my line of work, I see the other side of the coin all too often. But now, as I observe Drew and the way his entire body lights up from just one glance at those two little angels, I wonder if I've been too harsh on him.

"Daddy! Daddy!" Charlotte says, snapping me out of my thoughts. I turn my eyes to see her tugging on Drew's arm, Alyssa right beside her, as is typically the case. "Can we go see the Butterfly Gardens next?"

"Absolutely." His eyes float to mine. "Is that okay with you?"

"Of course." I nod. "It's their day, not mine."

"No. It's yours, too." His voice is contemplative as he holds my gaze for a moment, then smiles at his girls. "Okay. Hands." He holds both of his hands out to them. Charlotte eagerly takes one, grinning. Alyssa sneers in disgust, giving us a preview of what we have to look forward to as she nears adolescence.

"I'm eight, Dad," she reminds him, placing her hands on her hips, mustering all the attitude she can at her age, which is quite a lot. "I'm past the holding hands stage."

"Then maybe you're too old for ice cream, too?"

"We have ice cream all the time."

"Then, of course, you're too old for our trip to Disney World this summer, aren't you? I'm sure Auntie Molly will be more than happy to watch you while Charlotte and I go."

Her expression is priceless, her eyes bulging, her jaw practically hitting the floor.

"Because Disney World will be a lot more crowded than this place, and you'd better believe I'll be making you hold my hand there, too."

Her lips curl, and I can sense the wheels turning in her head as she tries to come up with an argument, but she eventually relents.

"Fine." She stomps over to him and grabs his other hand.

"Love ya, Lyss."

"I love you, too, Dad." She sighs, pretending to be irritated at the thought of having to hold his hand. I sigh along with her, a lightness in my chest as I watch how devoted Drew is to these girls. I've been lucky enough to witness him grow into his role as a dad. Now, as I watch the three of them walk hand-in-hand, I can barely even see the Drew I knew him to be during his hockey days. I see a different Drew...one who may be deserving of another chance.

"We can't leave you out," Charlotte says, reaching for my hand and grasping it in hers so the four of us can walk with our hands linked. My breath catches as I look from Charlotte to Drew. It's such a simple gesture, but it speaks volumes of the little person she's becoming. "You're part of our family, too, Auntie Brook!" Then she shoots her wide eyes to Drew's as we maneuver through the large crowds. "Daddy, since Auntie Brook's part of our family, she should come to Disney World with us! Auntie Molly was supposed to, but she can't anymore because she's cooking our cousin in her tummy."

"She's not cooking—" He stops himself. I can only imagine what happened to cause Charlotte to think Molly's cooking their cousin. By the flustered look on Drew's face, I can only imagine it's one conversation he has no desire to relive anytime soon. "Auntie Brook has her own commitments. She'll be taking a lot of time off from work for her wedding and honeymoon."

He looks to me for confirmation. A heaviness settles in my chest. I still don't know my status with Wes. I haven't spoken to him since our phone call yesterday. For all intents and purposes, he expected me to show up at ten o'clock this morning to have our engagement photos taken. Instead, I turned my cell phone off without a single word to him about my whereabouts. It's childish, but he deserves a taste of his own medicine. Moreover, it gives me time to figure out what I want. I'm not sure what that is anymore.

As much as I want to agree to Charlotte's idea, I

simply smile a tight smile, giving nothing away. To be truthful, a week at Disney World with Drew and the girls sounds infinitely more exciting than spending several weeks in Africa, which Wes planned without consulting me.

"What's a honeymoon?" Charlotte asks.

"It's a vacation a couple takes after they get married," I reply.

Charlotte shifts her eyes to me, considering my response. "You should marry Daddy instead. Then you can come to Disney World on your moon trip."

"It doesn't work like that, sweetie," I say, doing everything not to show any unease about the subject. As far as everyone else is concerned, I'm hopelessly in love with Wes. For now, I need them all to continue thinking just that. "But I know you're going to have an incredible time with your daddy. When you come home, I want to hear all about it."

"Okay," she replies, a bit of despondency in her tone. Thankfully, the butterfly exhibit looms in front of us, and all talk of my marrying Drew disappears as we enter the conservatory.

Now that the crowd has dissipated and we're in a smaller space, Drew allows the girls to walk farther ahead while we hang back. He still keeps his eyes trained on them as they roam the tropical oasis, pointing out all the different flowers, grinning when a butterfly floats around them.

"Sorry about that," he says after a while, breaking the silence between us. "I didn't mean for her to put you on the spot like that or for you to be uncomfortable, especially after——"

"Hey." I grab his arm and we both stop walking.

Facing him, I meet his eyes, my hand still holding onto him. Just the feel of him makes my heart rate speed up. His body tenses, his bicep bulging under my touch. I watch as his Adam's apple bobs up and down, a hard swallow.

"She's a kid. She doesn't know any better. She's so used to seeing us together, her logical conclusion is that I'd want to go with you guys. Kids Charlotte's age don't understand the concept that there are different kinds of love."

I squeeze his bicep, then drop my hold and head deeper into the gardens before glancing over my shoulder. "Remember, Drew…"

"What's that?" He hurries to catch up to me.

"I work with children for a living." I pause, contemplating for a moment before continuing. "And adults who act like children, now that I think about it. You never have to worry about what those girls say around me. In fact, I want them to say whatever pops into their minds." My expression turns serious, solemn, as I shift my focus straight ahead.

I rarely speak of my work with anyone apart from my colleagues at DCF and occasionally my father. It's too sad, too tragic. No one needs to face the things I do on a daily basis unless they're ready for it. When I first started, I went to sleep with tears in my eyes, unable to wrap my head around some of the abuse I witnessed. It still gets to me, but I remind myself that I'm there to help, to do everything in my power to give them the second chance they deserve.

"Many of the kids I work with are so scared and vulnerable. They've never known happiness. They've never been able to say whatever they wanted, do whatever they wanted without fear of repercussion." I stop walking and face him once more. "Can you imagine growing up in a house where you were scared to breathe because of what those entrusted to care for you might do?" My eyes become intense, my voice impassioned. Drew simply remains silent, seemingly unsure how to respond.

"So many of my kids have gone through that. My latest one, her 'parents' were meth addicts, always had people over, and were usually too high to take care of her or her little sister. They did everything to pretend the kids didn't exist, even going so far as beating them if they stepped foot out of their rooms when their friends were over. She was scared to leave her bed to go to the bathroom because of what they might do, so she would wet the bed. As you can imagine, they didn't like that, either. She's been in foster care for three years now. She's starting to make improvements, but that fear is still present, regardless of how loving and caring her foster family is. She still wets the bed. She's still scared to say what she wants, to talk about her feelings. She's still petrified of retribution."

His lips part as he swallows hard. "My god…"

"I know."

"I can't imagine doing anything that would put my girls in harm's way." His voice is quiet so the two girls currently squealing with delight as a butterfly lands on Charlotte's shoulder can't hear us. "I'll do anything for

315

them. Nothing is off-limits when it comes to those girls. They're my life. How can anyone treat their kids like they're disposable?"

"I wish I knew."

"I guess that's why I still struggle with what Carla did...what my own mother did. I'll never let anything come between me and those two girls. I'd rather die."

I reach for his hand, grasping it in mine. I'm sending mixed signals, but something about this moment, about being here with Drew and the girls, makes this feel right.

"And that's only one story. I have thousands more exactly like that one...or worse. So please, Drew, don't ever feel the need to apologize for anything your girls say." My face brightens as we turn the corner, our fingers entwined, heading down the row of flowers Alyssa and Charlotte are now exploring. "Nothing should discourage them from saying whatever pops into their mind. And, if I'm being honest..." I tilt my head, meeting his dark eyes. "I think it's sweet they want me to go to Disney World with you."

He licks his lips, a yearning in his gaze. "And, if I'm being honest, I'd want you to come with us, too."

We stop walking and I face him, smiling a wide smile. I don't want to put too much hope into his words. I've made that mistake before. But right now, a part of me wants to believe they have meaning. "Me, too, Drew."

We spend the next twenty minutes following Alyssa and Charlotte through the butterfly exhibit. When they seem to have had enough, we make our way toward the exit, my hand still enclosed in Drew's. Everything is perfect as I look between him and the girls, who walk ahead of us, a map of the museum stretched out in front of them, arguing over where to go next.

As Alyssa points to the space exhibit, they nearly ram into a woman. Drew and I are so lost in our own conversation, he almost doesn't realize it himself, pulling them back just in the nick of time.

"Lyss, Char, watch where you're going." He scolds them mildly. "You need to be mindful of other people when we're in public."

I turn my eyes toward the woman at the same time Drew does. In an instant, every muscle in his body becomes rigid. It feels like all the oxygen has been sucked from the area, my own heart squeezing, a pain in my throat. As I look to Drew, I know my pain is no match for the agony covering him as he's forced to face the one woman who broke him, who ruined him, who destroyed him. And in doing so, she destroyed me, too.

Chapter Nineteen

DREW

EVERYTHING AROUND ME SEEMS to fade as I stare into a pair of brown eyes I thought I'd never see again, that I *hoped* I'd never see again. Six years of wondering, of questioning, of agonizing, and not a single word from this woman who was supposed to love me in sickness and health, in good times and bad.

In retrospect, the odds were stacked against us. I just didn't want to believe it at the time. I was young, going through life with blinders on. Having just signed a ridiculously large contract for the hockey year, I was on top of the world. I was hockey's "it" boy. Sponsors were knocking down my agent's door. My face was plastered on magazines, billboards, t-shirts. So when a petite brunette sauntered up to me as I had a post-game drink at a New York hotel bar, her eyes trained on me and me alone, and asked if she could come back to my room, I was only too happy to oblige.

But I'm not the type of person who can just hook up with someone with no emotional attachment, at least I didn't use to be. My mother's sudden disappearance from our lives all those years ago affected Molly and me differently. Molly went through her adult life shunning all forms of committed relationships, thinking real love wasn't real life, whereas I coped another way. While Molly ran from love, I ran toward it, clung to it, hungered for it. That's why having to stay away from Brooklyn destroyed me. When Carla entered my life, I was convinced she was precisely what I needed to forget, to finally move on. But it wasn't enough. No matter what I gave her — the house of her dreams, a car that turned heads whenever she drove down the street, jewelry — it didn't make her happy. I didn't make her happy.

We didn't make her happy.

It took me months to get over the anger she caused when I learned she'd been cheating on me with one of my teammates, then left with no remorse for her actions. I'd just lost the one thing I was good at, being forced into retirement from one too many injuries. Losing her almost killed me. It wasn't her lack of love that affected me. It was the idea that I'd never feel love again. All it took was one look at my girls to make me realize I would. They were all I needed back then. And they still are today.

"Carla," I breathe, forcing her to tear her attention away from my daughters, my arms protectively in front of them, shielding them from her...her lack of empathy, her lack of compassion, her lack of love.

Overwhelmed with animosity, I don't even notice the little boy clutching her hand or the man at her side until he speaks. "Come on, bubba. Mama will be along." He nods at me, almost offering a silent apology. He must know who I am, why the tension in this small space is as thick as lava. Then Carla lets go of the little boy's hand, tousling his hair as he walks away with the man. Is she planning on abandoning them, too? Will she wake up one morning miserable with her life and decide to start over, leaving a tornado in her wake?

When she lifts her gaze to mine, tears are visible in the corners of her eyes. Her lips part, but no words come. I should walk away, but I'm glued to this spot. It's vindictive, but I want her to see how perfect the girls she tossed aside are. Want her to regret what she did to them, to me, to us. Want to take the knife she stabbed into our hearts and return the favor tenfold.

"Daddy?" Charlotte says, and we all snap our eyes to her. "Are we in trouble?"

Carla's lower lip quivers, having difficulty containing her emotions at the sound of Charlotte's angelic voice. She doesn't deserve to hear it, to be near her, to even see her.

Seemingly able to read my thoughts, Brooklyn steps forward, pulling Charlotte and Alyssa close to her. "Of course not. Why don't you two come with your auntie Brook and we'll go see the prisms, okay?" She steers them away from me, then glances over her shoulder. "Daddy will meet up with us in a minute."

Nodding, I offer her a smile, watching as three of the most important women in my life head away from the one woman I'd hoped to never see again.

"I can't…" There's a tremble in Carla's tone. I whip my fiery eyes back to her. She always was a good actress. She made me think she loved those girls when she never did. "They're so beautiful, Andrew."

All the anger I've suppressed the past six years

bubbles to the surface in the blink of an eye. I can get over the fact that she didn't love me, and I have. But I can never forgive her for what she did to those girls.

"Don't," I bark, my voice louder than I want, but I can't control it, not when it comes to protecting my girls from this woman. My jaw tightens, my fists clenching and unclenching as I struggle to work through the feelings rushing forward. "You don't get to say that about them. You lost that right years ago."

"I understand how you must feel," she responds softly. Her tone is a stark contrast to the woman I remember her to be.

When we first met, she carried herself in a way that made everyone notice her. She craved the attention, didn't care what she had to do to garner that attention. Now, she seems like a different person — reserved, aloof, withdrawn. While she once wore the tightest pair of pants and shirts that showed off her tiny stomach, she now dresses in more conservative attire — a sweater and jeans that don't look like they were painted on her skin. Her hair, no longer streaked with blonde highlights, is a deep chestnut. Her face isn't hidden behind layers of makeup. Gone is the dark eye shadowing and bright lips. In its place is just a subtle bit of color to bring out her eyes, cheekbones, and mouth. If I didn't say good night to two little girls who bear a striking resemblance to her every night for the past six years, I probably wouldn't have even recognized her.

"I don't think you do!" A heat fills me, my heart pounding in my chest, a vein twitching in my neck.

"I made some horrible mistakes when I was young." Her expression remains calm, unlike the Carla I married who would argue over the littlest things. She got upset easily, but that was one of the things I was drawn to...her passion. The sex when she was angry was incredible. But a relationship isn't sustainable on skin clawing and hair pulling. We're proof of that. "My biggest regret is..." She trails off, her lower lip quivering.

The old Carla never cried. She didn't get sad. She got angry. Closing her eyes, she draws in a deep breath to compose herself. When she opens them, there's a glint within, moisture pooling in the corners.

"My biggest regret is abandoning you and those girls. We weren't right for each other. We both knew that. At the time, all I cared about was myself. The only reason I even liked being pregnant was the attention I got at games because I was carrying Andrew Brinks' baby. In my mind, it made not being able to drink worth it. Nothing I say can ever make up for what I did."

"Six...years," I interrupt, an ache in my throat, in my chest, in my heart. "Six *fucking* years, Carla, without a single word. Six birthdays. Six Christmases. Six Easters. Nothing. Not even a goddamn card." My nostrils flare as I breathe in and out through my nose. Tears form in my eyes. Not at what I've had to endure because of her selfishness, but at what my girls did, although they don't know it. I've made sure of that. "At least they were both too young to remember you. At first, Alyssa would say 'Mama' every time I walked into her room to get her up from her crib. Thankfully, after a while, she stopped."

"I've wanted to reach out the past few years...once

I got my life together. My sponsor at AA suggested I do that, but I didn't know how, had no idea what to say. When I became a mother again, the guilt grew even more. I can't tell you how many times I took the train into the city and made my way to your father's café—"

"*My* café," I interrupt.

"Yes. Your café," she corrects. "But I could never work up the courage to go through those doors. I'd see you in there, and you looked happy. I didn't want to ruin that." She pauses, tilting her head as she surveys me. "And you look happy now, too."

"I am. Because of those two little girls you decided were forgettable. They're not. They're my world. I won't let you hurt them." Acid burning my stomach the longer I stay in this woman's presence, I push past her. When I sense her watching me, I pause, glancing over my shoulder. "So don't get any ideas that you can be a part of their lives now, even if you've finally realized leaving was a mistake. Those girls haven't needed you for the past six years. And they don't need you now."

I storm off, drawing in deep breath after deep breath to compose myself. The last thing I want is my girls to see me so worked up, wondering who that woman is and why she upset me.

As I approach the exhibit where Alyssa and Charlotte are *ooh*ing and *ahh*ing over all the colors reflected on the wall and floors by the prisms, Brooklyn senses my presence and snaps her attention away from them. Dropping their hands, she walks toward me, her analytical eyes seeming to assess every inch of me.

Without saying a word, she wraps her arms around my waist, squeezing me tightly. I momentarily still, then

323

pull her closer, sighing. I need this. The feeling of her warm, lithe body against me calms the fire raging within. It always has. Whenever I felt like my world was falling apart around me, she was the person I always went to. Right now, she's exactly what I need.

"Oh, Drew," she breathes. "I am *so* sorry." She pulls back, cupping my cheeks in her hands. "I can't even imagine what you're feeling right now."

I look deep into her eyes. "It's okay." While seeing Carla was the last thing I ever wanted, I refuse to let her get to me. I refuse to let the memories bring up everything I thought I finally buried. "Those girls are better off without her. They don't need her. They've had a better upbringing than she ever could have given them, thanks to Aunt Gigi, Molly...and you."

She brings herself onto her toes and places a tender kiss on my cheek. "Thank you." It's a simple gesture, but the feel of her soft, pink lips on my skin forces a tingle to run down my spine, easing my worry.

"Daddy?" Alyssa approaches, and Brooklyn steps away. "Are you okay?"

"Of course I am."

"But that woman...," she begins, always the observant one.

"She's no one, sweetie." When I grab her hand, she doesn't protest. "She's absolutely no one."

Chapter Twenty

BROOKLYN

BY THE TIME I pull up in front of my townhouse, the sun has long since disappeared beyond the horizon. I spent more time with Drew than I planned, but I didn't want to leave him. After his run-in with Carla, I could tell he was shaken up, regardless of his assurances that he was okay, that she didn't matter, but it wasn't true.

When she vanished from his life without a single word, other than divorce papers requesting no financial support, he never got any closure. To anyone else in a loveless marriage, as theirs had become, it would have been a proverbial "get out of jail free" card. But to Drew, it was another thing he lost. As much as he wanted to pretend he was all right, that the pain of what Carla did was nothing but a distant memory, it was obvious by his morose attitude the rest of the day that wasn't the case.

As I head up the walkway toward my front door, my own steps sluggish from the mere thought of how much Drew's hurting right now, I come to an abrupt stop when I see Wes sitting on the top step, leaning back against the newel post. I consider leaving, maybe driving back to Drew's to keep him company. A part of me worries he'll have Molly or Gigi come watch the girls so he can go see the woman he's been sleeping with. It's a physical relationship with no commitment, but I still hate the idea of them together, of her touching him, kissing him, screwing him. I've never been jealous of her before, but now, it irks me, even though I'm in a relationship myself...at least I'm supposed to be. I'm not sure anymore.

"Where were you today?" Wes asks in a low voice when I remain frozen.

I hesitate before answering, then blow out a breath, heading toward him. I could lie, but I won't do that to him, even if he deserves it. "At the science museum."

"With him?" He lifts his eyes to mine and my heart falls at the pain I see. His voice is tearful, his expression slack.

"Who?"

"You know who." He raises himself to his feet. "Were you with Drew?" There's a subtle tremble in his chin as he pulls his lips between his teeth, his entire body seeming to tighten.

I hate that he's hurting, but he brought this on himself. Even if he's not cheating on me with whomever I heard on the other end of the phone, he still lied. I can put up with a lot, and I have, but I refuse to be lied to, to be made a fool of. I've already hit my lifetime quota of that.

"Not that it's any of your business, but yes." I hold my chin high. "I went with him and his girls."

His shoulders deflate as he absorbs my response.

"Why?"

"It sucks, doesn't it? Expecting someone to be somewhere and finding out they're not," I bite back.

His spine straightens as he furrows his brow. "What's that supposed to mean?"

"Don't play dumb." I slip past him, heading toward the front door.

"Play dumb?" He follows close on my heels. "I don't know what you're talking about, Brooklyn. Do you have any idea how worried I've been? I tried calling. Repeatedly. We all did." He grips my arm, forcing me to face him. I gasp, about to berate him for touching me when he continues. "When I couldn't get a hold of you, I ended up calling every hospital in the greater Boston area."

"You did?" I swallow hard.

"Christ. Of course I did!" He releases his grip on me and paces my tiny porch, tugging on his hair. I study him, noticing how disheveled and weary he appears, a stark contrast to the put-together man I thought him to be. His tie is loose, his crisp white shirt untucked from a pair of wrinkled suit pants. "You weren't answering your phone. You weren't here. I kept thinking that something happened to you, and I had no way of knowing, of getting to you."

I peer into his pale blue eyes, his concern clear. But is it real? Or has it all been an act? Reminded why I chose this course of action, I shake off the regret at the idea of being the cause for his worry, firming my resolve. "Why? Guilty conscience?"

"About what?"

I cross my arms in front of my chest. "About where you were last night when you blew me off for dinner…a dinner I was looking forward to, considering how little time we seem to spend with each other these days."

He blinks, averting his eyes. "I told you. I had to work late."

"That *is* what you said." I lean into him, my proximity forcing his eyes back to mine. "After you canceled on me… I don't know." I throw up my hands in frustration. "I got this crazy notion in my head to surprise you at work. If you couldn't go out, I figured I could at least bring food to you. So imagine *my* surprise when I learned you hadn't been in the office since lunch." I press my lips into a tight line, my heart shrinking in my chest. "Care to tell me the name of whatever bimbo I heard in the background when you called?" I barely manage to choke out.

He keeps staring at me, a deer in the headlights, his mouth agape. I can sense the wheels turning, as if he's wracking his brain to come up with some excuse. But now that I've caught him in his lie, nothing can excuse his behavior. I should be grateful I learned the truth before giving my life to someone who would lie to me so recklessly, so carelessly. But I'm not. His lie makes me feel like a failure, like I'm not worth the truth. Like every other man has made me feel.

"So *that's* why I didn't show up today. And you know what? I'm done showing up. I'm…done. I deserve to be someone's priority, not just something else they have to deal with. I refuse to be an item on a to-do list." I spin around and retrieve my keys from my purse, inserting them into the doorknob.

Just as I open the door, Wes says, "Her name's Christy. She's a realtor the company works with on commercial plots."

I glance over my shoulder. "Then I suppose your mother will see that as a step up from a state employee from a blue-collar family."

"No. That's not what I mean." He grabs my arm, preventing me from hiding away inside my house. "The reason I lied to you, the reason I haven't been around much this week, is because I've been driving all over the greater Boston area looking for the perfect place for us."

I arch an eyebrow. "For us?"

"Yes." He releases his grasp on me and withdraws his phone from his pocket. After typing on it, he holds it out for me. I see an aerial view of a large parcel of land. "That's four acres in Wellesley for us to build our dream house."

"Our dream house?" I swallow through the tightness in my throat, my eyes glued to the image of the wooded area with a lake.

"I've searched everywhere for a house like the one you'd want."

"How do you know what house I'd want?" I press, still unsure if I should believe him.

"Because I listen to you, Brooklyn," he insists, his eyes intense. "You love where you grew up but wish you had more room to run around as a kid. You want a kitchen with a farmhouse sink overlooking the back yard, a large island, distressed white cabinets, and a wine cellar. The décor should be rustic chic, lots of metal and reclaimed wood. The master bedroom should be separate from the rest of the house, a private recluse, somewhere you can relax and unwind after a stressful day of saving the world, one abused kid at a time."

With each word, my guilt for ditching him today increases. There's a thickness in my throat as my stiff posture loosens, my shoulders drooping.

Noticing my anger waning, he steps toward me, his hand finding mine. He runs his fingers across my knuckles, the gesture soothing. "You want your own private study with built-in bookshelves, a large wrap-around porch, and a big tree in the front yard with a swing, like you had growing up."

My lips part as I stare at him, overwhelmed. "How did you know all that?"

"I told you, Brooklyn. I *listen*. Every word that has ever come out of that beautiful mouth has been permanently etched in my mind. Regardless of how trivial you may think they were, there's no such thing when it comes to you."

"But I never spoke about what I imagined for my dream house…"

"You didn't have to. How many times have you forced me to watch home improvement shows?"

I blush, smiling as I swallow my tears. But they're no longer tears of anger, of disgust. They're tears of happiness… Of love?

"A lot."

"And just by the look on your face, I could tell what you liked and what you didn't. I wanted to surprise you on our wedding day." He laughs slightly. "I had this vision in my head of leaving the reception, but instead of going to a hotel, I'd pull up to this breathtaking home."

"Oh, Wes..." I bring my body closer and he cups my cheeks in his hands, leaning his forehead on mine.

"You'd ask me where we were and I'd grin, not saying a word. You'd be wary at first, as you usually are, but your curiosity would get the better of you, as it usually does. You'd step out of the car and walk up the steps of the front porch, hoping your premonition was right. Your eyes would fall on a small, gift-wrapped box just in front of the door, your name on the tag. Inside would be a key, no other explanation."

I bite my lip to stop my chin from quivering, and Wes kisses the tear that escapes.

"I'd tell you to try it. You'd be skeptical, but you'd eventually put the key into the knob." He releases a short breath, a smile crossing his mouth, as if imagining it in his mind. "Your face would light up when it turned. The extra hours I spent making this happen would be worth it when you realized this was our home. Where we would build a life. Where we would raise our children. Where we would grow old together."

"My god, I'm so sorry," I exhale, pressing my lips to his, overwhelmed by how much this man cares for me. And what did I give him in return? Nothing. We've been dating the better part of a year. He's never shown any indication that he's the type of person to be unfaithful. In fact, his devotion has been nothing less than unwavering. But I was so eager to assume the worst, almost like I was looking for any excuse to walk away from him and straight into the arms of a man who's only caused me heartache. That ends today. From this moment on, Wes deserves every single bit of my attention, every ounce of devotion, every assurance of my love. Not Drew. That ship sailed years ago. And it needs to stay far off shore.

"No, *I'm* sorry. I never should have lied to you."

"You weren't lying. You were trying to surprise me. And I ruined that."

He smirks, the heat of his mouth so close to mine sending a shiver through me. "I'll just have to come up with something else to surprise you," he says flirtatiously.

"Oh yeah?" As I grip the lapels of his suit jacket, he pushes me back into the house, his lips never far from mine. "Like what?"

"I wouldn't want to ruin the surprise. But I do have something that might hold you over for the time being."

"And what's that?"

"This." In an instant, he gets down on one knee in front of me, grabbing my left hand in his. "I was just saying how I know you, how I listen to you, even when you're not talking. But I messed up."

"No, you didn't. I'm the one——"

"I'm not talking about that. I'm talking about last week when I asked you to marry me. Most of the girls I've dated would have wanted to be proposed to in public with people watching. And I thought since that's what they'd want, you'd want that to. But you're not them. Believe me. That's a good thing," he adds quickly. "You're unassuming, caring, and so beautifully pure. You don't care about money, about material things, about flying away to Paris for the weekend."

"True, but I did enjoy Paris." I chew on my bottom lip, immediately transported to the City of Lights, of kissing Wes in front of the Eiffel Tower. It didn't matter that there were hundreds of other couples snapping selfies as they did the same thing. In that moment, I felt like it was just us. I want to get back to that feeling. I *need* to get back to that feeling.

"I'm glad. But I still messed up the first time I got down on one knee and asked you to marry me. When the ring didn't fit, I worried it was a sign that our marriage was doomed. It *was* a sign, but not about our relationship. It was the kick in the pants I needed to realize that you're not like most women. It gave me the opportunity to give you the proposal you deserve...and the ring you deserve."

In one smooth motion, he withdraws a black velvet box from his jacket and flips it open. This time, instead of an over-the-top marquis-cut diamond with stones covering the wide band, I stare at a simple round-cut diamond. It's a decent-sized stone, but the band is thin, tiny diamonds inlaid into the entire circumference. It's exactly what I've always pictured.

"Brooklyn Rose Tanner," he begins and I stare at him. "I am madly, completely, irrationally in love with you. It doesn't make sense, but I guess love never does. I love the way you make my entire body perk up when you walk into a room. I don't even have to see you to know you're near, your mere presence causing an electricity to flow through me, a buzz in the air."

My lips lift as his words bathe me with the love I need from him right now. I'm no longer thinking that I've experienced the same reaction to another man. No more. This man kneeling before me is proposing again…for me. Because it's what *I* need. And he knows this without me even saying a word. This is the man I should devote my time and energy to, not someone who's perpetually emotionally unavailable, or at least he conveniently was until I got engaged.

"I love the way you hold your breath when you're excited about something, and I hope I can always make you excited…in more ways than one." He winks. I can't help but laugh. It's like the missing piece in the puzzle of my life has finally snapped into place.

"But mostly, I love the way you care for others." He takes the ring out of the box and brings it up to my finger. This time, there's no hesitation or anxiety filling me. There's no darting eyes at my surroundings. Even if we were in public, it wouldn't matter. Wes is all I see. And he's all I want to see for the rest of my life.

"All those children under your supervision are blessed to have you looking out for them, for advocating on their behalf so they have a chance at a better future than what they were initially handed. The world needs more people with a heart as pure as yours. And I'm forever blessed that you found it in that heart to let me in, to show me how beautiful it truly is. And I'll be eternally grateful if you find room in your heart to love me for the rest of your life."

Tears obscure my vision, a kaleidoscope of prisms distorting everything. Everything except Wes.

"So please, my amazing Brooklyn Rose, choose me,

love me…" He meets my eyes, his own awash with emotion. This moment is perfection. I don't even ponder why he asked me to choose him. It doesn't matter. All that does is how his words make me feel. For the first time, I feel venerated, adored…loved. Wes is right. This is what I deserve. "Marry me," he finishes with a quiver.

There's not so much as a hint of hesitation this time. "Yes."

He slides the ring onto my finger. A perfect fit. When he stands, I clutch his cheeks in my hands, kissing him, my tears continuing to fall. He pulls me to him, his tongue brushing against my lips. I open for him and he kisses me in a way he never has, leaving me breathless, thoughtless, mindless.

When he pulls away, his clear blue eyes meet mine. "I'll admit, I was kind of nervous you wouldn't say yes."

I laugh, wiping at my tears. "After that proposal? No girl in her right mind would say no to that." My arms wrap around his neck, my lips hovering near his.

"I don't care what most women would say. All I care is what *you* would say. And I'm so glad you gave me a chance to make it right."

"Me, too." I bite my lip, passing him a demure look as I reach for the buttons on his shirt, slowly undoing the top one. "Now, let *me* have a chance to make it right."

He cocks a brow. "What did you have in mind?"

When I finish unbuttoning his shirt, I run my hands down his firm chest. "You'll see," I murmur, then grab his hand, tugging him up the stairs and into the bedroom.

The instant we cross the threshold, I drop my hold on him and spin around. My eyes trained on his, I lift my shirt over my head. This is a dance we've done many times before, but it feels different. I'm finally ready to give him all of me, even that piece of myself that's been holding out hope for someone else. I'm ready to give Wes my heart.

I lower my jeans and panties down my long legs, then unfasten my bra, allowing it to fall to the floor. A heat builds in his eyes as I stand exposed before him. Fisting the fabric of his open shirt, I bring him toward me. Our mouths find each other and he breathes into me. My chest presses against his, our kiss an erotic filling of lungs.

"Make love to me," I beg.

Without a word, he gently pushes me back until my legs hit the mattress, his eyes never leaving mine. And I don't want them to. I never want to stop staring into his peaceful deep pools of blue, the connection keeping me here with him, keeping me from thinking of anyone but him. He shrugs off his shirt, then steps out of his pants before lowering me onto the mattress. My heart pounds in my chest as he crawls on top of me, his mouth on my neck, hands on my skin. I claw at his back, finding the waistband of his boxers and pushing them down.

"I need to feel you." I pulse against him, running my fingers through his hair.

He pulls back, peering down at me, a playful look about him. I like this. He's not the serious man I know him to be in his professional life. He's the hopeless romantic who stalked me at the café until I finally agreed to go out with him. He's the charismatic man who called in a favor so my dad could throw a pitch at Fenway Park after hours. And he's the devoted man who's willing to give me the rest of his days.

"I love you so much, Brooklyn."

I smile, my body relaxing. "I love you, too."

"I'll never tire of hearing you say that."

Opening the nightstand drawer, he reaches for a condom and rolls it on. The instant he enters me, all my tension disintegrates, the bliss and ecstasy coursing through me exactly what I need right now. *Wes* is exactly what I need.

No one else.

Chapter Twenty-One

DREW

I STARE AT THE calendar on the desk in my office, looking at today's date — April twenty-sixth. It's been nearly four weeks since I've last seen Brooklyn. I don't know what to make of it. We left each other on good terms. She even hugged me, kissing my cheek, encouraging me to brush off our surprise visit with Carla.

Since then, she's disappeared from my life, from all our lives. There's been no more Friday morning coffee at the café. She even canceled on Sunday dinner the past four weeks, texting Molly an excuse about working overtime. Whenever I've tried calling, she messaged back, claiming she couldn't talk, that she was with a client or in court. I even dropped by her house several times, but her place was dark, no life to be seen.

Maybe I'm over-analyzing the situation, but I can't shake the feeling she's trying to avoid me. I thought we made progress that day at the science museum. If I didn't know any better, I would have thought I dreamt it all.

As I reach for my cell, about to try to get a hold of

her, there's a knock on my office door.

"Come in," I call out, expecting it to be one of the assistant coaches or players needing something from me. When the door opens, I glance up, doing a double take when Skylar saunters toward me.

"Sky, what are you doing here?" I quickly stand, my brows furrowed. I shoot my eyes to my phone, clicking off the screen, hiding Brooklyn's contact. Why does it matter? Brooklyn's a friend. And Sky... Well, she's... I'm not even sure. Fuck-buddy sounds crass, but I suppose that's what she is.

"You've been avoiding me, Andrew Brinks," she coos, pressing her hands to my chest as she lifts her lips to meet mine.

The past month seems to evaporate from my mind as my body's autopilot turns on, my mouth lowering to hers. The instant our lips touch, the tension that's been building over the past several weeks lessens.

"Any reason in particular?" she asks, taking my bottom lip between her teeth, tugging at it. That's all it takes to cause a slight twitching in my pants. I'm nowhere near as turned on as I was the few times Brooklyn and I almost kissed, but it's still something.

"I've been busy."

"Too busy to stop by when I invite you over?" she pouts.

I inwardly groan. This is why I've always avoided serious relationships. My girls come first, no question. Not many women understand that. Or maybe just not many of the types of women I typically date do.

339

"I've had a lot going on." I withdraw from her, running my hand through my hair.

"Like what?" She sits on the corner of my desk, the short skirt she's wearing riding up even more.

"I won't bore you with the details." I return to my chair, rearranging the files scattered all over the surface of the desk to make it look like I'm busy so she'd leave. Unfortunately, she doesn't get the hint.

"I don't mind. I want you to share these things with me, Andrew." She inches toward me, her voice borderline whiny.

"You do?" I lift my eyes to hers, arching a single brow.

"Of course." She pauses, taking a deep breath.

For an instant, I see a bit of vulnerability. It's a different look for her. She's usually confident. It's one of the things that attracted me to her when we first met. She knows what she wants and goes after it. She wanted me, but not the trappings of a traditional relationship. I wanted the same things. It was the perfect arrangement. But after the way we left things the last time we saw each other, I get the feeling it's no longer enough for her, that we've hit our expiration date.

"These past several weeks I haven't seen you made me realize how much I do care for you."

"You do?"

"I know this was just supposed to be fun, a way for both of us to blow off some steam, but I've missed you." Peering at me through seductive eyes, she hooks her foot in my rolling chair and drags me closer. "Didn't you miss me?" She wraps her arms around my neck, slithering off the desk and onto my lap, straddling me.

A few weeks ago, I would have pushed her panties aside and screwed her in this very position, not caring who might hear us. But I haven't given Skylar a second thought since the morning Brooklyn stopped by the hockey rink and I almost kissed her. The only woman on my mind lately, the only woman who matters, is Brooklyn. I suppose she always has been.

"Skylar…"

She pulls back, shaking her head in what I can only describe as disappointment mixed with a side of confirmation. "I've heard that tone before. Why do I get the feeling I won't like what you're about to say?"

"Because you probably won't."

She raises herself off me and crosses her arms in front of her chest, glaring. "Well then, get on with it."

I stand, looking at her with a mixture of compassion and indifference. "I told you from the beginning I wasn't looking for a serious relationship."

Her expression softening, she approaches me once more, running her hand down my chest. "And I thought the same thing. But it seems more girls I went to college with are settling down, having families. It got me thinking about what's next for me. We could be good together, if you just give me a chance, Andrew."

I release a heavy sigh, rubbing my temples. "That may be so," I agree, not wanting to tell her she's not even close to the type of woman I see myself forming a long-term relationship with. She's exactly like every other girl I've dated — pretty, young, petite, and somewhat lacking in the intelligence department. I suppose not feeling any more than a physical attraction has always helped me guard my heart. "But there are other considerations I need to think about."

"Of course," she sneers, rolling her eyes. "Your kids."

My jaw firms, my position unwavering. "Yes. They're young. They need stability."

A hand caresses my arm, her gesture unlike her normal advances toward me. She's compassionate, warm, at complete odds with the almost predatory woman I thought her to be. "I can give you that."

I stare deep into her pleading eyes, wishing I could believe her. She reminds me too much of Carla. Skylar's young, a dancer for the Celtics. I know her type. She's interested in me now because she likes being able to attach her name to mine. Eventually, someone with more star power will come along and she'll trade up. I can't put my girls through that again.

"Maybe you can, but I'm not willing to take the risk."

"So… What?" She reels back, her eyes on fire, her voice a high-pitched shriek. It's a complete one-eighty from her kindhearted demeanor a second ago. "That's it? All you were interested in was an occasional booty call whenever it suited you?"

"You knew what this was when you signed up, Skylar. I never misled you."

In a last-ditch effort, she grabs my belt, tugging me toward her. She palms my crotch, but my body refuses to ignite. "Can you really stand there and tell me you're

342

willing to walk away from this?" She lifts herself onto her toes, her lips trailing along my neck. It still does nothing for me. "Even you have to admit the sex has been amazing."

"Yes, it has." I grasp her hand and remove it, stepping away. "But I've had amazing sex before. Hell, I *married* amazing sex. And it walked out on me, on all of us, when something better came along. I'm glad you're looking for something more serious, and I'm sure you'll make another man very happy. I won't lie to you and promise to try when my heart isn't in it. No one deserves to be played with, and that wasn't my intention. If you feel I did, I apologize, but I can't give you what you want. If you can't accept that, I don't know what else to say."

Her lip curls, the coldness in her eyes causing a chill to trickle down my spine. Before I can placate her further, she reels back, landing a hard slap to my cheek, momentarily surprising me. It stings, but I suffered much more brutal attacks on the ice. Her palm against my face is no more than a pinprick in comparison.

"What was that for?" I ask, unfazed.

"For using me."

"I'm sorry you think that," I answer in a calm tone, which only makes her even more upset, the vein in her forehead twitching, her face reddening.

"You think you can just fuck me for six months, then when I want to get serious, use those kids as an excuse?"

I remain silent, refusing to respond to her outburst. This isn't the first time a woman I'm casually seeing

343

wants to take things to the next level. It usually happens around the four-month mark. But I've always remained clear in my intentions. I've never engaged in conversations regarding any dreams for a future. I even told them they were free to move on or see other people when they felt the need. It may make me sound like a prick, but it's the best I can offer anyone at this point in my life.

"Well, I have news for you. You won't always be able to use them as an excuse. One day, they'll be adults and in relationships of their own, leaving you all alone, wishing you didn't turn me down."

"Perhaps, but right now, those kids *are* my priority. And as long as they remain my responsibility, my stance on this is firm."

She pauses, stammering, trying to come up with anything to convince me to reconsider my position, but nothing will. Realizing that, she huffs, stomping toward the doorway. As she's about to disappear down the hallway, she whirls around, her eyes on fire.

"For the record, I've had better sex."

"Duly noted."

My response not what she expected, she opens her mouth, then snaps it shut, storming off.

I hold my breath, waiting to see if she's going to stomp back in for yet another attempt to persuade me to change my mind. When she doesn't, I slump into my chair with a sigh, rubbing my temples.

"I've got to stop sleeping with girls under thirty," I mutter to myself.

"That's probably a good idea," a female voice quips.

I whip my head up. My heart immediately drops to the pit of my stomach, and I can't help but think I did something to piss off the big man upstairs. First, Skylar shows up to convince me to take things to the next level. And now Carla. Again.

"What do you want?" I bark.

She hesitates, chewing on her bottom lip, tugging on the hem of her suit jacket. The way she carries herself makes her appear nervous. When we were together, she didn't have a shy or uncertain bone in her body. She did what she wanted without a care for what anyone thought.

"Do you mind if I sit?"

I glower at her. "It doesn't matter what I want. You'll do whatever you want, regardless of my feelings."

Her hopeful expression falls as she averts her eyes. "Please, Andrew. I've been trying to work up the courage to come here ever since I ran into you almost a month ago."

"Back in the area now, are you? Last I heard, you'd left Chase and were working as a waitress in one of the Indian casinos in Connecticut."

"Yes. That's where I met Rob, my husband. We relocated here for his work a few years ago."

"How nice." My tone is filled with sarcasm. "So tell me what you want, then leave. And next time you get the urge to come see me, I recommend you skip the family reunion because I'm not interested in catching up." I cross my arms in front of my chest, leaning back in my large chair.

She rocks on her heels, taking a moment to collect her thoughts. "I've been doing a lot of thinking over the past few weeks. After seeing you and the girls, the guilt and regret..." She meets my hardened stare, undeterred by the harshness in my gaze. "I've often wondered about them. What shows they like to watch. What their favorite colors are. If you taught them how to skate, like I have a feeling you did, considering you bought Alyssa skates when she wasn't even born yet." Her lips lift slightly in the corners.

"All things you would have known if you weren't selfish and abandoned them." Standing, I place my palms on the desk, leaning into her, my imposing frame dwarfing hers. I hate that she's here, that she's speaking so fondly of my kids. "After learning I couldn't play hockey anymore, I was going through the worst time in my life. Instead of being there for us, you checked out, started sleeping with the guy who took my place on the ice." My jaw clenches and my nose turns up in disgust. "So I don't owe you anything, not a single iota of information about how those girls are thriving, what they like to do, what they like to eat. The minute you disappeared, having full knowledge of what my mother had done to us, how it affected us, you were dead to me."

She shifts on her feet, stepping away from the large wooden desk and toward a sitting area containing a couch and a love seat. Her eyes scan the framed photos and newspaper clippings hanging there, many of which used to adorn the walls of the café. Once I took this job,

I brought them here so the place would seem more like a trendy coffee shop and bar rather than a memorial to my fallen hockey career.

"Do you miss it?" She glances over her shoulder, then fully turns toward me. "The thrill of the ice? Hearing tens of thousands of people cheering your name?"

"Of course I do." My expression softens, my voice laced with longing. "For as long as I can remember, the only thing I wanted was to play hockey. I worked my tail off, sacrificing everything to make that happen. So when I had to retire after a few seasons..." I shake my head, the anger bubbling back to the surface. "It killed me." I look away, feeling exposed. Clearing my throat, I straighten my spine, returning my emotionless eyes to hers. "So, as much as I've enjoyed this little trip down memory lane, why don't you tell me why you're here."

She squares her shoulders, drawing in a deep breath. I have a feeling I'm not going to like whatever she's about to say, but nothing could have prepared me for the words that fall from her mouth.

"I'd like to get to know them. Alyssa and Charlotte. I'd like to be a part of their lives. I'd like them to get to know their brother."

I stare at her, mouth agape, eyes wide. Then I break out into a laugh, thinking I must be in some alternate universe. "You're joking, right?"

"You have to realize how difficult it was for me to come here and ask this of you. I know I haven't given you any reason to want to grant my request, but—"

"You're right," I interrupt with a snarl. "You

347

haven't. And if you think I'll ever let you near those two girls just so you can destroy them, you're sadly mistaken." My voice booms against the walls of my office. I'm sure the other members of the athletic staff can hear, but I don't care. I can't control my emotions, not when it comes to those girls. Especially when it comes to what Carla did to them. "So get out of my sight right now or I will call security and have you escorted out of here."

She raises her palms toward me in a sign of surrender. "Fine. At least I know I tried to do the right thing." She heads toward the door.

"The right thing?" I shoot back in disbelief, following her. "So now you're interested in doing the right thing? You're about six years too late for that, Carla."

She faces me, her expression still calm, despite my outburst. "I get that I hurt you, Andrew. And you can hate me every day for the rest of your life. But don't those girls deserve to know their mother?"

"Mother? Are you seriously referring to yourself as their mother? That term deserves respect, admiration. You are *not* their mother. Even though you gave birth to them, that does not make you their mom."

"At some point, they're going to have questions and will no longer be satisfied with whatever answer you've been giving them. You can't keep them from me forever."

I widen my stance, my fiery eyes glaring down on her. Like the Carla I used to know, she doesn't flinch. "Is that a threat? Because I assure you, I will do whatever it takes to keep those girls safe, to protect

348

them from feeling even an ounce of pain."

"It's not a threat," she sighs, her tone even. "I'm simply stating a fact. They'll eventually wonder where they came from, who their biological mother is. They'll want to know more than that I left. What are you going to tell them then?"

"The same thing I have for years. That they don't need to worry about that because their mother was a fucking coward. The only mothers they need to concern themselves with are the women in my life who stepped in when *you* bailed."

"You claim I was selfish to leave like I did. And I was. I admit that." She briefly looks to the ceiling, blowing out a small breath. "God, I'd do anything to go back in time and tell my younger self to think about what she's doing, but I can't. I don't have a machine that can send me back to the day I made the worst decision of my life. I can't take it back. But I can try to make it right going forward. So please. I beg you, Andrew. Stop thinking about how much I hurt you. Instead, think about what's best for the girls. I'm sure you've made mistakes you regret, things you wish you could change. Just… Just think about it."

Her words ring in the air between us for a moment before she turns, leaving me alone to stew. If I hated her before, my animosity has increased at the thought of her being a part of my girls' lives. I was the one who changed their diapers, who sang them to sleep when they woke from a nightmare, who cleaned their cuts and scrapes when they fell. She doesn't get to waltz back into their lives and pretend the last six years never happened.

Fuming, I slam the door, the impact causing one of the framed photos to fall to the floor, the glass shattering. It takes all the restraint I possess to not punch the cement wall and scream. That woman is delusional if she thinks I'll willingly allow her access to *my* girls. I don't care what it takes. I'll fight her every step of the way.

Chapter Twenty-Two

BROOKLYN

PINKS AND PURPLES FILL my vision. A floral arrangement here. A serviette there. Polite chatter surrounds me, but I don't hear a word that's said. Instead, I smile, feigning interest as Mrs. Bradford parades me in front of her friends who have assembled at the Cambridge Tea Room for my bridal shower. Every single one of them is unfamiliar, many having flown here from Georgia just for the occasion. Mrs. Bradford doesn't let me forget that fact, either, repeatedly commenting it would have been easier on all involved if I had agreed to have the bridal shower and wedding down south.

As I listen to their conversations, I have to fight my desire to roll my eyes. These women are well-off members of southern social circles. They speak of their vacation homes in Palm Beach or the Hamptons, their ski chalets in Aspen or Sun Valley, their yachts and cars. This lifestyle is so foreign. I feel like I have nothing to add to the conversation. Worse, some of them look upon me, their noses raised, as if I'm nothing more than another one of Wes' charity projects, like he found me in the slums and provided a chance at a better life. Is that how he sees me? As just another charity project?

Over the past several weeks, I've devoted all my attention to Wes and making things work between us. After his beautiful second proposal, he deserved nothing less. As he made love to me over and over again that night, I was convinced we had finally found our place as a couple, that our love would be strong enough to survive anything life threw at us.

But the following morning, it felt like the night before never happened. Wes was back to being the serious workaholic I knew him to be. I imagined spending a lazy Sunday in bed with him, something we'd never done. Instead, he got up early and went into the office, saying he was behind on a bunch of projects. I tried not to act disappointed, tried not to be overly clingy, but I needed Wes. Being with him is the only thing that quiets the doubts. With him, I'm at peace in the path I've chosen. Away from him, turmoil clouds everything else. Am I doing the right thing? Am I willing to forgo excitement and passion for dependability?

"And you're still planning to start school in the fall?" an annoyingly pleasant voice asks, bringing my attention away from the overtly feminine decorations that seem more suitable for a baby shower. Even the mountain of gifts adorning the long table at the head of the room are wrapped in shades of purple and pink. My two least favorite colors.

I smile at the petite woman with blonde hair wearing a floral dress. I can't remember her name, but Mrs. Bradford introduced her as the wife of one of their high-paying clients at the architecture firm. "Yes, I am."

"That's admirable, what with Wes soon taking the helm at the company and everything."

I furrow my brow. "He is?"

"Of course, dear. At least that's my understanding." She nods toward Mrs. Bradford. "Joel says your husband is ready to retire and hand the reins over."

"That's correct," she confirms in that smooth southern accent of hers. "My dear James claims work's impeded his golf game."

There's a fluttering of polite laughter as I stand there, a deer caught in the headlights. Why didn't Wes say anything? This is a big deal. He's worked his entire life to follow in his father's footsteps. He studied hard, graduating at the top of his class. He does everything he can to bring new and innovative ideas to the firm, hoping to show his father he's ready to take over. Why didn't he share this important development with me? Then again, I've kept so much from him, too, but I'm trying to get better. I'm trying to make an effort. Is he?

"Now that you mention it, he may have said something to that effect." I grit a fake smile. "We've just been so busy with agreeing on blueprints for the new house and getting all the contractors lined up, it must have slipped my mind."

"I don't know why he's even going through the trouble when he'll need to move back to Atlanta if he wants to run the company," Mrs. Bradford interjects. This time, I can't hide my surprise, shooting wide eyes to hers. Her expression is self-righteous and smug. "You can't expect him to run things from here, can you?"

"I…"

I feel blindsided, unsure what to say. From the beginning, I've known Wes had his sights set on taking over the company, of propelling it to the next level, focusing on greater sustainability and less environmental impact. Never did I think he'd have to go back to Atlanta to do that.

Does he think I'll just leave my home? Sacrifice the work I've put in to get this far in my career just to give it up, like his mother hopes I will? Is this why he wanted to get married so soon? So he could trap me into the marriage, leaving me no choice but to follow him wherever he wants to go? The idea makes me sick.

"Dear me…," the woman says, appearing genuinely remorseful. "It's not my place to say. I should never have opened my mouth, considering how full your hands are with planning a wedding."

I force a smile, pretending this news doesn't hit me in the gut like it does. "It's all right." I raise my lemonade to my lips, bracing for the sugary concoction to assault my taste buds. I would give anything to have a flask of rum or vodka. Hopefully Molly will come better prepared than me, even though she's pregnant. "Thankfully, Mrs. Bradford's been an enormous help in that regard. She's taken the guesswork out of everything." I try to hide the annoyance in my tone. "All I have to do is show up when she tells me. She even made sure I had the perfect dress to wear today."

I survey the bright white, A-line sundress with more layers of tulle than necessary. She claims she'd bought it for Julia, Wes' sister, to wear to her bridal shower. That was before she up and eloped. When I first heard the story, I wondered why anyone would give up having the wedding of their dreams. However, after the past month of pre-wedding appointments and festivities, I know why she did it.

"Oh, come now," Mrs. Bradford interjects, her lips turning up into a smile as fake as most of these women's boobs. "You make it sound like I'm making *all* the decisions. We both know that's not true. You chose your own wedding dress, even after I spent hours pre-selecting ones that would complement the look the planner had envisioned. Now she has to scramble to change gears and redesign everything." She lowers her voice. "I'm still not sure *how* you were able to pay for the dress on your own."

"Like I told you, it was an early wedding gift from Molly." I take another sip of my lemonade, hoping she can't hear the shakiness in my tone. I can't exactly tell her Drew paid for the dress. She doesn't know our history, but it would only encourage questions...ones I don't want to answer. I still grow uneasy about how I'll feel walking down the aisle to Wes adorned in a dress Drew bought me.

"I guess there's quite a bit of money in writing porn," Mrs. Bradford comments rudely, making her distaste for my best friend clear. The instant she learned what Molly did for a living, she's harbored nothing but animosity for her.

"She doesn't write porn," I respond in an even tone. "She's a romance author. One of the most successful romance authors out there today, to be precise."

Mrs. Bradford looks back to her circle of friends and mutters, "Like I said, she writes porn."

"We prefer if you call it 'mommy porn'," a voice cuts through. I fling my eyes to where Molly stands, her arms crossed over her stomach that seems to have ballooned in size almost overnight. Then again, I haven't seen her much recently.

After Wes' proposal do-over, I realized spending time with Drew was clouding my rationale, messing with my brain. Never again did I want to see the pained expression that adorned Wes' face when he learned I ditched our wedding responsibilities to spend time with Drew. So I've kept my distance from him. Unfortunately, that also means keeping my distance from Molly, Gigi, and the girls. I haven't blown him off altogether, but our interactions are at a minimum, just enough so he doesn't get suspicious and try to ruin what I've been working on with Wes. I hate it, but I can't think of a better way.

"Actually, we prefer if you don't even use that term, since it degrades the amount of time, effort, and creativity it takes to write a book." Her statement is met with silence before she continues. "Have any of you ever written a book?"

The silence only grows as everyone avoids Molly's gaze, obviously embarrassed she overheard the conversation. This is one of the things about Molly I've always admired. She doesn't care what others think of her. And she has no problem speaking her mind. There are times I wish I could be more like that.

"By the lack of response, I'm assuming none of you have. So you have no idea how many hours go into crafting a story, developing characters, making the reader want to root for those characters, using the only tool you possess, your words, to make your reader physically feel the connection between your characters. Romance is one of the hardest genres to write, but I love it. And billions of readers love it, too. So you can stand there and pretend you're too good to read romance, but I'm pretty sure you all have so-called 'trashy' books downloaded onto your e-readers that you read one-handed."

Eyes widen in response as I struggle to stifle a laugh. I look at her, her lips formed into a satisfied smirk. I've never been more happy to see Molly. I need this right now, need to joke and laugh with my best friend like we used to before life got complicated.

"If you'll be so kind as to excuse us, I need to steal the bride for a minute. You know. Maid of honor stuff."

She grips my hand and tugs me away from Mrs. Bradford and her minions, heading straight to an *hors d'oeuvres* station. Without saying a word, she grabs a plate and proceeds to pile it high with every type of finger food available, sometimes taking two or three of each.

"Hungry?" I ask timidly, waiting for her to unleash her anger at my disappearing act over the past month.

"Starving. Fuck this eating for two bullshit. I feel like I'm eating for ten."

I look around the room, a few familiar faces still missing. "Is Aunt Gigi coming?" I wouldn't blame her if she doesn't show.

Molly narrows her eyes at me. "Why? Think she'll blow you off just because you've been avoiding us lately?"

"I haven't been avoiding you," I argue. "We've seen each other at least once a week."

"*We've* seen each other," she emphasizes, gesturing between our two bodies. "You haven't seen anyone else. Gigi, the girls... Drew."

"Like I told you. I've been swamped with work."

"Mmm-hmm. Good luck with that."

"With what?"

"With that story. You know how Gigi can be." She nods at the entrance. I follow her line of sight to see her aunt heading toward us, Alyssa and Charlotte on either side of her. The second Charlotte sees me, she breaks into a run, the joy on her face melting my heart.

I crouch down, taking her into my arms as she barrels into me. "Auntie Brook! I've missed you so much."

I sigh, basking in Charlotte's tiny arms squeezing me tightly. "I've missed you, too, peanut. So much." I pull back so she can see the sincerity in my eyes.

"Why haven't you been at dinner?" Her happy expression falls, and I hate that I'm the cause of it.

What can I possibly tell her? That her father's always been my one weakness and I need to stay as far away as possible for my own sanity? She'll never understand why I need to distance myself from him. No one will. No one knows about that one night I finally let my guard down only to learn the passing of the years hadn't changed anything. I was still just as invisible to to Drew as a twenty-five-year-old woman as when I was a fifteen-year-old girl. I almost made that same mistake again…before Wes reminded me of what's important.

"Auntie Brook's been very busy with work. Isn't that right?" Gigi says pointedly.

"That's right." I raise myself back to standing, meeting her eyes.

"Will you be coming tomorrow night?" Alyssa asks.

"Yes, Brooklyn." Gigi crosses her arms in front of her chest, giving me a sanctimonious smile. "Will you be attending family dinner tomorrow night? Or have you forgotten what's important?"

"I haven't forgotten what's important."

"So you'll be there then?" She arches a brow.

I refocus my attention on Alyssa and Charlotte. "I'll try my best."

Aunt Gigi lets out an irritated sigh just as Mrs. Bradford's voice cuts through the room, telling everyone to please find their assigned seats for the first course. I've never been more grateful for the interruption.

"Come on, girls." I reach toward Alyssa and Charlotte. They both take a hand without complaint. "You're at my table. And I want to hear everything you've been up to the past few weeks."

"Alyssa has a new boyfriend," Charlotte volunteers excitedly.

I look from Charlotte to Alyssa, both dressed in the same green and white floral dress. "You do?"

She shrugs sheepishly.

"And what's his name?"

359

"Connor."

"He has a Yankees backpack," Charlotte offers. "Daddy says he's not allowed in our house. *Ever*."

We all burst out laughing.

"If I know your father, I have a feeling he most likely wouldn't be allowed into your house anyway, but the Yankees thing makes it a certainty."

"Yeah," Alyssa agrees as we approach the table, the two girls sitting on either side of me. "At least he's not a Canadiens fan."

"That would not go over well with your father at all." I lift my water to my lips, basking in the familiarity of these people. A ball of regret forms in my stomach from avoiding them the past month, but what choice did I have? There isn't room in my heart for both Wes and Drew, so I had to make a decision…one I should have made a long time ago.

Chapter Twenty-Three

BROOKLYN

U NWRAPPED GIFTS LAY SCATTERED before me, like shells lost to the sea. I can't remember ever registering for anything. I didn't even know we had a registry. Again, Mrs. Bradford must have made all the decisions regarding what items her son and his future wife should have in their home. I'm not sure if I should be grateful or extremely creeped out by the idea that she picked out the expensive Egyptian cotton bedsheets we'll be having sex on.

The entire shower has seemed like one big spectacle, every woman in attendance trying to one up the other with the gift they bought, even though they barely know me. I've never wanted to be somewhere else more than I do right now. I pray this display is almost over so I can disappear into my townhouse for some much-needed "me" time. I eventually need to talk to Wes about what it means for us if he takes over the company, but after this afternoon, I just want to forget about everything…about the wedding, about the house, about my future.

I stand from the chair placed in the front of the room, plastering a fake smile on my face as I address everyone. "Thank you for coming today. Your generosity means so much to Wes and me." I swallow hard, heat rushing over me when I meet Aunt Gigi's eyes. This woman practically raised me. If anyone can sense the indecision plaguing me, she can. These past few weeks have been nothing short of an emotional roller coaster. One minute, I'm certain I'm on the right path. The next, I'm questioning everything. Now faced with the possibility of Wes relocating to Atlanta, I'm even more unsure. "I'm looking forward to celebrating our marriage with all of you, as well." My voice is anything but convincing.

A few guests in attendance begin to stir, the party winding down, when Molly jumps up from her seat beside mine. "Wait. The fun's not quite over yet. No bridal shower is complete without a game."

I fling my eyes to her, shooting daggers.

She ignores my stare, continuing to address the room. "To make this as authentic and entertaining as possible, we didn't tell the bride what we were up to. Thankfully, Mrs. Bradford offered her assistance." She nods at my future mother-in-law. I wonder why these two would willingly work together on anything, unless they had a common goal. My stomach rolls at what that could be.

From the beginning, Mrs. Bradford has made it clear she isn't exactly a fan of my marriage to Wes. And I know for a fact Molly thinks this is a bad idea, even though she's repeatedly stated if this is what I want, she'll support me. Now I worry I won't like what's about to take place.

"So everyone gather 'round and make sure you can

362

see." Molly claps excitedly, turning to set up her laptop on the table behind me. I approach her, leaning close.

"What are you doing?" I hiss under my breath. "I didn't want a shower in the first place, but Mrs. Bradford insisted. You said it would be okay, that you'd do everything to make it as enjoyable as possible. A stupid shower game is *not* enjoyable. You know this."

She faces me with a sigh, her eyes soothing. She runs her hands up and down my arms, comforting me. "I promise. This isn't a stupid shower game. Trust me. Do you think I'd resort to doing a lame scavenger hunt for items we find in people's purses?" she scoffs. "Give me a little credit. I'm much more creative than that."

"That's what scares me, Molly."

"Come on," she encourages. "Have I ever steered you wrong before?"

"I can name a few such occasions, like our weekend getaway to the Cape one summer during college. I'm pretty sure that place you found for us to stay in has since been condemned." My stare softens as the memory returns. I didn't grow up accustomed to the finer things in life, but I did like things clean, free from grime...and used condoms littering the floor. It wasn't amusing at the time, but now I look back and laugh at the memory of the dump she booked.

"True, but you trusted me when I said it would work out, and it did, didn't it?"

"I suppose." It's true. Instead of abandoning our plans, we found a campground on the beach and stayed there. We made friends with several other college students who were camping there, and are still in touch

363

with several of them.

"It just goes to show, you may not like my ideas, but you always learn to appreciate them. So please, play along. I promise, you'll appreciate this, too." She places her hands on my shoulders and forces me back into the chair decorated to look like a cheesy throne, streamers and bows adorning it with the word "bride" on the back.

Returning her attention to the guests, she smiles a fabricated smile, oozing excitement. "We're going to play a version of the *Newlywed Game*."

There's polite clapping, along with some laughs, a stark juxtaposition to the dread filling me at the idea of sitting here and answering questions about Wes. True, I've been trying to make time for him, but even when we're together, it doesn't seem like either one of us is present. My nose is usually stuck in a book, getting a jump-start on some recommended reading for my upcoming curriculum. Wes is typically glued to his tablet, drawing up plans or checking specs on whatever project has his attention that day. We never just sit and talk.

"First question." Molly's voice sounds muffled and far away. "What is Wes' favorite movie?"

I stare straight ahead, not seeing anyone. My chest tightening, I swallow hard, feeling like every muscle in my body is quivering. A sinking feeling forms in the pit of my stomach that this is Molly's way of demonstrating how little I know him. I search my memory for the answer. Surely, he must have mentioned it at some point over the past few months, but nothing comes to mind. I pride myself on my observational skills, yet I can't seem to come up with a single movie Wes might consider his favorite, my brain refusing to remember.

"Come on, the future Mrs. Bradford," Molly goads. She doesn't mean anything by it, but it still stings.

Having no clue, I blurt out the first thing that pops into my mind. "*The Godfather?*"

Molly gives me a sideways glance, knowing all too well why I chose that. It's her brother's favorite movie. "Hmm… Let's see what Wes has to say."

She presses a button on her laptop and Wes' voice fills the room. The sweet southern drawl that once soothed me only serves as a reminder of how inadequate I am. I shift my eyes to the screen, my stomach rolling when I take in his appearance in the prerecorded video. He's been so busy, yet he found the time to answer these questions for her…and for me. I couldn't even put in the effort to learn these things about him. Why do I feel like I'll never measure up to what Wes deserves?

"*It's a Wonderful Life,*" he answers with a charismatic smile. His hair is neatly groomed, his tie perfectly straight as he sits in front of the large windows in his office. "It's cheesy and nostalgic, but I'm a cheesy and nostalgic kind of guy. I like the idea that it's never too late for a second chance, that sometimes the people we surround ourselves with are more important than money or material possessions."

I swallow hard, studying my guests, who seem to be looking upon me with pity. You can hear a pin drop in the stiff silence. Gone is the polite chatter, the clinking of ice against glass, the shuffling of plates. I almost want to ask each of them if they know their significant other's favorite movie, but don't. They probably do.

"Well, let's move on," Molly says finally. "It's my fault. I put you on the spot. Just take a deep breath." She meets my eyes. "I'm sure you'll get the rest of them." She lifts the next note card and reads another question, the acid churning in my stomach burning a little more with each answer I can't give.

This goes on for several minutes. Molly asks a question, one I should know. Thankfully, some of them I do, like what side of the bed he prefers. But for many of the questions, the ones that would require some sort of conversation, I'm clueless. She said to trust her, that even though I may not initially agree with her ideas, I eventually learn to appreciate them. I doubt I'll ever appreciate her putting me on display in front of Mrs. Bradford's friends and family, confirming her belief that I'm not right for her son. At first, I wanted to prove her otherwise, but now I can't help but think I *am* wrong for Wes.

"Last question, and it's a good one."

I close my eyes, bracing for yet another one I won't be able to answer.

"When did you first say I love you?"

My shoulders fall and I shake my head. Tears prickle my eyes, a lump forming in my throat. Every person in a committed relationship with their soulmate should be able to answer this question with no problem. But not me.

I look at Molly, silently begging her to put an end to this. With a sympathetic smile, she hits the spacebar on her laptop.

"Last September when I took her to Paris," Wes answers with certainty. "We'd been dating for about two months. I had to go for work, so I asked her to come with me. One day, she said she wanted to see Père Lachaise cemetery, and I thought it was the perfect place to tell her." He laughs, looking into the distance, as if recalling the day. "I know it may sound weird to tell someone you love them in a cemetery, but people flock thousands of miles to see the tombs of Abelard and Héloïse, the two fated lovers who were forced to live apart. They wrote beautiful letters to each other until Abelard died. I couldn't think of a more fitting place."

"I was nervous as hell. I knew I loved her, even though things had been pretty casual up until that point. Regardless, she deserved to know how I felt, even if she didn't love me. In time, I knew she would. At least, I *hoped* she would." He flashes the camera his brilliant smile. "I've always worn my heart on my sleeve, but Brooklyn... She's always been more...guarded. I don't fault her. That's one of the things I love about her. She doesn't give her heart willingly. You have to earn it. I'm so glad she thought me deserving of her heart."

Molly hits the spacebar, pausing the video, the silence in the room deafening. "Oops," she says. "My finger slipped before I gave you a chance to answer."

I keep my head lowered, doing everything I can to not burst into tears in front of these strangers. It's what Mrs. Bradford expects. The sanctimonious smirk on her face as I return my eyes to the assembled guests confirms my suspicions.

367

But are those things *really* important? Does it matter whether I know his favorite holiday or food? Does it matter whether I know the name of his childhood pet or imaginary friend? Are these things a valid indicator of whether we're a good fit? I know several people who can answer these questions about their spouses but are miserable in their relationship. I'm not. Wes makes me happy, and I know I make him happy, even if I can't say with any certainty what his favorite type of beer is. These are just things that make up our history. All things we can continue to learn about each other over the years.

At least that's what I try to convince myself after I finally escape all the judgmental eyes, unable to even look at Molly, and drive back to my house. Most brides probably spend the evening of their shower going through the gifts they received. I don't. I spend it curled up on my couch, a pint of Ben & Jerry's in my hand, watching *It's a Wonderful Life*.

Chapter Twenty-Four

DREW

IT'S NOT OFTEN I find myself with a free day to do whatever I'd like. Usually, when Molly or Gigi watch the girls, it's because I have a game or work. But today, I have neither. The house is peaceful and serene. There are a hundred things I can do to occupy my time until the girls get home from Brooklyn's bridal shower, but I need to keep my mind off her approaching nuptials. I can't do that in my house, where every room holds a memory of her. Instead, I head out to meet an old hockey friend to have a drink and catch up.

"I couldn't believe my eyes when I saw your name pop up on my phone," Parker says when he sees me enter the bar area of the restaurant where we agreed to meet. He's almost as tall as me and even more muscular. We played together professionally until I no longer could.

I reach my hand toward him and we shake before patting each other on the back in a typical bro-hug. "What can I say? I had a free afternoon and knew I couldn't avoid you forever."

"Damn straight." He returns to his barstool and signals the bartender. "Don't worry. I ordered a few appetizers so they'd serve me a beer. Fucking puritanical laws."

I shake my head. "Part of me thinks the restaurants are the ones who convince the local lawmakers to keep those laws in place. They make even more money that way."

"Agreed." Parker picks up the pilsner glass containing an amber liquid as a bartender approaches and takes my order for a pale ale. When it arrives, I take a sip, relaxing. "So you're kid-free today?"

"I am." I return my glass to the bar. "It's weird. Usually the only time I have to myself is when the team's on the road."

"How old are they now?"

"Alyssa is eight and Charlotte is six," I respond with a gleam in my eyes. It always happens. No matter how crappy a day I'm having, I can't control the pride that fills me when someone asks about my kids.

"Wow." He shakes his head. "Has it been that long?"

I nod. "I still can't believe it."

"Man, it seems like just yesterday I was standing on the ice, watching them wheel you away on a stretcher."

Averting my gaze, I swallow hard. "Yeah. Last hockey game I ever played. It's a blessing in disguise Carla went into labor the same day." I return my eyes to his, gritting a smile. "At least I won't always remember February ninth as the day my career ended, but as the day Charlotte was born." I stare off into the distance. I never considered that, but it's true. Every year on February ninth, there's nothing but happiness and celebrations, not a stark reminder of the anniversary I lost the only thing I thought I loved. I was wrong. I have my daughters. That's all I need.

"So..." I clear my throat. "How do you like coaching? I'm surprised you retired from playing so soon." Parker's only a few years older and left the league not long after I did.

He shrugs. "You know how it is. Got married, had kids. Your priorities change."

"Your wife's Marisa, right?" I hate even having to ask, but it's been a few years since we've had the opportunity to just talk. During our days on the team, his girlfriend was one of the long-termers. Often, the section of the arena reserved for the wives and girlfriends...or WAGs, as we affectionately called them...was like a revolving door of women. But there were a few who had been there a while. Marisa was one. She was dating Parker before he hit it big in the pros. Their relationship gave me hope that my own tumultuous marriage to Carla would work. But some people can't be tamed. It took several years for me to learn that lesson, albeit the hard way.

"Yes. Marisa."

"You finally married her? We took bets on whether you'd ever pop the question."

He laughs as I sip my beer, happy I picked up the phone and reached out to him. I never take time for myself, unless it was to drop by Skylar's on my way home from a night game. I've missed being able to

371

relax with the guys like I did during my hockey days. Since then, my kids have been my focus, my only friends being my sister and Brooklyn. It's good to be doing something normal again. Once Carla left, my life became one crazy roller coaster ride after another. I need the normal, even if only for a few hours.

"Yeah, well, when she got pregnant, I decided it was time."

"And when was this?"

"Well, Aiden turned eighteen months a few weeks ago."

"You mean to tell me you *just* married her?" My eyebrows raise as I smirk.

He shrugs.

"Dude…" I shake my head. "You're lucky she stuck with you that long. Every other woman I know would have hightailed it out of there instead of dealing with your noncommittal ass."

"Like I've told Marisa, I was giving her ample opportunity to test drive me."

"Test drive?" I laugh harder. "Most test drives only last a few minutes, not ten years."

"I wanted to make sure she'd be satisfied with the product."

"Well, congratulations. I'm happy for you."

"Thanks, man." He brings his beer back to his mouth and drinks before returning his attention to me. "How about you? Anything serious?"

"Nah. It's tough when you have kids. Most women

my age aren't willing to deal with the baggage I come with."

"How about that friend of your sister's I met a few times? What was her name? Chelsea?"

"Brooklyn," I correct.

"That's right. I knew it was some neighborhood in New York. So, what's her deal? You still close? Man, Carla hated her." He chuckled, staring into the distance as he recalls the past. "Whenever she was at a game with your sister, Carla would shoot daggers at her, talk shit about her, stuff like that."

I arch a brow. "Really?"

"Yeah. Marisa used to give me all the gossip. Well, maybe not give me, per se, but you know Marisa. She has two levels of talking. Loud and louder. It was impossible not to listen in on her conversations when she was on the phone with one of the other WAGs."

"And Carla didn't like Brooklyn?" I knew she didn't, but the fact other people picked up on it made me feel a slight bit of vindication for no reason other than that Carla was jealous. And of Brooklyn, of all people. Sweet, innocent, unassuming Brooklyn.

"It's been a few years, but that little tidbit always stood out. Granted, Marisa was never a fan of Carla, either. Said you deserved better. She was thrilled when she overheard Carla talking to one of the other freeloader WAGs at one of the games, saying she was finally going to file for divorce. Well, she felt bad for you, but didn't want to see Carla continue to hurt you, since she'd been screwing Chase for God knows how long. But she always liked Brooklyn, said the idea of childhood friends ending up together warmed her soul and made her cynical heart do backflips."

"Wait. What?" I ask, unsure I heard him correctly.

"Oh, she was just playing, but she still asks about you and her, claims she gets a feeling from the two of you."

"No. I'm not talking about Brooklyn." I blink repeatedly, my mind reeling. My brain screams at me to change the subject, that it's not worth it, but I need to know more. I thought Carla started cheating on me after the injury forced me out of the game, after Charlotte was born. But if it had been going on longer… I don't want to think what that could mean. "About Carla. How long she was sleeping with Chase."

Parker's eyes widen. "Man, I'm sorry. I thought you knew. I mean, it was public knowledge she moved in with him right after you announced your retirement. We all thought it was a dick move, but—"

"No. I knew that. I just…" I lift my gaze back to his. "How would Marisa overhear Carla talking to one of the WAGs about filing for divorce then? She left me in August. The season didn't start until October. Even if she mentioned something months before, I was out for the season in February. She had no need to go to the games, not to mention she had just given birth. The only games she went to were the ones I attended, but she sat with me up in the owner's box. I watched every single game that season, even the ones I couldn't attend personally. If she went to one, I would have seen her. I would have known." I stare straight ahead, the labels on the liquor bottles behind the bar blurring together. "Unless Marisa's referring to the first time she filed for divorce," I say, my voice low.

"Eh, it doesn't matter," Parker encourages me, trying to lighten the atmosphere. "She's gone. And Chase is stuck selling used cars. They both got what they deserve for what they did to you."

I shake my head. "No. It's not that." I return my eyes to Parker, acid burning my throat at the mere idea. "I know she cheated on me. I didn't think it was until after my injury. After she had Charlotte. If she'd been cheating on me all along…"

"Oh, shit. No!" Parker blurts out, reading my thoughts. "Don't even go there."

"But she served me with divorce papers one day. The next, she told me she made a mistake, that she was pregnant and wanted to work things out for our baby. What if—"

"Andrew, look, I'm sorry. I never should have said anything. I was just wondering if you and Brooklyn ever hit it off. My intention was never to bring up all that drama. You're better off without it. I can see that. You had a great year of coaching, which is why I've been wanting to get together with you."

I stare at him, my mind still occupied with the idea of Carla sleeping with Chase before Charlotte was born. I don't want to consider the possible ramifications, bile rising at the mere thought.

"As you know, Coach Griffin is retiring after this season."

"I've heard."

Coach Griffin was the head coach when I joined the

team over ten years ago. He was a hard-ass, but one of the best coaches out there. If it weren't for his ability to see something in me, I never would have been put on the ice during the game that changed my career.

"The way the team's been playing, they could make it to the Stanley Cup. It'll be great to send him out on that note." I take another long sip of my beer, the taste suddenly sour.

"Yes, and that bonus in my paycheck will be nice, too. But they've been tossing some names around to replace him, have already talked to a few people, but no one seems to have the same passion."

I smile, but it's lacking, my focus still elsewhere. "Are you up for the position?"

He shakes his head. "I'm not interested. But your name's come up on more than one occasion."

I sit back, allowing that to sink in for a minute. "Huh."

"I offered to talk to you, feel you out. I know you're just getting back into the game after being gone for a few years, but you know your stuff. It's a fantastic opportunity, one that may not come around again."

"I don't know. I already hate being gone from my girls as much as I am."

"That's understandable. I hate being gone from Aiden, and I'm just one of the assistant coaches. But the love you have for the game... I think you owe it to yourself to at least listen to what they have to say. Can I tell them you'll do that? And when they offer you a position, I'd be grateful if you'd consider keeping me on as an assistant coach."

I'd be lying if I said the idea of coaching for the pros didn't attract me, especially as head coach. Coach Griffin had offered me a position as assistant coach several times in the past, but I always turned him down, making my girls a priority. And they're still my priority. But I've finally found a balance between being a good father and being a great coach. This can be a career-changing opportunity for me, one I'd be crazy not to consider.

"There's no guarantee they'll offer me the job or that I'll take it, but I'll at least hear them out."

"Great." Parker faces forward as the bartender drops off a few plates filled with finger foods. "And again, I'm sorry for bringing up Carla and Chase. I probably just misheard something Marisa said. You know how women can be with their gossip."

"Yeah." I'd love to believe it's only a misunderstanding, but I know Carla. Anything's possible.

Chapter Twenty-Five

BROOKLYN

A TAPPING RIPS THROUGH my living room and I fling my eyes open, staring at the home screen of *It's a Wonderful Life* on my television. An empty container of Ben & Jerry's sits on the coffee table, physical evidence of my evening of self-loathing and doubt. Exhaustion settling in my bones, my eyes start to close when I hear the tapping again. It finally sinks in it's coming from my front door. Although the last thing I want is to talk to anyone, I manage to pull myself from the couch and shuffle to the foyer, thinking perhaps it's Molly here to apologize.

I open the door and stare into apologetic blue eyes…but they don't belong to my best friend.

"Hey," Wes says in a timid voice. "I tried calling, but you weren't answering your phone."

"I fell asleep on the couch."

"I figured. I just… I wanted to talk to you about what I heard happened today."

I exhale, hanging my head, then step back, allowing him into my home. He walks to the living area, then hesitates. When I lower myself onto the couch, he does the same. His eyes float to the television, a smile crossing his expression.

"*It's a Wonderful Life.*"

"Yeah." I shrug. "It seemed like the right thing after today."

He draws in a deep breath as he runs his hands down his jeans. It takes me a minute to realize he's not in a suit. I've known Wes for almost a year and have rarely seen him in anything other than a suit. I have to admit, he makes a pair of jeans look fantastic. It has my mind going to places it shouldn't, especially after today.

"Listen," he begins. I do everything to brace myself for what I'm sure will follow. His mother probably couldn't wait to get back to her hotel so she could tell him what happened. In retrospect, I should have expected him to stop by much earlier. Maybe he needed time to figure out what to do.

"Wes, I—"

He holds up his hand, silently pleading with me to let him finish. After everything, it's the least I can do. I can apologize and make excuses, but it won't fix this disconnect between us. I don't think anything will. I've tried to convince myself I'm happy, but am I? Is he?

"I should have told you when I found out. I hate you had to stand there, surrounded by all my mother's stuck-up friends, and be put on the spot like that."

"It wasn't just your mother's friends. Molly, Gigi, and the girls were there, too."

"God..." He runs his hands through his hair,

379

tugging on it. It looks sexy on him. His disheveled hair reminds me he's not as perfect as I've always believed him to be. "I am so sorry, Brooklyn. I can't even imagine what you must be thinking right now."

"Probably the same thing you are." I pull my legs into my chest, resting my chin on my knees.

"And what *are* you thinking?" he asks guardedly.

I meet his peaceful eyes, his brows creased as he awaits my response like the accused awaiting the verdict. "That maybe we rushed into this. That maybe we should have taken the time to get to know each other a little better." I stare up at the ceiling to fight back the lump in my throat, then return my gaze to his. "How is this supposed to work if I can't even answer what your favorite movie is?"

Wes straightens, his eyes narrowing. "Wait. Is that what you think this is about? That stupid game Molly wanted to do?"

I subtly nod, my brows squeezing together. "Isn't it?"

He grasps my hands in his. "God, no. Do you think I care about some ridiculous shower game? My mother was the one who chose the questions, for crying out loud. I'm pretty sure she intentionally picked ones you wouldn't be able to answer. I should have stopped it when I figured that out, but I assumed it was all in good fun." Then concern fills his expression. "Why? What happened?"

Tears obscure my vision and I struggle to even form the words. "What happened?" I choke out. "What happened was I could only answer a few questions. And with each answer I got wrong, the smugness in your mother's expression only increased. I sat up there, the entire time thinking I don't deserve you. That you can probably remember what I wore on any given date, yet I can't even tell you when you first told me you loved me. Worse, I can't remember the first time I said it back."

"Oh, Brooklyn... I am so sorry." His arms envelope me in his warm embrace and he kisses the top of my head. "None of that matters. The only thing that does is that we love each other. Who cares when we said it, where we were, what we were doing? Who cares what you named your favorite doll or what you wanted to be when you were little? All I care about is this, what we have." He pulls back, his intense eyes focused on mine. "And I love what we have. Nothing can change that, not even my mother's petty little games."

I breathe a sigh of relief, resting my head against his chest and listening to the thrumming of his heart...tranquil, serene, familiar. The soothing rhythm is like a metronome, one I can tap out in my sleep. I pull away, my eyes zeroing in on him once more. "But if that's not why you came to talk to me, then—"

"Mother said you heard about my dad retiring, that I'd be taking over."

"Oh." My solace is short-lived as I'm reminded of that. "Yeah. I heard something to that effect."

His hands cup my cheeks as he brings my face toward his, resting his forehead on mine. "And like I told my father, my life is here. We're not in the dark ages of technology. I can just as easily run the company from up here as I can in Atlanta. My mother wants me to go back to Georgia, but I like it here, apart from the snow. But if suffering through a nor'easter means having you in my life, I'll gladly do it. Please know that."

I exhale a short breath, all the tension I've been bottling up since this afternoon melting away. All it takes is a few encouraging words and I'm reminded why marrying Wes is the right thing. He's faithful, honest, and devoted to ensuring my happiness. What else can I possibly ask for?

"God, your mother must really hate me," I joke, pulling away and wiping my tears.

"Nah." He winks. "Well, maybe a little, which is all the more reason for me to keep you up north, as far away from her as possible. Just wait. In a few more years, we'll go visit and I'll have picked up this Boston accent everyone seems to have."

I fling my arms around him, tackling him onto the couch. This is the most laid-back I've ever felt around him. It's what I've always wanted for us. I often admired the way Molly and Noah interacted with each other. Tonight, I finally feel some of that with Wes. He's right. We don't need to know pointless facts about each other to know this will work. This is easy. It's comfortable. It's effortless.

"You better not. Don't you ever lose that accent of yours."

"You like my accent?" he asks, his sweet Georgia drawl even more pronounced.

I hover over him, biting my lower lip. "You have no idea what it does to me."

"Well then…" He hooks a leg around my waist, pinning me against him and flipping me onto my back, his motions quick. "Perhaps you'd be so kind as to let me see exactly what it does to you."

The playfulness leaves, his eyes darkening with desire as his fingers dig into my sides. Keeping his gaze trained on me, he lowers my yoga pants down my legs, then stands, pushing down his jeans. After he fishes a condom out of his wallet, he returns to me. His mouth finds mine, his kiss soft, consuming me, exploring as if it were the first time our lips have met. Right now, it feels that way, like we're able to put aside all the troubles we thought plagued our survival, basking in this connection. When he enters me, his motions slow, languid, loving, I lose myself in him, in this moment, forgetting about everything and everyone else.

Well, almost everyone. Everyone except the one person I wish I could forget, the one person I need to forget. The one person I want to forget. The one person I *can't* forget.

Chapter Twenty-Six

BROOKLYN

T HIS IS A TERRIBLE *idea*, I think as I stare up at Drew's house Sunday evening. My subconscious is telling me to turn around and go back home, but I need to talk to Molly about what happened at the shower yesterday. All last night, I lay awake as Wes slept beside me, his arm draped across my body. I should have found comfort in his embrace, but I didn't. His touch bothered me. I don't want that to be the case. After his beautiful words, I should want…no, crave that man's touch. I shouldn't look into his eyes and wish they were brown, deep, and penetrating. It's time to leave the past in the past.

Lively voices fill the open space as I let myself into the house. It reminds me of so many other Sunday nights. No matter what's going on in our lives, no matter how busy we are, we always take the time to get together every Sunday night. Even when Drew was playing professional hockey, he made a point to come to Sunday dinner when he was in town. Back then, it was held at his father's house, but once he got sick and had to be put in a long-term care facility, Drew took over so the tradition didn't die. And it's a tradition I love, one I've missed over the past few weeks.

Drawing in a deep breath, I steel myself for what needs to be done and continue toward the frivolity. The instant I step into the kitchen, the boisterous voices quiet, several pairs of eyes looking my way. My heart rate picks up and I immediately regret coming. Then I remind myself why I'm here and offer a smile, pretending this is like every other Sunday dinner. By this point, I've mastered the art of pretending.

"Auntie Brook!" Alyssa's excited voice cuts through the awkward tension. I look in her direction to see two little girls running toward me. "You made it!"

"Of course I did." I crouch to their level, giving both girls a hug and a kiss.

"And you're wearing pants!" Charlotte says.

I furrow my brow. "Why wouldn't I be?"

"You weren't yesterday. You wore a dress. You don't like dresses."

"Why do you say that?"

"Because that's what Daddy said when I told him you were wearing a princess dress."

"Is that right?" I tear my eyes from Charlotte, meeting Drew's gaze.

"Glad you could finally fit us into your busy schedule." His tone is sardonic and biting.

"Yes." I straighten. "I'm sorry I haven't been around. I'll try to be better about managing my time." I look around the room, surveying all the familiar faces — Molly, Noah, Gigi, Leo. These people love and support me, even if they don't agree with all my decisions. "You're all very important to me. No matter what, you always will be."

"And you're important to us, Brook." Molly slings her arm across my shoulders, squeezing me. "More than you realize," she murmurs in a low voice. "Especially to some people."

I sigh, stepping back. This is precisely the kind of comment I've come here to stop. Keeping up this charade isn't fair to me, to Drew, to Wes.

"What is it?" Molly asks as the normal Sunday ritual of Gigi kicking Drew out of his own kitchen resumes. It's like I wasn't even missing over the past few weeks. Life went on without me. And it will go on without me again. It *has* to.

"Can we go out back and talk for a second?" I ask.

She narrows her eyes. "Is everything okay?"

"Yeah. I just…" I chew on my bottom lip, fidgeting with my hands. My mouth suddenly feels dry, my heart racing. "I need to talk to you. It's important."

"Okay." Her response is guarded, but she still loops her arm through mine.

We step out of the French doors into the cool air, heading toward the unlit fire pit. The final remnants of the day are visible, the sun casting an orange hue in the sky, a few birds chirping before settling in for the night. I sit on one of the cement benches surrounding the fire pit and Molly lowers herself beside me.

"What's going on, Brook?"

I draw in a deep breath as I turn my eyes toward

hers. "Did you know what Mrs. Bradford was trying to do yesterday?"

She straightens her spine, her brows furrowing. "What do you mean?"

"You know what I mean. The *Newlywed Game*. I'm getting married in a month. *Married*. And you should be supporting me, telling me how excited you are, not doing everything in your power to convince me it's a bad idea."

"Do *you* think it's a bad idea?" she asks, not answering my question.

"Of course not." My response is quick. Perhaps a little too quick. "But it's obvious you do. Why else would you concoct that game unless you wanted to remind me that I don't know who Wes is? Don't you think I already know that? I do! I get it. You think we're rushing into this. And maybe we are. But you can support me at least."

"I *do* support you, Brooklyn. And for the record, I honestly thought you'd know the answers to those questions. There was no ill-intent on my part. It's all stuff I know about Noah. But maybe you *should* consider the fact you might be rushing into this. It's obvious you don't even know him. Not like you should if you're willing to give him your future."

"Wes said he doesn't care about that stuff. And he's right. A relationship isn't built on knowing the other's likes and dislikes. It's built on love."

"That's true. And I'd gladly accept that if I were convinced you loved him." She assesses me, her gaze unnerving. "I don't think you do."

I shoot to my feet, glaring at her, my mouth agape. "How could you say such a thing?"

"Because it's true," she responds, standing, her eyes fierce. "You may think you're great at reading people, but so am I. I know what love looks like. I ran from it for years. Wes loves you. I'll admit that." She pauses, her lips pinching into a tight line. "But you don't love him. There's no spark, no gleam, no excitement. And I can't understand why you would marry someone you don't love."

I close my eyes, shaking my head, tears welling behind my lids. I refuse to say the words, even though she's right. You don't need to be a genius to see my feelings for Wes aren't as strong as they should be. But I appreciate him. I respect him. I admire him. Can't that be enough for us? Can't I *learn* to love him?

"Why?" she presses when I remain silent. "Why would you give up on the one thing you've always dreamed of?" Molly's voice grows louder with each word she speaks, leaning into me.

It doesn't matter that I'm outside in the open air, acres upon acres of trees and space surrounding me. I feel trapped, the world closing in, suffocating me. We're alone, but I feel the burn of a thousand eyes, threatening to expose the secret I've kept from everyone for years. There have been so many times I've almost told Molly everything, stopping at the last second. The pain of all those chances I gave him. The repeated rejections. The heart-shattering truth it's taken me years to learn. I've kept it buried. I need it to stay buried, not resurrect it for all to see. Everyone has a chapter they don't want to read out loud. Drew is mine.

"Why would you settle for anything less than what you deserve?" she continues. "What reason could you have for marrying someone who doesn't make your heart do somersaults whenever you see him? Why, Brooklyn? Please, tell me why so I can understand what's going on with you!"

Still vehemently shaking my head, I attempt to sidestep around her. "You'd never understand, Molly. You—"

"Just tell me!" she shrieks, gripping my biceps with a force I'm not expecting.

My face flames, all the stress, confusion, and despair that's been building since I agreed to marry Wes reaching a boiling point. My muscles tense, my nostrils flare as the words slip out far too easily.

"Because I'm in love with Drew!" I shout, then gasp, covering my mouth, just as surprised by my revelation as Molly.

She stares at me with wide eyes, her jaw dropping as my words ring in the air. I've kept it in so long, refused to admit it, even with all her teasing and prodding over the years. I've always been able to remain firm, claim I value my friendship with her above everything. But that's not the entire story. No one knows the entire story…even Drew.

"You mean you love him as friends, right? Like you've always said?"

I shake my head, collapsing onto one of the cement benches. "No, Molly. Not as a friend. I can't remember a time when I haven't been in love with him."

She sits beside me, bringing her hand to my arm. I

peer into her questioning eyes.

"But Drew doesn't love me." My voice shakes as I struggle to speak through the lump in my throat. It's one thing to think those words. To say them out loud gives them meaning, a truth it's time I learn to accept.

"You don't know that."

"Yes, I do. He's made that abundantly clear."

"When? Did something happen at the museum?" she asks, then lowers her voice. "Was it because of Carla? Drew said you ran into her."

I laugh sarcastically at the irony of her question, raising myself back to my feet. "It's always been because of Carla." I fight to stop my chin from quivering, the memories leaving me raw and gutted. "Or whatever other woman had his attention at the time. I just…" I inhale deeply, collecting my thoughts. "He never saw me, and it's taken me years to finally wake up and realize it."

"I don't understand."

"You don't need to." I start back toward the house, wanting to get out of this place and turn back the clock to my younger days. There are so many things I'd do differently. I never would have given Drew my first kiss. I never would have allowed him to flirt with me over the years, to get my hopes up, only to have him forget about me the next day. And I never would have allowed a very drunk version of him into my bedroom seven years ago.

Molly grips my arm, preventing me from walking away. "What did she say to you?"

"Nothing."

"Then what did Drew say to you?"

I snort a laugh. "It's what he *didn't* say, Molly. It's what he never says."

"Please, Brooklyn. I'm sick of all this talking in code bullshit. Just fucking tell me what happened, what Carla or Drew did to turn you into this." She gestures at me, wrinkling her nose in disgust.

"This?"

"Yes." She straightens her spine. "This. This woman who, over the past few years, exhibited my friend less and less. This woman who used to believe in the concept of love so fiercely, she made me believe in it, too." She pauses, her tone softening. "Do you remember what you said when I tried to deny I was falling for Noah?"

I blink, remaining mute.

"You said it was in our DNA to want to share our lives with someone, to fall in love, but not the kind of love I used to write about in my books. What did you call it?"

"The gritty kind of love," I answer, my voice barely audible, worried she would hear *my* truth in them.

"That's right, Brook. The kind of love you have to work for, that doesn't come easily, that has absolutely zero resemblance to a fucking fairy tale. The love that hurts, rips out your soul, stomping on it and bringing you to the lowest of your lows. The old Brooklyn would have crossed oceans and climbed mountains to find that kind of love. Where did *that* girl go?"

"She was forced to realize it wasn't in the cards for her to have what you have. Look at me, Molly." I gesture at my tall, lanky body. "I'm not the type of girl a guy like Drew will ever love. You've seen the girls he's dated, slept with. I'm not it. I'll always just be his sister's best friend. Nothing more."

I wipe at the tears streaming down my face, surprised at my sudden candor with her. For the longest time, I put her needs ahead of my own, never wanting her to pry too much into my personal life. Now everything I've kept from her for years is spewing forth like molten lava, burning and destroying everything in its path…burning and destroying me.

"Yes, you are, Brooklyn," she assures me with more compassion than I deserve, especially once she learns the truth. "You're so much more than that. Drew loves you. I know it. I see it in his eyes. I can feel his heart breaking at the idea of you marrying someone else. If you'll just give him a chance to prove this to you—"

"I did."

Molly steps back, a blank look on her face. "When?"

I blow out a laugh at how stupid and naïve I've been. "So many times."

"Give me an example."

I zero in on her, studying her hardened stare. I can't believe I'm actually going to do this. But I came here tonight to explain why marrying Wes is so important. This is a big part of that.

"One stands out, although I can bore you for hours with instances where Drew broke his promises me. But this one…" My voice wavers as I'm transported back to that night. "After finishing grad school, I was living with my dad so I could save money for my own place. I'd just dropped you off at your apartment from a night at the bars. When I was about to turn down the street, I saw Drew stumbling around the park. He could barely walk, and I was worried something would happen if I left him. I pretty much had to carry him to my car, which you can imagine was quite the feat with how tall and strong he is.

"I asked what he was doing back in the old neighborhood and that's when he told me Carla had filed for a divorce. He didn't know where else to go, so he went to the only place that felt like home. When I started to drive him to your dad's place, he told me *I* was the only place that felt like home, that he was there to see me."

I pause, leaving out the other things he said, namely how he wanted to make amends for standing me up the morning he left for college. I never told Molly about Drew being my first kiss. After the pain he caused, I didn't want anyone to know, wanted to forget about it.

"I knew he was drunk and hurting so I shouldn't believe a single word that came out of his mouth, but I wanted to." I look to the sky, tears streaming down my cheeks, before returning my eyes to hers. "God, Molly. I'd been waiting years to hear him say something like that. Do you have any idea how hard it was for me to watch him date woman after woman after woman, then learn he got married?"

Molly remains stunned mute by my story, the words I've been too scared to speak for years spilling forward.

"It was fucking torture. But what could I do? Tell him?" I swipe at my tears, wrapping my arms around my stomach. "He'd never choose me over the models he dated."

"What happened?"

"He made so many promises, told me he loved me, how it's only ever been me. We didn't sleep together, as much as I wanted to. We did...other things. A *lot* of other things. Everything except..." My face heats from the memory alone, but I push it down. "He said he wanted to be sober when he made love to me." The little composure I have left cracks, a new wave of tears spilling forward. I meet Molly's eyes and repeat the words he said, as if it happened just days ago, not years. "Because, with me, it would be so much more than sex. I was stupid and believed him when I should have been smart enough to know they were just the drunken ramblings of a man scared of losing everything."

She looks at me with an unfocused gaze. "Why didn't you say anything? Why didn't *he* say anything?"

A sudden chill envelopes me and I run my hands along my arms. "Because he doesn't know." I'm not sure what's worse. The fact that I kept this from Molly...or from Drew.

Her eyes widen, her jaw becoming slack. "What? How?"

"He was drunk. *Really* drunk."

Understanding washes over her expression. "And with his head injuries, excessive amounts of alcohol can severely impact his memory."

I nod. "When I was making breakfast the next

morning, I overheard him talking on the phone. A few things he said piqued my curiosity, so I crept down the hall and eavesdropped. I only heard his side of the conversation, but it didn't take a genius to figure out he was talking to Carla, that she told him she was pregnant, that she wanted to work things out for their kids' sakes. As much as I wanted to be angry, I couldn't, not when he was trying to do right by Alyssa and the baby on the way. He finished the phone call, then came into the living room and looked at me with so much guilt. I wasn't sure what to do, what to say. That's when he said he couldn't remember much of the night before and asked if we slept together. It was a logical assumption, I suppose, especially when you wake up in a girl's bed. God, it hurt so much to know he couldn't remember, to know I was that forgettable, even if there was a medical reason for it."

"What did you say?" Her voice is low, almost hesitant.

"I told him he passed out on my bed and I slept in my dad's room, that nothing happened."

Molly's lips parted and she shook her head, eyes wide. "Don't you think he deserves to know the truth, deserves a chance to make it right?"

"It doesn't matter anymore. Drew and me... We're like opposing magnets. No matter how hard you try to bring us together, an outside force will always pull us apart. But Wes... He's done something no other man ever has. I may not love him, but he has made me a priority. Do you know I thought he was cheating on me?"

Molly remains silent.

"After you orchestrated my dress shopping excursion with Drew, I decided to surprise Wes at his office. But even though he claimed he would be working late that night, he wasn't there. And after spending the day with Drew, I was happy he wasn't there. As ridiculous as it sounds, there was a part of me that *wanted* Wes to cheat on me. It would mean I'd be off the hook.

"When I got home that Saturday after going to the museum with Drew and the girls, Wes was sitting on my front stoop, worried sick about where I'd been since I'd shut off my phone. He told me what he was doing Friday afternoon when he lied about working late. Do you want to know what that was?"

She simply stares at me.

"Buying us a plot of land where he could build me my dream house. He wanted to surprise me on our wedding night. His plan was beautiful. And I *ruined* it. Then he got down on one knee and proposed all over again. This time with a ring that's exactly like the one I've always imagined instead of his original choice." I close my eyes, toying with the beautiful diamond sitting on my left hand. "Wes is a *good* man. He's done nothing but make me a priority, and I've done nothing but piss on his affection in the hopes that the promises Drew made would come to fruition." I shake my head.

"I can't do this anymore. Wes and Drew cannot coexist in my heart. The memory of Drew's words, of hearing him tell me he loved me as he gave me one of the most intense orgasms I've ever had, still tortures me. And he was too drunk to even fucking remember."

"But—"

Instantly, the sound of glass shattering rings from behind me. I whirl around, my heart plummeting to the pit of my stomach when I see Drew standing on the back deck. The remnants of a wine glass are broken around his feet, red wine dripping down the stairs.

His mouth is agape, his eyes wide, his legs frozen in place. Everything is still, no one moving as we all stand there, shocked, my truth lingering in the air.

His voice is quiet when he finally speaks. "I thought you might want a glass of wine." As much as I'd love to believe otherwise, his expression makes it obvious he heard enough to know what happened all those years ago.

I snap out of my shock and look at Molly. "I'll let you get back to your dinner, but now you know why things are the way they are." My gaze floats to Drew. "Why they *need* to be the way they are." Then I hurry up the steps, narrowly skirting Drew's hand, and rush inside the house, Gigi meeting me when she sees my bewildered expression.

"Is everything all right, dear?" She steps in front of me, placing her hands on my arms.

"I'm suddenly not feeling very well. I need to go home."

"Of course," she says, dropping her hold on me. I push past her, grateful she doesn't press the issue for once. Just as I'm about to disappear out of the house, she calls, "You can't run from love forever."

I pause in my steps, looking over my shoulder.

"It'll find you. It always does."

"Please, Gigi," I beg. "Now is not the time for yet another one of your pearls of wisdom."

"On the contrary. Apparently, now is the *perfect* time. The ones we love the hardest are the ones we hurt the most. He lost you once. Don't think for a second he'll make the same mistake again."

"I can't do this right now," I choke out and hurry away. Emptiness settles in the pit of my stomach as I rush out of the house, considering Gigi's words. What does she know? Was she listening in on my conversation with Molly?

As I dart down the steps and stride toward my car, my focus is elsewhere. I come to an abrupt stop when I practically slam into Drew as he stands by the driver's side door, his arms crossed, his stance wide.

Avoiding his eyes, I try to push him aside. "If you'll excuse me, I need to get home."

"Why didn't you tell me?" The pain in his voice forces my gaze to his. But that hurt is no match for the agony covering his entire body, his muscles tight, his stare filled with betrayal. He's barely holding it together. Just like me.

My stomach hardens as I part my lips, searching my brain for what to tell him. There were so many times I wish I'd been truthful with him about that night, so many times I almost *did* tell him. But I reminded myself keeping it a secret was the right thing to do. He just found out he was going to be a father again. What if I told him the truth and he abandoned Carla to pursue something with me? Worse, what if I told him and he still chose her? At the time, I had no reason to believe otherwise. I still don't.

With a quiver in my voice, I peer into his eyes. "You couldn't remember. I just wanted to forget. So please, Drew..." I swallow hard through the excruciating pain in my throat, in my chest, in my heart. "Let me forget you," I finish with a sob, pushing past him and opening the door to my car.

"I can't do that," he responds, his own voice filled with so much emotion, it cuts me in two. "I can't let you forget me, not when I care about you the way I do." His hand grips my bicep and I whirl around, staring at him with fiery eyes. He releases his hold on me, but our stare only intensifies, cutting and deep. "Please, Brooklyn. Give me a chance."

Our eyes remain locked as I stand motionless, wishing I could. I want that more than anything. But how do you give someone your heart when they're the reason it's shattered into thousands of pieces?

"Do you remember that party the night before you left for college?" I ask, needing him to understand exactly where I'm coming from, why I need to sever the chains he's shackled around me.

His expression softens and he nods, stepping back.

"Do you remember what happened that night?"

He nods again, swallowing hard as I slowly approach him. "You were about to take your top off in front of a group of complete pigs. I hauled you out of there before that could happen."

"Do you remember what happened after? Once we were outside?" I'm just inches away now. His chest heaves, his breathing increasing. There's a charge between us, raw and unstable, just like our entire relationship has been.

"I kissed you."

"That's right." I stop walking, my body a breath from his. He remains completely still, staring at me. I crane my head and his mouth lowers toward mine. "You were my first kiss, Drew." My voice trembles as I utter those words. His breath intermingles with mine, the heat of his lips warming me. "You were supposed to be my first everything — my first kiss, my first sexual experience, my first love."

Regret swirls deep in his eyes, the unmasked pain more real than any emotion I've ever seen from Wes. "I fucked up. I know that. I'm sorry I missed out on those firsts. But please, Brooklyn…" His hand lands on my hip, gripping me like I'm a lifesaver, the only thing keeping him afloat. "Let me be your last."

I meet his eyes, wanting to agree, but I can't forget the past. I can't give him yet another chance, only for him to abandon me. "I can't do that." With haste, I pull away, spinning around and darting toward my car.

"Brooklyn, please," Drew begs, rushing after me.

"No." I face him once more, my eyes on fire. "No, Drew. You're toxic to me. Did you know I waited for you the next day? I sat watching the street for hours, coming up with excuse after excuse as to why you weren't there when you promised you would be. I did my hair. I put on makeup. I stared at my closet for what seemed like an eternity trying to pick out the perfect outfit so I'd look good for you. But you never came. You broke your promise to me. And that's just the first time. There are so many others, Drew. So many…" I pull my lip between my teeth, shaking my head at how

400

stupid I'd been. "Then when you told me you loved me that night after Carla asked for a divorce the first time, I thought this was it, this was the start of us. Now I know—"

"If I knew—"

I hold up my hand, silencing him, needing to get this out. "Now I know it was the end of us. I've just been in denial for the past several years."

I allow my words to ring in the air for a moment, our two bodies motionless, frozen in time, in space, as if nothing else exists but the truth I finally had the courage to set free. The truth that has been holding me prisoner for too long now.

"Goodbye, Drew," I say, then whirl around and duck into my car. He hurries after me, trying to stop me, but my keys are in the ignition, cranking it in one quick motion. I peel out of the driveway without a single look back...something I should have done years ago.

Chapter Twenty-Seven

DREW

"**B**ROOKLYN!" I SHOUT AS she speeds away without so much as a glance back at me. My lungs constrict, making it nearly impossible to breathe, my vision spotty.

What do I do? What do I say? How do I even start to process this information? I stare into the distance, struggling to jump-start a memory that's long forgotten. All I know is Brooklyn and I hooked up the night Carla asked for a divorce the first time, but I was too drunk to remember.

I don't drink much these days, not like I did when I was playing hockey. Once Carla left and I was responsible for taking care of Alyssa and Charlotte, my priorities changed. Getting drunk with my buddies was no longer important, particularly considering my doctor's warnings about the detrimental effect alcohol has on someone like me, someone who's suffered numerous severe brain injuries.

Regardless, I clearly remember what happened the day after she served me with the first notice of dissolution. That was seven years ago. Has Brooklyn really been keeping this from me that long? I suppose I can't fault her. I've been keeping my secret for even longer.

I dig my fingers into my scalp, tugging at my hair, my stomach churning at what an asshole I am. How could I so easily take advantage of her, then have no memory of it? If it were anyone else, I'd question the veracity of the claim. But not Brooklyn. She has no motive to lie. She's always been one of the most truthful people I know. She wouldn't lie, especially about this.

My mind overrun with questions, I spin around, dashing into the house in search of my wallet and keys. I need answers. I need an opportunity to make things right.

"What's going on?" Molly asks the second I storm into the kitchen.

"I have to talk to her. Apologize for fu—" I stop myself short of swearing, my gaze shooting to my two little girls standing off to the side, their interests piqued at the sudden tension in the room.

"Did you piss off Auntie Brook?" Alyssa asks, her hands on her hips.

My eyes harden on her, doing my best to appear stern. "Watch your language, Lyss. We don't say that. And no, I didn't do anything to upset Auntie Brook."

"Bullshit," Molly coughs, and I dart my eyes to her, glaring.

"Girls," Aunt Gigi interrupts, addressing my daughters. "Why don't you go play in the den for a little while. It appears Auntie Molly needs to talk to your dad."

"Why can't we stay?" Charlotte asks. "Are you going to swear?"

"Your aunt Gigi doesn't swear," she responds, indignant, holding her head high.

"No, but Auntie Molly says bad words all the time. Like shit."

Gigi's eyes widen as she points a finger at Charlotte. "Don't you *ever* say that word again. When I was a little girl, if I were to swear, your *bisnonno* would wash my mouth out with soap."

Molly stifles a laugh and I do the same, thankful for the levity, despite how short-lived it is. I should be just as furious to hear sweet, innocent little Charlotte swear, but I can't help smiling at her adorable voice. I'll take anything to relieve the tension and confusion growing inside me with each passing second.

Gigi turns her attention on Molly. "And you!" Her eyes are on fire. "You know better than to swear in front of those girls. You should be teaching them by example!"

Molly snorts out a laugh through her nose, unable to control herself.

"Don't laugh! It's not funny!"

"It kind of is," she insists.

Sighing in exasperation, Gigi pinches the bridge of her nose. "I can't wait until you have that baby and realize how difficult it is to raise a child."

"I'm already prepared for all hell to break lose. I was a hellraiser." She rubs her stomach. "I'm sure this little boy is going to give me a run for my money."

"One can only hope."

"Come on, girls," Uncle Leo interrupts, scooting off the barstool. "Let's go make spaghetti out of Play-Doh while we wait for the real spaghetti." He grabs Charlotte's hand, leading her away from us.

Gigi begins to usher Alyssa along with her when I call out, "Wait, Gigi. Can you stay? I think…" I trail off. "I think you need to hear this." Other than my father and Mr. Tanner, she's the only other person who knows what happened before I left for college. She could offer the perspective I need to figure out this mess.

She turns, a small smile building on her lips as she heads back toward me. "Of course, Andrew."

"Well, I'll let you all have a minute," Noah says, leaving Molly with a kiss. She clutches his hand as he brushes her shoulder, smiling at him. Then he walks away with Alyssa, joining Uncle Leo and Charlotte in the family room.

Once we're alone and free from curious ears, Molly leans toward me. "Is it true?"

With a nod, I slump into one of the stools by the kitchen island and hang my head. "Brooklyn doesn't lie. It's not in her nature." I lift my eyes, staring at Molly and Gigi. "It was the night Carla asked for a divorce the first time. But I can't remember any of it. Well, nothing that matters anyway."

I'm not proud of it, but I made a lot of mistakes when I was younger, when I thought I was invincible, untouchable, that I could have anything and everything I wanted. Growing up, we didn't have much money, so when I signed that first big contract and saw all those zeros, I went overboard. There was more than one occasion I woke up with a woman whose name I couldn't remember, having no recollection of the night before or how she got there. It sickens me to think Brooklyn was another one of those girls. She doesn't deserve that. None of the women I used and tossed aside do, but Brooklyn... She's different. She deserves to be worshipped, adored, cherished, not used by a sleazeball like me.

"She said she found you stumbling through the park in our old neighborhood," Molly explains. "That after learning Carla wanted to leave, all you wanted was to go home. She thought you meant Dad's house, but—"

"I told her I was talking about her," I interrupt. That night's fuzzy, but I remember leaving that bar with the intention of going to see her, to make up for standing her up all those years ago. It's the last thing I can remember until the next morning.

It's silent for a moment as I process this, trying to force more of that night back to the surface, but nothing comes. I return my gaze to Molly. "What else did she say?" My eyes are pleading, desperate for even the most meaningless piece of information.

"She didn't go into detail, just that you told her you loved her."

"Fuck," I breathe, rubbing my temples. For once, Gigi doesn't admonish me for my language. Even she realizes the severity of the situation requires it.

"It sounded like things got hot and heavy, but you stopped just short of having sex. You told her you wanted to be sober the first time you made love."

If I felt like an ass before, it's worse now, knowing what I told her. I gave her hope only to destroy it. History repeating itself. No wonder Brooklyn wants nothing to do with me.

"The next morning, she got up to make breakfast. That's when she overheard you talking on your phone."

"To Carla," I say, resigned, the ache in my chest building with each passing moment.

Molly nods. "She was able to decipher enough of the conversation to learn Carla was pregnant."

I rubbed the back of my neck, trying to relieve the tension, to no avail. "I remember waking up in her bed and panicking. I was so worried I took advantage of her." I can only imagine what Brooklyn must have thought of me when I stumbled from her room after learning I was going to be a father again and asked if anything happened between us the night before.

"It sounds like you did," Gigi interjects. I shoot my eyes to her steely glare. "Just in a different way."

"I had no memory of how I got from the bar to her bed. I still don't. I was young and stupid. It's not an excuse, but alcohol was my go-to stress reliever, regardless of its detrimental effect on me. After a bad game. After a fight. After learning my wife wanted to leave me. I just... I lost it. I was a different person back then. I don't know how Brooklyn could have stayed my friend after everything."

"That's who she is," Molly remarks. "Loyal to a fault."

"Always putting other people's needs before her own."

407

"She probably didn't want to say anything because of our friendship," she states, then furrows her brow. "I just don't understand. Brooklyn's always been a bit guarded when it comes to offering her heart. If it was just one night... I guess I don't see why it affects her like it does."

I look from her toward Gigi, who nods, wordlessly telling me it's time to finally tell someone.

"Because it wasn't just one night."

Molly's brows furrow. "You hooked up with her again?"

"Kind of." Shaking my head, I prepare myself to finally talk about the night I first kissed Brooklyn, the night I thought I was flying, only to learn it was with broken wings. "Do you remember that party you went to the summer before your junior year of high school."

"I went to a lot of parties," she answers.

"I know, but this was the first one Brooklyn's father allowed her to attend."

Understanding washes over her face as the memory seems to return. "The Strip Uno incident."

"Yes." I run my hands along my jeans. "We kissed that night. Not just a peck, but a real kiss." My lips curve up slightly in the corners. "I was her first kiss. She wanted more, but she'd been drinking. I didn't want her first time to be at some high school party. We made plans to get together the following morning after her father left for work and before I had to leave for the airport to catch my flight to Minnesota.

"The next day, I got up early. As I was getting

ready, there was a knock on my door. It was Dad, asking me to come with him. I followed him into the kitchen, surprised to see Mr. Tanner."

"Brooklyn's dad?" Molly asks. "What was he doing there?"

I close my eyes, the ache of walking into my kitchen and seeing Mr. Tanner standing there returning full force, regardless of the passing of years. Gigi's hand clasps mine, encouraging me.

"One of Brooklyn's neighbors saw me dropping her off the night before. Since I'd hauled her out of that house right before she was about to strip to nothing, she was still just in her bra and panties, a blanket draped around her. I should have made her put her clothes back on in my car, but hindsight's always 20/20. I didn't. When I walked her up to the house, things got pretty heated again."

I bury my head in my hands, tugging at my hair. "The next morning, as Brooklyn's dad was bringing in the paper, a neighbor told him what she saw. So he went to look at the footage from the security cameras he'd installed."

Molly's mouth grows slack. "Oh shit."

"It didn't look good. And this wasn't the first time he'd caught us in a compromising position. Earlier that summer, we'd almost kissed before he interrupted. After that, he gave Dad a not-so-subtle reminder that I was eighteen and she was only fifteen. So when he saw that video…" I swallow hard through the lump in my throat. "He gave me a choice. Leave for college without seeing her or he'd go to the police. It didn't matter that we hadn't slept together. The video of us walking up to her house, her in just her bra and panties, then kissing her the way I did... It didn't look good. Even if I was innocent, he could make a lot of trouble. Just the appearance of wrongdoing could have ruined a lot of things for me. I hated doing it, but I didn't have a choice. So I got on that plane without saying another word to Brooklyn."

Molly slumps onto the stool beside me, her lower lip trembling. "Holy shit. It all makes sense now. Every time I teased her about her crush on you, she'd say how she valued our friendship above everything. Now I feel like an ass. I should have known there was something going on, something bigger than her not wanting to ruin our friendship. And these past few weeks..." She trails off.

"What?"

Cringing, she faces me. "I've been questioning her decision to marry Wes. And at her shower..." She chews on her lower lip.

"What did you do?" My voice is guarded. Knowing Molly like I do, I have a feeling I'm not going to like what she's about to tell me.

"It wasn't intentional. I thought it would be fun, but I surprised her with a shower game."

"What kind of shower game?"

"A modified version of the *Newlywed Game*." She's unnaturally shy as she avoids my gaze. "I reached out to Mrs. Bradford with the idea and she was on board. So I went to Wes' office and recorded him answering a few questions — his favorite movie, childhood pet, stuff like that. The goal was to see how well the couple knew each other." She looks at me through remorse-filled eyes. Just by her expression, I can tell her idea backfired. "But Brooklyn could only answer a few questions about him. And when I asked what Wes' favorite movie was, do you know what she said?"

I remain silent, swallowing hard.

"*The Godfather.* His favorite movie is *It's a Wonderful Life.* And if we're being honest, even I knew that answer. He said as much last Christmas."

"I remember."

"But she couldn't. When we were talking earlier…" She gestures with her head toward the French doors leading to the back yard. "I accused her of settling. That's when she told me everything."

"She's just marrying Wes because of me."

"It's possible," Molly responds. "I didn't have a chance to dig deeper before she ran off."

"No. She is," I state. "A few weeks ago, she mentioned something along the lines of settling being better for all involved." I pinch the bridge of my nose. "I guess I did the same thing with Carla, but Brooklyn deserves better. She deserves to marry someone who makes her happy."

"I think Wes *does* make her happy," Gigi interjects, joining the conversation.

"You do?"

She scrunches her brows, a moment of silent contemplation passing. "I do. He treats her well, dotes upon her as if she's a treasure, makes her a priority. For Brooklyn, maybe that is happiness."

411

"I've treated her well," I argue, shooting to my feet. "I've always treated her with respect."

"Except for the night you almost fucked her when you were hammered and can't remember even doing it," Molly bites out.

Gigi glares at her before returning her attention to me. "Look at things from Brooklyn's point of view. If you were in her shoes, knowing what you know now, what would you think?"

I open my mouth, then snap it shut. "That I've done nothing but disappoint her."

Placing her hand on mine, her lips form into a small smile full of compassion. "Brooklyn is...special."

"I know that."

"She processes things differently," she continues. "I'm not her mother, but once Molly brought her into our family, I like to think she became like another one of my kids. She's practical, but she's always had this romantic side to her, as well. She's always believed in the idea of finding a love so strong it hurts. And I think she did, but it hurt too much."

"I didn't mean to hurt her. I had no idea—"

"I know you didn't. But for Brooklyn, love isn't about showering her with gifts and flowers. It's about putting in the effort, about making her a priority. Unfortunately..."

"In her eyes, I never did that," I say, finishing her thought, sinking back onto the barstool.

"Imagine how Brooklyn felt that night, then the following morning, especially considering your history.

One minute, she thought all her dreams were finally coming true. The next, she learned your wife was pregnant. How did you expect her to react?"

"The truth might have been nice."

"Perhaps. It might be nice for Brooklyn, too."

"You know why I can't do that, Gigi," I remind her in a low voice.

"I understand you don't want to do anything to ruin her relationship with her father, and it's admirable. Just like you think you deserved to know the truth all those years ago, perhaps Brooklyn does, too." Her tone is harsher than usual, her dark eyes firm.

I sit still for several long moments, processing everything in my head, feeling like I'm seeing a completely different side of Brooklyn, of me, of us. Abruptly, I stand, heading toward the door.

"Ah, ah, ah." Gigi's in front of me before I can leave. "Where do you think you're going?"

"To find Brooklyn. To show her I'll make her a priority."

"But she's engaged." She smirks, crossing her arms over her chest.

"So? That didn't stop you from trying to play matchmaker a few weeks ago."

A sly grin builds on her lips as she raises herself onto her tiptoes, kissing my cheek. "Tread carefully, Andrew. You won't win her heart overnight. It's going to take some time."

"How long?"

413

She shrugs, then retreats, returning to check on the sauce simmering on the stove. "Does it matter?"

Grinning, I respond without a moment's hesitation. "No, it doesn't."

"Good answer."

Chapter Twenty-Eight

BROOKLYN

THE MOST DANGEROUS LIES are the ones you tell yourself. They fester and churn, burning like acid, painful and biting until the lie becomes who you are, becomes the only identity you know.

For the past seventeen years, I've been lying to myself, doing everything to convince myself I can move past everything I've endured. After all, Drew's just a friend. The problem is that's not true.

Drew and I have a history, one I once cherished and held dear, but now only want to forget. And it's this history and connection that's turned our friendship into something more. It gave me hope, gave me faith, gave me promise. Each smile, each hug, each wink misled me to have even more hope, more faith, more promise. I can't do this to myself anymore.

I *won't* do this to myself anymore.

My hands shake as I bring my keyring up to the lock on my front door, relentless tears still flowing down my cheeks as his words replay in my mind.

"Please, Brooklyn. Let me be your last."

It took every ounce of resolve not to fling myself into his arms at his heartfelt plea. But staying away is the only way I'll ever have a chance at repairing my damaged heart.

I disappear into my townhouse, blowing out a relieved breath once I'm secure in my own private sanctuary. I collapse onto the couch, only to come face-to-face with a framed photo of Drew, Molly, and me from our childhood. Drew's in his hockey gear, Molly and me on either side of him, his arms pulling both of us close. I've always loved this photo, but now it makes the tears fall even harder, my entire body trembling.

I thought I could escape him here, but I can't. He's everywhere. In the air. On the walls. In the foundation. This is the reason I need to marry Wes. Drew may not see it. Hell, even Molly may not see it. But it needs to happen. I need to move on, to forget the past and the unrequited love I've held onto for too long now.

As I lay there, struggling to pull myself together, a car door slams, jolting me. It could be one of my neighbors, but I recognize that particular car door…as ridiculous as that sounds. It's known and familiar, like the rhythm of a loved one's breathing. I shoot up, staring out the window behind the couch to see Drew walking toward the door. I scurry from the couch, unsure where to go, scanning the small living space for an escape plan.

His footsteps up the stairs and onto the porch echo, my breathing increasing with each one. I duck, hiding beneath the window of the front door. His fist pounds on the wood, making me jump.

"Brooklyn! Open up! I need to talk to you."

I hold my breath, praying he's unable to sense me sitting just on the other side of the door.

"I know you're in there. Your car's in the driveway."

"Shit," I mutter.

"Please," he begs, his voice growing soft. "I just... I just want to talk."

There's a pause and I hold still, trying not to move so much as a hair for fear he'll know. This behavior is childish. I should open the door and confront him, but I feel too vulnerable, too exposed. I've kept this secret from him for seven years. How can I look into his eyes now that he knows the truth? What will I see when I do? Regret? Remorse? Nothing? The idea of seeing nothing is more than I can bear.

When the porch creaks with his shifting weight, followed by a labored sigh, I slowly lift myself to peek outside, seeing a shaggy mess of dark hair below the window. His voice rings out as I crouch back to my hiding position.

"Remember when you had the chicken pox?"

My heart thumps in my chest and I blink, wondering what he's doing, why he's talking to my door. Then I pull my knees into my body, comforted by his proximity. Just like I can always sense when he enters a room without setting eyes on him, he can do the same with me. He must know I'm sitting less than a foot away, only a thick piece of wood between us.

"I think I was in fourth grade, so you would have been in second. Both you and Molly had it at the same time. Gigi offered to take care of you so your dad didn't have to miss any work. You stayed at our house for the week." He laughs slightly, his voice growing more animated. "And it was during our February break from school. Molly didn't shut up about it. Every other kid who caught the chicken pox got to miss a week of school. She was so pissed she couldn't. But you…" He pauses. I hear the faintest hint of a shallow sigh as I imagine his entire body relaxing. I've heard that sigh before when he settled onto the couch with me, effortlessly throwing an arm across my shoulders as we watched a movie with the girls. "You were relieved you got sick during the school break because you wouldn't have to miss anything."

The memory brings a smile to my face and I close my eyes, returning to that time in my life, a time when things were simple.

"Gigi told me to stay away from you two since I hadn't gotten chicken pox yet and had a big hockey tournament in a few weeks…or at least as big a hockey tournament as there can be when you're nine. Even when we were kids, there was something inside me. This innate need to take care of you. So I ignored Gigi's warnings and checked in on you, bringing you soup and watching TV with you. Do you remember?"

Tears prickle my eyes as I listen to him recount the bond we've always shared, even as kids. "Yes," I say in a soft voice. I can almost feel his smile.

"I was too young to know what love was, how complicated and fucked up it can be, how much it can hurt. But, even back then, I knew I cared for you, Brooklyn. I never…" He trails off, then draws in a deep breath, as if collecting himself.

418

"I never meant to hurt you. And I'm sorry things turned out like they did. That day I punched Damian Murphy and came to see you, I was so nervous. You may not believe me, but I was. As I pushed you on that swing in your front yard, this electricity filled me. And it hurt because I thought you were too good for me. I *still* think that. Still think I'm completely undeserving of any amount of time you'll give me. As much as I wish I could rewind the clock to simpler times, to go back to the day I left for college..." There's a pause and I hold my breath, waiting for his next words, craving them.

"I can't," he finally says, almost as if to himself. "We've grown up. We've both done things we regret. At least I have." His voice is quiet, contemplative.

"We've done things to hurt each other. I can sit here and apologize all I want, but my words don't mean shit to you, and rightly so. You don't have to open the door to talk to me. I'll give you the space you need to figure this out since being near me has caused you nothing but pain lately. But I want you to know I'll fight for you, Brooklyn. Just like I risked being sick and not playing in that tournament all those years ago, I'll put it all on the line again just to be with you. You have to decide what you want, what path to take."

I hug my knees tighter, my tears falling more steadily. I've been waiting years to hear him say something like this. I want to believe him, but he's fooled me so many times before. How can I put my faith in him now?

I remain motionless, lost to my thoughts, my heart and brain playing a tumultuous game of tug-of-war. Finally, the floorboards of the porch creak, followed by

419

feet walking down the steps. I raise myself, peering out the window to see Drew climbing into his SUV.

As he's about to drive off, he glances back at the house, meeting my eyes through the window. His lips turn up in the corners, a sweet smile. He's a few yards away, but close enough for me to make out his lips as he mouths, *I'm sorry*. He pauses for a moment, then drives away.

I collapse back against the door, allowing the events of the day...hell, the past several years...to wash over me in the hopes I find some sort of clarity. But confusion clouds everything, not one event indicating which is the correct path. Do I risk a life of security and contentment with Wes, a man who's been nothing but devoted to me, albeit in his own way? Or do I follow my heart and go to Drew, see if whatever I feel for him is real, is strong, is true?

When I went over to Drew's earlier this evening, I thought I had everything figured out. I'm engaged to a wonderful man, a man who will do anything to make me happy, even if it means staying up here in Boston instead of returning to Atlanta and running his company from there. We're just weeks away from being married. But now the secret I've been keeping for years is out there. I've spent years dreaming of the day Drew would notice me. If he never overheard me tell Molly the truth of that night, if I weren't about to marry another man, would he have come over here and poured his heart out?

Feeling like the walls of my house are suffocating me with memories of both Drew and Wes, I grab my purse and keys, then dash out the door. I jump into my car and crank the engine, reversing out of the driveway.

As I approach the stoplight at the on-ramp for I-93, I'm at a crossroads. Do I go south to Cambridge to see Wes, or head west to Drew's house in Needham? I can't help but feel this one decision will change everything. Do I settle for the safety of what I know to be a loveless marriage? Or take a risk, knowing Drew has the power to destroy me?

My heart pounds in my chest as my eyes glance between the on-ramp and the road ahead of me. Then, as if the universe is playing a cruel trick on me, Dave Matthews' voice singing the familiar first words of "Crash Into Me" fills the car. I'm instantly transported back to that night at Brody Carmichael's party before Drew went to college. The night I gave him my first kiss. The night we became something other than the friends we've been fooling ourselves into believing we are.

When the light turns red, I know where I need to go.

Thank you for reading COMMITMENT! Find out how Drew and Brooklyn's story ends in REDEMPTION, releasing SEPTEMBER 23, 2018!

"We always come back to our first love."

To be notified when it's available for preorder, as well as other information about new books, exclusive material, and giveaways, sign up for my mailing list:

www.tkleighauthor.com/mailing-list

If you enjoyed these characters and want to know more about how Molly met Noah, check out WRITING MR. RIGHT, a fun, sexy poignant tale about a romance author who doesn't believe real love is real life.

Playlist

Miss Invisible - Marie Digby
The Scientist - Coldplay
Crash Into Me - Dave Matthews Band
Smallest Light - Ingrid Michaelson
Already Gone - Sleeping At Last
Loved - Lucy Hale
Just Breathe - Pearl Jam
I Don't Wanna See You With Her - Maria Mena
Amnesia - Gavin Mikhail
Black and Blue Bird - Dave Matthews Band
Times Move Quickly - Noah Gundersen
Old Days - Ingrid Michaelson
I'm Lying to you Cause I'm Lost - The Paper Kites
Bitter Pill - Gavin James
The One That Got Away - The Civil Wars
We Can Never Go Back - Joy Williams
Can't You See - Matthew and the Atlas
Over and Over Again - Nathan Sykes
Horizon - Rachael Yamagata
In The Silence - JP Cooper
Killing Me - Luke Sital-Singh
Bumper Cars - Alex & Sierra
All You Never Say - Birdy
Heartfelt Lies - Ron Pope
I Won't Give Up - Jason Mraz
Breathe Me - Sia

T.K. Leigh

Acknowledgements

Book number fifteen. Holy crap. I honestly never thought I'd write ONE book, let alone FIFTEEN? This is absolutely crazy to me.

For those of you new to my work, this story is a spin-off of my romantic comedy, *Writing Mr. Right*. When I was writing that, I had no intention of working in a budding romance between Molly's brother and best friend. It just kind of happened. I don't really ever plot my books. I let the characters tell the story the way they think it should be told. Apparently, Drew and Brooklyn knew something I didn't. This was just supposed to be a stand-alone contemporary romance. Again, they knew something I didn't. Their story is filled with pain, heartache, and misunderstanding, but also hope.

None of this would be possible without the unwavering support of my husband Stan. He's been my biggest cheerleader since I told him I wrote a book back in 2013. Fifteen books later, he's still at my side. And I know he will be through the next fifteen, as well.

On that same note, thanks to my wonderful nannies, Sharon and Brooke, for taking care of Miss Harper Leigh so I have lots of time to write!

There's only one woman I ever trust with my book babies, and that's Kim Young. She's edited all fifteen books. Her keen eye and flexibility is invaluable. I can't wait to work on the next fifteen books with her, as well.

Thanks to my wonderful admin team who help me manage my social media presence — Melissa, Joelle, Vicky, Lea. And to my fabulous beta readers - Stacy, Lin, Melissa, Joelle, Vicky, Sylvia. #BurnhamBitches4Life

Thanks to Emily from Social Butterfly PR for dealing with all my craziness, especially when I tell her less than a month before release that I'm writing a prequel novella as well. No matter what my brain comes up with she's on board, often adjusting our original plan. You make this author job a lot less stressful for me, and I'll forever be grateful.

A special shout out to my street team. Thanks so much for taking time out of your busy schedules to help promote me! And to my lovely reader group! Thanks for giving me a place to be myself, horrible jokes and tasteless memes and all!

Last but not least, thanks to YOU! Without readers, I'd have no one to write for, so thanks for taking a chance on my books! Redemption is coming soon!

Peace & Love,

~ T.K.

Books by T.K. Leigh

The Beautiful Mess Series
A Beautiful Mess
A Tragic Wreck
Gorgeous Chaos

The Deception Duet
Chasing the Dragon
Slaying the Dragon

The Redemption Series
Promise: A Redemption Series Prologue
Commitment
Redemption

The Vault
Inferno

Stand Alone Titles

Heart of Light
Heart of Marley
The Other Side of Someday
Vanished
Writing Mr. Right

For more information on any of these titles and upcoming releases, please visit T.K.'s website:
www.tkleighauthor.com

About the Author

T.K. Leigh, otherwise known as Tracy Leigh Kellam, is the *USA Today* Bestselling author of the Beautiful Mess series, in addition to several other works. Originally from New England, she now resides in sunny Southern California with her husband, beautiful daughter, and three cats. When she's not planted in front of her computer, writing away, she can be found training for her next marathon (of which she has run over twenty fulls and far too many halfs to recall) or chasing her daughter around the house.

T.K. Leigh is represented by Jane Dystel of Dystel, Goderich & Bourret Literary Management. All publishing inquiries, including audio, foreign, and film rights, should be directed to her.